A deep rumble filled the air.

Bailey started as if the ground jolted under her, her arms flailing wildly. Jason and Trent stared as her body . . . and the rock she sat on . . . began to lift from the ground. She shrieked and grabbed for a piece of it that jutted up sharply next to her and hung on for dear life to the sun-warmed . . . no, hot! rock.

"My ear!" a thunderous voice complained, and the rock tossed about, and then sent Bailey tumbling head over heels in a somersault to the ground, her mouth wide open in a soundless cry. The scoop-shaped granite wavered a bit, morphing into the triangular shaped head of a lizard. A very large lizard.

"A . . . a . . . dragon!" Bailey got out. She scrambled backward, stopped only by Trent's stunned and frozen body.

Jason stood, one hand still out in gesture, the great lantern eye of the dragon now fixing on him. "Don't move," he said. "Really. Just . . . don't move."

THE DRAGON GUARD

THE MAGICKERS #3

EMILY DRAKE

DAW BOOKS, INC.

DONALD A. WOLLHEIM, FOUNDER

375 Hudson Street, New York, NY 10014

ELIZABETH R. WOLLHEIM
SHEILA E. GILBERT
PUBLISHERS
www.dawbooks.com

Dedicated to my lovely family
both the carrot and the stick
for my success.

Contents

THE DRAGON GUARD

THE MAGICKERS #3

BEGINNING

A TALL figure swathed in black stepped out of a corner door, his lean weight barely causing the floorboards to sound. He moved with the agility of a fighter, a ninja, and he knew it. The great room had been an old dance studio once, this cavernlike room with high windows covered in metal mesh, and creaking wooden floor. Mirrors, their silver backing tarnished in blackened streaks along the edges, lined one entire wall, with a barre fastened below them. He took a moment or two to stretch, only the top half of his face revealed by the ninja veil. His dark clothing moved freely with his agile form. The only color on his form at all came from the clear, prismatic crystal pendant hanging about his neck. After a moment or two of stretches, he reached up and tucked the pendant inside his clothing.

"Ready," he said flatly. He moved into a defensive

1

stance, alert, weight balanced slightly forward on his feet, hands in readiness. The room dropped into silence. He stood in anticipation.

Nothing happened. He tilted his head impatiently. "I am waiting."

A breathless voice answered him from beyond the glass wall. "Just a moment, Jonnard. A difficulty—" The speaker broke off with a pant and a curse, then all fell silent.

"I said, ready! Do you expect me to wait all morning?" His voice broke harshly, impatiently, through the air. He tilted his head, listening for further action.

More curses followed, punctuated by a sharp yelp of pain. Then, mirrored doors shimmered as they moved inward, and then . . . something . . . came through them.

It looked as if it could be his twin, but it moved . . . wrong. More fluidly, as if it had more joints than he did. It glided toward him, at the ready. The eyes revealed above the ninja wrapping over the face were flat, and filled with hunger.

"No weapons," Jonnard said firmly, "but those of your body." As if what he faced would heed rules of combat. He moved into a stance, and smiled, with an inward breath.

It was the only moment of stillness he had. The Leucator attacked, in a swirl of black and pale hands and face, and the two met in a flurry of hands, feet, arms, and legs, punch, parry, kick, block, attack, and retreat, then attack again. The floor accompanied them in muted thunder as Jonnard fought for his very life.

Then, slowly, the attacker began to give. It made

little noise other than a hissing and its own quickened breathing. Jonnard made noise enough for both of them. A triumphant "Hah!" when a blow hit hard, a grunt when the other hit him, a curse when a spinning kick missed.

Their shoes squeaked on the varnished floor when they touched, yet many of their movements seemed almost airborne. Thuds of flesh against flesh drove each back and forth. Yet slowly but surely Jonnard began to drive the Leucator back, back from the center of the huge practice area, toward the corner it had emerged from. His ribs hurt. His hands smarted from the lightning-fast boxing blows of the other, but he knew what his foe would do. It was like watching himself fight, the mirrors eerily reflecting four of him.

Exactly like watching himself, for the Leucator was himself, duplicated and thirsting to find him and rejoin him. It was a creation of Magick, meant to be a tireless Hunter and Seeker. It would not cease or stop its Hunt till rejoined with its Soulmate, although no one in his right mind would allow such a joining. It was a corrupt thing, and its very presence prickled the hair at the back of his neck. Even he, who would do much to achieve his goals, thought of the Leucator as sheer evil. But it knew what he knew, in many ways, and made the perfect opponent to practice against.

Jonnard smiled thinly as they met again in another flurry of moves. Hand to shoulder, other hand to rib, leg, spin, kick, balance, jab, punch, spin again, push away. He could scarcely see the moves, but they lay inside, in the memory of his muscles and his training, and if the Leucator was fast, he must be faster!

The thing caught him with a stunning blow to his temple. Jonnard fell back, his eyes swimming with unshed tears from the sting of it, his ears ringing. He shook his head, trying to clear his senses. The Leucator advanced on him, blows pummeling fast and furious, and Jonnard twisted away, his breath caught in his throat for a moment, as he realized his danger.

It would bring him near to death and then claim him, "reuniting" their selves. Then he would be gone forever, absorbed into the fiber of this corrupted being. He played a deadly game . . . and he was losing!

Jonnard touched the crystal he wore inside his shirt. It warmed, even through the fabric, steadying him. He danced back a step, out of range, and breathed carefully, balancing himself. The ringing in his ear disappeared and he rubbed at his eye, clearing it. The Leucator would not land another such blow! Jonnard inhaled deeply, then stepped forward and back into the attack.

He beat the creature into the corner, slowly, step by step, until suddenly it slipped and went down with an exhausted sound. Jonnard shook out his crystal, cupping it briefly, calling it to fiery life. A singular beam sizzled from it, his own personal light saber, and he sliced off the Leucator's head.

The thing curled into hissing black smoke, sucking inward, until it disappeared.

Jonnard grinned in triumph.

The mirrored doors opened and Antoine Brennard stepped forth, frowning. "Another one dead? These are expensive, my son."

"But worth it for training. I need two. I demand

two." Jonnard quelled the crystal sword and once again held an ordinary pendant in his hand. "Jason Adrian will not stand against me. I promise that!"

"Do you now? And what if I need him alive?"

Jonnard felt the heat of his triumph in his eyes as he looked at his father. "Then I promise that, as well. But get me two. I need two to continue training." With that, he pivoted away and slipped off through the corner door, with not a look back. His father would obtain the simulations for him. Expensive or not, they could not afford *not* to. Not if he wanted Jason Adrian defeated and helpless in their hands.

1

THE HURRIEDER
I GO. . . .

"ALL RIGHT! All right, listen up! One goal to tie, two to win! And that's how we get them, one at a time!" Coach's voice broke over the huddle, carrying to each of them, the soccer ball tucked under his arm. His voice carried over Jason like a wave of sound, shutting off the rest of the world. Coach broke off long enough to toss the ball to a waiting referee, then returned to his time-out speech. "Here's how we're going to do it . . ."

Jason grabbed a spare towel and mopped up his face, feeling the sweat trickle between his eyebrows, preparing to slide down his nose. He rubbed the towel through his hair, and waited. The towel felt damp in his hands, but he managed to scrub up the back of his neck before tossing it toward the benches.

7

A limp banner proclaiming "Go Chargers" waved in the spring breeze.

Todd, their goalie, muttered, "Easier said than done." Coach grabbed his shoulder and shook him lightly. The agile teen was already beet red from three quarters of a hard-played game, but his face darkened even more and showed through the roots of his black hair. "I know, one step at a time," the goalie amended quickly as the coach nearly growled.

"Exactly! Now the first step is this . . . I've been using Jason lightly . . ."

Jason looked at his soccer coach in surprise. He'd been running his legs off trying to guard the center, making sure their star forward got as many clear shots as he could, and the sweat plastering his jersey to his body was more than proof of that. Coach Wayne didn't seem to notice his look as he continued. "Jason has been passing to Bradley all day, but I'm gonna cut him loose now. He's up there in right wing on purpose, but the other team has relaxed, they don't know what he can do. So . . . pass the ball to Jason. Let's show 'em."

A burst of elation went through Jason, followed by a brief moment of despair. It was all on him . . . all he wanted and yet, all the responsibility. He made a fist and pumped his hand rather than letting the doubt shake him. He could do it. He would! Enthusiasm leaped through him, and with it his Magick awoke, like a lightning flash, though he quickly contained it. No Magick here, just athletic talent, but he might as well have told himself not to breathe. And his Magick called to the others. From the corner of his eye, he caught sight of his cheering section in the warped and faded wooden bleachers. Bailey, her golden-brown ponytail bouncing in enthusiasm, jumped to her feet and waved. Their quiet friend Ting sat next to her, her hands weaving in a silent cheer. There was a flash of something bright and shiny in her hands, and Jason grinned as he recognized the sparkle of her crystal jewelry. He quickly brought his attention back to the huddle and his teammates. The Wingnuts were already dancing impatiently on the line, as eager to bring the game to a triumphant end as they were.

Bradley gave him a nod. "Watch Karcher, the fullback. He's fast and he's rough." He considered a moment, then added, "I've been faking their goalie right all day. Might try something different."

"Gotcha."

Coach gave them a few more instructions, then ended up with, "Don't pass it to Jason till you know he's in the clear. I don't want to tip our hand too early. Their fullbacks are good, and their goalie is . . . well, he's the reason we're behind. But we won't stay that way!"

A sharp whistle signaled the end of their time, and the boys broke apart, wheeling back onto the field. From the bench, Jason's friend Sammee yelled "Go get 'em!" and snapped a team towel. Hiding his widening grin, Jason trotted back into his position as right wing and looked down the field for the kick. He took a deep breath. This was it. League semifinals. Chargers against the Wingnuts. This wasn't the school team where nearly everyone who tried out had a position somewhere on one of the strings. No, these players were serious, headed to high school and then college and maybe even the pros in soccer, and the competition was intense. They lost here, and they were out of the tournament. They won, and they went on to the finals. You couldn't get much closer to winning or losing it all than this.

He jogged in place a moment to loosen his calves up, then froze into position as the others lined up and the refs readied for the kick. Without seeming to, he scanned the faces of the opposite team. Like his own, they were bright with sun and sweat, a little tired, yet eager. They smelled victory in the air. He grinned, showing his teeth almost like a wolf, facing into the late afternoon breeze. He was going to do all he could to prove them wrong!

He looked to Bradley, though, stifling his impulse to look them in the eyes, and stare them down. The center nodded back at him. His would be the stealth attack, and he'd give it away if he challenged them. So he took one last stretch, and straightened, and waited for the whistle and kick.

It all seemed to happen at once, noise, sound, and movement as the teams both surged forward. His body carried him down the field, angling to both protect and take advantage of an opening, without him even thinking of doing it. Stiles, on the other team, buffeted him, and he dropped back, then cut away, leaving the defender far behind. Bradley glanced his way and darted around the defender Karcher, then saw him clear, and passed the ball to him sharply.

The black and white came at him. Jason considered passing it off, but he was close enough to try a goal and no one seemed to be taking him seriously . . .

yet. He could angle it as he received it, to the goalie's left. The soccer ball met his insole briskly and caromed off like a shot.

There was a long moment in which he just watched, turning his body to match the geometry of the kick, and the goalie, who had been heading the other way in his nets, saw his look but couldn't cut back in time. The ball went cleanly into the corner of the goal and the team and crowd roared. Bailey and Ting jumped up and down, waving in joy, although their voices were lost in the crowd. From the corner of his eye, he saw a man separate from the bleachers, camera in hand, clicking pictures. He seemed to focus on Bailey and Ting, snapping away. Who wouldn't? Their excitement bubbled everywhere. Bailey's golden-brown hair caught the sun as her ever-present ponytail bobbed with every celebrating bounce. Jason didn't try to hide his ear-to-ear grin.

One more to win.

They gathered for the kickoff. "That was quick," Allgood muttered. Bradley said, "He had it clear, why wait?"

Allgood grunted, his square face red with effort. " 'Cause now I've gotta defend again." He butted his shoulder into Bradley's, with another grunt. "Good pass."

The center grinned. "And it was a great goal." He slapped Jason's shoulder. "Now, let's hope they think that was an accident!"

They lined up and kicked off, and there were frantic, jostling, long moments as the Wingnuts drove downfield without mercy and a goal seemed inevitable. Then, suddenly, Allgood had the drive broken and headed down their way. Jason found his way blocked, then when he dodged away, Stiles picked him up, but not close enough to make physical contact. So, they were cautious but not convinced yet. The zone defense still concentrated on Bradley. He let himself run, feeling good, the tiredness feathering away, the afternoon sun slanting across the field. They didn't expect him to try again, and he tried to contain his fierce joy.

The ball went back in the other direction again for a bit and he had a breather as the Chargers defenders moved into position, and held off the challenge. It was long minutes those, before they regained possession and began passing the ball back toward Bradley. He dropped back, fresh and ready, surveying the Wingnuts defenders jostling around the Chargers center.

A long dark shadow fell across the grass. He jerked in reflex, then looked about, seeing nothing. He glanced upward and saw nothing. The moment cost him a step or two against Stiles, so he circled to regain his position. Something blurred at the corner of his eye, and the back of his left hand began to burn, an old scar turning an angry red. Jason rubbed it warily, and circled again, looking. That scar meant many things to him, but mostly it meant trouble.

It meant something was about that should not be, that had no business in his everyday world but to work evil.

He scrubbed the stinging scar again, searching the soccer field as carefully as he might, yet unable to see more than the milling bodies of the other players as the ball shot back and forth, heading toward his end of the field. No distractions! No Magick. And, hopefully, no Dark Hand of Brennard looking for him.

But his scar burned even more fiercely, telling him otherwise. A cold chill passed across the back of his neck. Jason spun about. A black splinter fell across the field and then, as he stared, it elongated and then widened into a figure. A figure through which he could still see goalposts and net and players wheeling about, a dark ghostly presence. His scar gave one last warning, burning pulse as he looked at the figure of Jonnard Albrite.

"Salutations, Jason. Did you think me gone for good?"

Jason had little time to look at the nearly man-sized boy who faced him, as the fullback Karcher came running at him, and he realized that Bradley had the ball, about to pass it to him. The dark apparition stood between them, wavered as Karcher tore through his presence, re-formed, and smiled. Jason dodged and turned about, trying to stay in his zone and trying to keep from being pulled offside. He frowned.

"I've been training," said the deceitful son of the Dark Hand. "I'm waiting for you."

Jason caught the pass and aimed it right back at Bradley, playing for both time and position. A look of surprise shot over the center's face, but he took the pass and dribbled it downfield, toward the goal and the Wingnuts' incredibly tough goalie.

Jason moved after, but as he approached the black ghost of Jonnard, he felt a pressure and an unyielding wall. He could not pass!

He moved to his right, but Jonnard moved that way, too, smoothly, laughing in a chill voice that no one but himself could hear. Unless, perhaps, Bailey and Ting . . .

Jason tossed a glance over his shoulder at the bleachers and saw the girls watching him, but neither seemed to sense what he faced. He was alone out here, with something that ought not to be and was, and used Magick to do it. The dark side of the Magick he loved, but Magick nonetheless.

He faked to his right and then moved left. Behind him, Karcher gave an exasperated grunt and Jason realized he'd thrown off both Dark Hand and Wingnut pursuers. He bolted into the clear. Bradley saw it and the ball came hurtling his way again.

Iciness ran across his back and down his shoulder, into his arm, a cold that brought a gripping pain with it.

"You'll not get away from me that easily," Jonnard hissed into his ear, and a freezing darkness blew across the back of his neck, ruffling his short hair.

Jason put his chin down with a sprint of speed, forcing his body across the soccer field with a tremendous effort, meeting Bradley's pass and intercepting the ball. His fingers had gone numb, but it wasn't his hands he needed, it was his legs and feet! He zigged away from Karcher and the other Wingnut defender, driving toward the goal and its nets, his jaw clenched in determination.

He could feel a dark cloud descending over him, shading his eyes, sucking away the air he needed to breathe. Jason had the goal in sight though, he knew where it was and just how the kick should be made.

He faked the goalie to the left, and watched the other react, heading to the wrong end of the nets. As the aching cold sank through him, into him, through his torso and down into his legs, stealing warmth, breath, and movement, he drew his foot back and sliced his kick to the right.

The Wingnuts goalie caught the change of momentum. With a midair twist, he threw himself, full body length, at the soccer ball, hands out in a desperate catch.

Jason stumbled to a halt, unable to move, let alone run, as the cold took him. The spinning black-and-white ball went through the goalie's fingertips and solidly into the deep corner of the nets, and a shout went up.

Then, and only then, did he fumble at the throat of his Chargers jersey and wrap his fingers about the crystal hanging tucked inside. It flared as he encircled the cage of wire holding it, and with that touch, all cold left him, that quickly.

A low laugh at the back of his neck, and Jason turned.

Jonnard gave a salute. "I will be seeing you soon enough. And when I do . . . all the crystals in the world won't be able to save you!" Still laughing, a black flame enveloped him, and then both were gone.

The game-ending whistle shrieked through the air a second before his teammates found him, and Jason collapsed under their weight as they threw themselves on him, and he should have laughed with the victory, but he could not.

The Dark Hand was reaching for him once again. He had a feeling the real game was just beginning.

NUTS AND CHEWS

BAILEY kept standing and watched as the boys trampled from the field, grinning as she turned to Ting. "They did it!"

"Did you doubt they would?" Ting swung her long dark hair from her shoulders as she tucked her crystal necklace back under the curve of her neckline, the second crystal winking from its charm holder on her bracelet.

Bailey turned her attention to Ting, and paused, thoughtfully. The happiness she felt, that the two of them had shared, seemed to have fled Ting quickly. There was a worried look in her almond eyes. Bailey put her hand out. "Ting . . . what's wrong?"

Ting flushed guiltily, and began to make her way down the weathered wooden bleachers. She stopped and looked back to Bailey. "Does it show? I don't want my mom to see."

Bailey gave a nod. "It shows. To anyone who knows you."

Ting sighed. "We had a call last night. It's my grandmother. She's out of remission."

"Oh, no!" Bailey sat down and pulled Ting down beside her. "But I thought the treatments were successful. You told me she should be in remission for years."

"That's what we all thought." Something very bright shone in the corner of Ting's eye as she sat. She brushed it away quickly.

"Will you be moving back up to be with her again?" Bailey tried not to look at her, not wanting Ting to see that the idea of losing her across the state once again upset her. After all, what was important here was Ting's grandmother, and her battle against cancer. Besides, what with computers and the Internet and all, San Francisco was not nearly as far away from Southern California as it could have been. She slid her hand over to grasp Ting's and hold on. Her friend's skin felt cold. "It'll be all right."

Ting made a small muffled sound. "My mom spent half the night talking with my father. I don't think it's going to be all right." She scrubbed at her face again. "Bailey, she's been working so hard with me on Magick. What if I wore her out? What if it's all *my* fault?"

Bailey squeezed her hand. "Ting! Cancer is not your fault."

"Nooo."

"I mean, you know that, right? Really know that?"

"Well, of course I know that." Ting squeezed her hand back. "But she's been so frail, and the follow-up treatments have been rough, and I just wonder if helping me has kept her too tired. I mean," she looked at Bailey. "I can't help but wonder."

"I know. I would think, if anything, you've helped her. Imagine going your whole life having a talent for Magick, and hiding it, and yet knowing it was your family's legacy. She got to share that with you . . . she's no longer one of the Hidden. I would think . . ." and Bailey took a deep breath. "I would think becoming a Magicker the best thing in the world."

A tiny smile flickered across Ting's face. "And, of course, no trouble at all."

"Well, not much. Except for the Dark Hand and wolfjackals. Getting lost in your own crystal. Watching Henry set himself on fire trying to focus his crystal. Having to weed FireAnn's herb garden for forgetting homework. Watching Stefan change into his bear shape unexpectedly . . ." Bailey paused, as if thinking of more as she ticked off the obstacles on her fingers.

Ting giggled, and put her hand up to cover it, in a shy gesture that was all too familiar and welcome.

Watching her friend laugh pleased Bailey more than anything. She hugged Ting. "Things," she promised, "will get better!" She considered. "Of course, my grandmother always used to say they had to get worse first. Let's hope she's wrong."

Ting stifled another laugh. "Bailey. You and your sayings." She stood up and dusted herself off tidily. "Let's go home. I'm getting hungry and I bet Lacey is, too." She tickled a fingertip against the pocket in Bailey's sweatshirt jacket, and was rewarded by a sleepy sounding *Meep.* Seconds later, a little kangaroo rat, more commonly known as a pack rat, poked her face out and sleepily wrinkled her whiskers. Seeing the bright afternoon sunlight, she dove back into Bailey's sweatshirt, leaving her tufted tail hanging out, twitching.

Both girls laughed, and climbed down the rest of the bleachers, aiming for the parking lot, where nearly all the cars and vans for the game had already pulled out. From the corner of her eye, Bailey noticed a lone man sitting in a car parked in the shady corner. He seemed totally uninterested in anything till he saw the girls walk by toward the bus stop.

Did she imagine it, or did his head whip around as if he'd just spotted what he was looking for?

The hair on the back of her neck crawled. She hooked her arm through Ting's elbow. "Let's jog to the stop, I'm getting a little chilly."

Always slimmer and colder, Ting broke into a loping step with her, and their speed carried them through the parking lot and out onto the main street. Something flashed in the corner of her eye, but she dared not look back to see what it was. Instead, Bailey searched the busy street and saw, to her joy, the bus going their way. "Just in time!" she cried out thankfully.

Ting brought their bus passes out of her backpack and they climbed on as soon as the bus door wheezed open. Bailey sat down on the other side, drawing Ting with her, far away from the windows facing the park. She didn't want to know if whoever it was watched them. And she didn't breathe a word to Ting about the thoughts running through her mind. After all, she didn't want Ting thinking she'd gone nuts. She ought to know, but she didn't want to. Anyway, it was probably just her imagination. If there was one thing she had plenty of, it was imagination.

Wasn't it?

Jason got out of the shower, dressed hurriedly, and ran downstairs for something to eat, knowing he wouldn't be able to bear it until dinnertime. His stepmother Joanna sat at the nook table, her reading glasses nearly at the end of her nose, as she worked on some note cards and a stack of lists, pen in one hand and paper in the other. Tiny fake sapphires sparkled all over the plastic frame of the glasses, as if they could make having to wear them much nicer and more fashionable.

"Hi, Mom. Anything to eat?"

"I left chicken salad sandwiches in there for you. And there are some Terra chips in the bread box. Just don't eat more than two sandwiches this close to dinner."

Jason yanked the refrigerator door open happily. Someone, somewhen, had had the good sense to sit Joanna down and explain teen appetites to her. A woman who could rarely be seen eating, and didn't particularly seem to enjoy it even when she did so, at least Joanna didn't make him go by the same rules. He retrieved the two allotted sandwiches, found a plate, poured a small mound of the colorful, all vege-table "potato"-like chips next to them, and trotted over.

She made a note on one of her cards. Jason looked

at everything curiously and decided she was working on organizing yet another charity function. She pushed her glasses partway up her nose. "How did you do?"

"We won!"

She looked up. "You did? That's great! What happens now?"

"We go to the finals, but I don't know yet which team we're playing. Their game is scheduled tomorrow."

She tapped her pencil thoughtfully. "Would you mind if we came to see the finals?"

"Mind? I'd love it!" Jason wolfed down half a sandwich and paused, chewing, while trying to think of the details she'd need to know. Where, when, how long, and so forth. He told her what little he knew, which was mainly that it would be one day next weekend, depending on when the park let them play.

Her mouth curved. "William will be so pleased, and I think he'll be able to get the day off."

"How's the new development going?"

She shook her head. "Some sort of trouble with the permits, and you know how he hates paperwork. But he'll get it smoothed out soon, I'm sure." She watched Jason polish off the first sandwich. "You have homework for tonight?"

He crunched down on a bright orange-red Terra Chip. Sweet potato, one of his favorites. His stepmother had this illusion that this variety was healthier than the old-fashioned potato chip, and she was probably right, but at least he didn't have to eat tofu. Too often. "Yup, and I have to finish the packet you gave me for next year."

"Can you finish that for me tonight?"

He didn't want to. It was thick, and dull. She saw him hesitate.

"You really need to get that done, Jason. You've passed the tests, but your high school is a magnet school—it will be attracting students from all over for its programs. You need to sit down, make some decisions, and finish filling out your paperwork. This is a serious time. You have to decide what to study, for what you want to be for the rest of your life."

Jason stopped in mid swallow. There was no way he could tell her he'd already decided what he wanted to be the rest of his life: a Magicker. There was no way she'd believe him, even if he could break the Vow of Silence and get the words out. Finally, he finished swallowing and said contritely, "I know. I'll get it done, I promise."

Joanne smiled brightly. "Good, good. I'm here, and William is here, if you want to ask us anything later. He has lots of good advice he wants to give you, but . . . well, he's waiting until you ask for it."

He gave a crooked smile. His stepfather, big, outdoorsman-looking William McIntire, often known as "the Dozer," had worked in construction all his life. He was a good man, and Jason couldn't ask for more, he supposed, unless it was the advice of his own mother and father, both dead. He dusted bread crumbs off his hand. "What do you think *my* dad would have said?"

Pain shot through Joanna's face. She looked down at her note cards as her right hand twitched slightly. Then she looked back up. "Jason," she said quietly.

"I didn't know him long enough to be able to answer that. I wish I could have."

His throat tightened, and he suddenly wasn't hungry anymore. "Me, too," he got out, standing up and taking his plate to the sink where he rinsed it once or twice. When he thought he could talk again, he set the sandwich plate down on the counter and said, "I better go get that stuff done," and headed upstairs without meeting her gaze.

His was the highest room in the house, the attic made into a large, sprawling bedroom reached only by a trapdoor ladder. He liked it . . . no, he loved it. It was his and his alone, private and unique. As if sensing his need for absolute solitude now and then, McIntire had had this room made for him and drawing the trapdoor ladder up after him and securing it had a medieval sense to it, like pulling up the drawbridge over a castle moat. He retreated into it now, picking up his clothes to be washed later, and stowing them in the laundry bag in the corner before dropping onto his bed.

He took a close look at his left hand. The crescent-shaped scar just under the knuckles along the back of it appeared as a thin white line and well healed. But he knew it could and would flare an angry red and ache beyond reason if anything evil approached him. It had before, and it would again. What he didn't know was *why*. Why had the wolfish beast marked him, and why did it never seem to really heal, and why did it hurt whenever they or the rogue sorcerers of the Dark Hand came near? Surely it hadn't meant it to be a warning to him, but it worked that way. Or did it? Sometimes it hurt so badly it made him cry out sharply, betraying his presence if he had been hidden. Did that make it a beacon to those evil things that searched for him? Had the wolfjackal bitten and chewed on him with a purpose, or just to savage him? He had no real answer. From what he'd seen of Magick, it could take a lifetime of study to answer this and other questions.

Jason dropped his hand down and nudged at a file folder of papers, neatly labeled by his stepmother, JASON'S HIGH SCHOOL FILE. He didn't know what studying to be a Magicker would make him. Gavan and the others said he was a Gatekeeper, but he really didn't know much about that either. Obviously, he found gateways to other realms of existence, but even that was a hit-and-miss occupation . . . and he had no idea what he did to find them. They were just sort of there when a moment came that he needed them. He knew there had to be more to it, and there was no one alive anymore among the elder Magickers who could train him. Their own lives had been torn apart in the war between Gregory and Brennard, and much had been lost.

He couldn't tell any of this to Joanna and William, of course. First, because he'd taken a Vow of Silence not to, but more importantly, it was because they wouldn't want to understand it. McIntire built real cities on solid ground, as he'd no doubt put it, and Joanna would be worried about the social and cultural implications. But is it wise, she'd say, to be involved in something like *that*? And her nose would wrinkle in disapproval. It was the wisdom of things that bothered her. Left with a son by a man she'd been married to all too briefly, she was worried about appearances. What if she neglected him or misguided him in any way? What would people think?

Jason sighed heavily. Actually, he'd never doubted Joanna's desire to make sure he was presentable. He just wished he had his dad, and his mom, back. That's all. Dirty floors and dishes would be fine with him, if he just had his *family* back. Love made up for the lack of many things, but things could never make up for the lack of love.

He nudged his folder again, halfheartedly. It fell open. There were pamphlets of core courses and pamphlets of electives. His core schedule had been arranged so completely that he had room for maybe one elective a semester, if that. And, that was if he got up and went to school early, taking the ever popular Zero Period for honor students, a whole hour before the rest of the school day started. Add after-school athletics to that . . . he'd be gone from six to six nearly every day. When would he have time to do what he really wanted to do . . . to become what he really wanted to be?

Jason flipped the folder shut, unable to look at the paperwork for the moment. Instead, he reached for his crystal, pulling it loose from its wire jewelry cage, and cradling it in his hands. Light flared through his room, cast from the clear part of the stone, its gold and dark streaks fracturing the pattern as if black lightning had struck. After long moments spent just meditating over its inner patterns, Jason reopened the jewelry cage and replaced it.

The room fell back into normal, everyday, electric lighting, and seemed much smaller and dimmer in comparison.

Then . . . something tapped at the porthole window.

as a crow flies

JASON swung open the porthole window. He'd
taken the screen out months ago, and worked on
oiling the hinges so it moved smoothly—and quietly.
His head followed the pathway of his hand, cautiously, into the dusk, as he peered out. Something
brushed at his head as it winged past, swift and dark
as the soon to fall night. He jerked back instinctively
as the crow gave a laughing CAW at him, and circled
around the corner beam of the roof.

Jason crawled out of the porthole, finding it a more
difficult job than he had many months ago when he'd
first left his room that way, and stood on the slanted
roof which made up the ceiling and walls of his attic
room. A figure sat, knees doubled up, arm out for
the crow to land on. With a smile, Jason went to join
him at the precarious edge of the house.

"Well met, Jason Adrian," said Tomaz Crow-feather solemnly, his rich deep voice full of the inflections of the southwest American Indian. His crow nibbled a bit on his denim sleeve, before tucking his head under his wing and resting.

"Fine," Jason said as he settled down next to his elder. "We won in the League semifinals today, going to the finals!"

"That is good. But you sent a message of worry?"

Jason nodded. Quickly and as clearly as he could paint the imagery, he told of the spectral Jonnard who'd challenged him on the soccer field. Tomaz listened with great interest, saying nothing till Jason had finished, and then asking him only a question or two to clarify. Then both fell into deep silence while Tomaz considered what had happened. Finally, he gave a low grunt. The very last of the sunlight caught the silver rowels on his belt and turquoise stone bracelet, as he gestured at Jason.

"Jonnard is not wise. He has given us forewarning that the Dark Hand is prepared to move again. We can use this in two ways: first, to tweak at Brennard that his son is a fool, and second, to ready ourselves. This is good you told us of this. Gavan will have to know as soon as possible."

"I tried contacting him, but I got no answer."

Tomaz nodded. Jason watched his face, noticing for the first time that a bit of gray had begun to show among the straight black strands of the Magicker's hair, and that the weathered lines in his strong face had grown deeper and sharper. A Magicker aging?

The thought almost chased away his other concerns. "Eleanora is ill, Jason."

"What's wrong? Cold or something?"

"We don't know what's wrong."

Those words, coupled with his noticing new signs of age on Crowfeather, made Jason grow very cold for a moment, and stopped his words in his throat. He thought of the Magicker Fizziwig, Gavan's classmate, who'd suddenly aged into a white-haired old man, and then into death. . . . He managed to take a breath. "Not . . . that . . ." he said.

Tomaz lifted and dropped a shoulder in a shrug. "We do not know yet." He stood, in a fluid movement that did not even disturb the crow on his forearm. "Jason, I will pass this on, but you must keep trying to contact Gavan or Eleanora or Freyah with this, in case I don't reach them. It's too important to let go."

"You won't be able to tell them."

"Possibly not." Crowfeather looked over the sea of ordinary rooftops, as night began to hide most of them well and truly, and treetops brushed about them in a gentle night breeze. "I have a project I must tend to, and will be gone a while."

"Where?"

Tomaz smiled slowly, and dropped his free hand, large and warm, on Jason's shoulder. "I follow the track of the wolfjackals, Jason. I trust you to keep this between us, but you, more than the others, may understand."

The scar on the back of his hand gave a tiny pulse of pain, and Jason flinched slightly. "Tracking them here?"

Tomaz shook his head. "No. Tracking them to where they came from, and where they go—and to what master they answer."

"But . . . but . . . they belong to the Dark Hand."

Tomaz shook his head again. "No, Jason, I do not think so. Although they seem to thrive on the evil and chaos the Dark Hand stirs up, events suggest that Brennard is no more in charge of them than we are. Then . . . who is? We need to know."

Jason shivered, in spite of himself. It sounded like something very dangerous. "Gavan knows you're going?"

"He alone knows. And now you do. This is not the kind of thing I wish shouted from the mountaintops." Tomaz squeezed Jason's shoulder. "I should be reachable by crystal, but I may not be able to answer, so you cannot depend on me for a while."

"I understand," Jason said quietly. He did understand, but he didn't like it. "Is there anything we can do to help Eleanora?"

"No answer there either. It may just be exhaustion from her working with Jennifer, or it may be . . . something else."

Jennifer was a young Magicker, like Jason, but she'd run into an edge of dark magic that had stunned her, terrified her, and made her shut all of them away. Eleanora was determined to heal the fear in Jennifer, even if she never returned to Magicking. Jennifer was older than all of them, nearly sixteen, and she'd been a summer camp counselor to Ting and Bailey. How far away last summer seemed now.

Tomaz tickled the chest feathers on his crow, waking him, and then turned his wrist and moved his arm, setting the bird into flight. The beat of wings filled the air for a moment, then the crow glided away sullenly to find a treetop for the night. "There is a Council meeting tonight, Jason. I suggest you go and tell them what you told me."

"Ugh. All that arguing."

Tomaz laughed. "That is true. But at least we all have free will to argue with, right?"

"We must have lots of free will, then." Jason shuddered again. "All those objections. I'll do what I can."

"Do that. And even more importantly, do what you are driven to do, as a Magicker. Find that last gate, Jason, that will open Haven fully and anchor it down. We need that, all of us."

Jason dropped his head down, and stared at his feet. "I'm trying," he answered. He felt unsure as a Gatekeeper, knowing little of how it worked or even if that was truly his calling. If every Magicker had a specialty, who was to say that was his? Magick seemed so vast.

"I know that. And I know that if I say to you, try harder, it would not make a difference because you are doing your best. Do not let the Dark Hand distract you. It may well be that that is one of their chief aims right now. Your vision needs to be the clearest of us all."

The house below him seemed to awaken.

"You'd better go," Tomaz agreed. "I think it is nearly dinnertime, and it is not wise for anyone to find you out here on the roof."

Jason hesitated, then gave Crowfeather a hug. "Be careful!"

Tomaz looked surprised for an instant, then pleased. "That I will be, young Magicker."

Jason crept along the eaves of the roof and wiggled back into his porthole window. His shoulders almost stuck for a moment, and he wondered how much longer he would even be able to wriggle through. Everything changes, he thought, as he dropped back into his room.

Joanna's voice sang up the stairwell. "Dinner!"

Had it been that long? His stomach growled impatiently, telling him that it had. Jason dropped his door down and open. Meeting the Magickers Council on anything less than a full stomach would be a terrible idea. Dinner first, definitely!

CHAMBERS OF SECRET

BRENNARD sat and stared at the evening sky overhead. It was not dark yet, but creeping toward it, even as its constellations edged toward those of spring and then summer. Time. Time was eternal and yet of the essence. For all his abilities, it eluded him. He was Time's prisoner, and would have to suffer its punishment the same as any other prisoner. Well . . . not quite the same. He'd already far outlived most of his contemporaries.

That, of course, had not been entirely his doing. In standing up to Gregory the Gray's tyranny and misguided direction of Magick, he'd set off a backlash of energy that had affected everyone alive with even a touch of Magick in them. There was no way he could have anticipated that. It killed many by stunning them and leaving them vulnerable to the harsh realities of life many centuries ago. Still others, it threw forward through time . . . and a few more were merely cushioned in a kind of void until they awoke now, in this time and place.

He'd been almost as big a fool as Gregory had been. Brennard would admit that, even if only to himself. Still, he had ambitions and a plan to achieve. He steepled his fingers, then heard a faint, escaping sigh from across the room and remembered he was not alone.

The Dark Hand sat arrayed about him, in various postures of meditation and attention, sprawled on their chairs and cushions. Seven of them, the elite of his followers. Four men, three women. And one of them obviously was yawning in his sleeves, tired of waiting for the statement that he'd almost forgotten he'd gathered them to make. He regathered his thoughts.

"It is important, at this time, to know our enemies as well as we know ourselves. I called you all together for an accounting." His gaze swept the room. His words brought alertness back to their faces as they turned to watch and listen. "First . . . Dr. Anita Patel, of Gregory's Council." He put his hand on a staff lying across his knees, a staff carved to look startlingly like a cobra with its hood spread, a crystal held in its fanged jaws. The crystal was fractured beyond repair, and dull, with black streaks coursing throughout it. He lifted the staff. "She betrayed them for us, but I do not trust traitors. I think I can say that she is of no worry to us now, however."

He dropped the staff on the floor. The crystal fractured even more, spidery lines opening up on its dulled surface. The Hand closest to Brennard shuddered involuntarily and looked away from the staff. Their crystals were their magickal life. Seeing one so destroyed was like seeing their own hearts break. Brennard smiled thinly.

He paused as Jonnard came in quietly, folded his long legs, and took up a large silken cushion in the corner of the atrium. His dark hair was slicked back wetly as if he had just bathed, his face tilted to watch the gathering sunset. However, he also watched his father warily out of the corner of his eyes, and Brennard knew he had his attention.

Brennard put a little more strength into his voice as he continued. "We have our enemies numbered, and knowing them as well as we know ourselves is the key to their undoing. Gregory's Council is unraveling, and we need to use that to our advantage."

"Gregory's lot are loyal," observed a quiet voice near Brennard. "Gavan Rainwater is his acknowledged heir, and holds the Council close."

"Are they? Are they now?" Brennard put the toe of his shoe out and nudged the cobra staff at his feet. "This one was not. She was theirs, then she became mine. What do we know of them now? We know Freyah has retreated to a pocket of her Magick, making a defense there, and that pocket takes most of the Magick she has available. She is Gregory's own sister, but still there is no help there for Rainwater." He looked about the room, hearing a soft murmur of agreement.

"Then there is Rainwater himself . . . well, Gavan is young, impulsive, and still lacks a polish to his training and talent, and he knows it. He leads because there is no one else who will do it, and the others know that as well, jeopardizing the very thing he has been forced to do. He won it by default and there are those who can . . . and may yet . . . take it away from him. He is distracted by his love for Eleanora, and her own well-being, I hear, is not good these days. They argue with me that Magick is not finite, and yet, my argument becomes more and more compelling that it *is*."

"As for the lovely Eleanora, her ailment takes her out of consideration. We will not face much when we face her." Brennard held his hand up, ticking his fingers off. His hands, like his features, were slender with a hint of underlying steely strength. The years of comatose isolation after his sorcerous battle with Gregory the Gray had taken their toll but he seemed, finally, to be regaining all that he had lost. He had begun to look dangerous again, like some shadowed creature just emerging into the light, and he smiled slightly as if prizing that image. He ruled strong people. He needed to be seen as one who could best them.

"There are four others who could worry us. The herbalist FireAnn will take Gavan's side, of that there is no doubt. Her abilities will make up for the loss of the physician Anita Patel was." Brennard put his hand to a thick bracelet wherein a huge, clear crystal was embedded, and he traced it lightly. It flared with a warm light in answer to his touch. "The Moor Khalil has never been transparent to me, and my understanding is that he has brooked some opposition to Rainwater's plans, as well. If I can't see into his motives, neither can Gregory's Council. Therefore, one may assume he has his own agenda. We all know of Isabella's indiscretions and her love of power and money. As for Tomaz Crowfeather . . . coming from the Hidden as he does, from talent that has not been nurtured or instructed by any of the Magickers we know . . . he is also unfathomable. He has been involved in activities Gavan Rainwater knows nothing of, and I know little. He is a dark crystal to be examined, and deciphered. These three then, we must watch and know. Isabella, Khalil . . . and Crowfeather." He lowered his hands.

A chorus of voices answered him. "It shall be done."

"Good," he said. "Very good." He stood then. "But first and most important is the One, the younger Magicker, Jason Adrian. He must be used, and if he cannot be used, he must be stopped." Brennard paused, his dark gaze sweeping the room. "My son Jonnard has been training to handle that One, under my strictest supervision. You will cooperate with him if he asks for your assistance." Then Brennard sketched his hand through the air, leaving behind a glowing symbol, stepped into the shadowed corner of the atrium, and seemed to disappear entirely from sight, although the weight of his presence took much longer to fade. No one said anything. Jonnard got to his feet and left by the main door, head thrown back, a slight, knowing smile on his face. Silence followed him.

PLANS AND MICE . . .
OR PACK RATS

SOMETIMES having dinner at the McIntire house was like running an obstacle course while carrying a hundred-pound cat who knows a bath is waiting for it at the end. Not that baths are a bad thing at all, although Jason preferred showers, but trying to get a big cat into one could be. And that's just how he felt as he tried to get through dinner, every word from Joanna or William an obstacle to be taken carefully, without dropping the cat. Or getting his eyes scratched out.

"Did you get your forms filled out?"

High jump! "Almost," Jason answered carefully as he speared a few green beans. He munched them and tried to look thoughtful. His stepsister eyed him.

"Electives are as important as core classes," she

38

offered helpfully. "They opened up my love of film and arts."

Dodging through cones! "I've looked through the brochures," Jason said truthfully. "There's a lot that look interesting, but I haven't that much time. I think I might have one slot."

Joanna looked fondly at her daughter. "With Alicia's success in filmmaking, we all know how important it is to find something that fulfills you."

Trip and fall! "It's not that I don't want to find something, it's that I . . . can't decide." Jason stabbed at a green bean, a little harder than he intended. The fork went squeaking shrilly across his plate. McIntire looked at him briefly, bushy eyebrow waggling up and down, but he said nothing. Jason shoved the captured green bean in his mouth and chewed vigorously, hoping he wouldn't be asked anything else, at least till he chewed and swallowed.

Alicia watched him, too, her fine blonde hair framing her face, and finally she said, "Must be an awfully tough string bean."

His face warmed. *Time for the sprint!* "I'm thinking of photography," he finally managed. He wasn't, but the words just sorta fell out of his mouth. He stared at his plate in slight amazement. Where had that come from?

McIntire cleared his throat. "A nice hobby. Not that many can make a living at it . . ."

"He could be a cameraman. Cinematographer. Or even go into digital effects," Alicia said, with a great deal of satisfaction on her face and her expression. Her forte in film work was directing, but she was always complaining she couldn't find anyone to set up the shots the way she wanted them. Jason was never sure if it was because Alicia was so particular or young or just hard to understand. He'd never quite understood her.

Joanna frowned slightly, saying, "Digital?" in a vaguely unsure voice.

"Computerized photography, Mom, or close enough. They use it in all kinds of special effects, like movies, commercials, and so on."

"Oh, my. That sounds as if it could be very promising. Combined with a good business mind and sense, of course." His stepmother beamed at him then, as she refolded her napkin over her lap.

"I was just looking at it like a hobby. Something fun, you know. To break up the day." Jason pushed a few more green beans around. His appetite seemed to have fled although he could almost guarantee it would return with a growl when he went back upstairs if he didn't eat now. Even if he did eat, he'd be back in the kitchen around ten for a snack before bedtime. Something to do with having the constitution of a fast growing weed.

"Sounds like you're into something interesting and fun. A boy needs a bit of fun now and then, along with the hard work." McIntire gave a deep noise of approval.

Jason felt almost trapped. "It's not a done deal," he said. "I might not have room in the right time period. It might fill early. I might not like it."

"Worrywart." Alicia cleared her plate, standing up. "There're other classes, too. Don't be a typical freshman, running around campus with that 'Bambi caught in the headlights stare' on your face."

"Alicia!"

She flipped her lanky blonde hair, as she turned to her mother. "Well, Mom, honestly, you ought to see them! It's pathetic."

"I won't be pathetic," Jason vowed. "Trust me." His words came out strongly, not at all affected by the strange quaver that sometimes hit his voice now and then.

Joanna looked at him a long moment, then smiled gently. "I think you'll do quite well." She stood, with a relieved expression, as if a heavy burden had been lifted from her shoulders.

Jason excused himself, cleared his place, and fled to the sanctity of his attic room. Was raising him really that big a problem? He had never even thought of getting into things some of the other guys did, but Magick now . . . that would be bad enough. He couldn't ever tell her. He wondered as he trudged up his attic stairs if he could have told his real mother. Or his father. His father he still had memories of, though they were getting fuzzy. From what he remembered of his dad, someone tall, with strong arms and big hands, and a bigger laugh . . . he thought he could have. He hoped he could have.

Jason dropped into his chair with a sigh, kicking the rungs as he did. One of the all-important papers he needed to fill out drifted off the desk and fell to the carpet in a slow-motion kind of billow. He stared at it, rather than picking it up.

He already felt bummed. So, maybe now was just

as good a time as any to drop into the Council and get that chore over with. After all, things couldn't get any worse, could they? He got his crystal out, focused on it, and found the plane where interminable Council meetings seemed to be taking place, and went there.

He was, of course, wrong.

Isabella swept in at about the same time he did, wearing a red satin hat with a veil across her face and strong nose, and some kind of feathery fan fastened to the brim of the hat that matched the fan in her gloved hands. She sat down at the conference table with a muffled noise rather like a haughty snort. "It would be nice if meetings started on time."

"There is always someone here at meeting," answered Allenby mildly. The gleaming skin of his bald head flushed pink next to the white fringe of hair that was all that he had left, nearly giving him the appearance of a fluffy halo. Allenby, however, wore a pinstriped business suit and a serious expression that Jason would never associate with any cherubs. His briefcase sat on the table in front of him, a calculator nudging it. His sharp-eyed gaze swept the room. "Well, well, young Jason. Welcome!"

Jason pulled out a chair near the end where Gavan usually sat, and perched on it warily, seeing no sign of Gavan or Eleanora, and knowing Tomaz wouldn't be around. "Good evening, sir," he said, and his voice broke slightly, so he cleared his throat and went silent. Aunt Freyah, another with white hair, looked up from across the table, lowering the knitting needles which had been flying in her hands, and smiled kindly at him. She had dimples in apple-red cheeks, smooth but older skin, fluffy hair, and sapphire eyes, and a small cottage full of animated tables, pictures, trays, teapots, and the like. Jason loved visiting her. He didn't know who baked the best fudge brownies he'd ever tasted, but she always had an ample supply of them! She dropped her project (scarf was it? Something long and narrow with lots of bright yarn, at any rate), reached down into her huge purse and pulled out a steaming cup of apple cider. "Here, dear," she said as she slid it across to him. "This should help."

Actually, from what he'd heard and seen and been told in health class, the only thing that would help would be outlawing or outliving puberty, but he took the cup without argument. The cider smelled great, anyway, apple-and-cinnamon aroma in the steam. He sipped at it cautiously.

Khalil sat kitty-cornered from him, his steepled hands masking his face. As usual, he wore sweeping desert robes, making him look like a Bedouin sheikh. "Small group tonight," he observed. "Are we expecting Rainwater and Eleanora?"

"We'll wait a bit longer," Aunt Freyah said, her knitting needles once again tip-tapping in a blur of movement. "My niece has been feeling a bit under the weather, so we'll give them the benefit of the doubt." Her bright blue eyes looked about the table sharply, as if inviting disagreement, but she got none. Allenby turned his attention to some papers inside his briefcase, Isabella fished out a small, neat book of French poetry from her purse, and Khalil merely closed his eyes as if he were meditating. Jason sat back in his chair, bored, and drank his cider, feeling the sweet tart warmth trickle down his throat, bringing a nice satisfaction with it. He wondered what, if anything, really ever got decided at a Council meeting.

Finally Allenby looked up from his stack of paperwork. "I don't believe they're coming."

"Then we might as well get started." Isabella snapped her book shut with a retort that sounded like a gunshot. Khalil's eyes flew open and then he frowned at her. "Some of us have places to be and things to do."

Jason didn't know much about Isabella except for her European background and residence and that she was a businesswoman, he'd heard, of some wealth. She'd taken advantage of her knowledge of the centuries to become rich, which was in a way using her Magick and in a way not. Most of the Elders had an unspoken creed not to use Magick publicly or for ill-gotten gain. There were those who vowed it couldn't be done anyway. It seemed to backfire, and horribly, rather like the Curse of Arkady. A shiver whispered down the back of Jason's neck at the thought of that one!

Arkady had been a Magicker back in the times when Gregory the Gray and Antoine Brennard were elder and student, and all the Magickers were truly young, sometime around the time of Elizabeth I, although Jason wasn't really sure of the year. Renaissance, that much he knew. The Magickers didn't like to talk about the terrible war between Gregory and Brennard which had killed many and sent the survivors hurtling through time and space. The war was why Gavan and the others today refused to face off with the Dark Hand, in hopes of avoiding another tragedy. Arkady, they did talk about, though. Arkady had been a rather talented but hapless Magicker who couldn't control what he did. Everything had backfired or exploded in his face, but mostly because he hadn't the confidence or discipline to learn what he was doing.

They'd all been warned about the terrible Curse, one that only practice, practice, practice, and confidence seemed to be able to avert!

"First thing, then. Eleanora is not here because she has been ailing a bit, and she is feeling quite drained working with young Jennifer Logan. Jennifer's shroud of corruption not only leeches the Magick out of her, but out of anyone near her. As I understand what Eleanora and Gavan have told me, it would be easier to purge the nastiness all at once, but that might damage Jennifer for life. So, at the moment, the going is slow and difficult for everyone."

There was a murmur of sympathy about the table for Eleanora. Jason joined in, but he worried about Jennifer, too. Poor Jenny. He put his empty cider glass down on the gleaming wood table.

At the sound of its thump on the wood, all heads turned to him quickly, eager for a distraction, and it was like a trap snapping shut on its victim! Jason sat back with a momentary feeling of worry over having attracted their attention. It didn't help that Allenby immediately said, "How about a report on Gating, Jason? How goes your training, and how close are you to stabilizing the Iron Gate?"

Aunt Freyah jabbed a pointy knitting needle skyward. "That's it, put the lad on the spit, first thing, and pump up the coals." She let out an unladylike snort and threw herself back in her chair, staring a challenge at Allenby with her bright blue eyes.

Khalil composed his robes a moment, then said, "Has to be done, Freyah. There are things we have to know."

Another snort, one that *pffuffed* her frothy bangs off her forehead. "Much more is kept secret than shared around here." Freyah wrapped up her knitting briskly and stowed it away in her carpetbag. "All right, then, Jason. Looks like you're going to roast till you talk. Anything you can tell us?"

Her kinder words barely took the edge off the question as everyone kept watching him. He shrugged. "I'm doing my best, but . . . it's not so much my finding a Gate as the Gate finding me . . . I think." His face warmed with embarrassment over his uncertainty. He had no one to train him, the only Magicker in this time who'd had the ability, Fizziwig, had died mysteriously before he could help Jason at all.

"Is that how it works, then?"

Jason looked to Khalil. "It seems to. I mean, that's what happened with the Iron Gate at Camp Ravenwyng and then the Water Gate when the Dark Hand tried to trap us."

Isabella shifted. "We cannot wait for happenstance." She touched her face briefly where lines had begun to etch the corners of her eyes.

"I'm doing everything I can. I practice focusing, I travel whenever I can . . . I try to pay attention to everything I see and touch. That's all I can do," Jason finished up, helplessly.

Allenby closed his briefcase with a snap. "And that's all we can ask of you, given the circumstances." He glanced at Isabella. "Surely all that money can buy you a decent eye cream?"

"It's not that," she snapped back, "and you know it."

"I know that we're all going to grow old, sooner or later. It's the way of things."

Isabella opened her mouth to shoot off another retort but Jason quickly said, "That's not the reason I'm here, though."

Again, all eyes turned to him, and he felt their burn, as he tried not to squirm in the hard wooden conference chair and took a deep breath. "I was playing on the soccer field when Jonnard showed up. He was there, but he wasn't. No one else could see him, not even Ting and Bailey who were watching in the bleachers."

"A Sending? That takes a bit of strength." Freyah watched him thoughtfully.

"I don't know what it was. He bumped me around a bit and talked trash."

Isabella frowned until Allenby leaned over to whisper something to her, his words fluttering the feathered fan on her hat, and then she laughed slightly. "Jonnard is more his mother's than his father's son." But she did not explain what she meant by that, as she redirected her attention down the table.

"What do you think he wanted?"

"I think he wanted me to know he was back, and it's war between us."

"This is, of course, not good."

Jason nodded in agreement.

"They could," Khalil said slowly, as if choosing his words very carefully, "end us all by forcing us out into the open. But I cannot feel they want to do that, for it reveals them, as well. And removes us as targets they can drain."

"War between us is what put all of us in jeopardy. You didn't react to him, did you, Jason?"

"I tried not to."

Allenby fussed with his briefcase, then took a handkerchief out of his coat's inner pocket and mopped his head with it. "Surely you know what you did."

"I was playing soccer," answered Jason firmly. "For the semifinals! I got around him as best as I could."

"Soccer is more important than your life as a Magicker?"

"No. Well, this time it was. But I couldn't reveal myself to anyone, and no one else saw he was even *there*."

"This is serious, Jason, and I'd like to think you took it seriously."

"I did!" Jason stood up. "What did you expect me to do? What he wanted me to? He wanted me to use Magick on him. He wanted me to break the rules. What would you do to me then?"

"Don't raise your voice, young man, we understand your point," Freyah said firmly.

"No, I don't think you do. Every night, you come in here and sit down and bicker, and get mad at me 'cause I'm not doing what you think I should, when you guys can't even agree what it is I should be doing. And, I'm out there, every day, trying to be myself *and* be a Magicker, without much help from anyone else. I'm just trying to warn everyone that the Dark Hand is ready to move again."

Isabella stood, with a swish of red satin, and a wavering of the fan in her hand. "Then, I suggest, young man, that you get ready to move us to safety!"

"I'm doing all I can." Jason stared at her.

"I'm too busy for this," Isabella announced to everyone and no one in the room. She pulled one dangling crystal earring from her ear, looked into it, and was gone.

Jason sighed. He stepped back as another argument erupted around the table as to Jonnard's intentions and the strategy for dealing with the Dark Hand. He'd done what Tomaz had asked him to, and what good had it done? No one had really listened. He rubbed his palm over the crystal he still gripped and in a long moment, he was gone, too.

He found himself standing on the fallen page in his bedroom. He moved off it. Photography and computer techniques, the page read. Jason sighed. He tucked his own crystal safely away and took out the lavender one.

After very long moments, he felt Tomaz's presence in it.

"Jason," Crowfeather said solemnly. "I can tell by your expression it did not go well."

"I think everyone is mad at me."

"Did you expect anything else? You brought news of a fight to them. No one in history has ever taken such news well." He smiled, and then behind him,

Jason could see a world, in dusk, and it was not the world he'd been born in. "I have many travels before I can return. Will you be all right until then?"

"Oh, I'll be fine. I always am." Jason managed a grin.

"That is good." Crowfeather turned his face a little then, as if listening to something behind him. He frowned. Then he said something very odd. "Whatever it is that happens to me, Jason, I ask you not to tell anyone of it."

"What are you talking about?"

"Do I have your word on this?"

"But—"

"You will keep this secret?"

"I guess, but—".

A howl cut off the rest of Tomaz Crowfeather's words. A great darkness swirled through the crystal and across the landscape where Crowfeather stood. In it Jason saw and could almost smell the running figures of wolfjackals, growling and snarling, their jaws gaping open and their teeth glowing an eerie yellow green. The immense beasts raced through ebony darkness, surrounding the elder Magicker. The cloud encircled Tomaz and then . . . he was gone.

"Tomaz!" Jason juggled his crystal in his hands, trying to locate him, trying to see more clearly.

He heard one last ringing howl, and then nothing.

HEAVY SECRETS

A DULL thump hit the carpet by the side of his foot, and Jason jumped. He looked down to see the lavender crystal roll to one side before settling. He didn't remember dropping it, he thought, as he stooped quickly to retrieve it. First law of Magicking was: Never Drop Your Crystal.

Of course, as he learned more, he realized that the quartzes and gemstones were just for focusing his own inner power, so it was really a matter of . . . Never Lose Yourself. And he had, if only for a moment or two, while watching Tomaz being swept away. He stroked his fingers over the faceted stone. He still didn't know much about the minerals, even though he'd always intended to study them. He though this might be a morganite. If so, it was valuable because of its size and nearly flawless planes.

51

Even more valuable was the presence of Gregory the Gray he could sense within, and the power that could flow through it. The crystal was far more powerful than his first bonded stone, and he'd admitted to Gavan that he was a little afraid of it.

Rainwater had teased him mildly about that, and then taught him another trick or two about meditating upon the object. Gavan Rainwater held a bit of showman about him, acted a little flamboyant. He was very young for the leadership he'd taken upon himself, and that was part of his cover. He knew the Dark Hand didn't take him as seriously as they should, and that was fine with Gavan. "Lad, there's nothing wrong with being underestimated, as long as you don't underestimate yourself! Know your strengths."

He didn't, yet, Jason thought, as he warmed the stone between his hands. He did know he wasn't strong enough to go after Tomaz and help. And he wasn't sure he could be strong enough to do as Tomaz asked, and tell no one, although knowing *why* might have made it a lot easier.

Why didn't Tomaz want anyone knowing what he was doing, and why would he not want help if something happened to him?

Jason shivered. He'd been so close to Tomaz, linked with him . . . and he'd never felt any fear, even as the beasts swept around him. Whatever it was, Tomaz seemed to know what he was doing, for Jason hadn't sensed a single wavering of the Magicker's strong will. He'd have to find hope in that. And, perhaps, even in another source.

He sat down at the computer and opened himself

up to a different kind of magic. With a few key taps, he found Rich online, with Stef almost certainly sitting on the overstuffed chair in the den behind him, probably munching on something and reading a sports magazine. Rich confirmed as much with a smiley face as he typed in,

"And Stef says Hi ☺."

Quick as a flash, Henry was on, with a new SN "theSquibbler." Despite his worries, that made Jason laugh aloud. He could almost see Henry peering at him, then taking notes as his habit had become. For without notes, his Magick (like his life) seemed to be in a chaotic jumble which Henry muddled through with typical good-naturedness, if slightly worried about the outcome. Quicker than he got in trouble, Henry greeted Jason and asked what was going on, and had he heard from Bailey and Ting.

"No," Jason typed back. "Not recently. I just had to attend a Council meeting, and I want everyone to join me in a chat."

"Ick! Council meetings are the pits."

"Tell me about it." Jason then messaged everyone to follow him to a chat room. As if knowing they were being thought about, Ting signed on, and then Bailey bounced into the chat room with a *"Hi! Hi!"*

Trent signed on last, his typing in spurts, just like his tendency to whistle or hum song snatches came and went, his fingers often drumming. **"What's happening? Do I sense trouble—➡ at Bailey. What did Lacey steal now? Heya, Henry. Ever get Lantern under control?"**

Lantern was the ability to send one's crystal into a well-lit glow, like lantern light. Henry often started a fire instead. He used to practice Lantern wearing heat-proof oven mitts at camp.

"Almost, Trent. I only burned my thumb this week! Soon!"

"Rut-roh," broke in Rich. "Stef wants the keyboard!"

Jason sat back in his chair as his computer screen filled with smiley faces and all sorts of other symbols and message jargon in a storm of color. He laughed, for Stef was more and more like the overgrown bear cub that was his shapeshifting other self, rather than the bear cub growing more like the teenager Stef. He waited till the flurry of symbols died away before typing, "Heya, Stef. Okay guys, this is a little serious. I had to go visit the Council tonight." He waited until they'd all communicated their sympathy for that one.

"So," Trent typed, "the real question is: what did they want?"

Jason found himself sighing as he responded. "They want a Gatekeeper who can actually find Gates."

"What? Two aren't enough for them!" He could practically hear Bailey's outraged huff.

"I understand what they're saying, though." That was Ting, thoughtful as always. "We need a place where we can safely go and train. Maybe even hide."

Amid a cloud of emote symbols, Stef managed to type, "Ida join the circus."

"Who's Ida?" asked theSquibbler.

"No one."

"Then how did Stef know her? And why did she join the circus."

"HENRY," wrote Bailey. "Stef means he would . . . I'd join . . . the circus."

"Oh."

"This is serious, guys."

"We know, Jason."

"I can't find it!"

"It's always the last place you look," Rich wrote, after successfully wrestling the computer keyboard away from Stef, for the snowfall of colorful smiling faces and other emotes disappeared and words took their place.

"This is serious, Rich. What if I can make Haven safe enough that any time Stef changed, the two of you could bolt there? And you wouldn't have to worry about being a freak?"

"I'm not the freak. He is. I'm just the friend of a freak."

"Yeah, yeah."

"Why can't you find it, do you think? Are you looking too hard?"

"Dunno, Ting. Wish I did. It's like the Gate is there, but I can't see it until I need to, or have to. But we can't wait for things to get worse."

"Explain," typed Trent.

And so Jason did, telling them all about the ninja-styled Jonnard who'd appeared and challenged him. That stunned them all into computer silence, except for Henry who typed "Woah" over and over. Or maybe he leaned on the repeat key by accident.

"What do you need us to do?"

"Anything! Everything." Jason stopped, and took a deep breath. What could they do? He didn't really know.

"First of all," Trent wrote, "we all need to be looking around carefully. Maybe we can spot something Jason can't, because he's blind to it. Second, we need to watch each other's backs if Jonnard and the Dark Hand are getting ready again. Third, we need to stay in touch with each other, no matter what."

"What kind of things, though?"

"Anything and everything," Trent shot back to Henry. "Something that is kinda out of place, but not really. Or something that should change, but doesn't."

"Like a broken clock?"

"Sorta. Look, we know that Haven is a step out of time with our own world. So, if it has another side to it that has to be anchored by a second Gate, like the elders are telling us, then it has to be somewhere. Sort of another dimension nudging us every once in a while."

Ting wrote, and Jason could also see her shy smile as she did, "Then Bailey had better clean her room so we can see better."

"Brat!"

"Brat times two!"

"And proud of it! Besides, this is so Lacey will feel at home <ducks>."

Rich wrote in, "So it's decided then. We keep our eyes peeled, and we leave messages for each other more often, so we know what's up. AND we don't let anyone bag on Jason, right?"

"Right!"

"Definitely!"

"Jason's our man, if he can't find a Gate, no one can!" And Bailey added a cheerleading pom-pom to that sentence, and Jason found himself rolling his eyes, but he felt better. They understood. They were with him. They'd help.

Now he had to do everything he could, even if it meant walking into Jonnard again.

Trent signed off and pulled back from the computer he and his father shared. From the living room, his father's soft snore sounded—he'd evidently fallen asleep in front of the TV again. Listening for a moment, Trent could hear the distinctive tones of a narrator on the Discovery Channel. The corner of his mouth twitched in a reluctant smile. Something interesting and intriguing but not interesting enough to keep him from falling asleep. Trent stood up in the nook they called a den and walked softly to his own room, the floor creaking slightly despite his care. He'd let his dad sleep until bedtime, then wake him up before doing dishes and going to bed himself.

Taking care of his dad, he knew how to do. Taking care of Jason, he wasn't sure about. Without Magick of his own, the only thing he could consistently offer was his knowledge of things. But that came from books and imagination . . . and the borderline between what mythology thought Magic could be and what Magick was . . . would soon be crossed. How much help could he be then? Friendship was probably one of the strongest forces he knew, but Jason needed more than that, and he had nothing else to give.

Trent made his room up, laid his clothes out for the next day, found a good book, and sat down to read for a few minutes, but he wasn't really reading. He thought a great deal more, and nothing helpful came up.

The phone rang, incredibly late. Bailey lifted her head from her pillow, half listening, wondering if something had gone wrong. Lacey rattled about in her cage in her usual nighttime activity. Bailey had hidden something sparkly in her container and the pack rat was happily nosing it out and reburying it elsewhere, in a different corner, under sawdust curls and shredded tissue paper. After a moment, Bailey's bedroom door pushed open slightly.

"Bailey? It's Henry. Normally I wouldn't let him talk to you, but he usually doesn't call."

"Is there a problem?"

"I don't know, dear. I have him on hold."

"Okay." Bailey wriggled out from her nest of warm blankets, reaching for the phone on her nightstand. "Henry? What's wrong?"

"I'm sorry, Bailey. I can call back tomorrow."

"No, no. I wasn't asleep yet. Quite." She stifled a yawn. Her bedroom door closed itself quietly, and Bailey punched her pillow into a more comfortable position under her head. "What's up?"

"D-did I wake you?"

"Nah, not yet. Lacey's running around her cage and all."

Henry let out a sigh of breathy relief that carried over the telephone.

"What is it, Henry?"

"I was thinking about what Jason said tonight. About Jonnard and all. Has he bothered you? And could you tell if he did?"

"Well . . ." Images of the stalking man went through her thoughts a moment and she shivered. Lacey stood up in her cage, looked her way, and made a soft, chittering noise as if in question. Moonlight dimly filtered through the curtains and she could barely see the tiny pack rat. "Not exactly."

"Maybe but you're not sure?"

She didn't want to cry wolf. That Jonnard might go after Jason, that all the Dark Hand might, she knew. Herself? No way was she that important. "Something like that, Henry. Has he bothered you?"

"Nothing like that."

"Then why did you call me?"

"I just wanted to, you know, make sure you were all right."

Because he wasn't. She sensed it. "You can tell me."

"No, I can't."

"Henry," she said firmly. "If it walks like a duck and quacks like a duck, then we're gonna eat Chinese. Was it Jonnard? You called me because you had to talk to someone, and you knew you could trust me, so spill it!"

"I . . . I'm not sure. I hear this voice all the time. I think it's him. If it's not—I'm going crazy."

"You're not going crazy."

"Then . . . I . . . I think so."

She sucked her breath in. Poor Henry! He'd been Jonnard's victim before. "Noooo, Henry."

"I'm not sure! And, and, if he is . . . I can handle it this time. We're a lot stronger, Bailey, all of us."

So why then was Henry calling her so late at night and sounding so worried? "Sure we can, Squibbler."

He let out a fidgety noise. "I just wanted you to know in case, well, in case you were in trouble, too, or if they decided I was crazy or something."

"You are definitely not crazy. You're a Magicker, and that's a heck of a something!"

"What about you?"

Bailey wrinkled her nose. "I don't have anything I can prove yet. So, no worries, but I'll keep my eyes peeled."

"Okay. Just don't tell anyone, will you?"

"My word on it. You tell everyone yourself when you're ready." Bailey crossed her fingers. That was, until Henry got in trouble and needed help.

"Thanks."

"And Henry—"

"Yeah?" he answered, as if finally very very tired.

"You're right. We're a lot stronger this time. And it's because we're a 'We.' Got that? Like the Musketeers, all for one and one for all."

Henry sounded cheered a little as he said, "Right! Night, then."

"Talk to you tomorrow."

"Okay. And . . . thanks, Bailey."

She hung up the phone, and squirmed around till she could lie on her back and stare up at the bedroom ceiling. Long ago, her mother had painted it a soft sky blue and added billowy clouds. This wasn't a place they owned, but it was their home. Right now, the sky looked awfully dark, maybe even stormy, but there were those beautiful silvery and white clouds.

Every one had a silver lining. Her mom had painted them like that.

Ting moving again. Jason challenged. Trent worried about being discovered, as was Stef, although for different reasons, and Rich unhappy at being a Magicker period. Henry with worries of his own, and she with . . . what? Had she seen someone following her or hadn't she? Without proof, she couldn't ask anyone for help. Not yet.

So they all had secrets, all around. Dark, heavy secrets. Would they have a silver lining?

Bailey closed her eyes and tried to fall back into sleep.

THINGS UNSAID

THE wind off the lake was mild and yet held a touch of chill from the past winter. Whimsically named for the life it held only in summer for campers, Lake Wannameecha was still a beautiful body of water. There would be fog along the rocky shore and pebbled beaches in the morning, Gavan thought, as he stood outside a weathered building and watched the waters. It was a moment of serenity, of peace, but he did not find he could hold onto it. The moment fled and worry filled him again, even with the sound of a door opening, and gold lantern light spilling over him, as someone joined him with a rustle of long skirts and lace. She carried the lantern light with her, cradled in the crystal upon her wrist. Like his heart, she'd filled her crystal with warmth and illumination and it spilled out now, showing the way.

"It's late," Eleanora said. "Come inside, I've just made a pot of tea." She put her hand through the crook of his arm, and drew close to his side.

Gavan Rainwater felt his heart do a quick double beat, and he turned his face, so that he could rest his chin on the top of her head, where her bountiful curls made a soft pillow. He felt overwhelmed by many things, but most especially by what he'd felt for years and hadn't had the nerve to say. It felt right to say it, never more right, in case he might not have another moment like this again. He remarked, very quietly, "You do know that I love you?"

"Yes. I have known that for quite some time." Her hand tightened on the back of his wrist. Then she said, "And I love you."

"Good. I'm glad that's out of the way!" And he let out a sigh of relief at having finally voiced his feelings, so long left unsaid. Now there was no regret.

Eleanora laughed. "Now we can move on to other things?"

"Precisely." He could feel her laughter vibrating through her body as he touched her. "We can't waste time."

"Such a romantic you are!" Eleanora ducked out from under his chin, and swung around to look up at him. She kissed a fingertip and pressed her delicate hand to his mouth.

He grabbed her hand and nibbled on those fingers before she managed to free herself, and he laughed then, as her eyes widened, and then the carefree moment passed, as he noted the silvery glints in her dark hair . . . just a strand here and there, but . . .

there were new lines about her eyes. He inhaled deeply at the sight of them. She'd always been older than he, but never old, never would be old, as he hoped not to be. Still, there was that fear that sudden aging, and death, could strike any of them at any time, as the centuries decided to gain their vengeance for the Magickers having skipped through them. A rift in magickal power had thrown many of them through time. Most had slept through the passing years. Some had been hurtled forward through the centuries as if picked up bodily and thrown. What had the war between Gregory the Gray and the Dark Hand of Brennard done to all of them, outside the laws of natural sciences, and what could it yet do? He thought of his friend Fizziwig, young yet silver-haired, young yet dying of old age, like a candle snuffed out. Young yet gone, unstoppably.

She sensed his sudden turn of mind. "Things," she said, "will work out."

"Not unless we work on working them out." Gavan frowned. His words sounded grimmer than he intended, but perhaps that was just. "I can't stand by, Eleanora, and hope. I have to find an action that works."

"War with our own kind, when there's still a chance we can reconcile with them?"

"I don't think Brennard will ever allow that chance. He wants it all or nothing, and if nothing—that will suit him fine. He wants the children, Eleanora. He's sent me a note asking me to turn them over, and if I do not, he will reveal us to the modern world."

"He has to be bluffing." Eleanora's face paled,

even in the moonlight which accented her fair skin. "He can't be serious, he'd give himself away, too. That would destroy all of us."

"Don't think he won't. I imagine he has his little bolt-holes, his hidden places, to keep himself and the others safe while we fall prey. He's as aware as I am what revealing us would do. Scientific inquiries, exams, scorn, imprisonment with fancy words, more that we can't begin to imagine, probably. I don't think he really cares if he ends Magick in this world, as long as he survives and proves his point that Gregory was wrong."

"My father," said Eleanora softly, "was wrong about many things."

He put his arm about her shoulder and pulled her close. "Not the important things," he replied to her.

"Let's hope not." She sighed. "We have to do whatever we can to keep the children safe."

"Even more so than ever. It's not a burden that I want to add to Jason's life, but Brennard has given me a deadline to respond, and after that, we'll all be in deadly peril. The sooner Jason can anchor Haven for us, the more chances we'll have. We need a safe place, a sanctuary, to step away to and educate them, give them a chance to know their Talents and use them." He tightened his hold on her. He could feel the weakness running through her. "How goes your work with Jennifer?"

"It goes very slowly. It's like wrestling an octopus of dark energy, and with every tentacle I free from her, one tries to attach to me." Eleanora seemed to repress a shudder.

"Let me help you."

She shook her head. "I don't think Jennifer or her family would let anyone else get close. She is terrified, Gavan."

"I can't blame her for that. We're going to lose her, aye?"

Eleanora nodded slowly. "I can't bring her back. She doesn't want it, and we both think she is probably too damaged."

He rubbed the palm of his hand over her shoulder in soothing motions. "Then we must make sure she is as free as she can be, and that we don't lose you as well."

She leaned on him. "I'm always so tired these days."

"Get Freyah to help you." The moment he said it, he knew he'd made a mistake. Eleanora stiffened.

"My aunt has her eccentricities."

"And helping us seems to be one of them." Gavan made a noise, rather like a huff, in spite of himself. He loved Freyah despite her quackery and sharp tongue—but if only she'd give more! What she'd been through after the magickal battle that had separated all of them, he could not begin to guess, but she had become secretive and practically a hermit, though just as sharp-witted as ever. Dragging her out of her tiny cottage home was a chore he never relished, nor would he try unless it were a necessity but the time had come when they were all needed. "You cannot be a Magicker," he commented, "without reaching out to others."

"She reaches."

"When it suits her. In the meantime, you're exhausted. The Council asks about you, and your absences. If not Freyah, then go to Khalil. Or Isabella. For advice, support, whatever you can get from them!"

"Allies I know very little about." Eleanora moved her hand from his arm long enough to tuck a curling strand of hair away from her face and behind her ear. "I know Khalil cares very intensely about the children, but Isabella's main concern seems to be the money she's put away over the years, money I think there is no doubt her abilities helped her earn. They have agendas, Gavan, which you and I don't understand yet. Until I know their motivations, I don't want to trust my life to them."

"Your health and Jennifer's are at stake. If it meant going to Brennard himself, I think I would."

"Bite your tongue!" Eleanora slapped the back of his wrist lightly. "Neither of us would, and we both know it."

"Not at any cost?" Gavan considered, then nodded in agreement. "But I won't see you suffer, Eleanora."

"The attacks are less frequent now. Either I am coping better or whatever it is loses strength."

He put his hand over hers, and squeezed gently. He had seen her under attack, and known how much it hurt, how hard it hit, seen her reel and gasp for breath and her skin go ashen, as if she fought for her very soul. As, from what she told him, she did. An evil fought to tear her apart from the inside out, and because of it, she refused to leave Jennifer in her dilemma. He agreed. How could you leave a fifteen-year-old to deal with something like that? Yet, despite their vows, they weren't winning, and Jennifer and Eleanora were slowly, painfully, slipping into shadow.

Jason had to find a sanctuary for all of them before it was too late, untrained though he was, alone in his talent though he was. Jason remained Gavan's main hope. "What do you think your father would have said?"

"Gregory," Eleanora answered firmly, "would say, 'stop scaring my daughter with worry about tomorrow, handle today, and, by the saints, it's about time you declared your love for her!'"

He laughed in spite of himself. He brushed his lips against Eleanora's temple. "There will be an answer," he promised. "And soon." He had no idea how, or when, but having made his promise to her, he'd find a way to keep it.

Both fell into quiet then, and looked out over the lake, where a calm night and good weather allowed a few more hours of serenity.

Henry did not sleep well, despite his talk with Bailey. He stared at the second-story window on the far side of his bedroom. Curtains painted with a scene of the elvish kingdom of Rivendell from *Lord of the Rings* covered the window, giving him a view of another land, far away, framed slightly by the bookends on his high bureau, copies of the tall statues on the river. But his thoughts were not in another world, they were mired in great muddy clumps of this one, and he wasn't happy.

He punched his pillow up, then threw his head back into it, and clenched his teeth. He listened. Far off, muffled, he could hear the beagle down the street barking at something, probably an opossum cautiously crossing the backyard fence. He could hear his toddler sister making restless noises in her sleep. All normal late night sounds. What Henry feared to hear were sounds he shouldn't, that no one else seemed to hear, but that he did. And the thing that frightened him most was that he could not tell if it came from within or without. Was he being haunted or was he going crazy? As Rich and Stef would tease him, what kind of freak had he turned into? Yet, after seeing Stef turn from a burly teen into a chubby bear cub, could Henry not expect that his Talents might transform him? Their Magick seemed to affect them all in ways they were still learning about.

Henry turned over with a sigh, burying his cheek into his pillow which had now gone lumpy. He punched it again, and squinched his eyes shut tightly. In a moment, his breathing had deepened and he lay at the very edge of sleep and dreams, and his body began to relax gratefully.

Then . . .

Henry . . . my preciousssssss.

The whisper went through him like an icicle. He sat bolt upright in bed. His breath knotted in his chest and he put his hands to his neck as if he could claw it free, pulling at his pajama T-shirt. A gasp or two and he breathed again, eyes blinking through the bedroom darkness at nothing. He grabbed for his spectacles and pulled them on. Still nothing. Then who or what was playing Gollum in his mind? Henry grabbed his blankets, pulling them close as if they were some kind of armor. He stared about his room.

He felt as if every muscle he had was being pulled out of his body, turned to mush. A great weakness swept over him and he fell back limply onto his bed. His eyelids drooped shut, too weary to remain open. What was happening to him? He felt as if he were nothing more than a limp noodle, boneless, heatless. He had but a heartbeat or two to think, then slipped into exhausted sleep. So deep was his sleep he did not hear the whisper come again. *Sssleeep, precioussssss*. Then a hard, dry laugh.

MONDAY, MONDAY

STEF groaned as he sat down on the locker room bench and looked about at the battered steel doors, towels thrown everywhere, his sneakers in his hand. "Mom said if I went up another size in shoes, I'd have to go barefoot." He looked at his scruffy athletic shoes in dismay.

Rich sat down opposite him, his red hair sticking out in every direction. He tried unsuccessfully to comb it down with his fingers, even as he looked at his friend's stockinged feet. "You're already a size twelve. How much bigger can you get?"

"Well, that's the point, isn't it?" Stef let out a disgusted grunt. "We don't know!"

"But you're worried about it before it happens."

Stefan tugged on his shoes gingerly, as if fearful they'd rip apart in his great hands. "You don't know

my mom, Rich. It's like I'm this big burden to them.
All she and my dad talk about is when I can finish
high school and get a football scholarship and go off
to college and they're on their own. Like they can't
wait or something."

Rich sighed. He couldn't dispute that. He did
know Stef's mom and dad, and that was exactly their
attitude. As much as his mom fussed over him and
his health, the Olsons grumbled over Stefan and the
dent the raising of him put into their lives. Person-
ally, he thought that both families deciding to have
only one child had been a pretty darn good decision.
The Olsons would have loathed more, and his mom
would have had a nervous breakdown if she'd had
other unhealthy Hawkinses to worry about.

He stared at Stef's shoes. "They'll hold. The only
thing wrong with them is their stench. They reek,
Stef. Doncha use that foot powder I bought you?"

"Sure I do. It's the bear. He likes to sleep on 'em
sometimes. And he's ripe, you know that. That's the
way bears are."

Rich half-smiled at the big square face of his longtime pal. He could see the bear in him, even without
knowing that was Stef's shapeshifted other form. Stef
was big, burly, strong, and grumbly, with a sweet
tooth. He often did not know his own strength, and
he had to really focus on something to pursue it, but
he'd been working on containing his ability to change
unexpectedly.

Rich stood up and began gathering towels, part of
his job as trainer to the boys' track team, before bas-
ketball shooting them into the canvas bins at the far
end of the locker room. Most of the towels made it.

The rest were close enough to count, he decided. Stef stood up with a grunt, and put his hands to his right knee. Immediately Rich was there, kneeling, his own hands going to the joint.

"Still swollen? Sore?"

"Nah. Just kinda tight."

"Ah." Rich nodded, his spiky red hair bobbing. "Okay. Just make sure to stretch it before you do anything, even walk, but don't stretch too much. Just kinda loosen it up, okay?"

"Gotcha."

"Good, 'cause this is Monday and we've got a track meeting Thursday."

Stef stared at him. "I know what day it is," he said flatly.

Rich flushed. "Well, I know you do. I was thinking, you know, four days to heal up some more."

"Sure you were." Stef's hand shot out and cuffed his shoulder. "I remember things."

Rich hoped Stef did. He'd spent almost the entire weekend as a bear, and Rich was exhausted trying to dodge parents and other hazards associated with keeping a half-grown bear under wraps. It was a good thing they'd been allowed to go camping by themselves at nearby Featherly Park. Stef's parents had been more than glad to let him go for the weekend, and Rich's mom had been talked into the tonic qualities of an early spring sleepover. "Yeah, well, next time remember bears can't climb eucalyptus trees, okay? Bark is really slippery and just kinda slides off the tree trunks!" He poked Stef in his meaty ribs. "Let's get out of here. I've got homework and you've got laundry and homework."

Stef grunted again, and ambled with him to the locker room door, pawing at his backpack and pulling out a brightly foil-wrapped protein bar that was nothing less than humongous. "Snack," he mumbled, with his mouth half full. "Jus' a little one."

Rich could not help but grin as Stef wadded up the wrapper and stuffed it back into his backpack. He knew that protein bar brand—made of soy and low carb, low sugar. He'd be willing to bet it was his own mom who'd given it to Stef. Health food nut all the way. Whatever worked to keep both Stef and the bear cub inside him happy. Keeping Stef happy meant keeping curiosity at bay, and of all the Magickers, Rich thought the two of them had the most to hide. Stef's family would probably throw him out if he was ever revealed and his mom . . . well, he just wasn't sure what might happen. He closed the school gym doors behind him, as Stef lumbered away, still happily munching.

On Tuesday, Jason dropped off his finally completed packet. He almost asked for a receipt from the guidance counselor's secretary, just so he could take it home and give it to Joanna, and his stepmother could see he'd finally taken care of business. It wasn't necessary, he knew, but the desire to do it seemed to keep him hanging around the office. The secretary took the big manila envelope from him and then looked up curiously as he just stood by her desk.

"Is there something else, Jason?"

"No, I guess not." He hesitated another moment. "When do we hear?"

"Unless you're taking summer courses, you won't hear until early August. That's when our computer sets all the schedules up, to be sent out. Not our computer here, but the district one, and the high school's department."

"What if I change my mind?"

"The first week after schedules are sent, you go into the high school office and petition to add or drop classes. And you'll be having orientation that week too." Cheerfully, she shuffled his envelope into a rather large stack already on her desk. "It's a big step, high school."

"Anyone ever make . . . you know . . . a really big mistake?"

"What do you mean?" She looked at him curiously from behind her glasses, the crow's-feet at the corners of her dark brown eyes deepening.

"Well. You know." He shifted uncomfortably. "Becoming someone they really didn't want to be."

She smiled. "You have years, Jason, before you're locked in. And anyway, in this country, you're never really locked in unless you want to be." She checked her watch, and without her saying another word, he knew he'd been dismissed. She was busy.

"Thanks," he said, and moved away, through the guidance part of the school office, where the walls were covered with posters of happy, well-adjusted schoolchildren. Not a one of them, he noticed, wore a crystal focus upon them. Not a one of them was worried about dodging a ninja-clad Jonnard or finding an abducted Magicker, and how that might fit neatly into their future.

On Wednesday, Ting sat down to do her homework, with the background noise of her mother making phone calls and arrangements to move back to San Francisco. She tried not to hear the soft, but decisive words that were shaping her future even as they were spoken. She sat at the dining table, her notebooks and books spread out in front of her, rather than in the solitude of her bedroom at her computer desk. The dining room table had more space, and there was something about the deeply polished cherrywood that made her feel good. She'd grown up with this table waxed to a high gleam, and she wondered if it was moving to San Francisco with her, or if her father would stay behind again with the young ones. No one had said much to her about the arrangements.

Not that she would really mind. She loved her grandmother dearly, and the house with the dragon upon the roof, and the city of San Francisco which was altogether different from any place she'd ever been. It was only that she hated changing schools again, and missing Bailey, and it seemed that the Magickers had more adventures when she was away—and without her. *That* she minded. Bailey seemed to be caught up in the thick of things and she was always hearing about it later. Although, Ting reflected, being attacked by wolfjackals and finding a dead body (poor old Fizziwig) were not exactly the kind of things she wanted to be doing. There were times, though, when she knew she could help, and learn, and she wanted to be close to do it!

Ting closed her hand about her crystal charm on her bracelet. The wire cage holding the crystal was flexible, almost springlike, and could be stretched out to let the crystal slip through, freeing it. It was her own design, the bracelet and cage, fashioned like a long, sinuous Chinese dragon holding a lantern. Chinese dragons were old, wise, and not at all prone to eating young maidens. She had been able to make the bracelet and cage quickly once she'd managed to visualize its design in her mind, and she liked the way it turned out. Even through its clever cage, the crystal warmed to her almost touch, and a feeling of well-being flooded her. With it came the tiniest caress of her grandmother's thoughts.

Ting gasped and freed her crystal so that she could cup it closer, peering into it. She looked up into her grandmother's etched face as if seeing her through water, which she probably was. Her grandmother used a teacup and leaves as a focus rather than a crystal, for that was how she'd been taught many, many years ago. Eleanora and FireAnn referred to Ting's grandmother as one of the Hidden Ones, people of magickal Talent who'd never been really found or taught, and yet used their own abilities in mystical ways. Her grandmother's father had been a Chinese magician and acrobat, and a revered performer who had never given out his many secrets. Ting sometimes wished that she could have seen him, as well, but the age difference was just too great. He had passed away long before she had been born. A very few faded and yellowing black-and-white photos were all her grandmother had left, and in those, he was already aged, and had stopped performing.

"Grandmother!" Ting said in soft delight. "How are you feeling?"

"I am feeling well enough. Do you have a moment to come speak with me?"

"Let me tell Mama." Ting got up, slipping from her chair, and walked to the other room. Her mother held up one finger, asking for a moment of silence while she finished talking, then lowered the phone. "I am going to talk to Grandmother."

Jiao Chuu smiled. "Give her a hug and kiss for me, but don't stay too long."

"I won't. I've homework." Ting cupped her crystal, centered herself for a moment, then stepped into the sharp coldness of the jewel and through its door into her grandmother's kitchen. The room smelled of jasmine tea and its well-steeped tea leaves, and she hugged her grandmother tightly before she even had a chance to lower her porcelain cup in welcome. It had only been a few months since she'd gone home, and yet the body she hugged seemed smaller, more frail than she remembered. Even if she hadn't been told, Ting thought, she'd have known the cancer was back. She kissed her grandmother's cheek.

"You have grown!" her grandmother said proudly as she stood back and looked at her.

"A little."

"That is the way it should be." Her grandmother pulled out a wooden chair for Ting, and then they both sat. New porcelain cups were turned over and filled with steaming hot tea and sugar passed around. Her grandmother never used any, as she had grown up that way, and Ting used only a little. For a few moments, they exchanged pleasantries, as was the custom although Ting fought to keep from squirming in her chair. What had been so important she had to visit like this?

At last, her grandmother set her teacup down. "You are patient with an old woman."

Ting felt her face grow warm. Well, she was *trying*. "I'm afraid I haven't much time today, Grandmother. Tests and papers, and homework."

"Then I shall get to the point. First, I wanted to tell you, alone, that I am sorry you must come back." Her grandmother's face wrinkled even deeper.

"Don't be! I don't mind, and we want to help."

"You are a far greater help than you understand. Just knowing that what runs in our blood is not lost . . ." Her grandmother's voice trailed off. Instead, she reached over and patted Ting's wrist. After a moment, she took a deep breath. "Secondly, something rare and strange has happened. The dragon that guards my house has spoken."

Ting almost dropped the delicate porcelain cup balanced in her hands. "It . . . what?" She resisted the impulse to run outside and look up at it.

"It has spoken."

"What did it say?"

"Not in words, Granddaughter. It hissed at me."

She did put her cup down then, even though her hands were cold and the cup warm. "Are you sure it was not the wind, or something? Maybe a possum or raccoon up on the roof?"

Her grandmother shook her head firmly. "It is made, as you know, to whistle in the wind, or clatter if a great breeze or earthquake shock rattles it. But no. I was in the garden, and looked up at it, and it turned its metal head and hissed down at me. A long, warning hiss."

"Warning you of what?"

Her grandmother shrugged. "I do not know. But I thought of you and your friends instantly and decided you should know what little I do."

Ting swung her legs around. "If I went out to look at it, do you think it would . . . ?"

"Do it again? I doubt it." Her grandmother smiled then. "But shall we look?"

They went out the door to the kitchen garden courtyard. The dragon was made so that it could be seen easily from that side, as well as on the roof ridge immediately over the entrance to the house. She looked up at it. Sinuous like the design of her bracelet, it was similar to a weather vane, but far more clever and sculpted than that. She had never really seen anything like it before coming here. They stood in silence for a few moments, until her grandmother gave a weary sigh. Ting put her arm about her shoulders, to steady her, as night crept close to the garden and she could feel the dampness of a Bay fog in the air. "When I come back," she said, "perhaps I'll hear it then."

They turned away, toward the golden doorway of the well lit kitchen. Metal creaked overhead. Ting looked up to see the chrysanthemum-holding dragon peering down at her. It let out a long hiss. Then went quiet. She blinked in amazement.

Her grandmother nodded. "Tell them," she said. "Warn them."

Ting's heart beat rapidly. Her younger ears had caught what her grandmother had not.

The metal dragon had not just hissed. It had said, "Jasssssssssssssson."

FRIDAY, FRIDAY

SOMETIMES Thursdays could be so bad, Trent thought, you just wanted them to sink into oblivion forever so you could get on into Friday, which always seemed to be better no matter *what* was happening. That, of course, was just one of his mistakes.

Along with reading Ting's e-mail about a mysterious warning from the roof dragon at her grandmother's to confound himself with, his father came home from work with a box full of personal things from his desk and an overloaded briefcase. He sat down, cradling the box on his knee, and looked at Trent sadly. "Business," he said, "is not going well."

"They fired you?"

"No," his father answered thoughtfully. "Not yet." He shuffled his carton over onto the free part of the couch. "We'll find out tomorrow if the company has found a buyer willing to take on the debt, or if we're all laid off. Laid off," his father repeated, "is not the same as being fired."

"If you're out of work . . ." Trent muttered, and stopped at the expression on his father's tired face.

"Fired means I did something wrong. Laid off means . . . the company is struggling and there's no work. It means I can get a job with someone else, hopefully quickly."

"A lot of people are getting laid off," Trent pointed out. "It's been on the news for months."

"I know." His father let his briefcase hit the floor. "That's why I started packing tonight. These are things I don't need at the office anyway, and if it comes to the worst, I'm ready to go. I'll know tomorrow."

"And what then?"

"Then, I bring home my good briefcase, and my last check, and I start sending out résumés. I understand it's done over the Internet now, a lot of the time."

And so on Friday night, Trent sat in his room, doing his homework, and listening for the front door. He didn't know when he finally heard his dad's key in the door if being late was good, bad, or worse. Shoving his desk chair away, he rolled across his bedroom floor, neck craned. His dad walked in with his regular briefcase, and Trent couldn't tell just from looking at him. He stood and went to the threshold of his bedroom. "Well?"

His father looked at him. "Well. I got three months' severance pay, which is really quite good, under the circumstances. But they're closed, and it's done." He just stood there for a moment, a rather dazed expression on his face. He added in a low voice, "I worked there for a long time. I met your mother there. Now they're both gone."

Trent got up and went to him, putting his arms around his dad. "It happens," he said, trying not to feel as scared as his father looked. "You needed a job change anyway! Everyone does, sometimes."

His father gripped his shoulder. "Yes, sometimes they do. I have the retirement funds, of course, although that's for . . . well, retirement. And you've your college money put away."

"That," said Trent, "is yours if you need it."

His father shook his head. "We should be just fine. I've got a lot of skills, and they gave me some excellent recommendations."

Trent managed a lopsided grin. "You're not the guy who put them out of business, then?"

"Let's hope not." His father looked around the apartment and into the tiny kitchen. "I think I can manage pizza tonight. It's too late to cook, and I think I might be famished."

"And I think I can manage to find a coupon or two. We need to save money!" Trent dashed off to the corner of the room where newspapers and old mail stacked up. He wasn't sure if he had any appetite for pizza, but his dad needed cheering up, and they could always bring home the leftovers. Pizza for breakfast was always nearly as good as the night before. As he rustled through, looking for the coupons he'd seen days ago, he added, "And after dinner, I'll let you get on-line to look that résumé over."

"I appreciate that."

Trent found what he was looking for, and held the flyer up triumphantly. "And I appreciate *pizza*."

His dad smiled briefly, and then they were headed out the door. Sometimes Fridays were even worse than Thursdays.

Friday night, Jason got word that the soccer championship being held the following Sunday afternoon might not have his coach on the sidelines. He'd broken his arm in a car accident and might or might not be able to be up and about, even with a sling on. The assistant coach promised to fill in and told everyone not to worry, but against a top notch team like they were playing, every little bump felt like a major mountain. Jason knew it was his team that had to face the other team, but not having the coach there would make a difference, no doubt about it. It was rather like Magicking, with Tomaz gone and no one training him right now and his not being able to tell anyone or having a backup. There were times when there was no substitute for the real thing.

He sat back on his bed, book across his knees, and looked at his porthole window, which framed the moon just perfectly and would do so for about thirty minutes. Then, as the world turned, the moon's position would change and he would eventually lose sight of it from his window. It was almost like the glimpses he had caught of Tomaz in his crystal once or twice this week. Neither time had the Magicker seemed to be aware of him, and both times, he had been enveloped in a stormy looking mist, his hands up, and his mouth opened as if chanting, with a pack of wolfjackals sulking at his booted feet, as if his chant and strength alone held them at bay.

Did he really see what was happening? Jason didn't know. Was he supposed to go and help? Was that the meaning of Ting's warning?

He rubbed his forehead. He hated not doing anything, but he knew he couldn't; none of them could afford it if he did something wrong. Too much depended on it. He tried not to imagine ruining the lives of people who had somehow lived across centuries only to be done in by him in one afternoon!

He got out his lavender crystal and rolled it lightly between his palms. The feeling of it was only slightly different from his first crystal, a banded quartz, and the only way he could describe it was the way he'd once told Trent: it was like holding an orange and a lemon with your eyes closed. You could tell they were different, but they were also very much the same. The crystal warmed to his touch and he looked into it, hoping for a glimpse of Tomaz and a knowledge of what he should do to help. Not going to Gavan grated on him every day, and he wasn't sure he could respect Tomaz's wishes much longer.

Finding no hint of the Magicker, Jason opened his mind to even harder things . . . Gates. After all, Tomaz had told him that finding the third Gate was the most important thing he could do, and everything might anchor on that. If only he could. Jason looked deep into the gemstone, sinking into its translucent beauty, and his own thoughts. For long moments he felt himself drift, barely aware that his body lay in his bed, propped up by doubled-over pillows,

with his stockinged feet tucked into covers folded at
the bottom. The distance between here and now and
wherever his thoughts were taking him seemed incredibly far. . . .

Something latched onto him. He had just a moment to realize he was no longer moving aimlessly,
but he was being tugged, pulled in a certain direction
through nothingness. He experienced a moment of
worry, as the tug became a yank and he felt himself
catapulting through space and then . . . THUD!

He hit something large and transparent and hard,
and slid down it as though it were ice. When he hit
bottom, he caught his breath, and stared at the other
side of the icy window.

A man lay as if in a tomb. Jason felt his whole
body freeze, but it was not the man of his many
nightmares, he already knew who that man was . . .
Antoine Brennard . . . no, this was someone else, and
he knew this man, too. And he did not lie atop a
stone tomb as Brennard had before finally awakening, but he lay on a lounge, covered with a warm
brown blanket, with a small pillow for his head, and
a blanket tucked over his body except for his out-
thrown arms, as if he'd been caught falling backward
for all time, and then laid down for that moment
when he would ultimately hit bottom.

Someone had also left a tray next to the lounge,
and there was a mug and a platter of biscuits, and a
small vase with fresh flowers. As if someone, somewhere, loved him and waited for him to wake up.
As if he had not died in that awful magickal duel.

He had no air to breathe even as he let out a startled gasp, and when he blinked and drew back,

everything had vanished, and he lay in his own bed again. No icy panels. No tray or lounge or blanketed Gregory, and he wondered if he had really *seen* it.

But what if he had?

This, after all, had been Gregory's own crystal. Jason held it tightly. But what did it all mean?

Before he could recover, the phone rang, its sound harsh and jangling in his room. He jumped, the open book across his lap falling to the floor in an angry rustle of pages. He picked the novel up, replacing the dust cover carefully and marking his page. The phone stopped abruptly halfway through its second ring and he knew someone in the house had answered it. To his surprise, though, he could hear Alicia's voice filtering down the hallway and up into his attic room.

"Ja-son! It's Trent, for you."

Jason picked the receiver up, said, "I've got it, thanks!" and waited for the click before he said, "Trent? What's up?"

"You don't know?"

"I guess not." He frowned. Gregory's crystal was still pressed into the palm of his hand, despite his having dropped the book and darn near everything else. He opened the drawer of his desk and deposited it carefully.

Words poured out of Trent in a rush. "My dad got laid off, and I don't know what we're going to do until he gets work again, and I just got e-mail from Eleanora. Jennifer Logan is leaving tonight, and we're all gathering to say good-bye. Were you asleep or something?" Trent stopped.

"No . . . I don't think so." Jason flicked a glance

at his desk clock. Not even eight o'clock yet. Downstairs the household would be gathering for their favorite TV show. They usually let him have an hour or two of game time upstairs with Trent and Henry. "She's going?"

"She's quitting. She wants to tell me good-bye, and Bailey, and all of us, Eleanora said. Bring me through, please?" With that, the phone line went dead.

He hadn't left Jason time to argue, and if Jennifer Logan was leaving Magick, Jason wasn't sure he wanted to argue. He got his own crystal out from inside his shirt where it always lay against his skin, and centered on it, reaching out for Trent.

HELLOS AND
GOOD-BYES

JASON pulled Trent through. "You're sure about this?" The clear crystal doorway shimmered like a bubble, stretched, and then popped slightly as Trent emerged entirely into his attic bedroom.

"As sure as I can be without being able to look through my own crystal." Trent scrubbed his hand through his hair, sending it in all directions. "And I'm beginning to wonder if Eleanora suspects about my talent, or lack of it. She sent me e-mail." He frowned. "You don't think Bailey could have let it slip?"

"Never. One problem at a time." It was odd that the Magicker hadn't used her own crystal to reach Trent, but Jason didn't have time to think about that now. He hadn't been reached that way either, but possibly being in Focus with Gregory's crystal had blocked him. "At least they're giving us the chance to say good-bye, and at least Jennifer asked for you, huh?" He punched Trent's arm lightly. His comment didn't seem to erase Trent's unhappiness. Jason cleared his throat. "Are we waiting for anyone?"

"Ting and Bailey are going to go through on their own. Don't know about Stef and Rich," Jason answered with a shrug. He grabbed a windbreaker off the back of his study chair. "Let's go. I can't afford to be missed."

"You know I hate this."

Jason stared at Trent. "Hate Jennifer's leaving?"

"Hate traveling like this." Trent suppressed a shudder. "Doesn't it ever give you the creeps? Stepping into a rock, for crying out loud. Remember when Bailey got lost in hers? Don't you worry about being trapped?"

"Ummm. No." Jason rubbed his crystal a moment. "Maybe you'd prefer a flying carpet?"

"Actually, a flying carpet has mythological substance to it." Trent leaned his lanky body against the bed frame. "If you could manage to conjure one up. But what I'd really, really prefer is a Pegasus. Great white, winged stallion with a bridle of sunlight, and a sword sheath on his saddle."

Jason laughed, then said, "Keep dreaming," and put his hand on Trent's shoulder, gripping tightly. He looked into his crystal, his rock of clear quartz, and gold flecks, banded with one outer wall of dark blue stone, and found a door, an entry to where the Magickers were gathered. Then he pressed through, feeling it stretch as he pulled Trent with him.

They emerged with a faint popping of ears, and for a brief second Jason thought that Trent might be right. Was this any way to travel? His doubt vanished the moment he saw everyone waiting for them on Jennifer's back lawn, illuminated by the porch lights. If he'd any doubt about where they were, the monstrous moving van parked out in the street in front of the house, and the House for Sale—SOLD sign dispelled it.

Jennifer, Ting, and Bailey sat on the lawn, reminding him a little of a pile of puppies . . . wiggling, cute, and excited. Jennifer was very much like his stepsister in that she was a few years older, willowy with long blonde hair, but the difference between the two was like night and day. He wanted to strangle Alicia. Jennifer, well, he didn't feel about her the way Trent did, but he would protect her any way he could. Alicia was quiet and a little calculating. When Jennifer smiled, it lit up her whole face. Although, since she lost her Magick, she hadn't been smiling much.

Gavan Rainwater and Eleanora stood over the girls . . . or rather, Gavan stood and Eleanora floated. Gavan carried his wolfhead cane, the instrument at odds with the soft shirt and jeans he wore, but the crystal gripped in the handle's pewter sculpture was one of his powers and would never be left behind. His dark hair had been brushed back from his face and fell in a wave to his collar, and the night reflected in his intense blue eyes, but he smiled at Jason.

"There you are. Took the long way round?" The wolf's jaws glittered as he swung about to wave at them. His other hand held a goblet with a deep red liquid in it, and Jason's heart did a funny skip beat thing. The Magicker held a drink that would not only wipe the memories clean but take Magick away with them. Jennifer was really, truly leaving them then.

"Is Henry coming?" Jason blurted out, his thoughts immediately full of their friend who'd drunk that brew once, and nearly lost everything, but he had been able to come back . . . well, nearly so. Magick with Henry was an off and on thing, but it had always been like that.

Eleanora put her hand, framed by soft white lace hanging down from her sleeve, upon Gavan's wrist. "No," she said softly. "We thought it kinder not to have him here." She looked . . . well, thin, Jason thought. Worn thin as if she might be looked all the way through. He turned his gaze away quickly to keep her from seeing the surprise in his eyes at the change in her.

Trent approached Jennifer silently and just stood for a long moment. Then he said, "I know you have to go, but do you have to leave . . . everything . . . behind?"

Jennifer looked up at him. She wore a lavender velvet jogging suit, and she had one arm about Ting's waist and one around Bailey's. She had been smiling, but now she stopped. "Eleanora and I talked about this. It seems the best thing to do. I can't hurt anyone this way." A strand of blonde hair curled about her face, catching the lights streaming through the night. It was still too chilly in the year for mosquitoes, yet early enough to feel that spring was definitely here.

"You couldn't hurt me," Trent protested, and then stopped at the surly sound of his own voice.

"I know it seems harsh." Eleanora moved to Trent,

in that odd floating way she had, for she used some of her power to keep herself elevated three to four inches taller than she really was. Petite and brunette and altogether lovely in an otherworldly sort of way, with her dulcimer and her lace and long skirts, and the cameo on a ribbon at her throat. It was no wonder Gavan loved her, for she was beautiful. They could all see it on his face as Rainwater looked at Eleanora, and he wondered if she knew it, too. Trent shrugged as she came near; fending off any kind of hug or comfort she might offer. He didn't want a hug. He wanted to know that Jennifer would stay. If not here, in this house, in this city, at least in the ring of Magickers, so that he would still be friends with her. Sometimes life just dealt too many low blows. First his dad, now Jennifer. Not that he ever expected anything to be easy, but at least a breathing space between catastrophes, please?

Eleanora looked at his face, as though reading his thoughts, and shook her head, sadness crossing her features. "I'm sorry, Trent."

"I'm sorry, too," he mumbled, and crossed his arms over his chest and retreated to stay at the edge of the shade where the porch lights did not reach. He didn't even know why they were all there, if Jennifer wouldn't even remember them or their good-byes!

Jason nudged him slightly, but Trent would not look up at him. He had known why they'd come, but he'd hoped it wouldn't happen.

Gavan leaned on his cane. Very quietly, he said, "The heart always remembers a little, Trent. And I cannot tell you that there won't be a day, sometime in the future, when Jennifer will remember us, need

us, even return to us. So good-byes are always hard
but not necessarily the last time we see someone."

Trent glanced up quickly. He traded a long look
with Gavan. Rainwater nodded slowly. Eleanora's
body shimmered as she rose even higher on her magickal tiptoes. She whispered in Trent's ear, "And I
wouldn't want you to remember that you made her
even sadder than she already is."

He took a deep breath, then moved to the group
on the grass and sat down behind Jennifer, putting
his arm about her shoulder. She smiled at him then,
and for a moment, he forgot everything but the
warmth that twinkled in her eyes.

Ting passed over a charm bracelet she had dangling from her fingers. Each tiny charm held an even
smaller piece of crystal. There was a frog, a bear cub,
a mouse, a lightning bug, and a heart. "The mouse,"
said Bailey, wrinkling her nose, "is really a pack rat."

Jennifer laughed. "As if I could forget!"

In answer to the sudden happy surge in their
voices, Bailey's shirt pocket rippled and Lacey stuck
her whiskered nose out, sniffing the early evening
air. The tiny pet/pest who had stolen whatever she
could from their summer camp cottage before being
captured and tamed by Bailey peered at all of them
curiously. The pack rat's eyes shone with what
seemed to be a laugh of her own, before she turned
tail and dove back into Bailey's pocket, leaving only
her tufted tail hanging out and twitching happily.

Jennifer hugged Ting and Bailey both. "Thank
you!" The bracelet chimed and twinkled as she
slipped it onto her slender wrist. Jason took her hand
and said, "Friends wherever," and she held his hand

for a very long moment. The crescent-shaped scar on the back of it burned sharply till she let go, and he sat back, a little confused.

"I haven't got anything," Trent said. "Really."

"That's all right. I do." She smiled faintly with the wisdom of an older woman, leaned around and kissed him, very gently, and very quickly. Trent's face immediately went fiery red.

Bailey, Ting, and Jason laughed.

Jennifer grinned, murmured, "Sorry . . ."

"Oh. I'm . . . I'm not. Kinda." Trent sat back a little, his face staying red hot, and his eyes watching her closely.

Eleanora, however, watched Jason. "What is it?" she asked quietly.

Casually, he moved his hands out of sight. "Nothing. Just the Draft of Forgetfulness and all that."

"Really."

He stood and moved to the side, Gavan giving him a judging look, and nodding to Eleanora. The lovely Magicker stood in the night shadows with Jason, as Rainwater began to weave a spell over Jennifer, to protect her however he might, although with her Magick gone, even the Dark Hand would no longer have an interest in her.

Jason watched. He rubbed the back of his hand. Eleanora touched it.

He took a deep breath as she repeated, "What is it?"

"My scar," he answered softly. "It's burning. Either something is very near or . . ."

Eleanora turned her head, in a tumble of brunette curls, and looked toward Jennifer. "Or it's her."

He swallowed. "Yes."

"I know. I've been fighting it with her since that awful night last fall. It's one of the reasons she's leaving. She's convinced something terrible may happen if she doesn't." Eleanora touched him again, and coolness slid over the back of his hand.

Gavan finished weaving his web of Magick, tapped his cane on the ground, and said, "Done." At his word, a spiderweb of incredible lightness seemed to fall like a gentle curtain over Jennifer and then fade away. He held out the goblet, and Ting and Bailey shrank away instinctively as Jennifer reached for it. Lacey gave a tiny squeak, and her tufted tail jerked and disappeared into Bailey's pocket. Jennifer took a deep breath. She said, in a faint, breathy voice that did not quite sound like her, "Good-bye all," before lifting the cup and drinking down the thick, syrupy juice as fast as she could.

The cup fell from her fingers as her face went pale. She swallowed a last time, as if fighting to keep the drink down. Jennifer shuddered, and Jason shivered with her. Ting and Bailey made a sandwich, with Jennifer held close between, and a tear slid down Ting's face.

Trent couldn't bear to watch any longer. He bolted to his feet. He took his crystal out as if to leave, then hesitated, with Bailey and Jason watching him. Only the three of them knew he wasn't going anywhere. Gavan took him aside, saying, "There are harder things to watch, lad, and I hope you never have to."

Jennifer got to her feet. "I must . . . I must go inside. I have to finish packing, and Mother and Father are waiting and . . . you are all very nice but . . .

I don't . . . quite . . . know you. What are you doing here?"

Eleanora tilted her face up, smiling. "We just came by to say farewell, dear, and wish you luck."

"Oh." Jennifer pushed her blonde hair away from one eye. "That's very . . . nice of you." She took a step toward her back porch, her charm bracelet jingling. Reluctantly, Bailey and Ting let her go.

"One last thing," Eleanora said.

"Yes?" Jennifer turned to face her, a bewildered look on her face.

"This," said Eleanora firmly. She reached up, spreading her hand, putting her fingers to Jennifer's forehead.

They all felt it. Later, Jason would wonder how it was Trent did, although it was like a lightning strike. You didn't have to be at ground zero to feel the zap, the power, the snap, and smell the ozone. It was almost exactly like that. Something dark and powerful surged at Eleanora, knocking her to her knees and crackling through the air with power and Magick that reeked and promised nothing but ill. She took it from Jennifer. It snaked through the air in smoky dark lines, fleeing the girl and shooting toward Eleanora, sinking into her before disappearing, one line after another. Eleanora put a hand to her chest as if shot as Gavan cried out in alarm.

She put her other hand up, trembling. "Get her into the house quickly, now!"

Trent took Jennifer by the hand, and found it cold as ice. He led her across the grassy lawn, up the porch, and into the house. Packed boxes lay everywhere, and furniture had been piled neatly as well. She sat down on a box, as someone called from another room, "Jennifer, is that you? Are your friends gone yet?"

"We're leaving now," Trent called back.

She looked up at him. "All of you are so very . . . nice." And she smiled.

He smiled in return, though it took all of his strength to do so. He backed toward the screen door, and out it, and pelted down the porch steps before he stopped breathing.

Eleanora lay on her side on the ground, and Gavan knelt beside her. He held both her hands tightly.

She panted. "It will go," she said. "It will."

The Magickers ringed her, crystals in every hand. In their jeweled light, Trent could see . . . see . . . gray sparkling in Eleanora's hair. Lines at the corners of her eyes and mouth. It was as if she had aged ten years in just the few moments he'd been gone.

Trent and Jason looked at each other. "Fizziwig," Jason mouthed.

Gavan heard them. "No! No, she's not going to . . ." His voice strangled in his throat. He held his cane up, and the moonlight caught the crystal gleaming. "No!"

The beam of light that shot out from the wolfhead cane spilled across the yard, and in the shadows, things fled, scattered, as if they had been gathered watching. He could hear hot breathing, and paws thundering across the street, and feel the disturbance of great bodies leaping through the night. Jason felt something prickle up the back of his neck as two great glowing green eyes winked and disappeared with a low growl.

He whirled about, searching, every hair on his

body tingling with the sense of evil and chaos that wolfjackals always brought with them. The night went very still for a moment. He opened his mouth to shout out a challenge, but something moved in the purple shadows. He spun to face it.

And someone stepped out.

Khalil gathered his desert shroud around him, looking at all of them down his hawk-bridged nose, dark eyes narrowed. "Hello again this eve, it seems," he said, in his deep, purring voice.

"Have you been there all the time?" Gavan gritted his teeth as if he wanted to say more, and had to force himself not to.

"More or less. I wanted to see how you were handling the situation." He came to the curled up Eleanora and gently put his hand on her head. "Very well, until this."

"Help her."

Khalil stared at Gavan. "Only one thing can I do."

"No!" cried Gavan.

Eleanora protested softly, weakly, as Khalil cupped her head carefully against his knee, as he joined Gavan beside her. "It's all right," she managed in a barely audible, breathy voice. "I will accept this," she said.

"No, you won't!" cried Gavan. "No."

Khalil murmured a sentence of words neither Jason nor any of the others could catch, but Gavan heard them, for he seemed to flinch with each one of them. When the tall Magicker stopped, Eleanora lay asleep on the ground, the blush gone from her cheeks, and the breath in her body barely moving through her chest.

"How long?" Gavan asked, looking at her.

"Till you find the cure or awaken her to let her die." Khalil lifted her body in his arms as he stood, Eleanora limp in sleep.

"Like Sleeping Beauty." Ting touched her fingers to the lace drifting over one still hand before drawing back, her face stricken with unhappiness.

"And the curse is our very own Magick," Gavan said bitterly.

"Perhaps not. Perhaps the curse is our not understanding. Take us away from here, before we are seen, and so that we may find a place for our sleeping Eleanora to rest safely."

But Rainwater wasn't done, his face tight with emotion. "Was that all you could do?" Gavan demanded of Khalil.

The two Magickers stared at each other in the darkness of the night.

"Yes," answered Khalil. "For now." He shifted, and handed her body to Gavan. "She is lucky. The rest of us . . . may not have a chance to sleep rather than face our deaths." He turned on his heel and disappeared in a crystal flash.

HOT POTATO

GAVAN stood uneasily, Eleanora draped in his arms. A faraway howl sounded through the late night air that might have been from a lonely dog down the streets, or from banished wolfjackals. It was difficult to tell. Bailey stepped close to brush a trailing lock of hair from Eleanora's face, and shivered slightly as her fingers touched.

"She's so cold already."

"It's what's keeping her alive."

"She looks like Sleeping Beauty," Bailey said wistfully. Ting caught her hand and held it between both of hers, as if warming her.

"Maybe that's where the story came from."

Bailey looked at Ting, baffled. "Just think," Ting said. "Magickers asleep, hidden down the centuries.

Maybe one of them was the original Sleeping Beauty.''

"One way or the other," Jason interrupted, "we have to do something about this one." He didn't like the sound of another faraway howl wavering on the night air and also fretted at the time. He didn't want to risk being missed at the McIntire household.

Gavan frowned. "I can't hold your hands, so hang on to me however you can. Make sure everyone is connected."

They gathered around him, and with a faint feeling of not being anywhere, they were suddenly at the edge of the lawn of Aunt Freyah's cottage, and it was daytime there, although late in the day, with the warmth of the sun still flooding across the green grass. The cottage looked as if it were caught in a ray, its whitewashed walls cozy, and its tiled roof sound, with two crooked chimneys and dark blue shutters swung wide open. A climbing rose covered a trellis by the east wall, and its blossoms of red and copper were everywhere. A picket fence, rather ramshackle, bordered the little haven, but Jason noted it was falling down in places and he wondered if that was just part of the charming atmosphere or if it meant Aunt Freyah's Magick had begun to fail.

Gavan shook them all off gently like a big dog getting out of a bath. He tossed his head back to clear his eyes, and took a deep breath before approaching the cottage. They all shadowed him, more than willing to let him take the lead, because even though they all loved Freyah, her temper could be uncertain, rather like anyone's eccentric but favorite aunt. Her sharp blue eyes never missed a thing, and she was apt to speak her mind. Bailey inhaled as her pocket fluttered and Lacey let out a timid squeak for both of them, poking her little face out of the flap and watching curiously. The kangaroo rat's little soft velvet ears were still all crumpled up from her nap in Bailey's pocket as she began to clean one whisker thoroughly.

Trent stirred. "What're we waiting for?"

"The best way to go in," Gavan muttered.

Jason said dryly, "I think she knows we're here." He pointed, as the apple-red and somewhat fruit-shaped door began to swing open slowly.

With a sigh, Gavan began to move forward, the others following him. Taking their cue from his attitude, they grew quiet, although visiting Aunt Freyah was generally a boisterous time. That he seemed unsure made them unsure. Lacey kept her head poked out, twittering anxiously and blinking in the sun, and Bailey thumbed her head gently a few times to soothe her. Ting made a quavery sound at the back of her throat, and Trent reached out to catch her hand. Jason kept his eyes on the apple door, and thought of the warmth he'd found inside that cottage a number of times, and wondered what he'd find tonight. Or today, as it seemed to be here.

The difference in time nagged at the back of his mind. What if finding a Gate wasn't a matter of *where* but *when*? What if that was why he'd hadn't been successful . . . and why Fizziwig had aged so much? Jason was so busy mulling over these thoughts that he almost stumbled into Gavan's back as the adult Magicker came to a sudden halt just inside the doorway.

Needless to say, the others piled into Jason as though it were a freeway traffic jam.

"Whiplash," muttered Trent, as they all halted abruptly and stood shoulder to shoulder, packed into the relatively tiny doorway.

They peered around Gavan to see what the problem was, and discovered that the problem was Aunt Freyah. She stood with her feet spread, and her cane in her hands, held across her body in a defensive stance that would have done a martial arts expert proud.

"You shall not pass," Trent whispered in Jason's ear. Jason bit his lip on that remark, but Aunt Freyah did look remarkably determined not to let them by.

"Freyah," said Gavan gently, "there was nothing else to be done."

"Nothing? Nothing? There is always something else that can be done!"

"We couldn't let Eleanora take any more . . . damage . . ." finished Gavan, as if he hadn't any other words.

"Don't mince words with me," Freyah snapped. "As far as I'm concerned, this whole matter of students has been bungled from the start. They need to be sequestered and protected, from themselves, each other, and the outside world, until they can master what flows through them. You have failed on all those counts, Gavan Rainwater, and it's my niece who suffers for it."

"I agree. Yet times are not what they were when you taught me, and Gregory taught. We can't just sweep these sons and daughters away from their families and have anyone understand or agree to it."

"So you teach them bits and drabbles and expose

everyone to a great deal of danger. Do you think that even bad Magick is better than no Magick at all?"

Gavan shifted his weight, and Jason couldn't tell if it was because Eleanora was getting heavy in his arms, or if he was getting a better defense against Freyah's sharp, blue-eyed wrath. "Magick," Gavan said calmly, "manifests itself regardless of what I think."

A long moment of silence. Then Freyah straightened with a hmmmpf, lowering her cane a bit. "First sensible thing you've said in a long time." She thumped her cane against the floor, and leaned on it. "Regardless. You cannot leave her here."

"What other safe home does she have, Freyah?"

"What makes you think this is a safe home?" Freyah's voice sounded a little weak, and she swayed a bit on the cane as if she had stood too long without its support and now paid for it.

Two things happened. Jason put his hand in his pocket and immediately the lavender crystal, already warm with power, fell into his palm as if seeking attention, and Jason thought of what Gavan had just said about Magick. Behind him, at his elbow, Jason became aware of a sudden wriggle from Bailey. Something furry darted across his shoulder and then down his leg and disappeared, running along the cottage baseboards. Lacey! And the tiny creature was off and running as though it was entered in a race.

"Cookie!" whispered Bailey urgently, but the pack rat didn't waver at all as she dove into the depths of the forbidden cottage and disappeared. She put her hand out, and then dropped it as Gavan spit out a curse.

"You'd turn down your own niece! And for what, to spite me? To prove me wrong?"

"No," answered Freyah, her lips tight. "To protect her. Understand me well. It is not safe here."

"Then where? Where?"

"That is not my concern right now." Freyah's knuckles were icy white as she gripped her cane. "Leave now, there is no welcome here for you!"

Gavan threw his head back with a roar, and disappeared in front of them. They stood, blinking, taking a step back at his sudden departure. Jason brought his hand and crystal out, as if to take them all with him and follow, but Bailey tugged on his elbow. "Lacey!" she hissed, but even as she did, the tiny fur ball rocketed out of the shadows and scrambled up her leg and dove headfirst into her pocket. After a second, she pulled her tufted tail in with a squeak.

"Hold on, everyone," Jason said. "Aunt Freyah, I hope we didn't bother you too much. Things have been . . . well, a bit . . . unusual."

She snapped him a sharp-eyed look, then her face softened into a smile. "Lad, get along with you. There is adventure waiting for you elsewhere."

Actually, that was something he'd rather *not* have heard, he thought, as he closed his hand about his crystal and sent them all tumbling after Gavan.

They fell out of nowhere, hard, as though someone had opened a sack and dumped them out, like potatoes rolling onto a kitchen floor. Appropriate, he thought, since they seemed to be in a kitchen, and Eleanora had been shuffled around like a hot potato no one wanted to hold.

He sat up, after removing Trent's elbow from his rib cage, and looked around.

"FireAnn!" Bailey blurted out, half a second before he recognized the camp kitchen as well. Of course, Bailey had spent far more time here than he had when they were at Ravenwyng together, but they'd all taken their turn helping the fiery-haired cook. He got to his feet and put a hand down to help Ting. Bailey had already bounded up, and Trent just stayed on his hands and knees, practicing some deep breathing it looked like.

He could hear muted voices around the corner of the kitchen, near the pantry. They all trailed after the sound as if following a delicious scent.

FireAnn already had Eleanora in a cushiony chair, with her feet up on a well-stuffed ottoman, and was tucking an afghan about her still form, as they finally caught up. FireAnn looked like a gypsy in a sweeping long skirt and peasant blouse, with a kelly green kerchief binding back her intensely red hair, as though anything could tame those boundless curls. She looked up and smiled at them all, and Jason jolted to a stop.

She'd always had laugh lines about her eyes and mouth, but in the less than a year he'd known her, those lines had become sharp and drawn. He closed his mouth, about to say something in surprise, and managing to halt the words in his throat. FireAnn mistook the look on his face.

"Now, lad, dinna be worrying. I'll take good care of Eleanora. Gavan will get things righted around, and she'll be up in no time at all!" FireAnn stood and patted Eleanora's limp hand as she settled her arm across her lap.

"No herbs, then?"

FireAnn turned her smile upon Bailey. "No lass, as you've already been guessin'. Herbs willna do it. Only Magick and time, and we've both."

Jason stared at Gavan's back. The Magicker stood at the door to FireAnn's tiny home, which shared a common wall with the mess hall, but little else, and they could only guess that something about Lake Wannameecha held Rainwater's intense attention.

But did they have both time and Magick? The only thing sure in life was that, sooner or later, they were all going to run out of it.

FireAnn smoothed her apron out. "Best get home with you all. I'd invite you to supper, but all I have is mushroom pie, and younguns need more than that!"

"I'll say," muttered Trent. His stomach made a noise as if emphasizing it.

Ting nudged him. "It's hours past dinner."

"Ten o'clock snack." Trent sighed wistfully.

"Right, then." FireAnn smiled brightly. "Along with you, or do you need a boost."

"No," said Jason. "I've got it." The lavender crystal in his hand still burned with an unexpected warmth. "Good night, Gavan. And to you, FireAnn."

"Night my lads and lassies," the Magicker called back, even as Jason sent them stepping into doorways to take them home. Gavan said nothing, and Jason felt that was possibly the most despairing part of the whole evening.

When even Gavan did not know where to go or what to do, the Magickers were troubled indeed.

THE NEWS JUST GETS BETTER

JASON sat down hard on the edge of his bed, his body shaking a little from the night's activities, and his mind reeling a bit from the time changes. Could he get jet lag from Crystaling back and forth? He wasn't sure, but he did know something. He was suddenly, incredibly, ravenously hungry. He listened a moment. The McIntire household seemed very quiet, as if everyone had settled down to sleep, so he got up and lowered his trapdoor silently to make his way down to the kitchen. He crept as softly as he could, and used what little he knew of Magickal stealth to keep the floorboards and doors from squeaking as he passed by.

Once in the kitchen, he breathed a little easier, as he rounded up a sandwich of baked turkey slices and provolone cheese, on fresh crusty shepherd's bread. He wrapped it in a thick paper napkin to take back upstairs, and was making his way back again, when he heard the soft murmur of voices from the Dozer's office study. He had no curiosity at all, his only intent was to get back up the stairs before he was heard, but then they said his name.

He stopped on the first step of the landing, his whole body poised to listen in spite of his intentions. He found his crystal with his free hand, and heard the noises around him sharpen a bit.

"He keeps secrets."

"Anyone that age has secrets, Joanna. He's a good boy. You need to relax and accept that. It would do you both good if you did."

A sigh. Even if he hadn't recognized his stepmother's voice, he'd know the long-suffering sigh. Part of him quailed. He really didn't want to know what he'd done lately that failed some impossible expectation she had of him that he didn't even understand! But part of him dug his heels in stubbornly.

"I just . . . I can't handle his sneaking out. What if he becomes like his father?"

"Jason's father had an enormous burden he didn't know how to carry. The boy is fine. Trust me."

Jason felt his face crease. What was that all about? What was Joanna talking about? All the times he'd wanted her to talk about his dad, and nothing, and now, in the shadows . . . what? What was she *saying?*

He fought to stay where he was, quiet, unseen, unheard, but his heart thumped as loudly as a drum in protest. Surely they'd hear that! And then he could demand to know what she was talking about. His hands tightened.

"As for sneaking out, do you even know if he's back yet? I should think that would be your first concern."

Movement in the study.

"You're right, of course."

Jason unfroze and took the stairs as quickly as he could, both landings, then sprinted up his trapdoor ladder. The sandwich, crumpled now in his fist, he shoved into his desk drawer. Then he shed his clothes as quickly as he could before diving into bed and had time to draw about four steadying breaths before; a knock sounded downstairs in the hallway.

"Jason?"

"Mmmphf?"

"May I come up?"

He rustled around in his blankets, trying to sound warm and sleepy. "Sure."

The trapdoor lowered and Joanna's face appeared as she climbed the first few steps. "Were you sleeping?"

"Yeah. Something wrong?" He scrubbed a hand over his face, trying to smudge his expression. He wasn't a good liar, never had been, and didn't want to try to get better if he could help it.

"In bed early."

"Oh." He made a noncommittal noise. "I fell asleep in the closet earlier, looking at . . . you know. Stuff."

He had a box, small, of a few of his father's things. Not much to remember anyone by, really, but she'd been careful to give it to him. He kept it in his closet. It had been years since he had slept next to the box, but he'd done it quite a lot in those first horribly empty months after his father had died. He hadn't done it but one other time, that he could remember, since moving into this house.

"In your closet, Jason?"

He nodded and stifled a yawn, a real one this time, and felt his face warm.

"Oh, hon." Joanna looked as if she wanted to say something more, but instead closed her mouth.

"I must have been really tired," he added, by way of explanation, sounding as embarrassed as he felt. "I haven't done that in years, you know? I was just looking at some things, and next thing I knew, I was all stiff and curled up on the closet floor."

"It's all the stress," Joanna said gently. "School, soccer, getting ready for high school." The trapdoor stair creaked and part of her face submerged as she took a step downward. "Jason, if you need to talk about anything, you know you can."

Actually, he couldn't, but it was nice to hear her say that. He took a deep breath. "Someday, I'd like to talk about my dad a little."

"How he died?"

Jason shook his head. "Nah, I know most of that. I want to know how he lived. You know, the day-to-day stuff. I'm forgetting."

She smiled sadly. "We all do, don't we? He was a good man to both of us. Someday, we'll talk." She disappeared entirely then, and the bedroom ladder swung back into place. Jason watched it for a long moment, before getting his sandwich out of the desk drawer, and wolfing it down. The crumpling hadn't hurt the flavor at all, although it seemed a bit chewier. Then, he scrunched down into his bed, and tried to find a way to sleep. He didn't know how he could bother Gavan now about Tomaz with Eleanora so ill, but it seemed to him that the longer things went, the worse they got.

Tomorrow he'd have to do something.

Consequently, it took him a long time to fall asleep as if tomorrow were determined never to arrive.

She'd returned about the time she left, Bailey noted on her watch, as she stepped out of the crystal at her front door. She gave a grin and let out an impish cheer. She had tried to imagine arriving just that way, and she had . . . given that time seemed to flow like an unpredictable river through crystal doorways. Of course, arriving outside her apartment instead of inside, was not a good idea. So the experiment hadn't been as successful as she'd hoped. Still, there were possibilities to consider.

She put her crystal bracelet back on and fumbled in her pocket for her apartment key. Behind her, she could hear someone moving in the corridor. Lacey chittered nervously from her pocket as she tried to fit the key in smoothly. A duplicate key, it hadn't been cut quite right and she always had to do a certain amount of jangling around to get the key in and turned. It stuck stubbornly.

The steps drew closer. Bailey looked over her shoulder. A dark-clothed man stood, watching her. He stepped back when he saw her spot him.

Cripes! She was being followed. No doubt about it now. She shoved her key in, hard, and turned it, praying it wouldn't snap off in the lock. The door opened and she flung herself inside, and quickly secured all the dead bolts. Nothing else happened. She waited a very long moment before looking out the peephole to an empty hallway.

A moan from her mother's bedroom answered her outburst, and Bailey tiptoed to the threshold.

"Mom?"

The room light was dimmed to barely on, and she could see her mother lying on the bed, a folded washrag across her eyes. "Mom? You've got a head-ache?" 'Cause if it wasn't a headache, and something bad had happened—Bailey's blood felt as though it could boil!

"Yes, hon, I'm sorry. One of my migraines. How is Ting?"

"She's fine, mostly. Really worried about her grandmother."

Her mother smiled wearily. "If you're hungry, there's some tuna casserole left. I'm sorry, I need to get over this headache, and I've got to go in to work tomorrow."

"Overtime!" said Bailey brightly. "That's always good." She entered the room quietly, lifted the wash-rag, and took it to the bathroom where she ran water as hot as she could stand it and wrung it out a few times before bringing it back steaming, and replacing it across her mother's forehead. "There, that should help."

"Thanks, baby," her mother said faintly, and then lapsed back into a limp heap on the bed, as if she could will the headache away by not really existing. Bailey closed the door nearly shut on her way out. Now was not the time to worry her mother further.

Tuna casserole was, like spaghetti, one of those

refrigerator items that often tasted better a day or two later. She crunched up a few stray potato chips from a bag in the bread box, and sat down to eat, mulling over the day's events. From a magickal point of view, it hadn't been a good week, so maybe it was just as well it was Friday and nearly over. She thought a moment, then left a note to her mom that Trent's father had been laid off, just in case there were any openings where she worked. It couldn't hurt.

She checked her watch. She couldn't talk to Ting because . . . if her watch was right . . . Ting and she were in Jennifer Logan's backyard saying good-bye. *If* her watch was right. It couldn't be, of course, because how could she be in two places at once? Or want to be, with someone stalking her.

Unsettled, Bailey paced around her bedroom a bit before grabbing up the dullest book she could find. She read ahead in her classic novel assigned for English, found the dreary book putting her to sleep, and decided to settle Lacey in her cage and herself down for the night when the phone began to ring. She grabbed it up before it could rouse her mother.

"Little girl!" someone said at the other end. "Happy Birthday."

Just when she thought Friday couldn't have gotten much worse. She hadn't heard that voice in nearly a year and a half, and in a few ways, had hoped she never would again, even if that made her a really awful daughter.

"Daddy," said Bailey flatly. "It's not my birthday, and you're drunk."

"Is that any way to talk to me, punkin?"

"Maybe not, but it's true. It's late, and I don't want to talk to you."

"But ish . . . it's your birthday!"

"No, Dad, it's not. My birthday was weeks ago." And he hadn't even sent her a card. Too busy with his new wife and probably a new kid by now, too. "Why don't you just leave me alone?"

"I'm your father!"

"Why is it you're drunk whenever I hear from you? Once a year or so, that is." She glared into the dark of her bedroom as if he could see the anger on her face.

"Baby girl, your mother makes it very difficult on me."

"I don't want to talk about it. I am going to bed. Don't call back." And Bailey hung up, hot tears smarting in her eyes, for the things she wanted to say, and couldn't, and for the things she wanted to hear him say, that he never would.

It was the perfect end to a disastrous week, she thought, as she threw herself backward onto her pillow.

13

a touch of pepper

BAILEY staggered to the kitchen table at what felt like the crack of dawn, her alarm clock having gone off with a furious blast of music. Her note was gone, with another in its place. **Don't forget, you have a half day at school for testing today!**

She had forgotten. Just peachy. She had just enough time to bolt down a bowl of cereal, dress, and dash to make the bus. She could use her crystal to arrive, but there was too much chance of her being seen and causing a riot, or at least a lot of questions. She didn't even take time to sit down but ate her cereal right at the counter standing up. Lacey never stirred as she made sure the cage held fresh water, but it seemed best to leave the tiny creature home this morning.

Bailey reflected—when she finally got to the assembly hall, and waited as they passed the tests out and explained the rules about filling in the tiny areas with a number two pencil and not going on to another section till told, and that they'd be there till noon—that on the other hand, having Lacey would keep her from being bored to tears. Still, this was serious business and she swung her backpack between her feet under the tiny dropdown desktop and tried to have the proper expression on her face when receiving her test booklet, scantron sheet, and number two pencil.

She sped through the sections and halted where instructed, bored and half asleep, until given the go-ahead to start the next. Luckily once the last section was begun, she could leave the minute she finished, and Bailey was one of the first to hand in her test and bolt from the stuffy hall. Outside, she took a deep breath. School buses stood waiting, but she hated to just go and sit, for it was obvious they wouldn't leave till near full. It was a beautiful spring day, with just a scattering of clouds. Sinking down onto the grass, she sat cross-legged, and enjoyed the feel of the breeze and sun on her face.

If she could manage it, she wanted to go to Jason's soccer game tomorrow. That meant a bit of planning on her part, because Sunday was laundry day, and catch-up day, and with her mom working today, it also meant a much needed rest day. She hated to ask her mom to drive her over and pick her up in the midst of all that. The temptation to just use her crystal to go back and forth grew stronger. After all, what could go wrong?

Bailey seemed to have sat on a rock, bruising her

left hip, and so she squirmed about slightly, resettling herself. The obvious problem, naturally, was
knowing where she would be Crystaling to. She
needed to either see it clearly, or have seen it before
well enough that she was fairly familiar with it. Otherwise, she could get in all sorts of trouble trans-
porting. She could end up in some sort of parallel
limbo where things were almost as she had pictured,
but *not quite*, and she'd be lost forever in that in-
between. She'd almost done that once before!

Bailey shivered despite the warming spring sun
beaming down on her. She could count on Jason to
anchor her, though, if he wasn't too busy getting
ready to play, and getting home should be no problem. The other difficulty would be in getting permission to go without telling her mom about the mode
of transportation. Her mom could be pretty trusting,
but there were days when Bailey thought she was
facing the Spanish Inquisition! And there was no way
she was going to be able to explain this convincingly.
So, if not by car or her crystal, how was she going
to get to the soccer game?

Kids had begun to drift out of the assembly hall
and down toward the parking lots and buses. Bailey
perked up. Hopefully, the downtown bus would fill
enough so that the first one could leave. With a grunt
as she hoisted her backpack and got to her feet, she
noticed the teachers' parking lot beyond the buses. It
was, as would befit a Saturday, nearly empty.

But not quite.

It wasn't so much the few cars parked there, but
that a man sat in one of them, a nondescript Taurus,
over by the treed edge of the lot. Or even that he sat

there, when he should have been in the school working, if he was here on a Saturday at all, but that he sat there with great dark sunglasses on and yet he seemed to be watching her. She couldn't be sure of it, actually, except for the tiny fine hairs on her arms that seemed to be standing on edge, or the way his face turned as she paced by the school buses impatiently, and he reminded her of one of those paintings. The creepy kind, where no matter where you stood in the room, the eyes in the painting always seemed to be looking at you.

She darted behind one of the buses and waited a few moments. Then she peered around the back fender to see if she could catch a closer glimpse of the watcher from another angle. She couldn't, really, but she did see him moving restlessly inside the car as if looking over the growing crowd of kids beginning to mill around the quad, his head swiveling back and forth.

Bailey ducked back.

This really couldn't be happening to her. Who could it be? It had to be one of Brennard's Dark Hands, but why. What had she done to attract notice? Was it because of Jason or something she herself had done? Since a wolfjackal had come sniffing at her door months ago and been dealt with, she'd had no other sign, no problems at all. Maybe her luck was just due to run out.

Bailey reemerged, trying to blend into a group. From the corner of her eyes, she saw the watcher in the Taurus stop shifting inside the car, and fix his attention on her, as though she were a target and he'd suddenly been able to home in on her again.

He *was* tracking her. Why, she had no idea, but that he was, she was sure.

She wasn't certain how she was going to get home without his following, but she immediately decided a bus was out of the question. Nothing like trying to be inconspicuous on a big fat yellow school bus. Her crystal jangled in its jewelry cage on her wrist. Buffeted by a growing crowd of kids who were now happy to be out of the test and eager to get home to lunch, she found herself carried along in a wave of T-shirts, backpacks, and denims. Bailey tossed a look toward the other parking lot. Whoever sat in the Taurus had opened the door and begun to swing out. Hidden eyes behind the sunglasses searched for her.

She had no time to lose.

Bailey took a deep breath. She darted between buses parked at the far end of the circle—empty buses—and cupped her crystal. *Home*, she thought desperately, as she looked into the amethyst. *Home!*

She had two crystal clear moments. The first was of being drawn into the purple facets of her gem. The other was of looking up, and seeing that what she had thought an empty bus was actually full of passengers looking down at her, their jaws agape as she vanished into thin air.

Bailey put her back to the door, bracing it. What had she done? She could see it now: Local Student Vanishes into Midair, Abducted by Aliens? Film at Eleven!

What to do now? What could she do? She didn't think the Dark Hand itself could have done much more damage. She sighed.

From the depths of her room came a metallic rattling and scrabbling. Lacey, usually nocturnal,
seemed to be awake with a vengeance. Bailey went
in to see what the matter was. The little pack rat sat
on her haunches, vigorously cleaning her face and
paws. She looked up with a soft chirr as Bailey
appeared.

She undid the latch and reached in. Lacey immediately jumped to her hand and then scrambled up her
arm to perch against the curve of Bailey's neck. She
knew the small rodent loved cookies and bright objects, but there were many times when she felt as
though Lacey also loved *her*. Bailey stroked her silky
flank, making Lacey's tufted tail twitch a few times
in pleasure. They stayed quiet for a few moments,
and then Lacey's tail went stiff in fear. Bailey swung
around on one heel.

Something trod down the outside hall. And fiddled
with the apartment door, as though trying to decide
if it were open or locked or could be opened. Not a
knock. But . . . something else.

An intrusion.

Already in trouble or not, she had nothing else she
could do. Bailey scooped up the pack rat and
dropped her in her shirt pocket, and clasped her
crystal tightly between both palms. She dared not
call on the elders. Gavan and FireAnn were probably
busy with Eleanora. Tomaz had gone who knows
where for a while. She reached out wildly for Trent
and Jason, and caught Trent in the net of her
thoughts. That was no good. Trent had no Talent.

Bailey let her crystal fall from her fingers, its purple facets sending a soft lavender light over the

closed door. She had never felt so alone. Lacey peeked out from her pocket, and gave a soft chirp. Bailey stroked her head gently, and the pack rat wiggled her whiskers before diving back to the bottom of the pocket. She could send Lacey out to take a look, if she could get the tiny creature out a side door, but they had none. The apartment door was all the entrance and exit and protection she had.

Why did she feel it wasn't enough?

The hall floor outside creaked, as if someone moved or took a step. Bailey inhaled deeply. This was not the first time she'd had an intruder at the door. Last time it had been a wolfjackal, noisily snuffling and clawing, until scared away. This time . . . this time it might be a member of the Dark Hand itself. She stared into her amethyst, and met nothing. It was as though something blocked her cry. She knew they were out there, but she couldn't reach out. Her call for elder help would go unheeded. That meant it was up to her.

And Jason and Trent and anyone else she could grab. There was no Magick that could ever seal away her friends. She cupped her crystal again, gazing deep into the planes of the rock, sending her thoughts spiraling after Jason. She Focused her gemstone until she found him, his image hazy, intertwined with Trent. The two had to be talking, which explained why she'd had a handle on Trent earlier. It was a package deal.

"Help!" Bailey cried through her crystal.

Trent could never get there on his own. He couldn't Crystal. But if something were setting up a magickal trap or net around her home, that he could see. He'd done it before. The Dark Hand couldn't hide their webs from Trent.

Trent stood blinking in her thoughts, a clear image even though Jason was not. The remains of a peanut butter and jelly sandwich dropped down the palm of his hands.

"Someone's stalking me."

"What the . . . Wolfjackals?"

"No, a man. He's been at school, everywhere, and I think he followed me home!"

"Get Jason! And pull us both through!"

Her hand shook so she could hardly hold her concentration. "I'm trying!" And then Bailey yanked.

ONE LUMP OR TWO, WITH a SLICE OF DRAGON

THE air filled with a prism, sparkling and shining in large waves, like windowpanes of color, and then everything went back to normal, leaving the two boys in its wake. Jason caught his balance, but Trent just gave Bailey a very baffled look, then put a hand to his ear and wiggled it, as if trying to pop it.

"This is so not my favorite way to travel," he said, and then gave a barely stifled yawn.

Jason put an elbow to his ribs. "I don't think you were invited."

"True." Both boys stared at Bailey. "How did you do that?"

"I didn't. I focused on Jason. You're just a bonus prize."

The taller and lankier of the two grunted and wiggled his ear again, then made a noise of relief as he half-yawned. He finished his sandwich, wiped up with a napkin that looked as if it had seen other sticky messes, and smiled with well-fed contentment. "There. About time." Trent stuck his hands in his jeans pocket. "What's up?"

Bailey's pocket wiggled. "I need help."

"We heard that coming through the crystal. What's wrong?" Jason frowned slightly. He was still wearing his practice uniform, although he stood in his stocking feet with his regular tennis shoes dangling from one hand.

"The stalker is back. It has to be someone from the Dark Hand. I couldn't get Gavan or any one. My crystal was blocked."

"Blocked?" Trent raised an eyebrow as Jason swiftly bent to pull on his shoes and tie them. "I didn't know Brennard's crew could do that. But then . . ." he flushed slightly at his own reference to being relatively Talentless. "I'm always blocked, huh." He shrugged.

"Something brought you through with me," Jason said pointedly. "I didn't do it, and Bailey didn't. So, enough of that. You've Talent, but just don't know what it is yet." He rubbed his hands together, pausing. "Uhh . . . Bailey. I don't think it's anyone from the Dark Hand." He stared at the back of the apartment door as if he could see through it, then shook his head. "No. If there's someone out there, it's not anyone with Magick."

"How can you tell?" Bailey looked at Jason curiously. Her pocket flapped about vigorously as Lacey appeared, then ran up to perch on her shoulder, and curled up against her neck. The tiny squeaker watched them with shining onyx-colored eyes.

Jason shifted his weight. "I just can. Besides, if there was anything really bad prowling out there, she'd still be hidden in your clothes." He flicked a finger at the pack rat who began to busily groom her whiskers as if she hadn't a care in the world, and hadn't appeared to have been listening.

Bailey stood on tiptoe and peered out the little spy hole in the apartment door. "Someone *was* here. Honestly."

"I don't doubt that." Jason nodded at her. "But you're all right?"

"Outside of being nearly spooked out of my ponytail." Bailey settled back onto her shoe soles. "I think he might have followed me from the bus stop this morning."

"That's not good." Trent scowled.

"What'll I do?"

"Well . . ." Jason scratched his head and from the expression on his face, he had begun formulating some sort of plan. His mouth opened as if he'd finished just as the door rattled under a heavy THUMP!

Bailey jumped back with a muffled squeak and Lacey dove nose first back into her pocket. Perhaps it was Lacey who'd squeaked, no one had the time to decide.

Jason grabbed Bailey's hand, then Trent's. "Whoever it is, we're not waiting around to see if it's trouble!" He grabbed the crystal pendant around his neck and, with a cradle of all their hands, peered intently into it.

No rainbow of color like Bailey's teleportion, just a rush of cold air, and they were elsewhere. Trent stumbled a bit upon the ground as they alit, but he gripped Jason's hand tightly, and then all three were on solid footing, and Bailey let out a soft sigh of relief as she saw where they were. Fresh air, green grass down slopes leading to a green valley and a deep blue pond, framed by the oddly colored and jagged Iron Mountains. Jason was the only one who could bring the younger Magickers into Haven, for the Gate into the valley hadn't stabilized yet, although the Elders could, and had, brought them all there from time to time. Someday, a school would stand down in the valley, with the Iron Mountains as its backdrop.

Trent said, "Bubble, bubble, toil and trouble . . . when will we three be met again?"

Bailey rolled her eyes and laughed at his poor imitation of a witch from Shakespeare's *Macbeth*, but the color returned to her face, and she let go of their hands, though not before they felt her trembling. Trent and Jason traded looks. It was not like Bailey to let anything rock her optimistic view of the world.

She wrinkled her nose. "I really, really, don't like being scared." A toss of her head, ponytail bouncing, punctuated that.

"I can tell that." Jason beckoned down the trail to the clear blue pond nestled in the valley. "Let's go sit and talk a bit, then we'll see if the coast is clear."

The three of them trotted down into the small valley that was all they knew of Haven, and Bailey threw herself on a scoop-shaped rock that lay close to the water, poking out of the fringe of trees that ringed one end. Its bumpy exterior disappeared, moss covered in the darker, cooler grove. As she settled down on the sun warmed rock in a late afternoon that had given the landscape a warm orange glow, Jason looked about.

"Time," he said, "isn't the same here. Ever notice that?"

Trent nodded. He folded up and sat on a patch of dry grass, facing the lake which formed from a long, thin waterfall tumbling out of the mountain, its spray keeping most of the shore a little damp. "It isn't the same and it doesn't pass the same way. If we study here, I don't know if we'll stay younger or grow older. I've been trying to think of a way to test it."

Jason sat down too, checking the ties on his hastily put on shoes.

Bailey blinked. "Not get older?"

"Something like that. Or maybe we get older faster, but I don't think so."

She considered first Jason, then Trent, then shook her head. "I would have noticed that. You'd have sprouted chin hairs or something."

Jason blushed, but Trent put his head back and laughed. A startled pair of birds took wing and flew off as his voice broke the silence of the small valley. Jason hid his reaction by combing his fingers through his hair. "If time does pass differently here, then chances are your stalker will be discouraged and gone if we go back in a few minutes. The trouble is, how do we keep you safe after that?"

"Depends, doesn't it, on what we're dealing with?

Dark Hand, someone following Bailey, or . . ." Trent paused and busied himself with picking strands of grass and braiding them into a grass chain.

"Or what?"

"Or something where we can't begin to know what we're dealing with. Maybe she's imagining something. Maybe someone from school is trailing her 'cause they're too shy to say hello. Or something." Trent did not look up from the strands he twisted through his nimble ringers.

Jason stared out over the valley, the pocket of land he'd found when he'd opened a magickal Gate. "That's just not good enough."

"Well, I know *that*." Trent looked up, grass lanyard dangling from his hand.

Bailey said, "You mean I could be scared over nothing?"

"It's not likely, but yeah, you could. Or something we don't want to deal with."

She frowned, her freckles seeming to dance over her nose as she did. "Like what?"

"Like someone who wants to know more about Magick and isn't magickal at all."

Bailey paled.

"I don't even want to think about that," Jason answered Trent.

"None of us do, but it's bound to happen sooner or later. I have less risk than any of you of being cooped up in some super secret government laboratory while they try to find out what makes me tick, but I'm in this as deep as anyone. So. We have to be careful, and we have to stay hidden and . . . we have to have a safe harbor somewhere."

"Someone saw me Crystaling. Maybe him. I'm almost sure." She knotted her forehead. "It may be too late already."

"You didn't."

"I was trying to get away!" Bailey looked at Trent in despair.

"What's done is done. We need a haven, and we need it now." Trent looked at Jason.

"I'm trying!" Jason bolted to his feet. "Don't think I'm not!"

"We all know you are. The point is, none of us is truly safe till that last Gate is opened. Iron Gate, Water Gate, and whatever it takes to stabilize our being here." Trent put his grass chain in his pocket, Bailey watching. He noticed her stare, and indicated the weaving. "It'll deteriorate at a certain rate. I want to see what it looks like when we get back, and how it dries out, and so forth."

Bailey grinned. "A walking scientific experiment." Trent nodded.

Jason was not so easily distracted. He seemed to be trying to breathe steadily, every once in a while rubbing the back of his left hand. Finally, he let out an exasperated *chuff*, sounding rather like her beloved bulldog friend, Ulysses S. Grunt. "It's not Dark Hand. So, there's no reason why the crystal would have been blocked for calling for elder help, unless you were so scared, you just couldn't Focus."

"That's a possibility." Bailey chewed on the corner of her lip.

"But, on the other hand, Trent has a point. There could be others out there, even more dangerous to us, people we haven't even been considering. We've all got to be a lot more careful with our Magick. The vows we took won't keep us from our own stupidity."

They all nodded in agreement.

"And . . ." Jason took a deep breath. "I need help and I'm going to be asking everyone for it. We have to have some place to go . . . and I don't think I can find it alone."

A deep rumble filled the air. Bailey started as if the ground jolted under her, her arms flailing wildly. Jason and Trent stared as her body . . . her rock . . . began to lift from the ground. She shrieked and grabbed for a piece of it that jutted up sharply next to her and hung on for dear life to the sun-warmed . . . no, hot! rock.

"My ear!" a thunderous voice complained, and the rock tossed about, and then sent Bailey tumbling head over heels in a somersault to the ground, her mouth wide open in a soundless cry. The scoop-shaped granite wavered a bit, morphing into the tri-angular shaped head of a lizard. A very large lizard.

"A . . . a . . . dragon!" Bailey got out. She scrambled backward, stopped only by Trent's stunned and frozen body.

Jason stood, one hand still out in gesture, the great lantern eye of the dragon now fixing on him. "Don't move," he said. "Really. Just . . . don't move."

The dragon's now sunrise orange-red body revealed itself, looped into the forest, his chin resting on the edge of the watery pool, a serpentine grin opening his toothy jaws. "It would be too late to move, anyway, if I were hungry." The beast flexed one taloned paw which moments before had looked like a tree's dead roots reaching down into the mud at water's edge. "Which I am, but not that hungry."

Bailey let out another shriek as if her throat had finally unfrozen. The dragon immediately swung his gaze on her, and hissed, steam boiling up, with the smell of sulfur. "Enough of that."

She snapped her mouth shut, her eyes getting very big. The dragon stared into her.

Trent managed to say, "Don't look in his eyes! Don't!" but it was too late. Bailey felt herself being drawn into those jewellike saucers, and for an eerie moment, she felt as she did when experiencing what it was like to be Lacey.

Only this was not Lacey. This was an immense, wise, and very old bescaled body lying upon what used to be a very pleasant area to sun oneself.

It is not that you should not be here, but that you should not be here NOW. Take yourself away to whence you came, and that other one with you, or great harm could come to all three of you.

Bailey gulped down a deep breath. There were more words, like a roaring surf breaking over the beach, but she didn't hear them, she experienced them, and she knew she wouldn't understand any of it till later, when she could be still and remember it. But that she did hear. *Leave now. Leave now and take Trent with you, or there will be disaster.*

And there was the picture of her apartment building hallway, and her apartment piercing her mind, and it was safe and clear and empty, and she knew it was all right to go. For now.

She cupped her amethyst. She held her hand out to Trent. "I have to go. We have to go." She looked into her crystal, wrenching her eyes away from the sight of the great orange-red dragon.

"But—" was all she heard Jason say, and then she whisked Trent and herself away.

Jason watched his friends disappear. He looked to the dragon.

"Hasty friends," the other said. "Too bad. I was going to invite them to tea." The beast laughed, forked tongue flickering in and out. "Just a light snack really."

"I never know," Jason said, "quite how to take you."

"Then sit a moment, and talk, for right now I am quite serious. And I cannot talk long, for I *am* indeed getting hungry and might forget myself."

Jason sat, taking the dragon's advice. He also took Trent's advice not to look the firedrake directly in the eyes. He wondered what dragons used to sweeten their tea with . . . one lump of Magickers, or two?

WARNING SHOTS

THE dragon put out a talon, stretching it from the scaled toe of its paw, rather like a cat might extend a claw lazily, stretching, yet still reflecting menace with its grace. So much power hidden, and yet a hint of it revealed to him with that movement. Jason caught himself staring at the highly polished surface, thinking that it must be able to cut and slash as if it were diamond. And maybe it was. He had no idea what dragons were made of.

The dragon settled then, putting his chin on that selfsame paw, his eyes on a level with Jason's head, making it even harder not to look directly at him. Jason could feel the heat radiating from the orange-red scales. It was rather like sitting next to the fireplace, when the logs had gone to crimson coals, and were best for marshmallow roasting. He rather hoped he couldn't be considered a marshmallow.

"Now, then," said the dragon. "Insofar as I can read the expressions of one of your sort, you look a bit troubled to me."

Of the three of them, he thought he'd probably looked the coolest, what with all Bailey and Trent had been through. Jason sneaked a look at the mirror-like surface of the pond, saw creases etched deeply across his forehead, and blinked in surprise. He looked . . . well, old. Like McIntire. Or his faint memories of his father. Yes, his father had had a knifelike wrinkle just like that across his forehead. He put his hand up and rubbed, just to check, and to see if he could rub it away. He saw himself do it, and felt his rough fingers, and the wrinkle stayed and obviously belonged to him.

"So it seems," he agreed, although sharing with a hungry dragon bothered him more than he'd let on, friends or not. Never was there a time when they visited that he was not aware that he sat with a vastly bigger and wiser and mostly unknowable being who tolerated him.

"And you come here looking for . . ." The dragon let his question dissolve into a low rumble, rather like a drawn out purr.

"Haven."

A muted thunderous chuckle. "I look safe to you?"

"Safe is not a word I'd use." Jason gazed along the serpentine body which now revealed itself threaded throughout the forest edging the pool, and he wondered how he could not have seen the dragon before. "You are awesome. But this place . . ." He beckoned along the valley's horizon. "I opened the Gate here, and it must have been for some reason. We need a corner of our own, and I think this is it."

"Forgive me if I do not quite get the history right, but isn't that rather like what the pilgrims thought when they came to the New World? All that land, and theirs for use as a Haven?"

Jason nodded.

"But let us not forget that continent was previously occupied, shall we?"

"Well. Um, yeah."

The dragon kneaded his claw a bit, pleased with himself, echoing the catlike image in Jason's thoughts. "So what threatens you?"

"The Dark Hand, for one."

"Sorcerers of opposing ideals?"

"In a nutshell, I guess that describes them."

"A balance of the Universes, Jason, my lad. For every up, a down. For every Light, a Dark. And so forth."

"Does that mean we have to tolerate them? Accept the fact they want to drain us dry even if it kills us?"

"Did I say that?"

"Well, no." Jason felt for a moment as if he sat on a slippery hillside and was trying unsuccessfully to keep from sliding down.

"Your own lands cannot stop this?"

"My own lands." He paused, then took a deep breath. "My own lands would probably crack us open like an eggshell so they could see inside to find out what Magick is."

"My." The dragon's forehead moved, as a scaly eyebrow rose. "You're sure?"

"Fairly sure. Nothing like Magick exists, except in dreams and fairy tales and wishes, for most people. Getting discovered is one of our biggest worries, I guess."

"I see." The dragon lifted its snout, and looked back to the pass where Jason came down from the Gate he had secured there. "Anyone follow you?"

Jason laughed. "No. Of course not." Then his laughter died in his throat, as he realized that was an honest question, not a dry remark from the beast. "No," he repeated quietly. "No one can follow." He left *yet* unsaid.

"You are a warrior?"

"Me?" Jason glanced down and then saw that he still wore his grass-and-mud-smeared soccer uniform, stained and sweat-marked from the day's practice for the big game the following day. He grinned. "Not exactly."

"Explain, then."

And for long moments, Jason tried to explain to the dragon the game of soccer, and for that matter, football and baseball, and sports in general. The dragon rumbled his questions back and forth. It knew about golf, to Jason's surprise, but the games had little comparison and so the two of them did not find much of a common ground. The dragon insisted that the sports Jason described was stylized warfare, with winning and losing sides and hostage taking (and sacrifices), and followers and alliances and so forth until Jason felt like surrendering himself.

"Maybe," Jason finally agreed, and sat back.

"Then," the dragon said firmly, "you are a warrior."

"Maybe."

"But for justice, not mayhem. There will be dark times ahead, Jason, when justice may be all that separates you from the very forces you think you are fighting. Very, very dark . . . perhaps even fatal times."

"But justice will stand?"

"One hopes."

That sounded better than he'd expected, so Jason let the argument drop at that. He lay back on the grass, staring at a fluffy cloud that seemed to be wandering overhead, and felt the tension go out of his body. A warrior for justice. Yeah, he could accept that, both in soccer and against the Dark Hand. It might call for a lot from him, but he thought he was prepared.

"It is time," the dragon said. "You must go. I hunger, and for you, your world turns."

He sat, then stood. "Did I miss much?" Anxious, then, having forgotten how different time could be from one place to the next.

The dragon tilted its great head. "Lunchtime," it said thoughtfully. "And perhaps an afternoon snack." Its stomach growled in confirmation.

"Not food!"

"Is there anything else?" The dragon gave him a wide, sharp-toothed grin.

He supposed that there were times when even a great intellect gave way to a great hunger . . . and so should he!

The dragon got to its feet, and shook itself, scales rattling, as if loose armor plating, its body shaking with a tremendous clanking and clattering. "A

game," it suggested. "Why don't you run as fast as
you can back to Iron Gate and see if you make it
before I . . ."

"Before you what?"

The dragon's eyes glinted sharply. "Get hungrier!"

Jason sprinted across the grass and up the slope to
Iron Gate. He could feel the ground tremble and the
heat wave across his back as the dragon chased him,
and its laughter, as he dove headfirst through the
Gate.

DARK TIES

HENRY stood by the washing machine, feeding in pairs of jeans, checking the pockets as he went and finding loose coins and even a dollar bill as he did. He piled up the booty on top of the dryer as he added detergent and softener, then started his wash. Not that he'd ever admit it to the guys, but he felt pretty good that he could do his own laundry. It was a big help around his busy house, where everyone had to pitch in or they'd all be buried inside of a week, he figured. With any luck, and if his toddler sister went down for a nap when she was finished with lunch, he could find a corner and read a bit or work on his D & D strategy for the next session with Trent and Jason.

And, with any luck, he'd stop hearing voices.

Henry leaned against the washing machine, letting

its cheerful noisy intake of water and its chugging about fill his mind, instead of that whisper . . . that sly, cold whisper, he heard so often.

He felt tired. He felt like . . . was it Bilbo Baggins in the books and movies who said, he felt thin . . . stretched out? He felt like that. It was not a good feeling, and he'd tried to tell others about it who might understand, but there was no one who could help. How many people could he tell that he felt like a hobbit, huh?

Henry rubbed his eyes at that one, laughing at himself, then replacing his glasses carefully. That made him feel a bit better. He couldn't laugh at himself if he was going crazy now, could he? Could he?

Henry.

He gripped the edge of the washing machine. It was scientific. It didn't use Magick, couldn't think, couldn't do anything but mechanically churn and swish away. It didn't use crystals to work, and move through air, and light up dials . . . or hiss cold thoughts through his mind. Oh, no!

Henry. Don't think you can ignore me, Henry.

His blood felt icy. Why would he ever think that? "Who are you?" he muttered fiercely. "What do you want from me?" He grabbed his glasses off his face again, the weight suddenly too heavy on the bridge of his nose.

You can't get away from me, Henry. I have you like a fish on a hook.

A weakness hit him, as if something had ripped him open and was draining everything out of him. He felt it flowing out and grabbed at his stomach, crushing his glasses. Barely standing, he leaned against the laundry room wall and felt everything begin to spin around him.

"What are you? Who are you?" he cried out desperately.

He couldn't be crazy. Because he remembered feeling like this before . . . at Camp Ravenwyng. Before, when Jonnard sucked all the Magick out of him and left him . . . almost like this!

He unclenched his fists. His glasses fell to the floor. He frantically dug his hands into his pockets, searching for his crystal. Gavan, someone, had to help him.

No crystal. Henry searched himself frantically even as his movements got more and more feeble. He could barely stand. Then, desperately and with blurred eyes, he spotted his crystal sitting atop a pile of loose change and crumpled bills on the dryer. He stabbed his fingers at it, and caught it up, sharp quartz edges digging into his fingers. Afternoon sunlight streaming through the laundry room lit it up like a fiery prism as he curled his hand about it tightly. Strength surged through him. He felt warm again suddenly.

For a moment he felt safe. Then he knew he wasn't, as the strength and weakness warred inside him, a tug-of-war, moving back and forth until he could hardly think. He wasn't going to lose this time . . . he couldn't! The crystal alone would not save him.

Nice try, but worthless.

No, not worthless, it couldn't be. Henry shot his mind through his gemstone, calling to anyone who could hear him for help. He sensed Gavan slipping past him, as though too far away to reach, and Tomaz became a black yawning canyon in his mind, but there was Bailey, and then Jason, and he reached eagerly for them. He found them both, and Trent, too, in that place he knew as the Iron Gate Haven. Then he lost Bailey and Trent and had only Jason to try to anchor on, but his attacker wrapped around his thoughts tightly. *Speak of this and they will take your Magick again. Stay silent, my little Squibb. Silent.* Helplessly, Henry gave up. He sank back, unshed tears in his eyes, his fists clenched.

Jonnard sat back and felt Henry's despair as he tried to elude the bond between them. He braided and unbraided a tiny coil of golden rope he held in his fingers, his strong but slender hands busy as he tied Henry ever closer to his wishes. It was only a Focus, but an apt one. He had Henry tied forever to his powers and there was nothing the other could do, no matter how he twisted and turned. Jon had never thought when he first bonded with Henry to take his power from him, that there could ever be more to it, but he'd discovered that they were still synchronized, and that Henry's slowly returning Magick was just as vulnerable and easy for him to drain as ever. It gave him potential that even his father did not have. *That's it, little Squibb, go and find Jason for me. Find him because now is the hour of my first attack. . . .*

With that, he stood, and a shadowy figure behind him stood as well, radiating the icy coldness as a Leucator will do. Jonnard smiled thinly. He had Jason now, had him at the Iron Gate, and he should have known his rival would be there, probably trying yet again to find the third gate he needed to anchor

that tiny Haven. Just as Jonnard obsessed about
Jason, Jason obsessed about the Gates.

Jonnard's mouth twisted in a shallow smile. He
crooked a finger at the Leucator. "It's time," he said.

The other looked at him with eyes that might as
well be dead. It reacted little as Jonnard pocketed his
golden rope and took the Leucator by the wrist as
he summoned his crystal.

A door opened at the end of his rooms. Brennard's
aura filled the room with power and anger before he
himself appeared. Jon looked up.

"What are you doing?" Brennard's face looked like
a storm cloud, his eyes dark with fury.

"I am, Father dear, doing what you need done.
Jason Adrian will be mine, one way or another." He
felt his crystal warm to his summoning and the chan-
neling of his energies through it.

"We're not ready yet."

Jon felt his father's unspoken anger rumbling
through the room, his aura spiking. So much more
powerful than Henry or a Leucator, Jon mused. If
only he could bottle it. Or tap it himself. Very quietly,
very carefully, he reached a thought toward it and
savored the pulse of it. His father neither noticed nor
stopped him as he drank of it. The action both fed
Jonnard and seemed to calm Brennard.

"Perhaps you are not, but I am. And with Jason
out of the way, don't you think our paths will be
much easier?"

"Fool! Destroy him, and you destroy my options."

"I don't intend to do that. I merely intend to . . .
how do they say it today? I intend to own him."

"Stop."

A tingle spread through Jonnard's body. He melted into transport even as he answered his father, "Too late."

Jason tumbled headfirst through the Iron Gate, body surfing thin air, driven by the heat and laughter of the dragon behind him. The ground and grass and dirt brought him to a skidding stop, out of breath and laughing himself. He sat up, looking back, but there was nothing to see beyond the Iron Gate. It looked like a rusted, old metal gate hanging between two derelict posts, at the far edge of the Ravenwyng campgrounds. Except, of course, Jason knew that if he stood and opened it with Magick, he would see a dragon with flames dancing about its merrily opened jaws laughing back at him.

He stood up to dust himself off. His stomach growled slightly, reminding him that lunchtime, wherever he was, had been missed. His left hand let out a tiny throb, and Jason spun around. He saw nothing odd, yet—

He rubbed the pesky scar on his hand. It was rarely wrong. It wouldn't be the first time he'd been attacked at Ravenwyng, by the Dark Hand or wolfjackals.

Without word or other sound, with nothing more than an uncanny feeling, Jason suddenly knew he was no longer alone at the edge of the campgrounds. The skin on his hand prickled, as did the fine hairs at the back of his neck, and he turned around very very slowly . . . to find himself staring at . . . himself.

A rushing filled his ears. For a moment, he felt himself back at summer camp, with the hot sun overhead tempered by a slight breeze off the lake, as they sat on the ground and various benches, log stumps, what-have-yous, as Tomaz paced in front of them. "Magick," he said in his slow, deliberate voice, "has many shapes, and many shapes can hold Magick. And Magick can shift shapes. Of all those who can and do, shapeshifters, skinwalkers . . . the one you never want to face is yourself. We call those Leucators and they are splinters of your soul. They have but one dark desire, and that is to become one with you again, but because they are evil, corrupt, you must never allow that."

Bailey's hand had shot up, waving. Tomaz had looked to her, a slight smile tugging at the deep etchings in his weathered Navajo face. "What is it, Miss Landau?"

"Where did they come from?"

"They were made," Tomaz answered, "to hunt Magickers down."

Jason had shivered then, as he shivered now.

Jonnard Albrite, too, stood there, a chilling smile across his face, his arms crossed over his chest, as he leaned back against the Iron Gate rails. He lifted one hand slightly, and gestured. "Our battle begins," he said. "Now."

He had only a moment to notice the Leucator was dressed in jeans and a shirt, like and unlike him, with cold eyes that seemed to see nothing, yet fixed on him. As Jonnard moved his hand, the thing darted at him.

Jason did the only thing he could think of. He ran.

The lakeshore was knotted with scrub grass and loose dirt, and evergreens sprawled and twisted by wind. He took off through them, cupping his hand around his crystal and sending out a call of alarm to any who could hear. At his heels the Leucator slowly caught up, so near he could hear his own breathing, doubled as the other echoed him. He pivoted and cut back, and he could hear the Leucator slip on the loose dirt, go to the ground, roll, and get back up, sprinting after him. Jason grinned. It knew his moves, yes, but . . . it didn't have his heart. If this were happening on a soccer field, he could outrun him, outplay him, out heart him! It would take a pack of Leucators to corner Jason.

He circled around, not eager to let Jonnard out of his sight, not knowing what the other might be up to while the Leucator did his dirty work for him. The Iron Gate sparkled like a rusty jewel in his eyes as he raced back toward it, marred by the dark-clothed figure of Jonnard leaning against it. Although there was no way Jon could get the Gate open, the thought of him that close to it, of the possibility of his using it, made Jason grit his teeth in determination.

Stall.

Stay away from both the Leucator and Jonnard till help could get there. Surely Magickers would arrive at any moment.

A movement in the corner of his eye warned him. The thing reached for him, catching him, running chilled hands down his arm and Jason let out a yelp. It felt as though something cold squeezed his heart. He swerved sharply, out of range, and the Leucator gave a howl of disappointment. Jason dipped his head to run faster, anything, before that thing could touch him again! He felt as if it had tried to tear a hole into him from the inside out and attempted to crawl in—this thing that seemed as loathsome as last week's garbage, foul and slimy.

Get Jonnard and the Leucator out of here, and away from his Gate. Away from Ravenwyng and the sleeping Eleanora. Away from here and now.

Jason tripped over a hummock of tangled grass. The Leucator dove at him, his body brushing past him, and he gasped at the pain of the coldness sweeping through him. He sprang to his feet and dashed the other way, suddenly afraid. What if he couldn't shake it? What if it caught him?

Jonnard straightened, smiling widely, as they ran past, as if reading the expression on his face.

Was he going to allow that? No!

Jason doubled back and sprinted right at the Leucator, then went into a sliding tackle, both feet aimed high at the knees. Dirty soccer. He'd had it done to him, he knew how it hurt. There was a cold shock as they touched, and then the thing tumbled over, hitting the rocky shore of Lake Wannameecha headfirst. It flopped and then lay very quiet. Jason rolled to his feet, catching his breath, after a look at it, realizing it wasn't dead but knocked cold.

He spun about to face Jonnard as the other boy moved forward, still smiling, his hands coming up.

"I never figured it would do my job," said Jonnard lazily. He attacked.

A blur of punches and kicks drove Jason back. Some hit hard, but he kept dodging, and mostly flesh grazed flesh, although he grunted with the impact. He ground his teeth to Focus, to stay within himself, and do what he knew he could do, despite the fact that Jon was nearly a man grown, taller than Jason, with greater reach and strength.

And another Magicker.

He brought his shield up, a flare of light from the crystal hanging about his neck. It came without his touch, but in mere answer to his thought. Was it his imagination or did Jonnard's expression widen with surprise at that? No time to really think about it. He whirled away from the next assault, and brought a lance of Light into his hand as he did. It flattened into another shield, sizzling as Jonnard connected, and the other let out a yelp of pain and surprise, leaping away.

The moment of surprise gave no advantage. Jonnard dove back in, a dark rippling light now filling his own hands. He closed on Jason and as their shields touched, lightning sparked across them with a nose-burning smell of ozone and a deafening hiss. Both of them sprang apart, shaken.

Jonnard circled him slowly. Jason watched him. "Not as easy as you think," he said tightly.

"Nothing ever is." The black shield came up again, reaching out toward him like a razor sharp pincer.

Jason moved with him, dodging and striking back only when the other struck first. The Magicks screamed whenever they touched, an earsplitting howl that kept him flinching. And then Jonnard jumped him, carrying him to the ground. The breath went out of him and he lay, looking into a shower of sparks, light, and darkness all about him. He could feel Jonnard pressing down on him, but Jason held him back and it was easier than he thought. His shield spit in cat-like fury as he sat up and got to his knees, then his feet, Jonnard moving with him, but it was Jon now on the defensive. What could Jason hope to do? Drive him back somewhere . . . but where?

The sky split over them. Gavan roared in wordless fury, his wolfhead cane in his hands like a wizard's staff, sending both boys flying back and into the dirt and grass. Jonnard's shadow-dark light sputtered and went out, even as he reached out and put a hand up.

"Touch me and everyone here dies," managed Jonnard, his voice stronger than the expression on his face, his chest heaving with exertion.

"No doubt," said Gavan dryly. "I can feel your father's presence. But is it worth it? You'd be as dead as the rest of us. And your father, too, I wager." Gavan settled to the ground, cape behind him floating into soft folds about his form, and the crystal ball his wolfhead cane held muted to a steady white glow.

The thing behind them, the being Jason had dropped, stirred then, and made a mewling noise like a small, blind kitten. The Magicker's head snapped around.

"God's blood, a Leucator." Gavan's eyes narrowed at Jonnard. "You brought that abomination here? I will call an accounting for this—from your hide and your father's!"

"All's fair in love and war," hissed Jonnard. He stood then, and half-turned, then his booted foot shot out, catching Jason across the chest.

Jason doubled over in searing pain. He looked down and his eyes met those of the Leucator as it

crawled toward him, hands gnarled in a greedy reach
for him.

Jason rolled back, his shoulder rattling against the
framework of the Iron Gate. *Haven*, he thought.
Safety. And with that thought, the Gate opened and
he fell through.

Not through, actually, he realized later. Into but
not in, up against, but yet not across the threshold.
He had no chance as the dragon came roaring out of
the gate, Jason cradled against its chest.

Flame licked the air and everyone froze.

The dragon dropped Jason unceremoniously. It
picked up the Leucator and tossed it . . . into nothingness. A slit in reality opened up and swallowed it
whole, without a yelp or a scrap of cloth to show it
had ever existed. Gavan raised his cane defensively,
but made no other move, his face gone white as if
knowing they had all roused some great, eternal fury.

"You shall not pass. Not again. The Gate is forbidden to you, to all of you!" the dragon thundered. "I
am the guard and none shall pass me by. Now this.
Your petty fighting, your petty wars will never cross
my boundaries!" As it opened its jaws to roar its
fiery anger, Jonnard made a pass with his hands and
disappeared into his crystal, leaving only Gavan and
Jason there.

Flame gouted and the dragon pointed his snout at
the sky, painting the heavens with his fury, pouring
forth anger in heat and fire until he was quite done,
and then, and only then, did he lower his head to
look once more at them.

Sadly, it repeated to Jason, "You shall not pass again."

Then it was through the Iron Gate, with a clank and a roar, and everything went still.

Gavan rocked back on his heels.

"What have you done?"

17

PACTS

"WHAT did I do?" Jason repeated, then inhaled sharply at the pain in his side, reeling back against the Iron Gate in an effort to keep standing.

"Aye, what did you do? Jonnard here, and the dragon." Gavan looked around, his shoulder length hair stirred by a wind caused by the passage of the angry beast, and only now settling down upon his neck. His eyes blazed fiercely crystal blue. "Ravenwyng is warded. Was warded. I threw everything I had into it to protect Eleanora, and the wards are shattered, worthless. It will take me, if I can even do it, quite a bit of effort to rebuild them."

He gazed into the sky as if he could see Brennard in front of him as well. "And what brought Brennard? I doubt if he needed to protect Jon. What were you meddling with? Had you opened a Gate that did all this?" He gestured wildly, then took a deep breath and folded both hands over the wolfhead of his cane, set it to ground and leaned on it, the emotion in his face slowly coming under control.

"How could I break a ward?" Uncomprehending, Jason stared, first at Gavan's face, then around him, as if he could see the shattered Magick lying about them, like splinters from a broken crystal. He could see nothing, of course, but he had almost expected to. "Gavan, I didn't try to do anything, except bring Bailey here for safety. We've come here before, the wards pass us by."

"Not this time. No one should have passed lightly, or without alerting me." Gavan took a deep breath as if still gathering himself, and rubbed his eyes wearily. "With FireAnn's help, I repaired the two immediately over Eleanora, but the others . . ." he shook his head.

"I'll help. Me, Bailey, Henry, Ting, we'll all help." Too late, he realized he'd left out Trent, but it didn't matter, Gavan gestured him away, dismissing his offer. Jason felt his jaw tighten. It was as if none of them were of any real use to the adult Magickers, nothing but a burden.

"Building a ward is a difficult task, Jason. It's a layering of Magicks, one over the other, and requires precision—"

"How would I know that? How would any of us? Have you taught us that yet? Do you let us work with you?" Words tumbled out of him, hot and angry. "Do you ever let us help? There are things we can do, you know, if you'd only let us try. And you keep things from us all the time, so how can we even know what we're capable of? You won't let us!"

They stared at each other, jaws clenched, angry, almost toe to toe. Then Gavan rocked back on his heels. "Magick is newly come to you, lad," he said slowly, as if trying to force a calm he did not feel. "A little patience would help."

"I don't think any of us have time for that." Jason caught a breath and forced it down, feeling almost shaky with spent anger.

"You're right, we don't." Gavan spun on one heel. He rubbed the wolfhead of his cane, and the crystal it held in its jaws flared with light. "Khalil. Isabella. I want you here, *now*."

And before Jason could say another word or take another breath, he stood with Gavan in the Gathering Hall of Camp Ravenwyng, with Isabella and Khalil both appearing at his heels.

Isabella gathered up the sweeping hem of a red satin skirt, glaring at Gavan. "Rainwater, your youth is exceeded only by your extreme rudeness. What is the meaning of this?"

Khalil still held an orange in one hand, and a small knife in the other, a neat ribbon of orange peel hanging down from the ripe orange fruit. He pocketed both objects in his robes and looked about, eyes narrowing. "Have you no sense, Gavan? This place is barely protected. What's happened to the wardings?" He pulled up a chair at the conference table, and sat down, staring at Gavan.

"I just quelled an altercation," Gavan answered,

both hands wrapped tightly about his cane as if he'd rather they were wrapped about Isabella's neck.

"You don't summon me for an altercation." The elegant woman stretched her neck where her pulse ticked angrily as she put her chin up in disdain. "This is the height of arrogance, to pull me through whether I wish it or not. Surely you could handle a petty argument on your own."

Rainwater looked at her. He opened his mouth as if to retort, but Khalil interrupted him. "Quiet down, Isabella. You know better than that, and although it's obvious you had plans for the evening—" Khalil gestured a hand at her fancy gown and attire—"it's just as apparent something here has gone wrong. I suggest we listen a moment."

She looked daggers at Khalil then, and even raked her angry gaze over Jason who took a step back in reaction. "You have about two minutes and then I am leaving."

"I'll have as much time as it takes," Gavan answered her. "The attack was on Jason, by Jon and Brennard, and Leucators were brought to the Iron Gate. Less than a handful of us can create a Leucator and I've two of them standing in front of me." He looked from Isabella to Khalil and then back to Isabella. "I want to know why someone is working with the enemy."

"Strong words if true," Khalil murmured, but Isabella's face paled and she seemed at a sudden loss for words.

She groped for a chair, sitting down heavily. "He wouldn't have been so stupid."

"You did this? You worked with those who've sworn to see us dead to the last one of us?"

"What of it? I saw a chink in their armor. What can any of us do against the Dark Hand? Open warfare? Send us all through horrible agony like the last time? No, I used my wit and talent to infiltrate them." She glared back at Gavan.

"A Leucator is a hunter, not a spy. And all this time, we've had no way to strike back at them because we did not know where they hid, but you did. You do business with them."

"They contact me through one of my investment addresses. I still have no inkling where Antoine calls home, nor is he likely to tell me. As for betraying you—"

All of them looked at her. She made an impatient movement of her hands. "Of course I made them for him, he paid quite well."

"Who paid?"

"Both of them, father and son. Brennard and Jon. I had no idea what they wanted Leucators of Jonnard for, but I figured if they would risk such foolishness, why not profit by it?"

"How can money be so important to you?"

Isabella shot a look at Khalil. "What? Do you think it's easy maintaining the estates I have about the world? Do you think time stands still while Magickers sleep? Time erodes all things, all havens, all monuments, all flesh. Who do you think hid most of us after the disaster, who paid for bribes and families to act as caretakers?"

"Your contribution is unquestioned, Isabella."

She glared back at Gavan. "And unappreciated, as

well. No matter. I profited by it, and I enjoy the fruits of that profit." She beckoned with one hand, her fingers flashing with rays of color from a number of very expensive gemstone rings. "As far as the Leucators go, Brennard ordered one of Jonnard, for Jonnard's use. I didn't ask him how it was to be used, nor did they tell me. It expired. They ordered two more. It seemed harmless to me, and why not drain money away from them? Less mischief for someone else later."

"The Dark Hand never does anything harmless." The wolfhead gleamed in Gavan's hold. "The Leucator we killed was of Jason's."

Isabella sat back in amazement. "No. That cannot be. I would not make a Leucator of one of us and give it to the Dark Hand."

"Someone did." Jason fought a shiver. "It tried to kill me."

"That's what they do," said Khalil quietly. "If allowed to get hold of you. Otherwise, they're rather like a hound running quarry to ground. They will hunt endlessly and tirelessly, till they find their other half, and are most commonly used this way and only out of desperation. This is serious, Isabella, and I have to say I am disappointed you dealt with Brennard in any way, for any reason."

Isabella made a noise that could only be described as French scorn, and settled down to tapping her polished nails on the conference table's gleaming wooden top. Her perfume had settled over the room like a cloud and it tickled at Jason's nose. He rubbed it to keep from sneezing, trying not to draw any notice as he did so. His calves ached from soccer prac-

tice and the fight, and he could smell himself under
the fancy aroma of the scented cloud. He had no idea
what time it was at home, but his stomach knew he'd
definitely missed a major meal and who knows how
much time at home, or how much trouble that would
cause. He'd almost forgotten that and now it gnawed
at him.

"Where is the Leucator now? Does Jason need to
worry about facing it again?"

Gavan shook his head at Khalil. "Dead, as far as I
could tell."

Khalil stood, his desert robes rippling about him.
"Good. I'd like a look at it."

Gavan cleared his throat. "It's gone."

"Hmmm. Too bad. A body might have been
most useful."

"For what?" Jason felt the fine hairs standing up
in goose bumps along his arms at the thought of
it. He had no desire at all to see what he'd look
like dead!

"To find out where it came from and who made
it," Khalil told him. "If Isabella here admits to making them of Jonnard, why not of you? So it came
from elsewhere, and that might be extremely important to know."

"Next one I face," Jason answered dryly, "I'll save
for you."

A grin blazed across the Magicker's face, rather
like the desert sun from the lands he lived in, and
he raised a hand in salute as he stepped into his
crystal and left.

Gavan frowned. "I wasn't done."

"It seems you are, for now." Isabella stood, the

fabric of her gown rustling. "I won't take a dressing-down from you, Gavan, so don't even think of trying."

"And don't be so foolish as to think I'm not furious."

She put her chin up. "You need my support."

"Your support is one thing, your out-and-out betrayal is another!"

"Don't try my patience, Gavan." She rubbed a fingertip across her crystal in preparation for leaving.

"Isabella."

"Yes?" She paused in the act of using her crystal, to look back at Rainwater.

"You will let us know if you make any more, won't you?"

"Of course. As Khalil said, it will be important to know if another of us is making them. It might be even more important to know if any of the Dark Hand is capable of turning one Leucator into another." With that, she disappeared as well, in a swish of satins, leaving only her perfume behind her.

Gavan closed his mouth firmly.

"What did she mean?"

Gavan sat down, his face creased in thought. "I think, Jason, that she meant the thing can be twisted from one into another. I've never heard of such a thing before. If she's right . . ." He shook his head. "She can't be. The very existence of a Leucator is a mirror image of the soul. A truly evil twin. It can't be shaped into the twin of another. That flies against all Magick I know." He tapped his cane on the floor.

"I need to get home. I've a game tomorrow and parents worrying."

He took out his own crystal.

"Jason."

He looked at Gavan Rainwater, who seemed measurably older than he had that first day when they'd met only a year and a few days ago.

"Most of what you said was true. We've been neglectful, and I will try to . . . when things get sorted out . . . make it all up. And you are part of a family, here. A strange family, but a family nonetheless." Gavan smiled ruefully. He stood, and straightened his cloak. "It won't make everything perfect, but things will be better once we get the academy built. There's much to learn, but it's difficult to teach Magick since it comes from within, and it's as individual as each and every one of us is different. Do you understand what I mean?"

"A little. I suppose you mean that Magick can't really be taught, but has to be guided."

"Guided," Gavan repeated. He nodded. "You've got a good mind. That's probably an almost perfect way to describe it."

"About the school." Jason shifted his weight from one foot to another. "I don't know if we can ever go back. The dragon said we couldn't."

"It's your Gate. That gives you a power the beast doesn't have, whether it likes it or not. He may guard the Gate with all he has, but it's yours to open and close."

"You're sure of that?"

"Well." Gavan fidgeted a little. "Pretty sure." He put his hand on Jason's shoulder. "Watch out for Bailey if you can. My hands are full here with Eleanora. Be careful. Isabella hasn't betrayed us—yet—

but that any of us would deal with the Dark Hand at all . . . I just don't understand it. There are pacts here, my lad, we know nothing of. The rest of us will help whenever we can, but we're stretched thin, and Tomaz has picked a bad time to be gone."

A pang of guilt arced through Jason, and he wanted to tell Gavan, but didn't. Instead he cupped his crystal tightly and went home.

STRANGERS IN THE NIGHT

NO ONE missed him. For once, all the fuss over Alicia's budding film career didn't bother him, for it seemed she had received some important mail, setting off a frenzy of activity in the McIntire household. The Dozer was at work on-site, but Joanna and Alicia had taken off for parts unknown, and his only clue was a torn-apart priority mail envelope, large-sized, that lay on the kitchen counter and had once been addressed to Alicia; kitchen dishes still out from lunch; a plate of covered sandwiches in the refrigerator for him; and no sign whatsoever of the two females of the house. Looking at the envelope, he noted that it came from some organization that called itself Young Filmmakers of America. Curiosity sated but not hunger, he poured a large glass of milk and sat down at the nook and devoured three sand-

164

wiches, the first so quickly he wasn't even sure what kind of sandwich it had been.

The other two were turkey, avocado, and Monterey Jack cheese and very good.

He cleaned up after everyone except for the remnants of the envelope, in case the address needed to be saved. Upstairs, he took a shower, wincing at the black-and-blue marks emerging on his body. He'd taken a beating from Jon and the Leucator, that was certain. The only good thing about playing soccer the way he did, was that no one would notice the bruises. Then he dressed in some old worn jeans and a shirt and sat down, barefooted, at the computer to talk to Trent. His usually unruffled friend sounded aghast at all that had gone on after Bailey spirited him away.

Keep your friends close, and your enemies closer, Trent wrote. **Sounds like really good advice about now. And what about Tomaz?**

I don't know, Jason responded. **His family was one of the Hidden Ones. I don't even know how he found Gavan and the others, but I'd trust everything I have with him.**

Me, too, agreed Trent. **It's scary though. First Anita goes wrong, and now Isabella, maybe. Everyone seems to have their own agenda. We have our own pact, the handful of us, like the Musketeers. You, me, Bailey, Ting, Henry . . . one for all, and all for one.**

Jason and Trent batted some ideas back and forth and came to no conclusion. Trent fretted about his dad and then signed off, saying they were working on résumés and he couldn't stay on the computer much longer. Jason sat back in his chair. He wondered if his dad were still alive, what they might be doing. He couldn't really remember what kind of work his father did. He'd worked in a large company, but doing what, Jason had never really taken the time to understand. It wouldn't be any help at all to say to Trent, "At least you've got a dad to worry about," because it wasn't the same, and he knew it. Just like he couldn't say to Bailey, "Don't make your mom worry about you so much!" He knew how lucky, and unlucky, they both were.

He rocked away from the computer and went through his closet, to make sure he had his gear all set for the game tomorrow. The late afternoon sun slanted heavily across the house, steeping part of his attic room in shadows. His meal sat in his stomach in a warm, comforting lump, and he fought being sleepy. One step at a time, one thing at a time. Time . . . if only he had enough Time. If Fizziwig had had the Time to teach him, to tell him what secrets he knew about the Gates.

He fell asleep thinking about Ting and her grandmother who was running out of time, and whose house dragon had hissed his name.

He woke to a quiet house and a dark room, his body all stiff and cramped in his chair. Yawning, Jason scrubbed a hand over his face. He stood and made his way to his bed. Moonlight caught the edge of a white object shoved through the crack of his trapdoor, and he leaned over to pull it loose. He had to squint in the dim light to read the words: Dinner is in the refrigerator. We decided to let you sleep. A flowery "J" signed it.

Wow. He'd slept through everyone coming home, all the excitement, whatever it was, and dinner. And, from the sound of it, it was late enough that everyone had gone to bed. He eased his door open and down, taking the creaking stairs with quiet caution. A funny thought hit him as he did so. As he grew, and growing he was . . . would this door still fit him? When he went away to college, would this still be his room? It was an odd thought to have, and he shook it off. Dinner seemed more important than philosophical ramblings at this hour, because after he'd eaten, he had something he needed to do . . . and he needed the strength and alertness to do it.

The microwave told him it was nearly eleven, not awfully late on a Saturday but McIntire worked hard on construction sites, and so it made sense that they were all asleep by now. He ate his dinner cold rather than send the microwave into peeping fits as it reheated it for him. It wasn't bad, cold meat loaf was nearly as good as warm, and he liked the smoky sweet tomato sauce Joanna always made it with. The potatoes and green beans he ignored, but he scarfed down the chunky applesauce. For good measure, he cut himself another slice of meat loaf and made a thick sandwich out of it, wrapped it in a baggie, and carted it back upstairs.

Upstairs, he dressed warmly, pulling a thick sweatshirt over everything, and shoved a small flashlight into his pants pocket just in case he couldn't use the Lantern spell with his crystals. Jason patted himself down. What had he forgotten? Ah.

He sat down at his computer which still hummed quietly on his desk, and sent a quick message to Trent, informing him of his intentions . . . just in case. Then he turned the machine off entirely. He thought for another few long moments about what he was going to do, and if he should, and came to the same decision he had earlier, and pulled out the lavender crystal.

He'd found this crystal on a world where wolfjackals roamed freely. With it, he'd seen Tomaz, at least once. Now, he was determined to find Tomaz. Jason held the quartz tightly and opened his mind in search.

Bailey felt very alone after she took Trent back, but there was no changing it, so she caught up on homework and cleaned Lacey's cage, and then her room, making time till her mother got off work. The stalker seemed to be gone, and she tried not to look out the window or the door peephole more than six million times to check. Nothing and no one, and even Lacey had settled down, although nighttime was her active time. They played chase the cookie which was one of the pack rat's favorite games, although she preferred chase the sparkly barrette more. Tomaz who trained her in animal senses thought it funny a creature would prefer a colorful yet inedible treasure to food. It went against the grain of survival needs, he'd explained.

Bailey tickled the little rodent's chest. Lacey seemed quite plump, so she guessed she wasn't missing any meals! Lacey's tufted tail twitched as if she read Bailey's thought, and the pack rat gave a tiny *chuffing* sound. Bailey laughed. The little kangaroo rat sounded almost like Isabella on the Council when she got irritated!

A faint warmth and purr seemed to flow out of the amethyst Bailey wore and she touched her crystal in answer. Ting's face and voice sprang into her mind as she did so. "Bailey!" A smile spread over her features, erasing what looked to have been a worried expression. "I've been trying all day to reach you. I have to leave tomorrow morning. I was so afraid I wouldn't get a chance to talk to you."

"So soon?"

"I know, I'm going to miss Jason's game and, and, well, everything. But Mom has everything set up."

Focused exclusively on her crystal, Bailey stepped into that plane where Ting was and just wasn't, and hugged her. "You won't be that far away."

It was like hugging a ghost. Something was almost there and yet not, for both of them, and Bailey tried not to shiver. Ting brushed a long strand of shimmering coal-dark hair from her temple. "It's the worst possible time for me to go."

"There's never a good time," Bailey said. "I know it seems worse, because of Jennifer and Eleanora, and stuff, but there's never a good time to say good-bye to friends. At least we have a way of staying really close. Lots of people don't have that."

"I know." Ting put her hand out, palm up, and touched it to Bailey's matching hand, briefly. The bracelet on her ankle shimmered. "Oh! I made you something. Father said he'd mail it for me."

"What is it?"

Ting grinned. "I can't tell you, it's a surprise!"

"You know I can't wait for a surprise."

"You're going to have to," teased Ting gently. "All right then . . . one hint. Keep it away from Lacey."

"Oh, you made me some jewelry!" Bailey gave a little bounce.

"I hope you like it."

"I know I will. I'll Crystal to you soon as I get it."

"All right." Ting frowned again. "Grandmother went into the hospital yesterday for her treatment and felt so ill they kept her overnight."

"You see? She needs you."

"I know she does. I know. But, Bailey . . ." Ting's voice trailed off.

Bailey looked at her, and saw her friend's lower lip quivering a little as if she couldn't get the words out. "What if she's dying?" Bailey said for her.

Ting nodded.

"First of all, she's not. Not yet. She's got years, even as sick as she is. And second, well, she's got Magick, too, and that's a gift the two of you can share with each other. It'll mean a lot, and probably give her strength right now."

"You think so?"

"Well. I can't promise it, but yeah, I think so!"

Ting smiled. "I guess that's good enough for me."

"Half a cookie is better than none, as my grandma always used to say. And twice as good as a bundt cake."

"Oh, Bailey!" Ting broke into laughter then. They hugged again, and then Bailey let her concentration on her crystal go, and both of them faded back into their own realities.

Bailey tucked her legs under her and curled up,

one shoulder next to Lacey's cage. She turned the TV on, clicking the remote over and over. It wasn't fair that Ting had such awful things to worry about, and Bailey didn't dare tell her about any of the strange things she'd been experiencing. That would have been asking too much of Ting's gentle nature. Bailey finally settled on the Discovery Channel, with one of its wildlife programs, and she sat watching until a key rattled in the apartment door lock and her mother finally walked in the door.

"Why such a long face?"

"Ting's leaving tomorrow. She's going to miss Jason's game, and everything."

"Ah." She gathered Bailey into a warm hug. She smelled of the office, faintly of cigarettes, and coffee, and ink from the copying machine, and she sounded tired. But her arms felt strong around Bailey, and she whispered into Bailey's ear, "I received two free movie passes today, and I thought we could go tonight . . . if you want to."

"What movie?"

"*Kiss Me Again, Kate.* It's a remake of an old musical. Should be funny, with lots of good singing and dancing." Rebecca Landau fished out two colorful pieces of cardboard and waved them through the air as proof.

"That would be great!" And welcome. Anything to get her mind off things. "Are we eating there?"

"We can grab a sandwich across the way at that tea shop, okay?"

"And popcorn?"

"Definitely popcorn. And . . . Junior Mints."

"Wahoo!" Bailey ran to get her jacket. Lacey made

a lot of rattling noises in her cage, and Rebecca stuck her finger in, and stroked the animal's side softly. "You get her all day, don't fuss at me."

Lacey dove headfirst into her pile of shredded tissue and wood chips, jerking her tufted tail in after as if insulted. Her mother stifled a laugh as Bailey dashed back in, carrying two jackets.

"Ready?"

"Am I!" Bailey bolted to the front door, and her mother followed after, still chuckling.

For dinner, they split a meatball sandwich with melted mozzarella that hung in strings from their mouths no matter how daintily they tried to eat, and an iced tea that came with two cherries and a slice of orange on a toothpick floating on the top.

"*Two* cherries," beamed Bailey and promptedly claimed one of the maraschinos as her own. "How did they know?"

"How indeed," Rebecca answered, and winked at the girl who had set the sandwich down in front of them.

The movie unfolded in marvelous color and song and dance and costume, and the two of them sat enchanted for nearly two hours till it was over, and Bailey slumped back in her comfortable movie seat and hid a yawn. Rebecca tried to hide her own, but couldn't. She leaned over and kissed the top of Bailey's head.

"One of the best Saturday night dates I've had in a long time. But I think the best thing now would be to go home and snuggle into bed."

Bailey yawned a second time. "I second that," she said. Then, "Any Junior Mints left?"

"Enough for you to have one on your pillow."

"Ew. They were getting kinda warm and gooey."

Rebecca Landau broke into laughter as they strode through the theater lobby and out into the cold, brisk early spring night. Car headlights blinded both of them slightly as they rounded the corner to the theater parking garage. Bailey thought she saw something, a shadow, behind them, but when she turned to look, another car cruised past and she could barely see anything beyond it, except the brilliant neon marquee for the multiplex.

Rebecca reached down and caught her hand. "Just think if everyone sang everything." She cleared her throat. "Baaaaailey. Where do you think we parked the car-aaar?"

Bailey turned two shades of red as other moviegoers passed them by, but she sang back, "Motheeer. I believe it's over heeere!"

They rushed the car and got inside it before anyone else could think them crazy, laughing so much they could hardly get their seat belts buckled. The car eased out of the garage, its engine chugging away and its heater soon pumping in warmed air. Bailey hunched into her jacket, feeling the cheer bubble over her, most of the past week's worries gone away.

They parked in their reserved spot at the apartment building, and Bailey bounced out first, calling dibs on the last of the Junior Mints.

"Not fair!"

"All's fair in candy and war!" Bailey informed her mother. She grinned mischievously over the car at Rebecca.

"Don't I get even one?"

"Oh, all riiiiight, most excellent motheeer," sang Bailey. "Just one!" Bailey did a little pirouette for emphasis. She stopped, gasping, rooted to the ground, as a dark, lanky figure reared out of the shadows. Her breath stuck in her throat as the man reached for her, and then she jarred her voice loose. "Run, Mom! RUN!!!"

The stalker was there, right there, closing on her. Bailey couldn't get another word out, couldn't breathe, as his hand stabbed through the air after her.

Rebecca Landau stood in shock. "Bailey—"

She dodged from the man at the last possible second, slamming her hip into the car fender. The pain wrenched her voice loose. "It's the stalker, Mom! *Run!*"

Rebecca Landau's face sank into fear and worry. "That's not a stalker, hon. That's . . . your father."

19

SURPRISE!

SHE ought to learn to listen first and use her crystal later, Bailey thought a moment too late, as she grabbed her mother's hand, rubbed her amethyst, and suddenly the two of them landed in the hallway outside their apartment door. Sometimes there just wasn't time to think like that! But she had to have been wrong, that couldn't have been her father. Her father wouldn't have *stalked* them.

Her mother paled. "Bailey . . . what on Earth just happened. . . ." She looked around in disbelief, nearly stumbling back a step.

"You blinked."

"I blinked?"

"You blinked and missed it. We ran for it." Bailey let go of her mother's suddenly cold hand and dug through her jeans to fetch her key out. The door key seemed to have a mind of its own, much like her little pack rat, and kept disappearing into deeper and deeper folds in her pocket. Finally she curled fingers around it stubbornly and got it out and in the lock. There it resisted her even more and managed to jam once or twice before turning smoothly and clicking the lock chambers into place.

Bailey put her hand on the door to push it open.

"Stop right there!"

Bailey froze, her heart bouncing inside her chest as if it were jumping rope.

"I don't know what's going on here," came a harried voice from behind them. The stalker slid to a stop in the hallway, polished floorboards squeaking under the soles of his shoes, and he pointed a shaking hand at Rebecca. "What have you done to her?" He paused to catch his breath. He must have taken the stairs in two-at-a-time leaps.

Bailey could almost see her father in the stranger. But she heard him clearly in the voice, loud, unhappy, accusing. She shrank back against the apartment door.

"Get inside, Bailey," her mother said tightly.

"Witch! You've made a damn witch out of her!" The shaking hand settled into a point, aimed right at Bailey's forehead.

"What are you talking about?"

"I don't know what else to call it."

"Inside," Rebecca ordered her firmly.

"Not without you."

"This isn't a democracy. I'm your mother, now go."

Bailey set her chin, and shook her head. The apartment door began to swing in anyway, creaking open behind her.

"I'm taking her back," Jerry Landau told them. "Before it's too late. I don't know—I can't explain what I've seen—but you've made a witch out of her."

Her mother looked down at Bailey, one eyebrow quirking in an unasked question.

"I'm not a witch. I'm . . . I . . . I . . . I . . ." Bailey's throat locked up. She couldn't get another word out, and she clenched one hand in fierce frustration. The Vow of Silence! She couldn't tell even loved ones, let alone enemies, what she was! She had no defense.

Rebecca put her hand around Bailey's. The crystal in her palm flared slightly with renewed warmth, and that made Bailey jump slightly in surprise. Her mother and father stared at each other from across the apartment building hallway, but Bailey had the feeling it might as well be across the world's deepest chasm. She'd never seen them fight when they were still a family, but she'd seen many nights of her mother crying, alone, after he'd stormed out. "I have a restraining order," Rebecca told him. "I want you to leave."

"I have an order in process to take custody," he answered. "I've had her watched, followed, and I've seen it myself as well. She leaves here at all times of the day and night, while you're at work, while you're sleeping. Do you even know where she goes? She goes to hang out with boys, several of them. And I've seen her disappear into thin air. Not once but a number of times." Her father narrowed his eyes at her. "I don't know what you've been teaching her, or maybe it's those friends of hers, but she'll be better off with me, before it's too late."

"Too late for what?"

"To be a decent person. She's a freak, Rebecca, like you."

Bailey started to lunge forward, but her mother's hold stopped her, but couldn't contain the words tumbling out of her throat. "Don't talk to her like that! She's the best mom in the world. We don't need you here, we don't want you here!"

"Ssssh," said Rebecca soothingly, and pulled her back against her body, her free hand brushing Bailey's hair back from her forehead. "I won't argue with you in the damn hallway. You want to try to get a court order, go ahead. I'll fight you every step of the way. Bailey's an outstanding student, and she has good friends, and there isn't anyone who can say otherwise. So bring it on, if you're going to. Otherwise, stay out of our lives. You wanted one of your own, you went and got it, and you're not welcome here." Rebecca took a deep breath, and Bailey could feel it shuddering all the way through her mother's body as they leaned close together. "Get out of here before I call the police. I've still got a restraining order."

"We'll see about this."

Bailey could feel the air crackle, as her mother began to draw her back into the apartment doorway, repeating, "Like I said, bring it on. If you can. Now go!"

The crystal went hot in her hand, in their clasped hands, and Jerry Landau reeled back as if shoved out of the way, freeing them to fall into the apartment and slam the door shut. Through the wood, they could hear his muffled shout. "I'll go, but I'll be back!"

Rebecca fumbled at the dead bolts, and the main lock, then stood, her face whiter than white, as she looked down at Bailey. She rubbed her hands together, the palm of one pink as if sunburned.

"What was that? And you have to tell me, tell me now, or I don't think there's any way I can protect you from your father."

Bailey stood, her jaw slowly dropping, as she stared back into her mother's shocked face. She didn't know what it was either, but the crystal had answered, to both of them. "I . . . don't know what you mean."

Rebecca Landau, her back to the now barred apartment door, slowly slid down it to the floor, and put her face in her hands. Voice muffled, she said, "Bailey. I haven't got the money to fight him in court, not if he really makes a fight out of it. Honey, I'm gonna lose you!"

"No, you won't. We'll think of something."

Rebecca looked up. She wasn't crying, not yet, not quite, but her nose had reddened slightly, and her eyes were very bright with unshed tears. "We always do, right?" She paused. "The boys he talked about?"

"Jason and Trent. Mom, you know them!"

"You know you're not supposed to leave the apartment when I'm at work."

Embarrassment flooded her face. "Things . . . happen. It wasn't anything bad, all right?"

"Then what was it?" Rebecca reached out, took

Bailey's chin in her fingers gently and tilted her face up, so they could look into each other's eyes. "I've seen things, too, honey. Strange things I can't explain, but because I know you're good, I never worried. I have to worry now, because if I can't fight your dad, I'm going to lose you."

"I haven't done anything wrong!"

"I don't think you have, but I don't think you've told me the truth, either. Now, you and I both know I didn't take a long blink. How did we get up here?"

"We . . . ran?"

"I don't think so." Her mother leveled both eyebrows into a frown, drilling her gaze into Bailey's.

There was no way she was going to be able to answer, no matter how badly she wanted to. Oh, to be like Ting with a grandmother of the Hidden Blood, and with whom she could share some of her wonderful secrets. Bailey swallowed, as if that could loosen the throat lock she was going to feel.

"I can't tell you."

"Can't or won't?"

"Can't."

"You're sure?"

Bailey tried not to squirm. "Pretty sure. I've tried to tell you before."

"Anything to do with your tutor from school?"

Eleanora had dropped in once or twice, under the guise of a school tutor. But Eleanora looked far from ordinary, and although she and Rebecca Landau had hit it off, Eleanora had decided that she could not risk drawing any more of Rebecca's attention. "Mom, I can't tell you, but it's nothing bad!"

"It's bad if it allows your father to take you away."

"He called a few days ago, late. He was really drunk again. It's not the divorce that makes him a terrible father, it's just the way he is. He wasn't good when he lived with us, and he's not good now." Bailey sighed. "I don't want him to have custody. If he gets it, I'll run away."

"Then they'll put you in a foster home, eventually. You can't run from this problem."

"Oh, yes, I can. They'd never know where to look." Once Jason had Haven open, she would never be found if she went there. Never. Not unless she wanted to be found.

Rebecca lost control of her tears then, and they cascaded slowly down her face.

"I wouldn't run from *you*!"

"Oh, Bailey!" Rebecca put her arms around her daughter and pulled her very close in a comforting hug. "Promise me you won't run away."

"It won't be running away. It'd be another home, only for Magickers—" Bailey stopped in shock.

"What did you say?" Rebecca pulled back and looked at her.

"I didn't—" She couldn't have, could she? "I didn't say anything."

"Magicers? What on earth do you mean?"

"Magickers," corrected Bailey, and took a deep breath. Her mouth didn't snap shut and stay that way, her lips didn't feel like they were glued shut. She blinked. "Magickers! Mom . . . I can say it. That's what I am, I found out last summer at camp, I'm a Magicker." She paused a moment, waiting for the world as she knew it to end. Nothing happened.

"What are you talking about?"

"It's what I do, it's what I am. I can . . . I can talk to Lacey." Bailey bolted to her feet, skidded around the corner to her bedroom, and came back, pack rat in hand. "It's part of my Talent, animal sense. I can make friends with them." She put Lacey down. The furry little rodent twitched her tufted tail once or twice, then sat up and looked at them, in between grooming her long, slender whiskers. "Lacey, go run to the kitchen and bring me back something shiny."

"Bailey . . ."

"It's okay, Mom." Bailey quirked a finger at the pack rat. Lacey twisted away from them, running along the baseboard of the apartment, and disappeared in the general direction of the kitchen. "She'll be back in a few minutes, soon as she finds something."

"What if she doesn't find anything?"

"Mom! She's a pack rat! She can find stuff we don't even know we've lost."

"All right. Now. The long blink?"

"Oh, that! That's Crystaling." Bailey held up her bracelet, with the cage dangling, and her amethyst shining through the thin, spiraled bars. "It's like a . . . a wand in Harry Potter, I'd guess you say. Only I don't have to waggle it and say something in Latin. It's a Focus for energy. I can teleport short distances, if I know exactly where I'm going, and I've trained well enough. Beam me up, Scotty!" Bailey finished with a wide grin.

"And you brought me with you?"

"Yeah. That was hard, made me kind of dizzy. I guess it helps when the person with you knows what you're doing and can't fight it, even self-consciously."

"Unconsciously."

"Whatever."

The sound of claws on the wood flooring interrupted them, and Lacey came barreling around the corner, a flashy piece of tinfoil in her mouth. She skittered up to Bailey, climbed into the hand held down to her, deposited a silvery gum wrapper in her palm, and made a satisfied chitter, as if she'd found a great treasure. Which, to a pack rat, she had. "Good girl," Bailey said, and rubbed her chin. The pack rat grabbed back the foil and tucked it against her body before climbing up to Bailey's shoulder and resting in the curve of her neck, holding on tightly to both her treasure and the shirt collar.

Rebecca leaned back against the wall as if even it might not be strong enough to support her. "And a Magicker is . . . someone who works . . . magic?"

"Exactly."

"That's not possible."

Bailey pursed her lips and made a guppy mouth for a moment in thought. "Well, Gavan explains it this way . . . Magick is derived from rarer laws of physics, many of which are incompletely understood or not discovered yet. Rather like genetics. A family of brown-eyed people can have a blue-eyed child, but it's a recessive gene and you might have to go back several generations to find the parent who had it originally, but it's still in the bloodline."

"Like that?"

Bailey nodded, her ponytail bouncing enthusiastically. "Something like that."

"Is there any limit to what you can do?"

"You mean, like, what's my kryptonite?"

"Sort of, yes."

"Oh, there's a lot we can't do. It depends on our individual Talents, and our stamina and energy, and concentration, and training."

"Ah." Rebecca let out her breath, and rubbed at a faint wrinkle across her forehead. "For a moment, I was hoping you could conjure up a lawyer to get us out of this."

"No. And I can't tell anyone I'm a Magicker either. We took a Vow, to keep the others safe. I mean, who wants to be dissected to find out how we do it, right?"

Rebecca shuddered. "Right." She put her hand on Bailey's knee. "Honey, somehow I think we just jumped from the frying pan into the fire. There could be a lot worse problems than your father trying to get custody."

MOONDANCE

HENRY slowly thawed. He had no other way to describe it. The feeling of thawing out crept over his body, leaving behind it the pins and needles of muscles and nerves awakening, and the awful chill of having been colder than he could ever remember. The terrible moment of anchoring to Jason had been followed by a near total nothingness. He remembered dragging himself upstairs to his room, complaining of a headache, then collapsing onto his bed. Night veiled it now, and he must have slept or been unconscious for hours. He hugged himself for a moment, then reached for his crystal, the citrine of yellow-red colors, and brought up the Lantern spell, bathing his darkened room in warm orange color. And it *was* warm, too, although his Focus should have only been for light, but he'd always had trouble keeping heat out of it.

He remembered with embarrassment the times in study when he'd worn one of FireAnn's oven mitts just to avoid burning himself whenever his crystal had exploded into flame as he'd tried for simple illumination. Now though . . . now the flame-warmed depths of his gemstone felt heaven sent. He held it tightly to his chest, feeling the delicious heat bathe him until his teeth finally stopped chattering and he could wiggle around, trying to stomp out the funky pins-and-needles feeling. He gestured his hand over his crystal then, shutting off the Lantern spell, as he sat up.

That *had* been Jonnard in his mind. Had to have been, couldn't have been anything else, unless he was crazy, but now Henry wondered. Being crazy didn't leave you limp as a rag and frozen, did it? But having your *Magick* drained from you did. *That* he remembered. Jonnard had done it before. And somehow, Henry thought frantically, he was doing it again! Squibb, you're not insane! Not yet, anyway.

That made him feel a little better. Not as good as the Light and Warmth spell, but better. The well-being didn't last. A sharp, sickening cramp seized him, like a fist grabbing him and squeezing him. He couldn't tell anyone. They wouldn't be able to help him and they might take what little Magick he had away from him again. He wrestled with that horrible thought. He *had* to be able to tell someone, didn't he?

He scrubbed a hand over his thick black hair, sending it in every direction, no doubt. He had to *think*. He should tell the older Magickers what was happening. They might be able to shield him. They ought to. On the other hand, if Jonnard had managed to reconnect to Henry, it made Henry a possible spy within Gavan's group. What if Jonnard had found a way, not only to tap Henry's Magick whenever he wanted, but to look around through Henry's eyes? Hear through his ears? To *spy* on the others anytime he wanted, without being caught, until Henry dropped in his tracks.

No. No, no. If Gavan and the Council knew that, they'd never trust Henry again. Not as long as Jonnard and the Dark Hand were a threat.

He had to tell them, didn't he? They'd be furious with him if he didn't.

And suspicious.

Henry sighed. He scratched his head. One of them might be able to help. Maybe FireAnn had a potion or something he could drink and it would block his thoughts from Jonnard. Or maybe Gavan could put a damper on his crystal. Or maybe Tomaz could fix him one of those neat fetish bag charms to wear like Jason often wore.

Or maybe they'd just make him drink that awful stuff again and shut him away from ever Magicking.

Neither prospect sounded good, but they might be better than letting Jon pick at him, unravel him, till there was nothing left, like some bony old scarecrow in a raggedy outfit. He needed to think about it, what he wanted to do, what he should do, and what he might expect. He hugged himself tightly, fighting off the last bit of cold.

He wanted to remain a Magicker. He just didn't know right now if anything he did would allow that.

After being forced to give it up once, he didn't think he could stand to go through that again. He couldn't ask Bailey or Ting what to do, because he'd be putting them into the same dilemma he was facing, whether to tell or not, and how to handle it. He couldn't put them in jeopardy. Jason or Trent might be more helpful, but they always seemed up to their necks in trouble with the Dark Hand as it was.

He had the eerie feeling that anchoring on Jason, rather than protecting Henry from that awful thing that was happening to him, had led the Dark Hand to the Iron Gate. What if he had somehow sent great trouble to Jason? What if the thing in his mind had left him only because, linking to Jason, it had found better, more important prey?

No, for the moment, he was in this alone. Till he knew what he was dealing with and how to strike back at it, Henry decided.

Somewhere outside his room, the world returned to normal. He could hear his toddler sister fussing in her bedroom. That he could handle. He got up and padded down the darkened hallway to her room, so his mom could sleep a little. It was either a diaper or bottle emergency and after what he'd just been through, he had no doubt he had the answer to *that* problem.

Jason felt a cold wind shear past him even as he stepped through his lavender crystal. It burned at his ears and nose and exposed throat and as soon as he could, he put the hood of his sweatshirt up and shoved hands and crystal deep into waiting pockets. The time shift here was not as obvious as expected, it was the dead of night on this world, too, color and shadows in shades of grays, blacks, and purples, and he wondered if there was ever a daytime here for he'd never seen one. But then, he'd only been here two or three other times, and all of them when he could sneak away, so if they ran in parallel, it would be nighttime here too. Still, it gave him the creeps. The moon overhead was not the moon of his time and place. It hung like a silver-bladed scimitar, low and curved and remarkably large in the sky, as though it could slice out and behead him.

Jason turned on his heel. This was the world where he'd found Gregory the Gray's crystal. The world where wolfjackals seemed to roam freely and, indeed, the place which might be their home. The world where, when he tried to contact Tomaz, he seemed to see him. All of which did not make him feel particularly good or safe. He hurt where the Leucator had grazed him. His skin burned with an icy coldness, and his body ached where Jon had pummeled him.

He'd had worse bruises and injuries in soccer, and he'd garner more the next day, but he hated to go into a game already aching. He'd no choice and it wouldn't slow him down, not with his teammates depending on him, and the fierce joy of the game awaiting him, but he moved deliberately and carefully now. In the darkness, he couldn't afford to slip on an unsteady stone and wrench a leg or knee, laming him. That would be unthinkable.

He picked his way down a slope where what looked like grass crackled under his feet like brittle frost, and from the sharpness on the evening wind, just might be. A tree reared up with stick branches hung with icicles and black skin wood, looking far more dead than alive. Surely this world had a spring awaiting it . . . didn't it? It would have to have a cycle of life and rest and seasons, wouldn't it? The wolfjackals, if they ranged here, would have to have food, and that prey would have to have food or vegetation to support it and so on. Nothing just existed.

Or did it?

Jason picked his way over a frozen brook, little more than a stride wide, cut into the bottom of the slope. He stepped onto a vast, open field, and imagined what it might be like at the height of springtime. It was nearly the size of a soccer field. Would it be filled with grass and grazing animals? Flowers? Small rodents tunneled into freshly turned soil, and birds pulling worms out of the ground, and bees drawn close by nectar. Now it was nothing more than a darkness around him, flat and almost mirror-like as if frozen like black marble.

Jason slowly turned about, casting his gaze over the desolate scenery. He could see from where he stood now, far in every direction, which was what he wanted. He had no wish for a wolfjackal to be able to spring upon him, unseen. If anything approached him now, he'd spot it.

He took his crystal out again. Jason looked into it and sent a call out for Tomaz. He put every fiber of his being into it with such force that when he finished, the spell flung him back a step, arms outstretched for balance, and he hung there a moment as if caught in midair. He fought to be centered before realizing his feet had never left the ground. Feeling as if he were a giant hawk either lifting into flight or swooping in to settle, Jason lowered his arms and just stood. The power of his call for Tomaz washed around him. His ears buzzed with it.

Gregory's crystal stayed warm in his hand, about the only warmth that could be found in the bleak landscape of this world. He brought both his hands together just for that heat and it flashed with an eerie glow as he did. Jason did a slow turn, looking about, listening to . . . nothing, yet the hair at the back of his neck prickled as if he sensed that he was being watched.

And he could be, anything could be possible. As bare as the landscape seemed to be, there were scraggly shrubs and winter-browned grasses, a boulder here and there. Yet anything that watched him could hardly be big enough to threaten. Unless it spied.

Jason finished his circle and took a deep slow breath. The Magick enveloping him from the call began to ease away. It left him with a faint tingle over his skin, making him want to scratch inside his heavy shirt and sweatshirt and unable to get at it. His ears stayed cold even inside the thick hood. The wind plucked at him as if knowing he hadn't really dressed for whatever winter and nighttime this world could hold. He danced in place to warm his legs up.

Then, a faint something reached his hearing. He could not quite identify it at once. Perhaps the thin, high screech of a hunting owl or the wind whistling through a skeletal branch. Jason turned to face it, trying to catch it better. He reached up and lowered his sweatshirt hood. After a long moment, he heard it again. Pitched almost too high for him to hear, something wailed in the night air. He did not think it could possibly be Tomaz answering his call. The Magick or perhaps his very presence seemed to have attracted something else. He shivered as much from the eerie sound of it as the cold. He could not identify it, but whatever it was, it sounded like it was headed his way.

He readied himself by stowing Gregory's crystal and getting out his own, because he knew how to Shield really well with it. If pressed, he could also bring up a sword of energy which, for lack of any other description, seemed to be something straight out of the *Star Wars* movies. But he did not come to fight, he'd come to find Tomaz. If he were attacked, he'd retreat and head home the same way he'd come. He'd come for answers, though, and he didn't want to leave until he had a few, and Tomaz needed to know about recent events. Crowfeather seemed to have blocked everyone from him but Jason, and that made his burden that much heavier.

The howling suddenly filled the air, keening, rising and falling in pitch, and sounding from all about him like a whirlwind of noise. Jason spun about, seeing nothing but dark clouds boiling in the sky. A tongue of silver lightning licked through them, yet it brought no thunder. He knew that sound now, and he did not wish to face it. As he recognized it, the scar on the back of his left hand twitched painfully.

Wolfjackals, running in the storm of their own chaotic Magick, rushed toward him. The last thing he wanted to meet here and now, and yet he'd expected it. Every time he'd glimpsed Tomaz, wolfjackals had been there. Lightning split the sky again and in its glare he could smell both the power of the natural phenomenon and the Magick it carried. With howls louder than thunder, the wolfjackal pack leaped out of the sky, eyes glowing like green moons, as they bounded to the ground and raced toward him.

He brought his Shield up immediately in expectation but nothing in his wildest thoughts prepared him for what he saw next.

Tomaz rode the pack leader, astride its powerful wolfish shoulders, his own dark mane of shoulder-length hair loose in the wind, a gleam in his eyes. Jason rocked back, steadied himself for anything, as the Navajo shouted words to him in his native tongue that Jason could barely hear above the wind and the howling. The wolfjackals swung about in a wide circle, racing about him, drawing closer with every pass until he could smell their hot breath, and their sharp claws flung pebbles and bits of frozen grass at him as they churned to a halt, growling low.

Jason faced most of them, although one or two snarled at his flank. He could not keep them all to the fore of him, and the beasts knew it, but it was Tomaz he wanted to look in the face.

Crowfeather raised a hand, and said only, "Jason."

What he wanted to answer boiled through his mind. What was Tomaz doing with these beasts, and why, and when was he coming back, and did he have the answers he was seeking and did he have any idea at all how badly things were going in his absence. But he said nothing for a long moment. Then he said, "Eleanora is in a deep sleep. Something dark attacked her, and it began to take her. Aging.

Other stuff, and the only thing Gavan and Khalil could do was put her to sleep."

Tomaz frowned. Here, in the barest of moonlight, Jason could see silvery streaks in his dark, unbound hair. The conchas on his belt and bracelet rattled, disks of silver studded with turquoise and other stones, little mirrors of light pooling about him. "How is Gavan taking it?"

"Not well. We tried to find sanctuary for her with Aunt Freyah and she turned us away. We need you, Tomaz. The Council is falling apart. Isabella has been making Leucators for Brennard." Jason gestured with one hand, realizing the spill of words held a sense of hopelessness. "And I can't find the Gate. There's only one of Gavan."

"I am not done here." Tomaz stroked the bristling neck of the beast he rode, and its growling stilled slightly as if soothed by his touch. "I can't come back yet, Jason, but I can, and will, send some strength with you for Eleanora's sake. Come here." He lifted a hand and reached out for Jason.

Jason hesitated. To approach Tomaz would be to enter the pack, for the beast he rode was now surrounded by its smaller pack mates, all growling hotly at him, their teeth gleaming whitely and drool falling to the ground in such warm drops that the frost melted where it touched. What if he saw an illusion? What if only wolfjackals awaited him? He felt his scar tighten and throb. *You are mine*, the wolfjackal who'd bitten him had said. Was he?

Jason stepped forward. The nearest wolfjackal spun on its haunches and snapped at him. Teeth clashed against his Shield and sparks flew with a stink of Magicks meeting. Jason looked at the beast as it cowered back, red slash of a tongue licking its chops in wounded surprise.

"Hurry," urged Crowfeather. "I cannot hold them long, if at all."

Jason leaped two strides, carrying him to Tomaz's side. The Magicker leaned out, and his rough callused finger traced a sign on Jason's forehead. "See clearly," he said as he did so. Molten heat singed Jason's skin, and then cooled as fiercely.

"It's all I can do," said Tomaz. They traded a long look.

"Hurry," answered Jason.

"I will. Send me word if things worsen." Tomaz paused. "Jason, I would never try to turn you against anyone, but be wary of Isabella. This is a bad thing she has done, and it may not be the worst of her actions. She is dealing with Chaos and every action swings the balance more and more out of control. Promise me you will stay clear of her."

"I will."

Tomaz dropped his hand and thumped the wolf-jackal on its flank. Turning its head, it snarled at Tomaz's booted foot, but whirled about in answer and flung itself across the ground, bounding away from Jason. The other wolfjackals yipped and howled in disappointment, then raced after their pack leader, leaving Jason alone in their wake.

He let his Shield drop and put his hand to his forehead. *See clearly.* If only he could!

Jason rubbed his crystal and thought of home.

21

BIG TROUBLE

"I DON'T know whether to commend you or punish you." Antoine Brennard sat in his great fan-backed chair which framed him rather like a throne, and let one hand drop over the arm of the chair as if pondering his own statement.

Jon stood in front of him, unimpressed at the moment because he knew his father's temperament. If he were going to have been rewarded or beaten, both would have happened on the spot, at Iron Gate itself, or a heartbeat away. Brennard was quick to anger and strike or shout, and just as swift in any other emotion, though few emotions ever held him for long. Jon knew it well, for he was just like his father, with a few exceptions.

He held his silence, watching his father's face. The weariness that had driven his breath clean away was gone, and he knew that he had but to reach out for Henry Squibb again and he would be charged. But from the way Henry had tried to fight him, he also knew he should not try again too soon, lest the bird figure out just how caged he was and how to escape as well. It would take Jon too long to find another Magicker to draw from as easily.

Unless . . . The temptation to drink from his father's aura again bathed him. Why not? It had been even easier the last time than draining Henry was, and Brennard had not even known. Jon felt spent, old, and so he reached out. He made contact so easily, because they were father and son, he supposed, and his father's angry energy rushed into him. Even as Jon felt its incandescence fill him, his father sat back with a calmed sigh. Perhaps, thought Jon, this was a thing that was good for both of them.

His father stirred from his thoughts. Brennard raised a finger. "None of us was prepared to do battle, yet we almost had them."

Jon gave a slow nod.

"The Leucator was a mistake."

"Perhaps." He would not admit more than that. He could not, and his father would be suspicious if he did. Turning a Leucator from one thing into another had never been done before, yet he *had* done it, if imperfectly, and he knew his father must be mulling that over in the back of his mind. How much effort, how much of a draining would such a thing take, and would it be worth it? Perhaps. Perhaps not. He waited. It was past his bedtime and although he didn't have a very great need for sleep, as he could easily get by on four or five hours, he looked forward to a rest this evening. The fight had taken more out of him than he'd wanted.

"I propose this to you: The best time to hit an enemy is when they are most vulnerable."

"That would seem obvious."

"Obvious, but not always possible." Brennard steepled his fingers and looked over them at Jon. "But if it can be done, we can break them, and once broken, the children will scatter. Once scattered, they will realize they are alone in a dark and hostile world and they will need aid. They might even be willing to accept it from us openly or by guile. Do you not agree?"

It seemed Brennard had been doing a lot of thinking in the past few hours. Openly? Never. But offered in disguise? Maybe. "I do," answered Jon cautiously.

"Good. Because it will tax you, and I want you to be prepared." Brennard then told him how and when and where he intended to strike.

"That soon?"

"If we are tired, they will be exhausted. There isn't a better time, for the moment."

Jon listened solemnly, bowed in understanding, and then left his father's presence for much needed rest, his thoughts tumbling in eagerness, even as he fought for the calm he needed to sleep.

Stef woke curled up around his battered sneakers, their overripe scent filling his nose. "Yuck." He groaned and rolled away. The room stank of bear cub and he knew he'd spent at least half the night in the furry hide of his other self. He sighed. They'd catch him one of these days, and what would he do then? Rich had told him just to say it was a big old dog, a stray, he took in sometimes and which followed him around, but jeez. How blind did his parents have to be to mistake a bear cub, half grown, for a dog? Not to mention the stench. Or the noise, if his cub self decided to start bawling for food. He had a sweet tooth in either form. Impossible, Stef thought, and sighed. They'd never think it was a dog.

Especially since neither animal had permission to be living at their house.

Stef rolled to his knees and then his feet. The smell of hotcakes and coffee filtered into his bedroom, the standard Sunday morning breakfast. His stomach rumbled loudly, in a familiar bearish way, and he decided he was starving. He pulled on pants and shirt, ran a comb through his hair and lumbered to the kitchen, ready to devour as big a stack as his mother could pile on a plate.

"Stefan! Sleepyhead! Ready to eat?"

"Smells great, Mom." He poured himself a glass of milk as his dad winked at him, and tugged a chair away from the kitchen table with his foot so that Stef could sit down.

"All American breakfast, eh? Bacon and pancakes."

He forked himself a few crisp pieces while she took a plate warmed on the stove and heaped it up. She set it down in front of him, saying, "Have you been using that foot powder I bought for you?"

He ladled syrup over the pile and watched the caramel stickiness drip everywhere. "Yes, ma'am."

"It stinks in there, Stefan."

"I'll clean it up tonight, Mom, after Jason's game,

okay? I've got laundry to do and stuff. And . . . and . . . I'll get one of those stick-up things, okay? It's just the football gear, it gets sweat in it, you know. I know it smells. I try to keep it clean."

She ruffled his hair. "You're a good son, Stefan. Don't worry. Someday you will be big football star and we can retire to Florida and watch your games on the TV." Her accent came out a little as she said that, wiping her hands on her apron, as she returned to the stove and poured a new batch of hotcakes onto the griddle.

"College first, Mom."

"Of course. Always the school. You must grow a little more, too. Eat up!" She gave the order with a wave of her pancake turner.

"If he grows any more, Mama, we'll have to buy more shoes," his father said, grinning as he stuffed a forkful of light, fluffy pancakes into his mouth. His eyes twinkled at Stef as he said that, and Stef just grunted at his father's teasing.

His mother let out a little huff, and said, reluctantly, "If he needs them. Only if he needs them!"

Now that she mentioned it . . . "I will soon, Mom," Stef said. He snapped a piece of bacon in two and devoured both halves at once.

"Fine, fine. It goes in the budget. Two weeks your father gives up beer and has liverwurst for lunch sandwiches, and you have new shoes."

His father opened his mouth to protest that, and stopped in mid-word as she turned and waggled the pancake turner menacingly again. "Made of money we are not," she scolded. "But we are your parents and will sacrifice for you. Those two weeks, I will skip bingo at the church, too. Everyone must give up something."

Whatever it was his father had intended to say, it had been stomped flat by the second flood of words from his mom. Instead, his father mopped his face with a napkin and said, "Not the bingo, Mama. I'll make do, but you go to bingo. Who knows? You could win the shoe money!"

Besides which, bingo nights were the only nights of peace at home for his father. Stef hid his grin by polishing off the last of the pancakes on his plate and asking for more. His mother's face flushed with pleasure. "You like my cooking?"

"It's the best, Mom." And it was, nearly.

"Good, good. You say there is a soccer game today?"

"Yup. Jason's team is in it. We're gonna go watch, if that's okay."

"As long as everything is cleaned later." She nodded, and fussed with the bow on her apron before pouring out yet another round of pancakes. "And as long as it is okay with your father."

"It's a big game, Stef?"

"Yup. Part of the championship."

"We should all go. Spring is outside, and we should go." His father stole a pancake off Stef's plate, winking again, his good humor recovering a bit.

"Oh, that might be fun." His mother wiped her hands on her apron. "I'd better start on some sandwiches for lunch!" Humming tunelessly but quite happily, she began to plan her assault on world hunger at lunchtime.

It wasn't quite what Stef had planned, but what

could the harm be? Rich's parents never went anywhere with him, his mother worried endlessly about germs and public exposure, so it wouldn't be too crowded.

Stef reached over and plucked a piece of bacon from his dad's plate, grinning, and winked at him. "Sounds like fun."

The early morning flight to San Francisco Bay landed in light fog, bathing the whole area in soft gray mist draped everywhere she could see from the plane window. The gloom held a beauty of its own, but Ting also found it saddening. She had had plans for the day, but they didn't matter, really. Jason would play super with or without her in the stands, and Bailey would cheer loud enough for both of them. It's just that she didn't think . . . she didn't believe . . . that her being with her grandmother would help. Magick couldn't fight cancer, as far as she knew. Being there seemed to be all she could do, and she would. It's just that she felt as if they were all fighting a losing battle. She didn't want to face that.

Ting touched the airplane window as if she could trace a pattern through the mist, to see things better. Jiao Chuu hugged her shoulders gently. "It'll be all right," she said softly, as if reading Ting's mind.

"I hope so." Ting felt the brush of her mother's kiss across the top of her head.

"We don't know if everything will turn out the way we want it to. But I do know that anything done in love will turn out all right."

Ting put her hand out and held her mother's,

tightly. Her mother was thinking the same thing, then. They might lose Grandmother, even after all they'd been through, and all they were going to try. She sighed, as the plane lurched downward and bumped on the landing strip and began to brake hard and fast, and her ears popped faintly. Sometimes you had to do things for the past and the present, and not think about the future, she guessed.

Bailey slept soundly all night despite the worry, and she only woke when she heard her mother making an early morning, hushed-voice phone call. She only caught a word here and there which sounded more like she was leaving a message than talking to anyone. Bailey punched her pillow back up and drifted off to sleep again for a little longer until a tiny fuss from the pack rat's cage woke her for the last time.

Lacey appeared to have eaten every tiny morsel of food in existence in the pack rat world. She lay in her empty food cup, her tail tucked around her body, with the tuft under her chin, and looked up with the saddest eyes imaginable.

"Like I would let you starve," Bailey scoffed at her. The fluffy rodent managed a faint chirp.

"Oh, really." Bailey rolled her eyes as she shuffled to the corner of her tiny bedroom where she kept the various packages of seeds and grains and pellets. Lacey got to her haunches at the familiar rattle of food packs. The black tufted tail twitched in eagerness. She barely waited for Bailey to lower the refilled cup into the cage before diving in nose first.

"You must be a stress eater," Bailey observed.

Lacey did not make a noise other than rattling through the food till she found what she wanted, stuffed her little cheeks full and then went into her sleep ball filled with freshly shredded tissue and chips. Then came the noise of sunflower seeds being noisily cracked open. Bailey grinned.

Bailey was dressed and halfway through her own breakfast when her mom called out, "What's the agenda for the day?"

"Jason's game, homework, laundry."

"Fun stuff." Rebecca yawned as she sat down opposite Bailey.

"Speak for yourself. I find homework and laundry kinda groadie, myself."

Her mother laughed. "That's why I'm the mom and you're not." She pulled over the teapot that Bailey had made up and poured herself a cup of tea. The teapot looked like the character teapot from Disney's *Beauty and the Beast*, but it reminded Bailey more of Aunt Freyah than anything. If Aunt Freyah ever became a teapot, which of course, she didn't, to Bailey's knowledge.

"Bailey?"

"Hmmm?" She looked back to her mother.

"I called Legal Aid this morning, but they were closed, of course, it being Sunday. So, I won't have any idea what we can do until tomorrow or even Tuesday."

"Okay." It wasn't really quite okay, and they both knew it, but it was all that could be done. From here on out, it was a "wait and see" deal. See what damage her father tried to do, and see if they could counter it somehow. She put a spoon in her teacup and stirred it around, a lot, before adding, "I don't want to live with him."

"He might be able to offer you things I can't."

"If he'd changed, maybe, but from what I can see, he hasn't changed at all. He's gotten worse." Bailey waggled her spoon at her mother. "Some people just shouldn't be parents. There ought to be a license or something where you apply before they let you, like driving school. And I don't want him to be a parent of *me*."

"You're sure?"

"He may walk like a duck and talk like a duck but that doesn't make him a good father."

"Mmmm," said her mother, the corner of her mouth twitching. "Right." She stood up. "I guess I'd better get going, then. Big day ahead of us."

Bailey finished her breakfast, got up, and loaded the small apartment dishwasher quickly while her mother ate, standing up, as she often did. Trent liked to tease her, "Mrs. Landau! All that food will go to your ankles!" whenever he and Jason came over and joined them. That would be the bright spot in her day, seeing Trent and Jason. She could tell them what had happened and they would tell her they'd help however she needed it. Things would be okay.

"Oh," said her mother, as if she'd remembered something she'd almost forgotten. "About that . . . other thing. Maybe you could . . . not do it? Just for a while, till this problem with your dad is resolved."

"Not do Magick, you mean?"

Rebecca nodded.

"I can try. I mean, most of the time, you have to really concentrate on it to do anything, you know?

It's like hard mental work. Sometimes, though, it just . . . pops out at you."

"No one's going to believe you're a witch, but I don't want anyone to be able to prove you do unusual things either."

"Understood." Bailey nodded vigorously, her ponytail bobbing.

"Although . . . if you could manage the laundry?" her mother added hopefully.

"Sorry. Magickers don't do laundry. We just summon up new clothes." Bailey fled the kitchen, followed by her mother's laughing disappointment.

In her room, as she sorted through her hamper and laid out various piles of clothes for the wash, she thought about that. She wondered if Gavan or Aunt Freyah were ever tempted to use their power for everyday things. Freyah did, in a way, in her little cottage, but Bailey thought she did what she did to make people feel at ease and taken care of. They all knew picnic hampers didn't really have personalities or dancing food trays really have names, even if they did in Freyah's corner of the world. Did they? Or did Freyah have so much power in her, and so much experience under her hat, that such things were second nature?

Wow. She might *not* have laundry in her future! Wait till she told Jason and Trent that.

Trent steered his father by the elbow the moment they neared the soccer bleachers, and he could see Jason's stepfather getting ready to be seated. "Mr. McIntire!"

The big man turned and smiled, laugh lines going deep around his heavily sun-tanned face. "Trent."

"You remember my dad, Frank Callahan?"

"Once in a rare while." McIntire smiled affably and put his hand out. Trent's father looked rather like a string bean next to him as they shook hands.

"Good to see you, sir. We both put in long weekends, these breaks are nice."

"Dad's gonna have a lot of long weekends," Trent interjected. "The company's laying everyone off."

McIntire frowned. "Are they? That's not good. A man of your experience shouldn't have too much trouble getting placed. Sit with me, and catch up."

"Well . . ." Frank traded a look with his son.

"I'm sitting with Bailey," Trent said firmly.

McIntire chuckled. "Jumping up and down cheering, is more like it. It'll be quieter here with us." He motioned to Callahan to sit, as he settled himself next to his wife. Before his dad could protest, Trent escaped.

"You've got the whole fam damly here, looks like," Trent said, as he sat down on the benches and watched Jason lacing up his shoes tightly. The soccer field rang with the noise of people ascending the aluminum bleachers, and kids shouting as they raced around on the spring grass in the midst of the teams trying to warm up a bit. The midafternoon sun shone down brightly, but there was a crisp spring breeze that would keep it from being too hot. All in all, it looked like a good day. "Joanna, Alicia, and the Dozer."

"No kidding. Alicia wanted to film it, and then splice some of the shots into this project she's been invited to do."

"Little Miss Spielberg, huh?"

"Looks like it." Jason straightened his shin guards. "I kinda like having everyone here to watch, though. I hope we give 'em a good game."

"Think you're gonna win it?"

"Hope so, but they're a tough team. They've won before, and we haven't. Depends if we get nervous and if we're good enough and want it enough."

Trent grinned at him. "Going to work for ESPN later, huh?"

Jason cuffed at him, and missed.

"Good thing you don't use your hands in soccer," Trent teased. He waved back at the bleachers. "Brought your dad?"

"Yup. Thought he might talk to your stepdad, maybe do a little networking."

"Hey." Jason tucked his shirt in. "You know, that's not a bad idea. McIntire might know of some jobs."

"That's what I thought. He could do worse than find Frank Callahan a job." Trent nodded confidently.

"Always thinking." Jason leaned forward, after gazing up into the stands. He could not help but feel tremendously happy seeing his friends gathering there. Henry sat next to Bailey and her mother, his round face very pale in the afternoon sun. Rich and Stefan sat a few rows down, with Stefan's foreign-born parents looking overly American and proud, and even Rich's parents, his mother with a tissue to her nose and trying not to get too close to people. "Rich's parents are here?"

"How can you miss that red hair?"

"I can't, but I thought his mother never went out." Mrs. Hawkins was a notorious hypochondriac, dreadfully afraid of catching some exotic disease or other.

"She doesn't, usually. I guess there's a health fair or something at the other end of the park, so they thought they'd come for the game and then go over and get their blood pressure taken." Trent's eyes sparkled with amusement as he speculated.

The only ones missing were Ting and Gavan. Gavan occasionally sneaked in a soccer game, although professing he knew that even soccer was out of his time, but quite popular now in England and Europe of course. Jason liked to rib Gavan that only golf and jousting had been invented when Gavan grew up, and for all he knew it was nearly true. Maybe croquet. He'd have to look it up on the Internet sometime, just to see. Ting would be in San Francisco now, so he'd catch her up on the news later either through his crystal or computer.

"Tell 'em, Trent," Jason said suddenly. "No Magick, no matter what happens to me."

It was something that never came up. "We wouldn't—"

"I know. Just . . . in case."

"Right. I'll pass the word." Trent backed away from the benches as more of the team began to gather, and the coach started barking out drills. "Luck." He touched his knuckles to Jason's shoulder.

Luck, indeed.

Trent wove his way through the now crowded bleachers, tapping the others on the shoulder and conferring with each of them the same way before sitting down next to Henry and Bailey. To them all, he whispered, "Hero boy says don't do anything, but we all know what to do if Jonnard shows up, right?"

They all gave him a nod and a wolfish grin of agreement.

Trent settled on the aluminum bleacher. Beautiful day for a championship game. He noticed his father sitting down with the McIntires where he and the Dozer seemed to be having a good conversation. Yup, a good day where a lot could go right.

22

FRIENDS AND OTHER ENEMIES

JASON bloodied his lip sometime in the second quarter. He couldn't quite remember when. It might have been when he tried to head the ball and missed, or it might have been when he got caught in a rundown or it might have been someone tossing an elbow during a throw-in. He didn't remember getting it, and he didn't mind it at all. It only hurt when he needed to suck down some water and he wouldn't even have noticed it at all except for Rich calling down from the bleachers, "Better get some ice on that, Jason!" Only then had he realized he'd split his lip.

He didn't feel it, any more than he felt the tiredness in his legs or the bruising in his ribs from the fight of the day before. He didn't feel anything but the sheer, fierce joy of running down the field, the

211

ball in his control, the goal net in sight. The rush of other bodies flying with him and the jostling contact with others, all intent on controlling that ball and scoring, filled his mind. Like a sharp-eyed eagle, he watched for the hand and body language signs of his teammates, knowing when and where to wheel about, and weave around, and take the pass or kick it off himself. They played like what they were . . . a team . . . and as the minutes ticked away and sweat darkened his shirt, the goals added up, three for each side.

As it should have been, he thought. They were all fighting hard and playing well, and he hadn't seen any mistakes. Sometimes a team got to the finals accidentally because it won on a freak day, but not these two teams. Both had earned it. His own Chargers against the Wolverines. Their banner held a depiction of the fearsome beast, a soccer ball being torn to shreds in its great jaws, while his team's showed a white charging medieval warhorse on a field of blue. He felt a keen sense of pride just being there, and a sharp jabbing wish to be the one who made his team the winner. They'd been all over him, though; word had gotten out since his last game, and he found himself bottled up regularly with little he could do but play decoy and defense. Everything he did helped, though, like a puzzle piece fitting in for a greater picture, or that was what the coach had told all of them at the break. Teamwork.

Sound broke over him with a roar like that of waves from the ocean. He could only make out a word now and then from the bleachers as the only voice he was really listening to was that of Coach

Wayne bellowing as he paced them up and down the sidelines. Bailey would chide him later. She would say, "Didn't you hear me tell you that a Wolverine was on your heels?" Or, "Didn't you hear us yelling, 'Go, Jason!' for the umpteenth time?" She'd know it if he said he had, she always knew it when he lied, which he rarely did. Maybe that's how she knew it, he hadn't enough practice.

A whistle blew sharply as the Wolverines called a time-out, and Coach Wayne waved at them to come in. He trotted off the field with Sam, his longtime friend, and headed for the big plastic tubs of water. Sam got little play time compared to Jason, but he'd been in for most of the fourth quarter to give other players a break. Coach Wayne pointed a finger at him.

"Good work, Sammee. Bench yourself now, and I want you to watch the defense carefully. See if you spot a chink, and let me know."

Sam tossed a grin. "Sure thing, Coach!"

Benched but with an important assignment. That was the way to do it, Jason thought. He grabbed one of the stiff white towels lying in a heap on the ground and scrubbed off his head and neck. Now that he was not running, he could feel a thin edge of ache along his shins, and his breathing burned a little in his lungs. He took a proffered cup of sports drink and chugged it down, even as Coach said, "All right, boys, gather round. I have something I want you to take a look at."

Without further notice, he lifted his clipboard and began to draw on it, his felt tip pen squeaking as he drew diagrams and line defenses on it. Jason grabbed a second, smaller white cup of sports drink and began to sip it slowly, feeling the mildly flavored fruit punch go down his throat.

"This is what they're doing," explained the coach, "and this is how we're gonna beat 'em while they do it."

Behind them, he could hear chanting. Without really listening, the words sounded a bit like, "The Chargers are cool, the team is gonna rule." He wasn't sure of the wording though, but he could hear Bailey's voice in loud enthusiasm. Jason found himself grinning even as he tried to concentrate on the coach and his assistant as they laid out strategy for this second part of the very last quarter. All too soon, their brief moments of recess were over.

Bradley and Todd bumped fists with him as they trotted back onto the field for the throw-in, Todd dropping back into his place as goalie and Bradley pacing him on the offensive line. The Wolverines joined them, looking appropriately sinister in their black and silver colors and frowning faces, having a much rougher time than they'd figured on. Everyone jogged in place impatiently. Game time was running out.

A dark cloud skittered across the brilliant blue California sky and gusted away as quickly as it had appeared. Its shadow grazed Jason and he looked up briefly. The ref's whistle blew, jerking his attention back just as the throw-in hurtled right at him. He headed it to Bradley and away they went.

Bailey sat back down, and glanced overhead. The dark splinter of cloud that pierced the afternoon brightness was gone, yet another followed on its heels, and a third. They gathered and hung low as if the bright sun and brisk spring breeze had no power over them. Trent followed her glance upward.

"Too late to rain the game out," he said. "Sides, soccer is like rugby. They play in anything, till it's over."

"No one said anything about rain though," Bailey muttered. She rubbed her bare arms. Lacey twittered in her shirt pocket, as though aggrieved by the motion or the coolness rapidly descending on them.

"Give her a cookie."

"She's had one whole one already. My pocket is full of oatmeal crumbs." Bailey wrinkled her nose. She spotted something on the field and jumped to her feet, yelling, "Go, Jason! Go!"

Rebecca Landau popped up at nearly the same time, the two so alike they might almost be thought twins. The bleachers rumbled with their excitement. A row or two forward, he could hear Alicia tell her mother confidently, "I'm getting great video of Jason. The automatic focus on this thing is following the action just great."

Dozer's heavy voice followed. "Good thing to have. Jason's in the thick of it now, he'll want to see it later."

"Got it," muttered Alicia, somewhat distractedly as she angled her camcorder through the shoulders of other watchers in the stands. "This should go great with my project, too." Joanna put a hand on her blonde daughter's shoulder, as much to steady her as she filmed, as to encourage her.

Trent frowned, though. He looked back at the sky.

A storm front gathered at the edges of the sky with incredible speed, yet the breeze barely ruffled the treetops. Charcoal clouds began to peak, like breakers gathering for high tide. He felt an uncomfortable prickling along his scalp as he often did when Jason or one of the others was working the Magick he didn't have. He shifted as a nervous edginess ran over him. Bailey would have said someone was tripping on his grave.

Trent looked about. The bleachers on this end were packed with families and friends of the Chargers. Parents he rarely saw were here, even . . . Rich's nervous mom and dad, his mother with a handkerchief to her nose as if trying to prevent inhaling any germs. Bailey's mom who often worked on weekends. His dad, who was now out of work indefinitely. Joanna and William McIntire and Jason's stepsister Alicia, her fine blonde hair tucked back from her face as she kept her attention intently on the miniature camcorder in her hands. Stefan's thick, rather dowdy looking parents who were immigrants and looked it, in an odd, 1950s sort of way. Henry Squibb sat on the other side of Rebecca Landau and he seemed to be the only one there without a parent in tow. Still, that didn't answer Trent's curiosity about the Magick he felt adrift. None of his friends had their hands on their crystals, essential for Focusing and using them, just as Jason had asked—for now. Still, just as Shakespeare had written, "By the pricking of my thumbs, something wicked this way comes."

He smelled, in his own unique way, the tainted

power of the Dark Hand reaching out toward them all. The others might have Magick, but there were times when he could *see* it and they could not, and now was one of them. As he glanced overhead again, gloom covered the sky and he could see lightning, dark green and blue, lancing above. Henry Squibb's face went white as a sheet. His face twitched toward Bailey. His lips moved as he mumbled something inaudible and then slumped to his side, hands jerking.

Bailey cried out, "Henry!" but no one heard her but her mother and Trent as the Chargers bleachers rose in a roar as someone in white and blue drove in a goal, sending the score to 4 and 3. From the corner of his eye, Trent thought the kicker might have been Jason who punched the air once or twice, but his friend was a team guy and his joy could have been for any one of his teammates who'd done a good job. Trent grabbed Bailey's arm.

"I see Magick," he hissed in her ear.

"What?" She blinked at him, confused, torn between Henry and Trent. Her mother had her arm about Henry and was trying to sit him up.

"Magick!" he repeated hoarsely at her ear, her tangle of golden-brown hair muffling his words.

"No one here . . ." Bailey plowed to a halt. She beckoned her hands helplessly. "Jason said we couldn't. Not to help him or endanger ourselves."

"I can see it!" Trent insisted. "If it's not us, then it has to be the Dark Hand."

Clouds overhead crackled now, their stormy charcoal depths sparkling with levin fire, and they could hear the sound of lightning bolts sizzling past, without seeing them clearly, and then the low rumble of thunder danced about them. Someone screamed.

"Lightning!"

In panic, people began to clamber from the aluminum bleachers. Trent rose, to protect Bailey and her mom, and Henry, as they did. No rain struck his face, but the sky had gone storm black and he stood, waiting, the hairs on the back of his neck standing up like an angry dog's. He could feel, however, the hot splatter like sparks of Magick falling. Pure, malicious Magick, directed at them. Stef turned to Rich. Trent could see the heaviness on his face blur, his expression rippling as if he were underwater, and the current obscuring him. Had he begun to shapeshift? Not a chance, no, not here, not now! Could he see that Magick, too?

The players on the field lined up for the kickoff, seemingly unaware of the unnatural weather, or perhaps uncaring as the Chargers moved ahead by one goal and the Wolverines swore to get even.

"Shields," Trent called out, knowing no one but themselves would understand. They were under attack!

He should have known that it was too much of a coincidence, too unusual, that all their families had decided on the same Sunday to be here and now. Everyone but Ting and her fragile grandmother was here. Bailey gripped her crystal. "Henry's fainted."

"Shield Stef."

"But—"

Trent tugged on her elbow. "Bailey, he's *shifting*. Shield Stef!" He drew her down the bleachers with him, through the crowd as people settled again, muttering, looking at the gathering storm.

Rich hurried Stef out of their row and onto the ground, behind the team benches. Trent could see the glow of crystal fire playing over both of them and knew Rich had sensed the same thing, and was trying to give Stef the control he needed to keep from morphing into the bear cub. Henry poured out of the bleachers like a wet noodle, still shaking and pale, barely able to stand, his crystal cupped in one fisted hand.

"It's like a . . . tug-of-war . . ." he managed, breathily, gasping for strength.

"What is?"

"They're pulling on me. We've got to . . . get out . . . of here!" Henry's eyes flickered, as if they might roll back in their sockets. Bailey threw an arm out to his shoulders to steady him.

Stef bleated. His bear voice rolled out of him, like a belch, and he turned desperately to Rich.

"Shields up, everyone, gather, and concentrate."

"Everyone is watching!" hissed Bailey, but she did as Trent ordered.

A sharp whistle sounded the end of the game. They could hear the shouts and yells, some happy, some outraged, as the teams wheeled across the field and turned back to their benches. Jason came running toward them, his face decorated with an ear-to-ear grin of sheer joy that turned stark as he saw them.

Lightning crackled overhead. A piercing scream set the crowd to running, pushing and scrambling to get clear of the metal stands. Jason immediately gathered his own crystal, and the sky flared with the white-gold of its shield. His power hung over the spectators like an unearthly umbrella, raining tiny sparks. Trent thought of a glorious fireworks display, exploding, flowering, and then drizzling out of the night sky. Jason had power, more than any of them, and to spare.

But not enough.

Stef bawled and fell to the ground, rolling under the crowded bleachers. Rich and Trent immediately went to his side, without hope of hiding much. The bear cub reared on its haunches, shredding clothing about it as it stood and pawed at its nose, in bewilderment and ursine anger. In seconds, nothing was left of Stef. Rich inhaled deeply and dove at his shape-shifted friend, hitting him in the shoulder and bowling the bear cub over, knocking him under the benches and out of sight.

The sky opened up. Jonnard's laughing voice echoed over them, mocking their pain, as the screams of their friends, family, and teammates surrounded them. Lightning sizzled and struck within inches of them. They could feel the Magick dancing off their skins painfully.

"Hold on a bit longer," Jason grunted. Sweat already darkened his jersey and smeared his hair to his head, and his arm trembled as though the weight of his crystal might be more than he could bear.

The roof of the sky became a field of lightning sparks. It exploded over and over, as if frustrated in reaching its targets on the ground. It drowned out the screams of the stampeding people getting out of the stands and to their cars, to safe places across the open field, away from those gathered in a closed circle and trying to protect them. Henry moaned softly and swayed on his feet. Then he gritted his teeth and said, "No!" as if arguing with someone.

One last lightning stroke blasted the edge of the bleachers with a deafening noise. The air stank with the melting of the aluminum. It ran white, and then melted into a blackened mess at the corner of it. The frightened bear cub let out a bawl of pain and terror, and crawled out from underneath, its fur singed, dragging Rich with it, his hand knotted in its hair. Into the crowd of fleeing people it bolted, Rich stumbling after his friend, yelling, "Stef! Come back!"

The duo raced with the crowd before veering away into the shrubbery and trees guarding the parklike edge of the soccer field. There was a loud noise, and one of the portapotty buildings toppled as the bear cub ran into it, full tilt. Rich shouted, "Stef! Leave the dog alone!" as if he could disguise what they were all seeing. Both boy and bear cub disappeared headlong into the shrubs.

Then, all went silent.

It lasted only a moment before Mrs. Olson cried, "What have you done to my son? What is that animal?"

"Just a stray dog," muttered Trent, somewhat helplessly. Jason looked up, to the flashes of cameras, and to his stepsister's face as she lowered her camcorder, and saw the expressions on the faces of those few left who now began to draw near. They all of them had been exposed. *Film at Eleven*, he thought in despair.

"Oh, my," said Bailey.

WHICH WITCH IS
WHICH

"IT'S a setup," said Jason. He lowered his aching arm slowly, the light from his Shield dimming as he released the power. He couldn't explain the soaring feeling he'd experienced for a moment, the sense of another figure standing with him, strengthening him. He could name that figure, the lost wizard Gregory, whom he'd never met except for an occasional fleeting glimpse in the lavender crystal.

All he knew was, when he'd tapped for power, both of the crystals on his body had answered, even though he'd only held one. And now, that power was diminished. He felt very alone. The pearl-and-gold glow which had covered them like an umbrella faded as he did, then disappeared with a sharp snap of energy. The soccer field, nearly empty, suddenly drained of its menace. "We were totally set up," Jason repeated.

"No kidding." Trent spun around on one heel, surveying the area, looking for the Dark Hand. He saw no sign of them now as the unnatural electrical storm rolled back, clouds tearing to wispy shreds and dissipating. As quickly as it had been called, it seemed to be blowing apart. Rich bolted into the park grounds at the edge of the soccer field, hot on Stef's furry heels.

Henry muttered, "It's like a tug-of-war." He rubbed his eyes, confused looking, unaware he'd been repeating that over and over.

Bailey rubbed his shoulder. "Stay together." She moved closer, trying to use her body to shield Stefcub from the sight of anyone still standing in the bleachers. The cub had lit out for the bushes, moving so quickly that it did look like a terrified big golden dog. Of course, nearly having been hit by lightning might have helped its speed, she thought, as the smell of burned hair stung her senses.

Jason realized from his heartbeats that only seconds had passed, though it felt much, much longer, as the remaining spectators came down from the bleachers, their attention fixed on them. Joanna stared at him, her face sheet white, one arm about Alicia's shoulders protectively while his stepsister held her camcorder to her chest as if someone might think of grabbing it away. McIntire's huge body seemed to frame them.

It's on tape, Jason thought, his heart sinking.

"Nobody move," called Trent's father, descending to the trampled earth at the foot of the stands. "That's ball lightning that struck them, and they could still be charged with static electricity."

Trent gave a lopsided grin, trading a look with Jason. Help where they hadn't expected any.

McIntire moved away from his wife and step-daughter. "It's like Saint Elmo's fire," he agreed. "I've seen the same thing, Frank. Rare as hell but scary. Still . . ." he shrugged heavy shoulders and looked overhead. "Freak storm. You kids okay?"

Someone had been repeatedly letting out high yelps of terror and Jason finally got a look at who—Stefan's mother. She stood with her purse clutched tightly, her frizzled hair practically standing on end. "Where is Stefan! Vhat have you done with him?"

"We're fine. He went after that stray dog." Jason cleared his throat uneasily.

"My boy!" Her hands went white-knuckle on her purse. "I saw no dog . . ."

"Liars. All of you, liars!"

Rebecca and Bailey both swung about, jaws drop-ping. Jerry Landau stood defiantly, camera in his hands. "It's witchcraft. I've got everything in pic-tures. The court's going to see everything!"

"Jerry," said Rebecca with forced calmness. "I hope you haven't been drinking. What you think of me is one thing, but let's not do this in front of the kids."

He shook his camera violently. "It's all on film! I've got all the evidence I need, and the court will get it first thing in the morning. You're not keeping Bailey."

Rebecca answered grimly, "I have attorneys, too."

"Oh, no, you don't," muttered Bailey. Her hand, clutched around her crystal, started to swing up.

"No." Jason caught her wrist, putting his body between her and her father. "Not here."

Bailey shot him an angry look, then sighed. She lowered her arm but not before Jason could feel the emotion trembling through her body.

McIntire and Callahan both moved to frame Bailey's father. "I think," said the Dozer slowly, "the kids have been through enough for one day, don't you?"

Trent's dad echoed with, "We need to find out who's been hurt and who's all right, first." Frank Callahan's gaze swept across them, then, a slight puzzled look on his face which he quickly shed for a neutral expression.

"You're all either blind or crazy." Jerry Landau swung about in a circle. "I know what I saw. So do you!"

The Wolverines defender who'd given Jason most of his trouble hung at the edges, listening, although most of his team had been hustled off the field as the storm had threatened. Frowning, he jerked his head toward his coach who also stood, watching. "Does that mean the game gets called? We won?"

"You lost, bud." Trent straightened and his voice went deep with menace.

"Not if he's a witch or something. That would be cheating."

The Wolverines coach suddenly looked as if he might be really interested. He nudged his player. "Don't hang around. Game's over. For now." He trotted off in the direction of the van where two of the black-and-white started refs were standing, papers in their hands, nervously glancing up now and then at the sky.

Jason throttled down the anger he felt, hard words bitten back behind his clenched teeth as Landau started again. "I saw what I saw. You've made some kind of witch out of her, and I'm taking her back. I'll have her exorcised if I need to!"

McIntire moved with astonishing quickness for a big, hefty man. He stepped in, blocking and over-shadowing Bailey's father. "I think it's time for you to leave."

"It's a free country!"

"It's never been free for harassment. You've got a lawyer, let him handle it. Now get in your car and go before I call the police."

Landau managed a gesture around McIntire. "This isn't the end of this!"

"No," said Rebecca quietly. "I don't imagine so." She watched as her ex-husband loped off the soccer field and disappeared into the parking lot. Moments later, a car peeled rubber.

McIntire rubbed his hands together and then reached for Joanna. "I'm sorry."

Joanna shook visibly, but the color began to return to her face. She kissed his cheek gently. "Thanks for getting rid of him." McIntire gave a satisfied rumbling which sounded almost like a purr. She said, in a dazed voice, "I don't know what I saw either."

Alicia looked down at her camcorder and up at Jason. She said nothing, but he could see a glint in her eyes.

She knew she had it on film. And he knew it, too. Jason took a deep breath, trying to think what he could do. Before an answer came to him, Frank Callahan suggested, "Isn't pizza the order of the day? After a victory like this?"

"I'm starving."

"You're always hungry." Henry stared at Trent with very round eyes behind his glasses. He took them off and rubbed his eyes carefully. He looked as if he wanted to say more but did not.

"We all have to talk," said Frank firmly.

Mr. and Mrs. Hawkins had said nothing, but she took her handkerchief down from her face at that. She shuddered as she got out, "Tell Rich that if he has so much as touched that filthy beast, he's not welcome home till he cleans up." She turned about smartly and marched off. Mr. Hawkins gave them an embarrassed shrug before trailing after his wife.

Mrs. Olson's eyes narrowed. "My son is not filthy. What he is, I am not sure. But not filthy."

"This conversation belongs elsewhere," echoed McIntire. "My home, I think." He beckoned toward the last remaining cars and vans in the parking lot. Jason realized bleakly that his team and coach had left without him.

"We're not freaks," Jason said flatly. Although the living room of the McIntire house was crowded, his voice seemed to echo all about those gathered. The muted, tasteful tones of Joanna's decorating in ivory and golds seemed overwhelmed by the people crowded in now, occupying every sitting space available and then the floor.

"Then what are you?"

"What happened out there was some kind of paranormal power, wasn't it?" Frank Callahan leaned a shoulder against the wall, slouched comfortably, both hands in his pockets.

Henry sat curled up on the end of the couch, his arms about his knees, looking rather like an over-stuffed sofa pillow. Some color had finally returned to his face. "We can't say what it was. But it wasn't us."

"Can't or won't?"

"Can't." Trent rubbed his nose. He reluctantly closed the last lid of the last empty pizza box. Rebecca had brought Rich and Stefan with her, after Bailey finally called Stef in with her Talent of animal sense, luring the bear cub close. Messages had been left for the Squibb family that Henry was with them and not to worry. Ravenous as usual, Stef had eaten nearly a whole pizza by himself. He tried to stifle a burp while licking a finger. No one else had had much appetite.

Joanna gazed at him. "I'm so sorry, Jason. All this time, all this time, I thought your father worried about you because of your heart, like your mother. Never did I think anything like this could . . ." Her voice trailed off, and she shook her head.

He stared at his stepmom a moment, struck by the realization that all her worry, all her care for him, had come out of her promise to protect and nurse a potential time bomb, as his mom had been with her heart defect. No wonder she'd practically suffocated him.

"I want an answer from this Rainwater," McIntire offered. "And I want it now." Joanna put her hand on her knee and shook her head.

"Actually," said Bailey, "so do I." Her usually cheerful expression was knotted in unhappiness. "I think he owes us that."

Jason got his crystal out. "Maybe he can say what we can't." He concentrated with the little strength he seemed to have left, and it was barely enough to bring Gavan to his mind. But the Magicker looked at him, and turned away, with a faint whispering thought that Eleanora had worsened, and he could not leave for the moment. He caught a shadowy vision of Eleanora lying cold and still as death, and he thought of his many nightmares of finding a body just like that. "Gavan, come back!" He clutched at the elder and found coldness blocking him, as Henry rolled back against his chair and grabbed at his temples. He tried to force the block, only to hear Henry moan loudly.

"Jason," said Trent, holding his wrist. "You're hurting him. Trouble?"

"Seems to be blocked." Jason retreated in his efforts and Henry sat up, forcing down a deep breath. "Henry's feeling it, too. I can't force it." Henry gave him a look of desperation, then hid his face in his hands.

"So. No help there, at least not yet." Jason rubbed his eyes. "We've got to buy some time."

Stefan's mom sat across from her rumpled son, looking at him with mournful brown eyes. "You cannot stay, my son."

"Mom . . ."

She shook her head. "You won't say what happened, but something did. All here saw it. Do you think I have no eyes? You will be a freak. American television will hunt you down, until someone makes up a crazy story about what happened. Then it will get even worse." She held her hand up, as he protested. "You know this is true! You know it."

"You've all been freaks since you got back from summer camp," stated Alicia. She balanced her camcorder on her knee.

"Alicia!"

She tilted her head at her mom. "Well, it's true." She turned back to Jason. "So what happened? Some kind of government experiment? Did you guys all get shot up with ESP or something? I mean, we all thought it was strange you guys got all rounded up as talented and stuff. Not that you aren't. But looking back, it's obvious you were recruited."

Rich's mother had taken up a guarded stance in the far corner of the living room, handkerchief to her nose, pausing only to pull out a horribly antiseptic smelling spray and spritzing it every ten minutes or so. She had only come because Rich had called and begged her to, and she'd acted as if they could all contaminate her the moment she'd walked in the front door. Now she let out a choked warble, and grabbed for her husband's arm. "Germ warfare!"

"Oh, don't be ridiculous," Joanna snapped. She blushed then, and leaned back against her sofa, unaccustomed to such outbursts. Jason grinned at her, thinking, *Way to go, Mom!*

"Obviously not," rumbled McIntire. He stared keenly at Jason. "But there have been odd happenings. The old house that burned down last Halloween, for instance."

"Nothing we did," Trent offered.

"Today looked like an attack." Trent's father straightened and walked across the room, as if not wanting to face his son. "In which case, there was nothing you started in October, or today. Would I be right in saying that?"

"We can't tell you," answered Bailey, Henry, and Trent in unison.

Rich bit his lip and Stef decided to check a different pizza box, on the off chance he'd overlooked a slice or two.

But Jason drew himself up. "Something like that," he got out, and waited for his throat to tighten and his jaws to lock, as the Vow of Silence promised it would. Other than the vague uneasiness of being in front of everyone, and in deep trouble, he felt nothing. Immediately, everyone's eyes seemed to be on him. He took a step back involuntarily. "We haven't started anything," he said, feeling a bit lame, and the cords in his neck did tighten then and he wasn't sure if he could get another word out or not.

Rebecca Landau made a small movement with one hand. "I know what it is they're facing, sort of, and they can't tell you, and I've promised not to, but yes . . . they're extraordinary, and they do have powers which will draw attention to them, and may be very dangerous for them. We live in a world which—" She paused. "Well, frankly, it may want to take them apart to see how they do what they do, and they don't even know for sure what they can do. Not to mention people who might want to use them for warfare or covert activities, or just misuse them altogether. I don't think any of us want to risk that."

Mrs. Olson stared at her son, a large tear sliding

down her cheek. "You must go," she said in her accented voice, words growing thick.

"Mom."

She shook her head. "No football here. But better than life in a cage."

"We don't know this," started Frank Callahan.

"Yeah, Dad, we do," Trent interrupted. "That's why we can't talk about it, for our own protection. It's *not* witchcraft. There's a good side and a bad side to this and we're on the good, and the others have come after us a couple of times. We don't know what to expect."

"They need a safe place," Rebecca said, drawing Bailey close to her and holding one of her hands tightly.

Henry squirmed. He ran a hand over his head, sending up a thatch of dark hair, but he remained silent.

"There isn't any place." Bailey bit her lip and fell silent.

"I can only think of one place to go," said Jason slowly. Haven was out. But he had places he could go where he wouldn't take no for an answer.

Trent looked at him. "Where?"

Jason shook his head slowly. There wasn't a lot he could say, in front of everyone.

"Richard!" cried Mrs. Hawkins.

The redhead made a gesture with his hand. "Forget it, Mom. You'd be better off without me, if people come hunting around, you know?"

Henry said, "They'd all be b-b-better off."

McIntire stood. "You're all leaving together, then?"

"I think we have to." Jason nodded at his stepfather.

Rebecca said fiercely, "You're not going without me." Bailey looked up at her mom, and began to cry, softly, silently. "I mean it. Not without me. I know, anyway, so I have to go, right?"

"That would probably be wise." Trent shifted uneasily. "Do you have a plan for all this, Jason?"

"Not yet. I don't know how to cover our tracks." He pulled his crystal out. "But I don't think we can wait around to see who else filmed us or took pictures."

"You just can't disappear," Rich's mom stammered. "There will be questions asked."

"We're not going forever. Just a few weeks or so, and nobody will ask questions."

"The schools . . ."

Trent flexed his fingers. "Schools have computer systems. They might think they know we're gone, but they won't be able to prove it."

Callahan cleared his throat. "If my son just mentioned hacking, I didn't hear it."

"I think," noted McIntire mildly, "that computer manipulation may be the least of his abilities right now. Is there a way we can get hold of you, wherever it is you're going?"

"Not easily, but there's a way." Jason looked at Bailey who turned red. "Some people have already popped in and out a bit."

"No." Joanna rubbed her slender hands together. "I can't do this. I can't just let you go, Jason."

"I think it's gone beyond your wishes or mine," McIntire told her.

She shook her head briskly, elegantly coiffed blonde hair flying. "I promised his father. There's a trust there that I have spent a lot of time making sure was met."

"You've been a great stepmom," Jason told her. *A little too great*, he thought to himself.

McIntire put his hand on Joanna's knee. "Honey, they all leave, sooner or later. This is sooner, and necessary. You've done what you promised Jarrod."

Joanna looked at him, her face with that brittle look that meant intense, held back emotions. He wasn't sure if she was going to cry or not. "You make sure," she said to him, "that you take care of yourself."

"I will." He took his crystal out. "Everyone who is going, join me."

"Wait." Alicia stood, and held out her camcorder. "Take the tape. Just in case, you know." She tucked a blonde wing of hair behind her ear.

Trent looked over her elbow. "What's it show, anyway?"

She lifted a shoulder and dropped it, then pushed a few buttons, and the camcorder whirled faintly as if rewinding the tape, and she pushed Preview Play, so that the tiny screen could show her what she'd filmed.

She fast forwarded through standards scenes of the soccer game, including Jason's winning goal, and then the tumble of the Magickers one by one out of the stands. The sky looked dark and very threatening.

Then her camcorder screen went white gold and

showed nothing. Frame after frame of . . . nothing. Trent let out a low whistle, and glanced at Jason.

"The energy appears to have wiped the tape out. And, I'll bet Krispy Kreme Doughnuts the cameras don't have a decent picture either."

"I . . . I didn't do that." Jason looked at the tiny camcorder screen.

"You can't wipe out memories, though. We still gotta go." Stef stood reluctantly, the last one to gather at Jason's side. He stared at his mother.

She nodded. "Go, Stefan. You must do this."

He made a noise that sounded as if the bear cub inside him mourned. "Awww, Stef!" Bailey cried and put one arm around him. The other she held tightly onto her mother with.

One by one, the Magickers linked hands.

"We'll be back," Jason told them, "when we can."

"When it's safe," Trent added.

If it ever would be.

24

CLEAN CUP, MOVE DOWN

THE moment of crossing from one door in the crystal to another only took seconds. Usually. Even in those seconds, he might feel a chill and a darkness as he traveled a strange *between* that did not quite really exist, nor Jason suspected, did he. That last thought would have raised the hair on his arms, but he didn't have time for it. Or rather, he had way too much time. He didn't bring the group through the way he thought he would. They seemed to hang in the void, the iciness and bleakness creeping in until he feared someone would let go, and he'd lose them.

Being lost inside his crystal was nothing he'd wish on anyone, but you wouldn't be lost permanently. At least, Jason didn't think so. On the other hand, it wasn't something he felt like testing. It had been bad enough when Bailey had fallen into her crystal those many many months ago and not only had she disappeared physically, but in time as well. Her disappearance had baffled every one of the Magickers for days and days, until he'd finally picked up on clues she was leaving them, and managed to find her.

Jason started to take a deep breath at the memory, and all that had changed for them, but the void held no air. There was nothing to suck in, and he panicked for a moment, gripping his crystal tightly and forcing them through and beyond.

The void fought back. It did not want to give him passage or let him go. Bailey let out a small noise, almost a whimper, and he realized they must all be feeling what he did. No light, no air.

The sharp edges of his gemstone cut into his palm as he punched his way through, forcing the void to let them go. He could feel the *between* give way suddenly, and then they emerged, his ears popping, his step settling onto solid ground. They all stepped down onto the lawn, shaking themselves like a dog after an unwanted bath, jostling each other around.

"Wow," said Bailey. "You take the scenic route?"

"I really, really hate traveling this way," muttered Trent. He tapped his fingers on his jeans pocket, his hand moving to a musical beat only he could hear, betraying his nervousness.

"I hate planes," Stef said. He scrubbed at his eyes, and then his crew cut, and it looked for a moment as if the bear cub looked out, too, unhappily.

Jason's stomach growled. They'd all been too nervous to eat more than a single slice of pizza, and now, after Crystaling, his stomach seemed to know what his mind could only sense. They'd been in the void a good deal of time. He was *starving*.

Rebecca Landau just stood there as they regrouped, her mouth half-open as if she wanted to say something, and couldn't. Bailey joggled her mother's arm.

"Mom? You okay?" She frowned. "Jason didn't leave your brain back there, or anything, did he?"

Rebecca moved. "Not . . . quite. This is how you travel?"

"Sometimes. Most of the time, we just get in a car and have a parent drive us."

Rebecca looked at her daughter as if she'd sprouted a second head. Then she shook her own, dispersing thoughts. "How we could have missed this, I'll never know."

"We're not supposed to do it in public," Bailey told her.

"I guess not." Rebecca hugged her. "I can see I have a lot to learn."

Bailey nibbled her lip. "Ummm . . . I don't think I can teach you this."

Rebecca laughed. "That's not what I meant, and I think I agree with Trent. I don't think I want to travel this way."

Jason looked about at the midsummer night sky. Early spring in Irvine, step through a crystal to this place, and the seasons had changed. Possibly even the hemisphere, if this place was even on Earth. "Hopefully, we won't have but one or two more Crystalings to go." Even more hopefully, this would be the last one for a while, but he didn't know if he'd brought them to sanctuary or not.

Henry took his glasses off and cleaned them before putting them back on with a sigh. "I don't think this is a good idea. I shouldn't be here. I shouldn't be here at all," he finished, sounding miserable.

Rich elbowed him. "Course you should, Squibb."

"I didn't get to say good-bye."

"You can Crystal back as soon as we have everyone settled. I'll go with you if you want company," Bailey told him.

He nodded, his face still knotted with unhappiness.

"We'd better get inside," Jason said, "before we attract any more attention." He beckoned at the cottage.

"She didn't welcome us last time. What makes you think she will this time?"

"There's no other place to go. Either she's a Magicker, or she isn't," stated Jason flatly.

They straggled through the sagging picket fence and across the grass, with a keen sense of the hour being very late as a high, bright summer moon shone down on them from overhead. Stars twinkled blue and white in the sky, and the aroma of night-blooming flowers lay about them, although he could not see the hedges where they grew. The other side of the cottage maybe. It occurred to him that Freyah's cottage was very like the moon in that he'd only ever seen the one face of it. Did it have a face toward the sun and one toward the dark side? Had anyone ever seen the other side of that cottage?

The door snatched open just as he reached his hand to knock. Aunt Freyah looked out, her blue eyes flashing with intensity, her silvery hair fluffed about her face, her apple cheeks blazing with blush. "Come in, quickly, don't dawdle. I've got the tea-kettles whistling." She counted briskly as they walked past her into the cheerful abode. "Seven of you, altogether? An auspicious number. Sit, sit, find chairs and pull ups. We'll have a bite to eat first, and then we'll talk about why you're pounding on my door at midnight on the summer's eve. And yes, yes, I know it isn't midsummer's eve where you're from, but it is *here*, and that makes it a bit of an omen, don't you agree?" Without waiting for agreement, she beckoned them briskly inside.

Jason lowered his hand. He hadn't pounded, but he wasn't about to dispute the elder Magicker. Everyone filed past him quickly, Bailey saying to her mother, "She has this picnic hamper that makes meals, and a serving tray, his name is George, who serves them. George likes company and will dance for us, I hope."

"Oh, really?" answered Rebecca faintly. She tossed Jason a somewhat desperate look as she moved into the depths of the cottage sitting room.

Trent came through the doorway last. His chest still thumped a bit from Crystaling, and it made no difference whether he liked to travel that way or not, because he couldn't, and he knew he was at the mercy of the others who could. It was not a big deal to any of them to leave their homes or their family because if they wished, and the coast was clear, they could just pop back for a few. He couldn't. Their flight had cut him off from his dad totally, and he felt that loss inside him now. What would his dad do without him? Would he go out and get that new job he needed, or would he fall into a depression as he had years ago when it had first been just the two of them? How would his father get along without him, and how would he get along without his dad? Everyone else here had the ties of Magick which not only linked them to each other, but to every other Magick user across the years, known or unknown. He was alone.

He sat on the ottoman and watched as Aunt Freyah cleared a small table, bistro size, and snapped a fresh white tablecloth over it. A metallic rattle came from the corner leading to the kitchen and George strode out, his burnished surface gleaming, fairly dancing with happiness at the presence of company, his tray laden down with teacups and spoons and sugar jars, and two teapots. For all his skittering about, he spilled not a drop as he settled into place, and well, for lack of a better description, Trent thought, kind of percolated in place. Rather like a car idled, moving yet not going anywhere, just vibrating loudly.

Trent waited for everyone else to serve themselves. Freyah bustled off to the kitchen, leaving them to themselves, but her business around the corner was punctuated with the clatter of crockery and the tinkling of more silverware. He wondered if her famed picnic hamper no longer worked and she was making food the old-fashioned way. As he touched George to retrieve his own cup and saucer, he noticed the aura about the tray. Silvery like the metal tray itself, it sparkled about the serving tray as if dusted lightly over it, but he could see it.

Trent turned to Jason and said softly, "See that?"

He poked his finger at George's aura. The tray quivered a little, then settled back to its idling.

Jason tore his attention away from Bailey and her mom, as Bailey tried to explain Magick in her usual tangle and enthusiastic spill of words. "See what?"

"That." Trent rubbed the edge of the serving tray. George let out a catlike purr as if stroked.

"It's George," said Jason.

"I know that. Do you see this?" And he tapped the aura a third time. George made a little move, scooting over toward Trent, still like a cat getting a good ear rub and enjoying it thoroughly.

"I don't see anything but George."

"Surrounding him. This. It's like a ring of color."

"Not a thing."

"You're sure."

"Trent."

"Okay, okay, I was just checking. Don't see anything, huh?" Trent finished.

Jason just shrugged in bewilderment and turned back to Bailey, who flourished her hands and said, "And that's how I had a whole herd of frogs in a chorus after me!"

"And that's how you tamed Lacey, undoubtedly," her mother said. She glanced at the tiny pack rat who'd ventured from Bailey's pocket and now sat perched on her knee, awaiting treats.

Freyah bustled back into the room, demanded introductions all the way around and sat down amid a great deal of loud conversation. She seemed delighted to meet Bailey's mother and not at all perturbed that Bailey's plight had drawn in Rebecca.

Trent leaned forward a little, observing the cottage,

trying to do it without attracting attention. He'd gone for a very very long time without any of the Magickers noticing that he had no Magick. For that time, he'd thought it was because of his cleverness and his reading. He loved the idea of magic and mythology and fantasy. He'd read everything on it he could get his hands on, and some of his favorites he read over and over. So when the Magickers had held their little tests to ferret out ability, he'd passed easily. They'd never questioned him in camp or after. He'd finally told Jason about it when they'd been backed into a corner and he'd had no choice, but Jason had never rejected him over it, nor had Bailey later when she'd learned.

Jason once pointed out that Trent had a crystal after all. He'd been bonded to it, even if it was not a clear crystal as they all used; it was a translucent, mingled gem and mineral chunk. Nor had Gavan and Eleanora taken it away from him or tried to change it for another, as they had Jason's. Jason's was flawed, badly, and they seemed to worry about that, but they'd never fussed over Trent's choice. So what did that mean, if anything? He was great at lying and posing? Or did he have a buried Talent as Jason thought and they knew that, and had the patience of saints waiting for it to surface.

In the meantime, he could see Magick where the others couldn't. He couldn't manipulate it or create it, but he could see it from time to time. Was that enough of a Talent to be of any worth? He didn't think so. You could see the effects of the wind, but unless you could harness it, as in sails or windmills, what use was it to see it?

Freyah called out, "Eat hearty, dears!" just as the picnic hamper came waddling out, its woven sides bulging here and there as if laboring to contain every dish stuffed into it. It huffed and chuffed and came to a stop at the foot of the bistro table, and its lid flew open with a loud BANG! "Serves 10 or more" read the sticker on its inner label.

Stef reached in and started to pull out plates of food beginning with a platter heaped with chicken pot pies no bigger than the palm of Bailey's hand, steaming with a mouthwatering aroma. A plate of strawberry tarts followed that, and a third plate of wafer thin cheese pizza slices. Then a kettle of stewed apples fragrant with cinnamon came after, and with a hiccup from the hamper, a pan of frosted chocolate brownies. After that, Trent rather lost count of the goodness overflowing, but he thought he managed to get at least two of everything on his plate.

When he'd finished, he brushed George a last time, done and satisfied. He felt a tingle, and the tray lost both its aura and animation, slowly, like a tire leaking out air until it inevitably became flat. Trent stared at the serving tray in fascination as no one else seemed to notice. He slid his empty plate onto the tray. It was odd, and he wanted to point it out to Jason but since Jason hadn't seen it in the first place, well, there you were. How do you say something is gone that no one else knew was there but him?

He cast a glance about the cottage. Was Freyah's Magick fading? He knew that this bit of existence came out of her creation and she held it together by Talent and strength of will. He could see the signs of Magick here and there, but nothing seemed to be nickering or fading. Other than poor George who'd gone quite to sleep.

Stef let out a belch. He sat on the floor, his back to the ottoman Rich perched on, and stretched. "Man. That was good."

"Just think." Rich stared at his friend. "He'll be hungry again in a few hours."

"Then, by all means," Freyah said, "we'll pack him some food to go."

"Go?" Jason looked at the elder.

"You're not staying here, dears. Surely you didn't think you were." Freyah balanced her teacup on her palm. "It's out of the question."

"Maybe for Eleanora, but there's no place for us now, and you haven't a choice," said Jason. His voice broke a little on the last of his sentence and he flushed.

"There is always a choice, Jason, my lad."

"Not if you're a Magicker."

"Now this is just what I've been arguing with Gavan about. This is no time to be gathering a gaggle of students and hoping to educate them. Taking one in at a time would have been the best we could do. Educate and protect that student among ourselves. Now we're strung out so thin we can't help any of you."

"If you'd only taken one of us," said Bailey quietly, her eyes on Freyah, "what would the rest of us have done?"

"We would never have known we were Magickers, that's what," stated Rich. "And, frankly, that sucks." His red hair made him look a tad angrier than perhaps he was.

"Perhaps, but that one Magicker would have been safe, and none of you are now, to my read." Freyah put her teacup down on George. She frowned a moment as she touched the dormant serving tray, then tapped the surface three times and George woke up a little, although greatly subdued. Trent thought it safer to say nothing and just observe.

"Wrong. That one Magicker would have been with one of you, but the rest of us would have been pursued by the Dark Hand. They want us, even if you do not."

"Jason, is that fair?" Bailey blurted out.

He didn't take his eyes off Freyah. "I don't think we're talking fair here. We're talking survival."

Freyah glared back at him. "There are many of us who survived without help."

"So you pass it on? Are you trying to get even with someone? And you had your power. From everything I see here, you were fully grown into it."

Her mouth tightened. It made sharp knifelike wrinkles in her face. "I won't discuss that with you."

"Gregory the Gray couldn't handle Brennard, what makes you think any one of us alone could? But we're not alone. We have each other. And you're not alone either, Freyah, and you know it. You choose to live here alone, but you can reach out and touch a dozen Magickers in a wink if you wish." Jason took a deep breath then, and Trent saw his left hand tremble a bit. The scar on the back of it looked angry and pink although it had healed last summer.

"I'll get Gavan." Freyah stood. "You need to go now."

Jason stood as well. "Get him then, but we're not

leaving. You say we'd drain you. I say we can help sustain this place."

Freyah ignored him. She pulled a long hairpin from her silvery coif, glaring into its gemstone butterfly decoration, and Gavan appeared with a blink.

He looked a bit rumpled as if he'd fallen asleep with his clothes on, a faint shadowy beard on his cheeks, his hair mussed, and deep lines across his face. "Auntie dear," he said, bemused. Then his eyebrow went up as he caught sight of everyone gathering around him. Four or five voices broke into explanations. He did not listen but raised a finger, and as everything became quiet, he said, "Now I understand. As a popular movie once stated, 'There was a great trembling in the force.' "

Gavan straightened a little. "I felt it, of course, but not in the way you did. The dark curtain that shrouds Eleanora suddenly got stronger. Deadlier. It took everything FireAnn and I had to hold it back."

The teacup in Freyah's hand rattled in its saucer. "Is she all right, then?"

"She is holding. Not better than that, but at least, not worse. I am beginning to think there is much about Magick we all don't know, and that the ignorance of it could be fatal."

"All the more reason they cannot hide with me."

Bailey had jumped to her feet, dumping little Lacey unceremoniously to the cottage floor. The wee pack rat scampered here and there, gathering flaky crumbs from dropped food and then bolted off altogether, disappearing into the unknown depths of Freyah's abode as she had once before. Bailey's jaws opened and shut, and she looked desperately at Jason who merely shook his head. She wrung her hands and stood still as Freyah and Gavan yelled at each other a bit.

"I have important work going on, not the least of which is warding Eleanora."

"They are your charges, and it was your headstrong decision that put them in jeopardy."

"For pity's sake, woman, I cannot be everywhere all the time!"

"If not Ravenwyng, then perhaps Tomaz can take them. Surely he has a hidden nook or two in the desert." Freyah drew herself up stubbornly.

"Tomaz is missing and has been for days." Gavan ran his hand through his hair. He looked much older than Trent remembered, with lines in his face and weariness about his eyes. The care of Eleanora had taken a toll on him.

"Nonetheless, they are not staying here." Freyah folded her arms over her chest and looked stubborn.

"No," answered Gavan sadly. "It is apparent they are not. I don't know what happened to you, Freyah, or when, but a great selfish thing has crept into you and taken possession. Eleanora loves you, and I have always respected you, but turning the children out is an act I can't forgive."

Freyah's expression hardened. "There are reasons, Gavan, you know nothing of."

"I know only that you used to be a pillar of the side we thought was good." Gavan held his hands out. "Gather round, everyone. Time to go."

"I can't!" wailed Bailey.

"Of course you can," snapped Freyah. "And the sooner the better."

"Not without Lacey."

Rebecca put her hand on her daughter's shoulder. "Honey, I don't pretend to understand most of this, but we can't stay where we're not wanted."

Freyah sighed, and sat down heavily. "It's not that I don't want you." She waved a tired hand. "I can't possibly explain, but someday maybe all of you will understand. Even you, Gavan," and she looked at the other sadly.

"A little late to get the sympathetic vote, Auntie." He rubbed the pewter-and-crystal head of his cane. "Leave the beast. As I noted, the trembling in the force could be felt by many, and I for one do not want to see what reaction it may bring. There are other things besides the Dark Hand and wolfjackals to fear."

Bailey closed her eyes tightly. "Just one minute more. Please! I can call her back."

"She's a little wild thing," her mother soothed. "You were bound to lose her sooner or later." She patted Bailey's shoulder.

"Mrs. Landau, I don't think you quite understand," Gavan began, but Bailey's squeal interrupted him.

"She's coming! Hold on, wait!" She bounced in place a moment as the others gathered in a circle, holding hands as they needed to. With a frantic skittering of nails on the wooden floorboards, the pack rat scampered into sight and then up Bailey's leg.

"Now!" she cried out triumphantly, clasping Lacey's furred body close.

"Now, indeed," said Gavan and waved his cane before Trent could even take a gulp and pray he wouldn't lose his meal.

How he *hated* Crystaling.

25

ANTIQUES AND OTHER VALUABLES

THE step through with Gavan was barely more than a blink. It left only a moment of disorientation, and his stomach did not seem to notice it as it stayed pleasantly full from Freyah's midnight supper. If that gave him a hint of the relationship on other planes of Ravenwyng to Freyah's cottage he didn't trust it. More likely, Jason thought, it was sheer skill and experience on Gavan's part.

They stood outside the Gathering Hall of Camp Ravenwyng, and he felt for a moment as though it were a year ago and they were all just arriving for a summer of unknown adventure. The bright blue wooden cutout of Lake Wannameecha hung on its nail below the camp emblem. Some things never seemed to change, and some things he could barely recognize.

Bailey said quietly, "Ting should know." She stroked Lacey between her hands and was rewarded with a contented chirping. The pack rat's tufted tail hung between Bailey's fingers and swung back and forth in a slow wag, the little black knot of a tuft emphasizing each swing.

"We'll have some time to tell her. In the meanwhile," Gavan rubbed his face. "I think a good night's sleep is in order. The cabins and cottages aren't ready for summer campers yet, so we'll have to rough it in the Hall."

"Just like old times." Trent grinned. He nudged Henry. "Remember that down sleeping bag you had? The one that kept exploding like an air bag and swallowing you whole."

Henry managed a smile for the first time. "Yeah," he said. "Rolling that back up . . ." he shook his head at the thought.

"All I've got are blankets, but you'll be inside the wards, and nothing will disturb you." Gavan glanced at Stef. "Unless someone cannot keep control of himself."

Stef muffled a belch. Rich thumped him between the shoulder blades. "I've noted," offered Rich, "that being well fed seems to help."

"Well, that's something, then. I think Stef polished off most of the hamper all by himself."

Stef's face reddened. "Did not!" He pointed. "Trent helped."

Trent grinned, and straightened his lanky body. "Prove it." Of all of them, he had a body type that would probably never exhibit what he ate.

"Inside, all of you!" With a roll of his eyes, Gavan

waved them inside. He touched Rebecca on her arm. "And you, dear lady, are welcome to have the chair in my office or the cot near Eleanora in FireAnn's cottage, if you wish."

"She's in a coma?"

"She's lovely," breathed Bailey. "Just like Sleeping Beauty."

Rebecca shifted uncomfortably and then said, "I think I'll stay with the kids, if you don't mind."

"Extra blankets, then. You should not have to sleep on floors." Gavan frowned slightly, as he unlocked the great doors to the Gathering Hall and flung them open. The air inside smelled a little of old wax and old stuffiness, having been shut away for a long time.

Jason rubbed his crystal, murmuring the Lantern enchantment, and it set off a warm yellow glow that illuminated all of the Hall. There were chairs pushed to one side of it, but basically it was just a large, wooden-floored room, rather like a dance hall or some such, with a small stage at the far end. Gavan left and returned with an overflowing armful of blankets and began handing them out to everyone.

They were suddenly, eye-drooping, bone-aching tired. Stef plopped down first, hugging a blanket to his chest, and settling in rather like a big dog. He let out a wide, pink-mouthed yawn and fell immediately into sleep. Bailey blinked at him.

"Is it just me, or . . ."

Rich shook his head. "He gets more bearlike every day." He sighed, and unfolded his blanket neatly. "I think, even if things settle down, he might not ever be able to go back home. Medically, it's fascinating, but realistically, he doesn't want a life as a freak."

"We'll cross that bridge when we come to it." Gavan handed the last three blankets to Rebecca. "Rest well. FireAnn will be around in the morning, with shower towels and breakfast call. I'll be here if you need me." He rubbed his eyes. "Even if you don't."

"Good night, and thank you." Rebecca Landau paused, then added, "Eleanora is very lucky, I think."

Gavan cleared his throat and looked a tad embarrassed before striding out of the Hall. His cloak, so much a part of him, as were the blue jeans, swirled about and then hid his passing.

After a few trips to the lavatories down the passageway and some muted talking while Stef began to snore as soon as his eyes closed, everyone seemed to settle down except for Bailey who had developed a rather odd eye twitch every time she looked at Jason.

Finally he stood up and gave a twitch of his own to the corridor, went out and waited for her.

She bounced in.

"What is it? We're all tired."

"I . . . we . . . that is, Lacey . . . saw something at Aunt Freyah's."

He stared at her. "I'm tired."

"You're tired, I'm tired, we're all tired. But she saw something."

"What?"

"That's just it, I don't know."

He leaned against the wall. "Give me a little hint. Something big and furry with fangs or maybe a human or what." Lacey was more than a pet, she was a familiar to Bailey's budding Talents, but the two of them were far from sure what their partnership could do.

"Well, it was downstairs. Down into a creepy cellar like. Lots of stuff was stored down there, old vases, trunks, lamps, you know. A wine rack, I think."

"Like antiques and stuff put away?"

"Exactly. And something else, something big, something that scared her a lot. It had power to it. She ran off before she could give me a clear look at it, but even then, I don't know that I could be sure what it was. Seeing what a pack rat sees is kinda difficult."

"It's not like you've had a lot of practice at it yet, anyway." He rubbed his nose which felt as though he was on the verge of a sneeze or snort. "That does explain why she doesn't want us, or anyone, there. She might have a power source or something to keep her little place going. From what I've seen, most Magickers would love to have some sort of battery that boosts power."

"You think?"

"I only think I don't know what it is she's hiding down there. What I do know is that she doesn't care if it costs Eleanora her life or hurts us to keep it secret." He let out a short breath of disappointment. "So it must be pretty important to her, at least." And something that the Dark Hand might well kill for.

"I wouldn't normally believe in blackmail," said Bailey, frowning. "But the next time one of us needs help, I'm gonna pull her chain."

"Not yet, Bailey. You don't know how strong or desperate Aunt Freyah is, and I don't think you want to learn."

"She should be helping us!"

"Bailey, we can't make someone feel that kind of obligation. You know that. There's a lot of that going around in the world, and nobody's been able to solve that problem yet." He put a hand on her shoulder. "What you found might matter later, but we have to see how without hurting her. Let's keep it quiet for now and see what tomorrow brings."

"What will tomorrow bring?" She looked at him. The Lantern spell on his crystal had nearly worn off, and the glow it cast was down to a faint, but steady gold. It brought out the gold in her hair and made the dusting of freckles across her nose look like pixie dust.

"I wish I knew," he said. "But then again, the way things have been going, maybe it's a good thing we don't!" He turned her around and pointed her back in the direction of the Hall. "One disaster at a time."

He trotted down to the bathrooms where he scrubbed himself as clean of the soccer game and all that had followed as best he could. He'd changed his clothes at his home, but there'd been no time for a shower. Coming back to the Hall with his hair still wet and plastered to his skull, he could see Bailey sitting up, her amethyst cupped in her hand, an intense look on her face and her mouth moving a bit as if she whispered to herself.

Telling Ting, no doubt, most of what had gone on. She finished as he settled down on his spread blanket, waved at him, and curled up next to her mother's back.

He settled back on his blanket, which did little or nothing to pad the hardwood floor underneath. If he weren't so tired, he didn't think he'd ever be able to sleep, but the last few days had made him feel worn and edgy. If he'd learned anything, it was that he had to trust himself. He had to trust his instinct that Tomaz knew what he was doing, and it was vitally important, despite the fact they all desperately needed him. He trusted Trent, after all, had never doubted his friend's value as a Magicker. He trusted Bailey, with her boundless enthusiasm for everything, and quiet Ting who was often Bailey's shadow—yet so much more. He trusted Gavan's vision for an academy to both hold Magickers secure and educate them. His instincts, surely, were guiding him where he needed to go. Jason dropped into dreams, wondering what he could do next.

In the morning, he knew. The sound of FireAnn's percussion on pots and pans and yelling, "Breakfast, come and get it, lads and lassies!" permeated the dawn. He waited until after they'd all eaten and stood in the cafeteria kitchen, washing and cleaning up.

"I'm going back to Haven," he announced, "and opening the last Gate there. It's where we need to be."

"But you said we were cut off."

He nodded. "We were forbidden."

"Then . . ." Henry stopped cleaning the pot he held and stood, dish towel in one hand and pot in the other.

"And we're going. Everyone but Rebecca."

Bailey's mother frowned. "If it's something dangerous—"

"It is, but I need you here as an anchor for Bailey. The two of you are very close, and if we get in trouble, she'll be able to reach and get you, and . . ." he paused. "It's like throwing a line to someone, and having them pull it over, see?"

"I see," she answered slowly. "What is it that could be that dangerous?"

"Just a dragon," answered Trent.

Stef grunted and rolled his shoulders. "Big one, too."

"A . . . dragon." Rebecca sat down on a kitchen chair, her face pale.

Jason hesitated. She'd taken everything so well up till now.

"Mom, really, it's okay." Bailey hugged her mother tightly about the neck. "If Jason says it is, it will be."

"Well, I don't know . . . that much . . ." Jason faltered. "I just know it's what I have to do." He looked round the kitchen. FireAnn, her bounteous red hair bound back in a soft green bandanna, stood at the kitchen doorway, twisting bundles of herbs to dry on the many hooks about the kitchen walls and beams.

"Sounds dire, lad," she said, in her soft Irish voice. She wiped her hands on her apron. She was thin and wiry and had a strong nose, and her love was in her herbs and cooking. "He closed the Gate, as I hear tell. Ye're not to trespass there, ever again."

"But that's just it." He faced FireAnn and then swung about to look at all of them. "He had no right to close the Gate. I opened it. I opened the Iron Gate and the Water Gate, there. Twice I was led there, and all of you said I had to find the third way there to stabilize it. It's te only place Magickers can go to be safe right now. And I belong there. It's where my senses, my thoughts, take me. And I have to trust that. I have to trust myself."

"Think he'll listen to reason?"

Jason shrugged at Trent's question. "I have no idea. We've had a lot of conversations. I used to think he was my friend. But I just don't know. You all can come with me, and help—and I do need your help— or you can stay and wait to see if I do it. Either way, I'm going."

"Count me in," said Bailey.

"Me too, bro." Trent waggled his fingers against the thigh of his pants, tapping out a heroic ballad of some sort, heard only by himself.

"The two of us, of course," Rich said, putting an elbow into Stef who seemed a bit stunned by the idea of facing the dragon.

"And me," Henry finally offered, although he seemed to have gone pasty white again.

"Should I get Ting?" Bailey started to uncage her amethyst.

"No. She can anchor us, if needed. Ting and your mom. Best that way, I think."

Bailey waggled an eyebrow. "She's gonna be so peeved. She keeps saying she is missing all the excitement."

"Ye'll be creating a backwash here," FireAnn stated. "The best I can do is to stay and try to dampen that, so nothing comes to feed on th' energy or any of ye in a weakened state."

"Ummm . . . thanks."

"Think nothing of it, lad." She winked at Jason.

"Ready, then?" Jason fingered his crystal. He wasn't sure he was, but he didn't think it was the kind of moment anyone could actually be ready for. You either took a deep breath and plunged in or you didn't. Sometimes the things you did were life altering and they had to be handled that way, because if you thought about it too much, you'd never do anything. You'd freeze in indecision.

"Go for it," Trent told him. He looped an elbow with Jason and reached for Stefan.

In moments, he could feel them all joining him. As he opened the Iron Gate and brought them through, he could hear Rebecca Landau cry out softly, "Bailey, I love you!"

Her gentle words were drowned out by the roar of the beast bearing down on them, jaws open, huge eyes glaring.

"You shall not pass!"

26

DRAGON EYES

THE orange-red guardian of the Gate rushed them. Its scales glittered brilliantly in the morning sun, but not as brightly as its bared fangs. Jason fought not to back up as he said, "Steady," to his friends. He could feel the molten breath of the dragon as it flew down upon them.

All hope for a talk first fled. So many times he had come here, just to talk, and now there seemed no chance of it. It would be war between them. He brought his gemstone up, readying to Shield.

"Hold it," muttered Trent. "Something's not quite right."

They had maybe two heartbeats before the dragon would be upon them.

"What is it?"

"Illusion. I think."

"You think?" Rich countered, his voice breaking off on a high-pitched note, as he and Stef jostled their elbows.

"Note to self: illusions difficult to perceive under pressure," cracked Trent, even as the beast swooped directly overhead, its passage buffeting them with a hot wind as it . . . disappeared.

They blinked.

"Gone." Jason turned in his tracks, surveying the area.

"Told ya."

Bailey let out a quivery breath. "What do we do now?"

"Do you have a p-plan?" asked Henry as he pushed his glasses squarely back onto his nose with a nervous gesture.

"I think his plan is to use us all as dragon bait while he finds the Gate he needs," Rich told Squibb. He steadied Stef who'd gone to his knees, body torn between staying human and going bear, at the sight of the menacing dragon.

"That works for me," Jason said lightly. He looked down the pass into the valley where they'd always hoped to build Iron Mountain Academy. Bailey punched him in the arm.

"You wouldn't!"

"Of course he wouldn't," said Trent. "I would, but he wouldn't." He ducked as Bailey swung a nudge his way.

"Seriously," Jason told them, leading them down into the valley. "I haven't much to go on but a gut feeling, and that means unless I find the Gate right away, we may all become dragon bait. It will know we're here, if it doesn't already."

"Think that illusion would be tripped by anyone here in the pass?"

Jason nodded. "Probably."

"Wouldn't a doorbell be just as good? Or maybe a big brass door knocker?" Bailey swung her head about vigorously, ponytail bobbing.

"I think a two-thousand-pound dragon can pretty well use anything it wants for an alarm."

Lacey let out a few sharp chitters as if feeling as disagreeable about the whole matter as Bailey did. "It's not like we've ever done anything to *it*." Bailey rubbed the little creature's nearly transparent pink ears.

"Guys," Jason began and then stopped.

"What?" They all halted in their footsteps, turned, and looked at him.

His face flushed with a slight embarrassment. "Well. It's kind of hard to concentrate with everyone talking and arguing."

Trent put a hand up. "Pipe down, everyone. Shaddup, in other words."

Stef grunted, ducking his big square head down between his shoulders. Rich, though, did not grow still. "Just tell us what we're looking for here, okay? I mean, I could stumble over buried treasure here or something and not know it."

"I'm not sure what we're looking for. All I know is, I'll know it when we find it."

Trent gestured. "How about everybody spread out a little bit, like we did when we had to find the ley lines?"

Stef groaned. He scrubbed both hands up the sides

of his head and over his crew cut. He rolled his shoulders from side to side and began a reluctant, lumbering walk. Rich caught up with him and thumped his back. "It's all right, big guy. I've got you covered."

"It's not that I can't find 'em," Stef muttered. "It's because they make me itchy all over, like a spider-web, you know? And I *hate* that." He scratched his head again.

"They do?" Trent stared with obvious fascination.

"Yeah, they do."

"That's great!"

"It is?" Stef stopped in disbelief and squinted at them.

"It has to be. Ley lines are natural energy lines of Magick running over the Earth, right? And we're all in tune to them, but if you can feel them without any dowsing rods or gear like that, you're really sen-sitive. Call me stupid, but I think what Jason needs here is probably going to be at the center of a nest of ley lines. Power, you see? And if you can feel it that well, you can lead Jason right to it!"

Stef grunted. "It'll be like a beehive," he muttered. "Stinging me all over. The bear won't like it."

"Then we'll keep a grip on him, Stef," Rich prom-ised his friend. Steering his friend down the grass and rock slope to the valley below, he chanted foot-ball plays and facts back and forth, keeping Stef's mind off the unseen power that webbed the area. They trotted slowly away from the rest of the group.

Henry shadowed Bailey. He still looked uncertain of events as he did. Trent fell into step with Jason. "Stands to reason, doesn't it?"

"It does. I should have thought of that."

"Not bad for a guy with no Talent." Trent gave him a grin.

"You've got tons of Talent," Jason told him. "We just don't know what it is yet." He rubbed his crystal.

"It has to be here, right?"

"It has to be," agreed Jason. "All the time I've been looking, every time I was worried or tired or whatever, this is where I came. It's like part of me knows instinctively what the rest of me is fighting to figure out. It *has* to be here."

Trent nodded in agreement as he agilely negotiated the downslope with Jason. "Have any idea how big it is, here?" He surveyed the valley. "Is it just a tidy little land basin or are we looking at a continent here? Or an entirely new world?"

"I don't know. Not sure if it'll make a difference. The Gate, till it's anchored, probably exists everywhere and nowhere. It's like a . . . a shadow. All I have to do is catch a corner of it . . ." Jason's voice trailed off in thought as he trotted closer to the clear blue pool of water, the lake that took up much of the valley's area. He wondered how close he was to that description. Could something as important as a Gate begin as insubstantial and wispy as a shadow? Or had he already seen the Gate and just not recognized it for what it was?

Jason made a fist about his crystal and stumbled to a halt. No. No, it couldn't be. He looked around at the spine of the Iron Mountains edging the valley, and the faint spray off the long waterfall that fell from it into the pool, and across the rolling slopes of soft, green grass.

What he'd said to Trent wasn't quite right. Every time he sought the gate, he came to the valley—and the dragon.

No. And yet . . .

"Everyone stop," he called out. "I've found it. Or rather, I know what it is."

The Magickers halted. Rich and Stef perched on one of the big broken boulders at the foot of the mountains, while Bailey delicately chose a patch of clover and sat down cross-legged. They all found a place to rest and turned to look at him.

"I need the dragon," Jason told them.

"Frankly, Jase, I thought our strategy here was to avoid the dragon, and maybe not get eaten or flamed while we did it." Trent watched him.

"I'm serious."

"I don't think this is a good idea." Henry took his glasses off and cleaned them vigorously. "I'm with Trent. I thought we wanted to stay away from it."

"Things change. Look, I know what I know, when I know it. And what I know is that, just like it's right coming here to find the Gate, it's right to find the dragon."

"If it has closed off the Iron Gate to you, what makes you think it'll let you open another?"

"That, I don't know. Yet." Jason shaded his eyes to scan the horizon.

"Any way you can call it?" Bailey paused to tighten the laces on her sneakers. Lacey perched on her thigh, and nibbled on what looked like a bit of raisin scone. Breakfast from that morning, courtesy of FireAnn.

Jason watched the two of them, a thought nibbling

on the edge of his mind, much as the pack rat did on her crumb of scone. "Nooooo," he said, finally. "But . . ."

Trent's attention snapped to him. "But what?" He followed Jason's stare. "Oh. Ummm."

Bailey scratched her pet's chin with a fingertip. "Umm, what?"

"Remember how you called the frogs? And Lacey? And Stef as a bear cub?"

"Cut to the chase," Trent told him. He pointed at Bailey. "Jason wants you to call the dragon."

"Oh." Bailey rocked back on her elbows.

"I don't think you want to do that," offered Henry.

Both Rich and Stef grabbed Henry up, mock growling at him, "Shaddup!" Henry made an aggrieved growl of his own and the three of them rolled around on the grass.

Bailey stuck her foot out and nudged at all of them. "Honestly. As if I can't make up my own mind."

"Look," said Jason to her. "This is what we came for. Now, I can't promise that the dragon won't eat every one of us, because I don't know what it'll do. But we've been talking for months and it should know what I won't do, and I won't harm it, not on purpose. Or any of you."

"That," said Bailey, "is good enough for me." She uncaged her amethyst from its wire cage. "What do you think a dragon answers to?"

"Probably something sharp and scaly with fire-breathing jaws," Trent noted.

"You think?"

He nodded sagely. Bailey snorted, *pfuffing* her bangs off her forehead as she did. "Give me a few minutes." As she concentrated, her face knotted more and more. Lacey scampered back into the pocket of her shirt, but hung there, looking out, resting her chin on her tail tuft.

"Now is probably a really good time to work on your Shields," reflected Trent.

Instantly other hands came out, gripping crystals, and light flared around them.

"Not that anything we can put out yet will stop a dragon," added Trent, and he grinned. The Shields stayed up, sparkling in the daylight like some vast soap bubble.

Long moments crawled past. A cloud of gnats flew by after darting once or twice at Stef, circling, and then leaving as they all flailed about and waved their hands frantically to chase off the flying pests. A cloud drifted over and scattered in the bright sun. Rich wandered off to "visit a private bush" and came back and still nothing had happened.

Jason sat down, his knees under his chin. His rib cage still hurt from the various attacks and the soccer game, but not as much as the knowledge that he could never go back and be the same Jason he'd been before. He hadn't noticed it at the time, but, thinking about it later, he'd realized that his coach and Sammee had just walked away from the soccer field while everyone was still ranting and raving, as if he'd done something wrong. The memory was tucked in the corner of his mind and he hadn't even really seen it till he was trying to go to sleep on the

Hall's wooden floor. That and other things had circled round and round in his mind, but the dragon had ruled everything.

Sun beat down on his sneakered feet in a warm band. He looked down and saw a small orange lizard lying comfortably across the laces on his right foot. A salamander, a tiny fire lizard, like he'd seen a few times at camp. He looked at it, smiling. It, too, seemed to enjoy soaking up the sun. Then the reptile lifted its head and looked right at him, and Jason froze.

"Nobody move," he said quietly. "It's here." He put his hands back, debating over standing or not.

"What is?"

"Dragon."

"Oh-kay. How invisible is it?"

But Bailey followed his glance downward to his shoe. "Jason, that's a lizard, and it's not any bigger than Lacey." The pack rat gave a chirp as if insulted. "Not that there's anything wrong with that, but . . ."

"It's not the size." Jason looked at the salamander. "I know what I know." He stood slowly. The lizard uncoiled, yawned lazily, and crawled off Jason's shoe. It stretched, catlike, in the grasses, and it began to grow.

And grow.

And grow.

Until it dwarfed all of them by ten or twelve times, its head alone bigger than two or three of them put together. It cocked its head, and rattled the spiny plates on its back. "Smart, lad." Its crimson forked tongue slithered in and out of its teeth a few times, testing the air.

"Not smart enough, sometimes. Anyway. It's like this. I want the Gate."

"You cannot pass."

He shook his head. "Not good enough. This isn't a game anymore. Our lives depend on it."

"You cannot pass." The dragon's eyes glared a bit, but he did not dare look straight into them, wisdom passed on from Trent and the tricky ways of mythological beasts.

"You cannot stop me. I opened the Iron Gate, and the Water Gate, and I'll open the third Gate, too."

The dragon bellowed. The noise shivered off the very mountains, sending clusters of rocks tumbling down, and thundering off their eardrums, all but Jason throwing their arms about their heads to shut the sound away. He took a deep breath.

"I know what I know."

"You know nothing if you do not understand what you are opening this time."

"A sanctuary, a haven, a school."

"Think that, do you?" The dragon shifted around, coiling its tail across its haunches. It hunkered down, chin on the ground before Jason. "Are you a warrior or a guardian?"

"We've talked about this before. I'll fight if I need to." He rubbed his hand across his ribs. "If I need to," he repeated.

"Find the Gate if you can," hissed the great beast. "And my wrath if you cannot, because a Gate is the only way you'll escape me." His gemlike eyes blazed with defiance, and heat rolled off the creature's body like a cloud of steam. The dragon could be deadly, and left no doubt of that.

Jason opened his mouth to retort again, then closed it. His crystal felt hot in his hand. He turned his head slightly. "Get back, all of you."

"What are you going to do?"

"Open a Gate." He stepped forward. He put his hand out, on the Dragon's head to steady himself, as he leaned in and looked deeply into the gleaming eyes of the beast. "You, my friend, do not only guard the Gate. You *are* the Gate." And he fell into its depths.

27

SMOKE AND MIRRORS

H E FELT the heat. Amber color swallowed Jason whole, and it carried the warmth of a fiery forge with it, shimmering off his skin like the sun off a sandy beach. That was the first essence of the dragon he perceived. Hidden inside the warmth came a sharpness like that of knives, slicing against him, not deep enough to cut but enough to feel their many edges. The dragon's talons and teeth, he thought. And more than that, he felt the profound intellect surrounding him, weighing him, judging him. He walked carefully forward, making sure not to slip, for any false move would drop him into the fire, into the sharp edge, into trouble.

He walked into an inner chamber and stood inside the lanternlike glowing amber, and stopped there. He could hear the thunderous yet slow and steady beat

271

of a faraway drum. It pulsed with a steady sureness. Jason listened, baffled a moment, and then realized it was the dragon's heart he heard.

He wondered what was happening outside. Had he disappeared to them or did he stand paralyzed next to the beast, drawn in by its glorious eyes? And were they safe? Had he abandoned them?

Jason frowned and turned around slowly, looking all about the honey-gold cavern. He had not a clue what to do next, but he knew he had to be right. The dragon was the Gate itself, or at least so deeply wound into it that he could not separate one from the other. The rightness of it seeped into him.

Golden-orange coils began to separate from the wall facing him. In a moment or two, the sinuous beast extracted itself to face Jason, just a little taller but a Chinese dragon of length and grace as well as strength, its jaws and claws no less impressive as it studied him.

"You cannot pass."

"No matter how many times you say it, it doesn't make it true." Jason looked at the dragon.

"Then you will have to fight your way through." The dragon had whiskers, not at all catlike, but fine, strong whiskers for all that, and they bristled as it looked at Jason.

Jason shook his head. "I can't do that."

"Why not?"

"You're my friend. At least, I always thought you were. But even if you weren't, I can't just attack something. I fight if I have to, not before."

"Warrior or guardian," the dragon stubbornly insisted.

"There's no right answer there."

"There is more of an answer than you think." The dragon reared back, then struck at him.

Jason threw himself to his right. He slid on his elbow and came up rolling. As soon as he could get to his feet, the beast struck again. He dodged in the other direction. Its fang caught his sleeve as he did, ripping through. Pain scraped him as he landed on one knee and thrust himself out of range as the dragon recoiled and then snapped at him again. Its scaly body cut the air with a sharp hiss. It missed him again and again and again, every strike closer and faster until he panted.

He couldn't do this all day until it caught him. Jason rolled over and gathered himself, watching, waiting for the next snap. When it came, he leaped, not away but at it, catching the beast at the back of the head and wrapping his arms and legs about its body with all the strength he had left.

The dragon reacted like a bucking bronco. It reared and flung him back and forth to shake him off. Jason clung with everything he had. He pushed his voice through clenched teeth.

"This . . . is not . . . about fighting! If it were, you'd . . . have me . . . beat!"

The dragon rattled him as though he were a rag doll. He couldn't let go now. If he did, he'd be thrown across the cavern with such force, he'd break in two when he hit the wall. "Listen! You win!"

The dragon reared up, balancing on its haunches, panting a little itself, its blood racing like fire through its scaly body. Jason felt as though he were hugging a furnace. "But it is you who has me."

"I'm just holding on, trying not to get hurt." Jason sucked in a breath. "You're my friend! There has to be a way to make you see what I have to do."

"Get down," the dragon ordered quietly.

After a moment of hesitation, Jason let go and slid down. His arms and hands felt as though they had been sandpapered with a thousand small, stinging cuts. He'd read once that a shark's skin was like that . . . tiny scales that were miniatures of its dangerous teeth.

"Tell me." The dragon settled then, curling up in front of him.

Jason fell onto his butt, too weary to stand. He tried to sit cross-legged. "This Haven feels right. I can't explain it better than that. It's like when you walk into a room, and you know you belong there. Not because you own it, but because you . . . created it. And you love it, and you care for it. Does that make any sense?"

The dragon pulled at a whisker, curling it against its sharp obsidian claw. "And?"

"And whether you try to deny me or not, you can't deny the rightness of it, do you see?"

The beast lowered its head until their chins were nearly level. It said quietly, "Warrior or guardian?"

Jason rolled his eyes. "How should I know? You're the being with an ancient mind, full of riddles and history."

"Ah!" It drew back, grinning in a draconic way. "A riddle then? I win, you go, you win, you . . . go through. Agreed?"

Jason rubbed his eyebrow. He could almost hear Trent in the back of his mind saying, "Careful!"

Maybe he did hear Trent. And Bailey, too, saying, "You can do it." He nodded. "Okay."

"Good. This riddle is a story." The dragon rubbed his claws. "Centuries ago, in a land you may or may not have heard of, a mighty emperor was told by his astrologer that his days were coming to an end. He was a great ruler, and a great warrior, and had lived long, so he was not sad. But he had a burden in picking someone to rule after him, as he had no family. He had built an empire that was good for its people, and he wanted that to live on after him. After thinking long, he devised a test. He picked six candidates for this test. One of his generals, one of his priests, one of his accountants, two of his mayors, and the sixth, a common man who had been in his army and was now his gardener."

"All were humbled at being summoned to the emperor's court. Even more humbled when told why. 'But,' he said to them, 'I have a test and the one who passes best will be my successor,' and they all agreed to abide by it.

"To each man he gave a nest with an egg in it. 'Take care of this egg, and hatch it, and return in six months' time with what you have nurtured.' And he sent each man away, even the gardener who was named Ding.

"Ding had traveled far and been a solider and knew the ways of the civilized world before returning to the land and becoming a gardener. He knew how to care for his nest. He kept the egg just warm enough and turned it as a mother bird would, and yet it never hatched. Long day after long day passed and nothing emerged from the emperor's egg.

The dawn came when all the candidates were summoned back to the emperor's court, and each was to present his nest with its bounty."

The dragon looked keenly at Jason. It indicated him with a toe claw. "Think of what you would do if you were Ding.

"The general came forth. He showed the emperor a mighty falcon, hooded and resting on his wrist. 'Young but eager for the hunt,' the general said proudly. The emperor nodded and waved the general to one side.

"The accountant approached next. He held a woven cage of small size, efficient and neat. A sparrow sat inside, picking insects out of the air. He said nothing, but put the cage on the floor at the emperor's feet, bowed deeply and backed away. Sparrow and emperor looked at one another a moment.

"Beautiful birdsong came through the air, as the third candidate brought in his cage, far bigger and prettier, containing a lovely canary who sang as if for the gods themselves, or so the priest maintained. He too set his cage on the floor.

"The mayors came in together. They presented a large clay pot. 'We both hatched ducks,' they said proudly. 'And in alliance with one another, have butchered them and cooked them, in a dish fit for an emperor. Thus may all eat and prosper.'

"Indeed, smell from the clay pot was wonderful!

"Ding waited to go last for his turn. The emperor turned expectantly to him."

The dragon motioned to Jason. "You with your empty nest. What do you do?"

Jason blinked.

"Quickly," said the dragon. "What do you do?"

"I enter, and put the nest on the floor and tell the emperor I failed," said Jason finally. There were a thousand clever things that came to mind, but he did not like lying, never had, and not even as the humble gardener could he see doing it.

"Nothing else. Excuses?"

"I have none. I did my best, but I failed." Jason shrugged.

"And that is what Ding did, and said," the dragon told him. "The mayors told him out of the sides of their mouths that he was a fool, and could have described a mighty phoenix, but that the bird had escaped him. The others just stared. The emperor rose to announce, 'I have chosen my heir, and it is Ding. The eggs I gave you all were infertile. He presented no grand illusions or imposters, but told the truth and showed no fear in presenting it. I wished to choose an honest man, and a man who is not afraid to judge himself.' And so, in due time, Ding became an emperor."

"I guessed the riddle?"

"Not quite." The dragon tapped his claws together. "Warrior or guardian?"

Impossible! thought Jason. Would the dragon never give up? "Guardian," Jason finally, reluctantly, told him. "I would only fight if I had to, and to protect those I needed to, I guess."

The sinuous serpent drew back, coiling, as if for one last fatal strike. It looked at Jason, its eyes gleaming.

"The Gate is Open," the dragon said. "Pass it if you dare."

WHOOPS

LIGHT blazed around him. Jason lost his vision as he fell through it. The air smelled of fire and copper, burning away all his senses as Magick roared past him, over him, *through* him. He tumbled in mid-air, as though caught up in the winds of a hurricane, all the power swirling around him. It made him want to scream in fear and shout for joy and roar in triumph, all at once, and he could not make a sound. Instead, he seized it. Jason spread his arms and rode it, surfing across the Magick as if it were a vast, curling wave.

He had never felt anything like this before, and knew his world had changed, and as it bore him through the void, it began to lose strength, and he realized he would probably never feel anything so fierce, so pure again.

And it was his. He was part of it, braided into it, held up by it.

He threw his arms up, fists clenched in sheer joy. The Magick carried him through forever, then began to lower him, and his voice came back, shouting aloud in victory, as it washed onto an edge of now, and deposited him gently there.

Jason dropped his arms. He felt incredibly weak from the rush, and his heartbeat surged in his throat painfully, subsiding slowly as he took a few great breaths. He stood in a dirt cave and he walked out of it, ducking his head to avoid sharp outcroppings of rock. Outside, the sunlight made him squint as he turned back around to see where he'd come from.

He'd walked out of the Iron Mountains, through a cave he'd no idea had existed. Or maybe it hadn't, before. He'd opened a Gate, after all. Jason stood, swaying, his knees still weak, his whole body feeling limp with the effort, but he put his chin up and looked at the Gate.

Chiseled out of the rough, rust-red stone of the mountain, was a pouncing dragon, jaws opened wide to gather up any who dared to enter, with sharp teeth of stone. It looked awesome. Jason grinned broadly.

"Jason!" Bailey tackled him and he went to the ground, laughing. The others dog-piled on, all screaming and pummeling him.

"Did you see that? A Dragon Gate! Did you see what you made?"

"We didn't know! You disappeared and then the dragon, and then everything got really quiet. Then we could hear the mountain moaning."

"We all thought, 'Earthquake!' "

Jason rolled over, still grinning, and trying to protect his ribs from the hugs and pinches and nudges of his buddies. "And then what?"

"Don't you know?" Bailey stared at him, aghast.

"I," Jason told her, "was on the inside, don't forget."

"Oh!" She tossed her head.

"Whole mountain shook," Stef grumbled. "Dust and pebbles poured down. We figured it was all over, place was coming apart. We figured you were done for."

"Woah." He rubbed his face. He hadn't thought of that, of what might happen to the unstable Haven if he failed.

Rich sat back on his heels, his normally pale face reddening from being out in the sun so long, his freckles standing out as though he'd been hit with chocolate chips. "So you killed the dragon?"

"I don't think so. I hope not. We were friends." Jason struggled and managed to sit up. Everything looked as if it was going to spin around, and he closed his eyes.

"Friends don't eat friends," Bailey said firmly.

"Did you get eaten?"

"Noooo."

"Well, then." Jason opened one eye to peer at her.

Trent leaped to his feet. "So. We're good here?"

"Should be."

Stef let out a bearlike grunt. "We'd better be, because you let off so much power, it's like attracting flies."

"Or something like that." Rich stood, too. "Is it

always like that when you open a Gate? I don't remember feeling anything before."

"Never," vowed Jason, "like that." And it probably never would be again, and that was fine with him. Some things should be a once in a lifetime experience. He still felt overwhelmed. He tried to stand. "I think you guys need to . . ." He paused. He wobbled to his feet.

Henry put his arm out to try and catch Jason. "Do what?"

"Camp. Or something." Jason swayed on his feet, and his ears roared, and blackness threatened to gobble all his thoughts. He pulled Rebecca Landau through and knew he had to shut the Gate because of the backlash crashing down on him. He left a tiny crack open for Ting and only hoped she could find it, and them. Jason felt the weakness surge back through him, and fell into darkness. Something squeaked and he hoped it was Bailey in surprise and not the pack rat as he fell.

Ting sat in the client lobby, waiting for both her mother and grandmother. Her mother had gone to move the car around, and her grandmother was being wheeled into the reception area even as Ting shifted restlessly, trying to ignore the other outpatients and their families. It was like a library in that no one wanted to speak above a whisper, and the marble flooring held a chill that the sun glinting through the corridor couldn't warm, and there was a feeling that several of those waiting held little faith in the treatment they'd received that morning. Waiting for the end, her grandmother had told her, walking in. "They have no faith!" She'd swung her cane about vigorously. "Even if I go, I live on. In your mother, in you. That is faith enough."

And now, just a bare hour later, she was being wheeled back out, the color behind her naturally tanned and Asian-pigmented skin gone pale, her arm bandaged where the IV had been, and one of those paper cup masks over the lower half of her face. She raised a hand to grasp Ting's firmly as the nurse said, "I'll be back when the car is here."

Ting's grandmother hardly took up any room at all in the wheelchair. Ting slid in next to her, pressing against her so she could lend her own body's warmth. "How do you feel?"

Ting's grandmother wrinkled her nose. "Bad taste in my mouth. Even my best tea leaves will taste awful for days." She rubbed Ting's hand in her own. Her hand held strength in it still, although it was wrinkled and somewhat shrunken by her illness and age. "But what can one do?"

"Mom'll be out front in a minute. Then we'll go home and you can rest." Ting leaned her head against that of her grandmother's. She smelled of medicine and antiseptics and it would be good to get her home where she could brew ginger tea against the nausea and she would smell of that goodness instead. They were sitting that way when the wave of power hit them.

It rippled through the clinic lobby like a shock wave. Ting sat back in the wheelchair with a smothered gasp as it lanced through her as though it were pure sunlight, almost blinding. It gripped them both so strongly neither one could move and they could hardly breathe—and it continued to just pour through them. Ting's eyes stung with the brilliance that no one but the two of them seemed to see!

Her grandmother's hand curled tighter over hers. "What is it?" she managed.

"I don't know!" Ting wanted to shout with joy though as it soared around her. She tasted Magick in it. In fact, it *sang* with Magick. But where it came from, or what caused it, she had no idea. She put her chin up to face it, seeking it as a flower did the sun. It felt glorious, and her grandmother gave a soft sound, rather like a purr, as they clasped hands.

"Someone is a master," her grandmother said. They breathed in the Magick for another few, long moments before it began to fade and then was gone.

Ting blinked and realized someone had honked a car horn out front, at the doors. She let go of her grandmother's hand and went to the back of the wheelchair to push it out in answer. "I wonder what happened."

"We must go there."

"Where?"

"You can find it," her grandmother said confidently.

"But Mom . . ."

"She will understand." Her grandmother got to her feet. She wore silk trousers and a black silk jacket quilted in gold thread with a small tiger embroidered over her left pocket. She tugged her clothes into place. "Leave a note."

Ting fished around in her purse, scribbled something quickly, and left it on the wheelchair seat. She took her grandmother into the empty corridor, got her crystal out and Focused. After a shaky try, she found the trail of Magick and, gripping her grandmother's hand firmly, took her there.

Gavan woke with a jerk. He leaped to his feet, dismayed at having slept so soundly or so late, and being awoken so abruptly. He swung his cane about, searching for intruders, for trouble. Then he stopped, puzzled. Nothing or no one to sense. He took a deep breath, and sat back down by Eleanora's side. "Alarms over nothing." He touched her cold, still hand, then added, "Not nothing if it's over you, that's not what I meant." He rubbed the wolfhead on his cane as if gathering his thoughts. "Aunt Freyah kept me awake half the night raving over the kids. Worry over you kept me awake for most of the rest of the night. I am up against a rock here, Eleanora, without any answers. I keep asking myself what your father would have done, and yet I cannot help having angry thoughts that Gregory put us in this position. If only he'd dealt with Brennard instead of seeing him get stronger and darker every day . . ." Gavan paused. He traced a finger down the side of Eleanora's sleep-frozen face. "Of course, that wasn't his way, nor yours. I'll admit my position varies from day to day. There are days when I'd seek Brennard out now just for the satisfaction." He took a deep breath, which was good, because when the wave hit him, it was so strong, such a lash of power, that he could not breathe again for many long moments. It flared through the diamond gemstone gripped by the wolf's pewter jaws of his cane, and shone through like a laser beam, sharp and glaring white, and he'd no doubt if he Focused it, it would cut through steel. He sat pushed back in his chair with the force of it, felt it part every fiber of his body and flow through him unstoppably. When it had gone and he could finally breathe again, he took two or three whooping gulps of air, then knelt down beside Eleanora.

Its passing had tousled her long brunette hair into a jumble, but other than that, she seemed untouched. Perhaps not entirely untouched. The lines on her face seemed to have relaxed, and she wore more of a serene expression in her deep rest. Nothing untoward, though, and for that he gave many thanks.

He stood and shook his cane. He had no idea what had just happened, but he *would* find out.

Khalil paused in his study, his hand stretched out to take down a dusty leather book fastened with cords of twisted gold, and felt the power sweep over him. He considered it for a moment until he had absorbed its strength, its flavor, and its portent. He smiled slowly. The act would have come sooner or later, but the consequences of the chaos it would rip loose by its doing . . . He shook his head. They had no consideration about what it was they were doing. He had some research to conduct, then he would look into the matter.

He continued smoothly reaching to take his book down, and opened it carefully, for the pages were greatly aged and written many a century ago. He sat down under a strong electric light and began to read.

In dark chambers halfway across the world, Brennard jumped to his feet. The power that had swept through left him chilled and shaking in his chair. He put his hands to his face, cupping his eyes a moment, for the Magick had nearly blinded him, and it took him a while to recover. Then he threw his head back and let out an angry roar. He flung his hand out, swiping a Ming vase aside and smashing it to the floor where porcelain centuries old and valuable beyond compare shattered into a thousand pieces.

At the sound of the crash, Jon ran in, and stopped amid the rubble, his face chalk white. He looked down. "What happened?"

"Did you not feel it?"

Jon looked as though searching for an answer, then said, "How could it not be felt? It roared through here like a typhoon or cyclone."

"Backtrace it."

"I cannot. It recoils from me as if knowing my power and its are opposite from each other."

"Find someone who can!" Brennard bellowed. "I want to know who unleashed that kind of Magick on the world."

"Want to . . . or need to?" asked Jonnard quietly, studying his father's face.

"You can be a fool."

"We are both fools if you think you can chase that down, and triumph against whomever sent it."

"I do not think it an attack."

"But you do not know for sure."

"No." Brennard clenched one hand. "It could have been deliberate or the residue from some deliberate act, a backlash they had no idea would occur. Either way, I need to know who did it."

Jon inclined his head. "I will find out." His ties with Henry Squibb had been very weak the last day or so, but only because he hadn't tried to reinforce them. Squibb had been fighting him, and it seemed wiser to conserve his strength for other problems. Now he had other priorities and Squibb could be useful again. "Anything else?"

"The vase," Brennard answered, looking down on the floor as if in sudden recognition of the accident.

Jon waved his hand. A thousand fine pieces of porcelain rose in the air, circling about aimlessly and then more and more into a maelstrom pattern that grew closer and closer together until the vase reformed itself. Jon dropped his hand and the Ming vase settled to once again to rule a corner of his father's desk in dark blues and milky whites and incomparable porcelain. "Please be careful, Father," Jon noted mildly. "You could have cut yourself." He turned and left the inner offices of his father's domain.

An excitement woke in him. He could do something Brennard could not. The days of his father's unlimited power seemed to be drawing to a close. He would need Jonnard more than ever, and perhaps even finish his training, and confide in him.

And then the day when Jon could take over entirely would be that much nearer. He wanted the power, and he wanted it now.

He'd had a taste of his father's strength, and knew the rest of it could be his any time he wanted. When he had it, he could then command the army his father had assembled over the years, mercenaries from lost wars over the centuries, lean and hungry men who slept in the catacombs below their estate, ready to be awakened and used however necessary.

They had not been born in modern times. Like Brennard, like Jon, they did not have a fondness for modern sensibilities. They had all sprung from eras in which survival of the fittest was the highest code. Thanks to Isabella's unwitting help, Jon could now make Leucators of any of them, not to hunt down its twin, but to hunt with it. Unstoppable.

Jon smiled slowly. They had the means to make the world theirs, whether by might or Magick. It was up to him to make sure that the time was now theirs as well.

NOT IN KANSAS

GAVAN bent over his crystals, sifting, searching, and finally found the thread he looked for. He seized it with a shout of joy, bounded to his feet and ran through the corridors of the Gathering Hall and out to FireAnn's cottage where the herbalist sat in a rocking chair, making notes in a cookbook the size of a massive dictionary as she watched Eleanora.

"It's the kids," he announced.

"We thought as much, since they were gone."

"True, but now I can locate them."

FireAnn had her kerchief off, and her luxurious red hair had fallen to her shoulders in a fiery mass of curls. "And the power, lad? Either they got the dragon or it got them."

"Possibly."

"Ye're not about to go charging in there by your-self, are you?"

"Not that I want to, but it seems wisest."

FireAnn put her fountain pen in her book and closed it thoughtfully. " 'Tis a sad day when we canna trust our allies, Gavan."

"I know. But who on the Council would you call in? Other than Tomaz."

"I'd have to say, we're pretty much it, as it stands. What do you expect to find?"

"Trouble, one way or the other. An unleashing of power like that could mean anything, although I hope not what it might mean."

FireAnn raised an eyebrow over her sparkling green eye. "Not the Forbidden."

"We have no idea what resources Brennard has hidden, although Gregory told me he feared the worst when Antoine turned." Gavan rubbed his wolfhead cane. "To my way of thinking, I don't see how Brennard could hope to get away with it. This is a different world. We balance on science instead of superstition. Our shadows are too well lit. And anything he could raise that was Forbidden would bring attention to him he wouldn't want. My real fear is that he would stop at nothing to expose us, and then flee to leave us facing the con-sequences, as he has already tried with the children."

"Then he has to be stopped. Am I going or staying with our lass?"

"Staying. Here's the thread of power I'm following . . ." Gavan let it graze FireAnn's mind and thoughts till he felt she could grasp it herself if needed. "I'll send word one way or the other. If I can't come back." He stopped.

"She'll know how much ye loved her, and I'll see to her. We'll beat this, I promise." FireAnn rubbed her hands together lightly, wincing at the pain of the arthritis-swollen joints. "Perhaps it's only right that time catches up with some of us, eh? We've been a tricksy lot."

"Not like this, FireAnn, not like this." He kissed her forehead, then bent down and kissed Eleanora's mouth gently. Standing, he grasped the thread he intended to follow and Crystaled out of the existence of Camp Ravenwyng.

Ting's grandmother leaned heavily on her, as they burst through the plane of her crystal, and emerged in a green valley she knew well. "Haven!" cried Ting happily as her feet touched ground, and she tightened her arm about her grandmother's waist. A rainbow of color met their eyes from the grove at the edge of the deep blue pond, where shirts appeared to have been knotted together. From under their canopy, Bailey burst out, shouting, "Ting! Ting!"

She ran across the ground and gathered both of them in joy, her ponytail bouncing. "What are you doing here!" Into her ear, she whispered confidentially, "This place is awesome. We are definitely not in Kansas anymore."

Ting shook her lightly before letting go and giving a little, formal bow. "Bailey Landau, I wish you to meet my grandmother, Qi Zhang. Grandmother, this is my best friend, Bailey."

Bailey gave a little bow back, saying, "I am hon-

ored to finally meet you, Ting's esteemed grandmother." She tilted a glance at Ting as if asking if
she'd done it properly.

Ting grinned. "Qi means fine jade, Bailey."

"Cool name! Are you feeling better?"

Ting's grandmother lowered the paper mask from
her mouth, and took a deep breath. "Much better,"
she announced. "Can you not feel the power in the
dragon bones of this earth?"

"Not exactly," Bailey admitted, "although we did
see the dragon. He seemed pretty well fed, too, not
at all bony, mostly teeth and claws and bright shining eyes. That was just before Jason opened the
Dragon Gate."

"And I missed it!" Ting gave a hop. "Is that what
hit us? We felt it all the way in San Francisco!"

"It was incredible," Bailey said to her, as Lacey
poked her head out of her pocket, whiskers shaking
as she gave a pack rat squeak of agreement.

"Tell us about it! But first, we need a place for
Grandmother to sit. She had chemo this morning,
and sometimes . . ." Ting gave her grandmother a
worried look.

Qi, however, shook her head as she leaned on her
bamboo cane. "I am fine, Granddaughter. However,
I want to listen to this tale being told, and I see others
waiting for us."

Bailey took each by the hand and led them to the
canopy under the treetops, where Rebecca sat beside
a sleeping Jason who looked pale even in the shade.
Ting came to an uncertain halt. "Ooooh . . . what
happened?"

Qi leaned over and touched his forehead. "He is

fine. Much power went through and out of him."
The tiny Chinese woman frowned. "I shall have to
teach him the ways of Wu Shu. He must be a fighter
inside and outside of his body."

"Wu Shu?"

"Martial arts. You Westerners have many names
for it, but in northern China, I was taught the Wu
Shu. It disciplines your mind and soul and health as
well as your body. It makes one a whole person,
in order to live well, not just fight a little better."
She winked.

She sat down on a small, flat rock, tucking her silk
trousers around her, and laying her cane across her
lap. She put her hand on Rebecca Landau's knee.
"You must be the mother of Bailey. I see a resem-
blance of face and soul."

Rebecca smiled. "Thank you. Are you one of . . ."
She stopped helplessly and made a gesture.

Qi inclined her chin. "I am honored you think so,
but my abilities are small compared to the others
gathered here."

"Not true!" Ting protested. "Eleanora calls her a
Hidden One, one of Talent although untrained."

"Blood runs true to blood, do you not think so,
Mother of Bailey? She favors you in Talent as well
as heart."

"Oh, I'm not." Rebecca paused, and got a thoughtful expression on her face. "At least, I never thought
I was." She leaned back and grew very silent.

Qi smiled at her granddaughter. Her paper mask
hung about her neck now, like an odd necklace, and
her dark eyes snapped with humor. "I am trained,"
she corrected softly, "although perhaps not in the

way of the long noses." Her wrinkles creased deeply with her silent laugh at that. "So, now, the tale."

Ting sank onto the grass and pulled Bailey down with her. "Spill it! Everything."

Bailey opened her mouth to say something, interrupted by the bawling of a bear cub as it barreled past them, Rich chasing in hot pursuit. No one but Ting's grandmother seemed to think it odd, as the two raced past and into the woods, Rich yelling, "Stef! Darn it! Come back here!"

Three or four paces behind them trotted Trent and Henry. At the sight of the girls, they stopped their pursuit and dropped to the grass as well, both boys a little out of breath. No one wore shirts because it was their garb that made the canopy overhead that shaded them without being deeper in the colder woods. "That cub can run!"

"Maybe he'd stop, if he were not chased?"

Trent thought over Rebecca's statement before shrugging. "Stef is out of control right now. I think it's the surge we had through here. He went bear and can't get back, and he's terrified."

"Another who could use training in the ways of Wu Shu," said Ting's grandmother wisely.

Squibb said nothing, except that he gave Ting a beaming smile. He sat back uneasily, braced against a tree trunk. "I think we're safe here," he told Ting.

"If Jason opened the Gate, we are."

Bailey pointed at the Iron Mountains, with the massive dragon carved out of rock at its foot, darkness in its yawning jaws.

"Wow." Ting stared in unabashed amazement. "Okay, now I *have* to know what happened." She scooted over to her grandmother's knee, and touched her, as if checking to see all was well. Qi smiled down on her.

Trent grinned at Bailey. "You tell it and I'll fill in the blanks when you get excited."

Bailey turned blazing pink, but that did not stop her from flinging herself headfirst into the tale, starting at the soccer game. No one spoke for long moments after she finally finished, with occasional explanations inserted from Trent in a strictly helpful way. "And then he keeled over, nearly squashing Lacey, and that's it."

"Exhausted," said Rebecca. She nodded. "I don't think it's anything worse than that."

Ting stood and dusted herself off. "We should get back, then. We can leave, can't we?"

"No one's tried yet. We all seem kinda burned out for the moment. I can't reach anyone, but it's coming back. I think we just have to wait."

Qi put her hand out to Ting. "I am staying, Granddaughter. Tell your mother that I love her and gather up my things."

She blinked. "What?"

"My father, the magician and acrobat Jinsong, had a prophecy when I was born. It was told that I would spend my last days in the shadow of the red dragon. He feared it meant the communism that gripped our country and sent me to the United States when he could. I was a woman grown then and he old and dying, and we did not understand the prophecy at all, and so feared it. But now I believe . . ." Qi looked at the rusty cliffside with its sculpture. "I believe that this is my destiny, and a worthy one. There is work

to do here, am I right? A haven, a school to be built.
And I have strength here, Ting. I can feel it.''

"Grandmother, your medicine . . .''

"My medicine works by killing me little by little
and hoping that my body can survive it longer than
the illness. But it cannot give me more than a few
more years, even if it works. Here, I feel strength.
My soul has purpose rather than merely surviving.''

"Yes, but—''

"I wish to stay.''

Ting stammered a bit. Her eyes sparkled brightly.
Bailey jumped to her feet. "You'll be back!''

"I will?''

"How could you not? You're a Magicker!''

"But . . . my mom . . . but . . .''

"Jiao is a wise woman,'' her grandmother told her.
"She knows I will need you, and she knows you
have your own growing to do. Trust her, trust yourself. You will be back.''

Ting looked down at the ground, her wings of lus-
trous dark hair hiding her face for a moment, before
she put her chin back up. "I will see you soon, then,
Grandmother!'' She hugged Qi fiercely, cupped her
crystal and disappeared before anyone could say another word.

She found the Gate open only a tiny splinter, and
it frightened her for a moment. Would she even be
able to return? She brushed Jason's thoughts as she
tried to Focus. *Go*, he whispered wearily. *I will try
and let you back through.* Then he faded a little, as if
tired even beyond the help of sleep and dreams, and
she Crystaled anyway, for if Jason did not keep his
word, who would? She trusted him.

Qi settled back as her granddaughter shimmered out of sight. "Now," she stated, "I am old and have been through a great deal. I must rest my body. Do not disturb me or the boy, as I have much teaching to do, and he much training."

"In his sleep?" Rebecca stood gracefully.

"For now, yes. It is best for the two of us. He has much to learn. If his mind knows how to do it, his body will follow." Qi nodded sagely. "We shall see if the bones of the dragon in this earth aid him as they do me." She leaned back against the tree trunk, put her small hand on Jason's forehead, and closed her eyes.

"Wonder where your ex-wife and daughter went to?"

Jerry Landau slowly slid upright in the seat of his car. The upholstery creaked under him, papers from fast food dinners crackling under his feet as he moved. He rubbed his eyes. Everything felt crusty. Late afternoon sun arced through the dusty windshield, and the street had begun to pick up traffic, heading into the hour when nearly everyone got off work.

He looked at the slender, dark-haired man leaning against the fender of his car. "Who in the hell are you?"

"Maybe someone who wants to help."

"Yeah? Or maybe not. No one knows where they went, least of all me." He eyed the apartment building which he'd been waiting outside of since Sunday afternoon. Several days now. "The w-w-w-" He cursed and gave up trying to say witch. He hadn't been able to speak about anything straight since he'd seen it. And it hadn't been on the news or in the papers. It was as if everyone who'd witnessed it had been cursed. No pictures, nothing. As if a hurricane had hit the county and no one knew or admitted anything about it. He rubbed his jaw, which ached with the effort of trying to get the word out.

"Too bad," the stranger said smoothly. "Here you are, a father, just trying to see your kid get raised properly, despite the ex. And she runs out on you again."

"Got that right. The school won't even tell me anything. She's got a restraining order against me. All the rules and lawyers in a row on her side." Jerry leaned on his elbow, against the rolled down car window. He didn't remember having left it down, but it was electric and couldn't have come down on its own. The restraining order had been in effect for a few years, but Landau saw no reason to muddy the waters here. He was the victim, after all.

"So that's why I'm here. Figured we could help each other."

Jerry looked at the man. Well dressed. Hadn't seen a lot of sun, or hard work either, for that matter, but probably had money. Never hurt to have money on your side. Once he had custody of Bailey, his new wife could raise her however she wanted, religious freak that she was, and he could get the support payments off his back. That would be a miracle in itself. "How's that?" he asked.

The stranger smiled. "Ever notice how we all saw something but none of us can talk about it?"

Jerry nodded.

"I think it's a kind of mass hypnosis. A crowd hysteria kind of thing, you know? Controlling what we saw or thought we saw."

Jerry wasn't quite sure, but he wouldn't admit he couldn't keep up with the dark-haired man, so he nodded again. The stranger smiled again, slowly. "Now, some of us are harder to hypnotize than others. Stronger wills."

Now that, Jerry understood. He had a will of iron. Except maybe when it came to wanting a drink now and then, but that was different. That was because he deserved it, for all he went through. It wasn't easy working and providing.

"So what's that mean?"

"That means that one of us is going to be able to break the control. Could be any minute now, could be a few days. Those kids are missing. No one seems to know anything about it, but—" His new friend paused. He rubbed his gloved hands together. "Someone has to know something. And I want to be there when everything cracks open. My kid deserves that."

"So . . . what do we do?"

"All I ask of you is that when you learn something, anything at all, you share it with me. And in return, I'll use all my resources to see you get your daughter back."

Jerry's eyes narrowed. "She's not supposed to take Bailey out of state, restraining order or not."

"There you go. You're in the right, and you know it."

The stranger stepped away from the car, into a dark shadow cast upon the street.

"But how do I get hold of you—"

"Don't worry. You will."

Jerry sneezed suddenly, grabbing for a paper napkin on the dashboard, and when he'd finished mopping up, the man had gone. Jerry wadded up the napkin and tossed it out the window. About damn time someone had listened to his side. He glared out at the apartment building. There wasn't a place Bailey could hide now.

FORGOTTEN AND FORBIDDEN

GAVAN knew the moment something went wrong. The thread he followed twisted and then turned on him, as though it were some great snake coiling and fighting with him. He growled back at it and yanked, then immediately felt a chill of fear. The void he tried to enter shut on him. Jason's thread snapped and disappeared. Gavan often likened Crystaling to jumping from an airplane. There was that moment of plunging off and then just hanging, before reaching for the parachute cord and deploying it. His cord had just broken away and he had no place to go. He drifted in the cold nothingness of *between* and tried to search out a true path. That which he had sensed before stayed as if it had never existed at all. Instead, he found Eleanora, faint and weak, beckoning him. He concentrated on her then and even as he emerged, he knew he was not at Ravenwyng.

Nor was it truly Eleanora who'd caught him.

Something waited for him, wanted him, hungrily. Too late to stop Crystaling, Gavan went through. He landed at the ready, eyes narrowed, weight balanced, awaiting anything. A faint, damp breeze lifted the cape on his shoulders and let it drop as quickly as if sulking.

He murmured a word to Lantern the darkness. Gavan looked about, not sensing Jason or Bailey or any of the others, but the hungry presence hovered nearby, and Gavan juggled a thought of leaving as quickly as he'd come, but curiosity got the better of him. He'd felt Eleanora calling. He couldn't be wrong about that. Had she been taken? Had she led him here? Or did something dark and sinister mock his love for her? His thread had been tangled or captured, his journey detoured and he wanted to know by what.

The glow from his crystal fell on cave walls and crude drawings jumped into sight. He stepped closer to look at renditions of hunters depicting the hunt of thousands of years ago, paint fading yet still preserved. He put a hand up, and then dropped it, knowing his touch could disintegrate that record of a struggle immemorial. The caves led deeper into stillness and Gavan followed the cave wall cautiously. "Eleanora?" he called lightly, quietly, not expecting an answer, hoping fervently there would be none. She did not belong here. Yet a small sense of her lingered, and it bothered him, drove him deeper into the caverns. Lichen growing here and there seemed to glow with its own phosphorescence as his Lantern light touched it. He trod carefully, making as little noise as he could, yet knew that would not help. Whatever it was he approached knew as well as he did that he sought it even as it sought him.

Gavan brushed the essence of Eleanora again and recoiled from it. It couldn't be her and yet it was, and he feared that she had fallen into true darkness. It was as though nothing had been left of her but an aching need.

So hungry it was! And tired and cold, but most of all thirsting for him. It pulled him nearer and nearer relentlessly and Gavan had no doubt that it would savage him if they met. Yet though he sensed he was moving nearer to it, he could not feel that it was moving toward him. Did it wait in shadowy ambush? Was there a Gateway here he had no knowledge of? Had that been a Gate he felt opening? Yet, if it had been, it should not have led to this.

Gavan slipped through the caves into a labyrinth, a catacomb passage that he could see had been carved both by hands and time. There were traces along the way of what it had once been. A broken crate, old and weathered, rotting away. Old rope. Rutted wheel marks ground into the dirt and stone below his feet. He could smell, faintly, the dampness of a river or perhaps a seacoast. A smuggler's passageway.

The cave drawings brought Lascaux, in the south of France to mind, although he doubted that these drawings had ever been found by those of archaeological academia. He had a pretty good idea whose domain he trespassed in. He had to be underneath an estate, a manor house or perhaps what might even pass for a castle in these days, built over hidden caves and passages and the smuggling trade along the waterways. He could not imagine why the remnant of his Eleanora would be here in the shadow of another Magicker except that it had to be a trap or worse, and he could not turn back now.

He rounded a corner, and lantern light bounced back at him, dazzling him for a moment as the catacombs opened into an immense cavern, studded with oil burning sconces and hung with prisms to reflect and increase the meager light. Heavy chain rattled amidst teakettle loud hissing at his stumbling entry and Gavan halted, and stood, surrounded.

Dead eyes watched him from all around the cavern. The captives tried their chains and shackles, reaching for him and failing, their faces hungry to touch him. He shuddered as he turned about slowly, taking the horrible sight in. Leucators filled the room. Their mouths *sissed* at him in anger and need. They clawed the air trying to reach him, their white-gray bodies clothed in the crudest of rags, gnawed bones scattered at their feet, and everywhere felt icy cold.

"Eleanora!" He raised his cane, letting light fall on her, but it wasn't her. The Leucator reared back in its chains, its brunette hair in greasy disarray about its face, like the youthful Eleanora when he'd first fallen in love with her but horribly, terribly wrong. And yet the Leucator retained the youth she herself had lost. The bitterness of it filled his mouth, and he spat. It raised a shaking hand at him in entreaty, then dropped it, and its eyes looked at him hopelessly. He would have wept but something tugged viciously at his ankle nearly pulling his leg out from under him.

Gavan spun about. Another Leucator crawled back, whimpering, and slyly covered its head with one arm, and he stared in shock. "My God," he whispered. "Fizziwig." It couldn't be, but it was. His study partner, his colleague, his best friend from days he could hardly remember anymore looked back at him. His friend from before the battle, before the great jump across time, before he'd become old and cheerful and spritely and then had suddenly died. No, this Fizziwig had the mop of unruly golden curls which had later gone to shocked white, and his unhealthy Leucator skin remained free of wrinkles. The creature grinned back at him mockingly. If only it knew how terrible it was.

Unable to face either it or the doppelganger of El-eanora, Gavan turned again, slowly. He looked into parodies of faces he recognized and felt bile rise at the back of his throat in disgust and fear. Someone had made doubles of them all, as well as doubles of strangers.

This had been Forbidden. Gregory had made it clear in no uncertain terms. Leucators should not be created but if they were, a Magicker should never fall into the delusion that it can be fed from.

Yet, as Gavan swung about, it was clear someone had. Like a vampire with its own herd of cattle hidden in these caves, someone had been feeding. He clenched his teeth. No wonder Eleanora lay near death, her soul being drained through the Leucator and its Maker. And perhaps that had killed Fizziwig as well, or at least haunted him all the days he'd had left after the disaster, for a Leucator was a mirror, and this one had been made *before* the War of the Wizards. Fizziwig had been doomed even before the rest of them. As for Eleanora, did she sense it? She had pushed him this way, and then the Leucator had drawn him the rest of it. She must have! She must lie in her sleep and know that she was being fed upon and drained and helpless. Anger shot through him.

The sound of a chain rattled in his ear. Gavan jerked away, shuddering at the thought of being touched by one. A pebble rolled under the heel of his shoe and he went to one knee. A shadow fell over him.

Gavan twisted his head to look up, and his heart stilled for the barest of moments.

Not all the Leucators were chained.

He pushed himself away, rolling, and came up, back to part of the cavern wall. Three closed in on him. Their howls of hunger filled the air and the chained ones added their own hissing excitement. Gavan put his Shield up and waited, his heartbeat having recovered and now racing in his throat. Cornered and likely outnumbered, he was not sure if he would have time to Crystal elsewhere or not.

Silence filled the cavern. Dead silence. The Leucators all retreated a step, their mouths writhing in un-uttered distress as someone entered the cavern.

"Well, well, my beauties. Look what you have found."

Bailey woke. She didn't know why, because she'd been in such a deep sleep that she'd forgotten she was on the ground in a strange place. Everyone around her appeared to be lost in dreams, too, their breathing deep and strong. Stef, back in human form, snuffled a bit in his sleep.

Bailey rolled to her knees and got up quietly. She went to Jason and stood at his side a long moment, listening. He appeared to be in regular sleep now. Before he had been fitful and hot, as though fighting a cold or something, and they'd finally put damp cloths across his forehead to bring down his temperature a bit. He looked better now though, his face turned to one side, lit by the low silvery moon.

Madame Qi opened one eye and smiled at Bailey. "Let him sleep," she said. "He is still learning much."

"How do you do that?"

"Teach? Tell me, when you learn something new, something important, do you not dream of doing it?"

Bailey looked closely at Ting's grandmother. "Sometimes. Yeah, I do." She grinned in sudden realization.

"So, you see." Qi smiled and closed her eye, leaning back securely against the tree once more.

Bailey thought everything was going to be all right. She walked quietly to the edge of the pond and pulled up the bucket Ting's grandmother had woven for them out of green sticks and lined with mosses. It didn't stay full of water, about half would drain through but it made for a good catch and drink. When it was safer, Rebecca and Bailey had already decided to sneak back for their camping things and extra clothes and other necessities.

She drank deeply of water that tasted more heav-

enly than anything out of a faucet or fancy plastic
bottle before dropping the bucket back into place at
the shore. With a hand covering her yawn, she made
her way back to the little hollow on the ground next
to her mother's sleeping form. Then her eyes opened
wide in surprise.

Where she'd been sleeping but a few minutes before now rested . . . well . . . things. Bailey sat down.
She combed through the items. Three onions. A small
cloth bag with a dozen eggs in it. Three applelike
looking fruits. And a stack of four crudely woven
but ever so soft blankets. She unfolded one and a
tiny bunch of herbs fell out. She picked them up
and sniffed. The sachets smelled faintly like flowers
and cinnamon.

Bailey looked around. Leaves shifted and twigs
cracked in the grove but she saw nothing.

Obviously the items were presents and welcome
ones, too, for it meant a breakfast awaited them in
the morning. She thought a moment, then slid her
bracelet off her wrist, jewelry Ting had made, and
she laid it out on a flat rock nearby. "Thank you,"
she said softly to the evening air. Quietly Bailey took
out the blankets and covered those she could, before
crawling back next to her mother and taking a corner
of the last blanket. Its scent drifted over her as she
fell back into sleep, wondering who had visited them.

Gavan still could not see who approached, but he
rubbed his wolfhead cane and said, amiably, "Well,
then, Isabella. I was wondering how long before you
would know I was here."

"Always astute." With a rustle of satin, Isabella

stepped out of the shadows. She lifted a gloved hand, and the Leucators slunk away, sinking onto their haunches, still watching him avidly but cowed by her presence. "A little too late, but a very clever lad nonetheless."

"This is an abomination," Gavan told her. "And it *will* be stopped."

"Stopped?" She paused, in her elegant designer gown, its hem dragging the filthy floor, jewels sparkling at her throat, ears, and wrists. "By whom? You?"

"Me and the Council. Whatever it takes."

Isabella laughed softly. The sound of it was colder than the flesh of the Leucators about her. "I see no Council. In fact, I barely see a Magicker." She rustled a step nearer. "Do you really think you need a Shield between us?"

"I'll stand with it," Gavan said.

She moved again, imperceptibly nearer. He watched her face. Could he tell, with a master of Magick such as she, if this were really Isabella or yet another Leucator? He stared at her eyes. He thought he could. His life might well depend upon it. The problem with dueling another Magicker is that the power they wielded carried more chance of destroying whatever it was they fought for, and themselves, than of saving it. It was best never to come to blows at all.

He didn't think he'd get out of here without a fight, however. His mouth went dry.

Isabella put her hand up, and made a small, elegant gesture with her gloved fingers. The Lantern light from his crystal dimmed.

It could be coincidence, because the spell only lasted so long once cast or it could be that she drained it away. Amusement danced over Isabella's face as she read the expression on his.

"I wouldn't want to be down here in the dark," she observed.

He had no intention of lingering that much longer. To his flank, he could hear the creatures stirring, growing restless in their chains once more. "How could you have done this?" he asked of her.

She made a noise of scorn. "And why not? It is Magick, to be used whenever it is necessary. I could help Eleanora, you know." She inched forward again.

"Eleanora?" That did catch him by surprise.

"They have their uses, Leucators, besides running their prey to the ground."

"I can see how you used them," he answered stiffly.

"Bah. You see nothing!" She gathered her hem up with her left hand, freeing her legs a bit from the sweeping folds of her dress gown. "Do you think we all slept after Brennard defeated Gregory? Are you really that naïve, Gavan? Some were physically hurtled through the centuries but some of us," and her voice dropped to a low hiss. "Some of us had to live the decades."

Her sibilant voice echoed in the cavern about her, picked up and hissed softly by the Leucators.

"What are you talking about?"

"This." Isabella beckoned. "The Forbidden. Yes, I create them and then I draw on them. They have no life but what I give them, and so it is only just that I take it back! Look at me!" She cried out, and dropped her Magicks and he saw her then . . . saw her aged but proud face, deeply lined by the years, the true color of her vibrant hair turn to thinning gray, liver spots multiplying along her porcelain flesh to muddy it. He saw an antique, an old woman of great strength who had once been young but was no longer, even with her powers.

Yet Isabella stood triumphantly, for she might look every day of ninety years old, yet she had lived four hundred years or more getting there.

"Now do you see? Think on Eleanora, Gavan. Do you wish her to sleep forever? I can give her a century or two, even without glamour to hide her years. I can save her for you!" And Isabella laughed again, her voice rising until it sounded shrill.

"At the cost of her sanity? Her soul? Like yours? And the Leucators you gave to the Dark Hand. Do they feed on them as well, or just use them to harass us? Do you even know or care?"

Isabella waved her hand. Her glamour rose again, concealing her, and she became once again the handsome woman he knew. But now, as if she wore a transparent mask, he could see the truth beneath it, if he tried. The illusion was eerie.

Gavan gathered himself. He put the thought of Eleanora away, for even if Isabella told the truth, and he doubted that, he knew his beloved would never choose to stay alive that way. He would find another answer for Eleanora. But first, he had to get out of here *alive*.

He threw his hands up in summoning. The Lantern spell flared out in a brilliant, crystalline burst even as Isabella moved to counter him. "If I die here, you and your works are going with me," he said grimly.

31

CLEVER IS as CLEVER DOES

JASON'S eyes flew open. He sucked down a deep breath feeling as if he had been drowning. For a moment, he thought he really *had* been as something very wet and sloppy slid off his face and plopped onto his chest as he sat up. The sodden rag looked (and smelled) as though it had lately been part of one of Stef's T-shirts. Jason held it up and off to the side, puzzled. Water ran off it into a little puddle.

"Young master awakes."

Jason swiveled around. Ting's grandmother sat, a bamboo cane across her knees, watching him, a twinkle in her deep-set eyes as if she saw something that gave her great pleasure. "Grandmother," he smiled. "Am I still dreaming?"

"Do you think so?"

"I don't know." He rubbed the bridge of his nose.

Sunlight glanced off deep blue water and he winced at its brightness even as he yawned. A look at the Iron Mountains told him he was where he remembered, great stone dragon crouched and roaring out of the cliff side. He hadn't done that, the dragon had, as a reminder he supposed of what they had shared and what it expected out of Jason. Warrior or guard. It looked as awesome as the dragon itself. He stood.

"Where is everyone?"

"Rich and the one known as Stefan-cub are off gathering wood, with Trent guiding. Henry, Bailey, and her mother are trading."

"Trading?"

Ting's grandmother inclined her head. That made no sense to Jason, but then he wasn't sure if he were truly awake yet and into that state where anything would make sense.

"And Ting?"

"My granddaughter is making arrangements to return. She brings my things and things of her own. Much work to do here." The wizened Chinese woman looked about.

"Bringing your things?"

Grandmother stood as he did. She planted her feet firmly on either side of the bamboo cane. "I stay. The bones of this earth are powerful, and give me strength."

"That's great!"

She winked at him. "So you say now. When I am done with you, you may not feel the same."

"Ummm . . . why?"

She raised her cane and tapped him on the side of his leg, lightly slapping his calf. "Great power means great discipline. You must learn it inside and out, or the power will use you rather than you it. With what you know comes great responsibility. I will teach you Wu Shu, the martial art of my province, which is more than fighting. It is a discipline for the mind and soul."

"I can use all the help I can get." He stretched gingerly, still feeling sore from the soccer game.

"You will have more help from me than you want," Ting's grandmother promised him. She gave a giggle that reminded him intensely of Ting. "Here. We saved a bit of breakfast for you."

She passed him a speckled brown egg and part of what might have been an apple on a broad green leaf and motioned for him to sit again. He did so. The egg was hard-boiled, so he peeled it and found it chewy and good. The fruit wasn't quite an apple. It reminded him how near and far from home they were. He chased it down with a few swallows of water. She watched him intensely, then leaped to her feet. The gold threads in her black silken outfit glittered. "Now. I am Madame Qi Zhang. You will call me Master Qi."

He bowed back. "Pleased to know your name, Ting's grandmother."

That mischievous grin flashed. "So we hope."

He remembered his dreams. Without more than a touch of thought in introduction, she'd appeared to him. Very soon, he thanked his soccer coaches for making him run circuits all day long, for she had him trotting about the valley of Haven till the breath knotted in hot little pinches in his lungs and he staggered to a stop, hands on his knees. Madame Qi would give him five breaths, before stamping her cane, and he'd bolt off again feeling like a skittish thoroughbred colt in its pasture. When she'd run his legs off, she made him stand and just center himself.

With legs like rubber, he wondered that he could stand at all. She spoke to him as he stood, with a voice barely audible, until it was as much a part of him as the racing pulse that slowly calmed to where it should and then quieted even more. He could feel the blood river inside him, cleansing and feeding his body from within, and Qi's words helped him look inside to see that. He stood so long he felt as if he were part of the Iron Mountains itself: tall, still, quiet, and strong.

It was sometime in that moment when he felt the bones of the earth, as Qi called them, the natural power of merely being that sank deep into this corner of the world. Sank deep and strong, yes, and allowed him to touch and draw from it. He opened his eyes then, to see Qi sitting on the grass watching him yet again. The sun slanted steeply across the sky.

She smiled, deepening the many lines in her face. "You are a good student."

"You are a masterful teacher."

She winked. "Ready for more?"

"I . . . think so."

"Good." She tapped her cane and stood. "Show me."

Jason took a deep breath, then let his mind drop his body into a nimbleness he didn't know he had, somersaulted and tumbled his way across the grass with such speed and vigor he couldn't stop himself in time and bowled into the small Chinese elder. She wobbled a bit and paled, then caught herself.

"Master Qi!"

She held her hand up. "I will be fine. It is true that this old body would prefer not to be an acrobat. Yours, however, should not argue with you."

Jason readied himself. "Tell me and I'll do it."

He was limper than a noodle when she finished and let him fall to the grass. She stood over him.

"Tomorrow," she promised, "you will do better."

Jason managed a groan.

The valley filled with voices.

"Jason! Jason, you're awake!"

He got up on one elbow to see Bailey racing toward him. He threw his hand up. "Don't touch me. I hurt all over."

"And you smell all over, too." She came to a stop, ponytail bouncing, and wrinkled her nose.

"That is good all-American sweat." He straightened. "I think Ting's grandmother used to build pyramids in a former life." He stretched carefully, muscles aching where he didn't know he had muscles. Even his toes hurt.

Madame Qi smiled. "This one has enough strength left to complain. Tomorrow I should work him harder." She giggled before ducking her head and retreating back to the canopy which seemed to be their camp. After a few strong steps, her body seemed to cave and she leaned heavily on her cane, as Rebecca came to her aid and helped her.

"I missed a lot. What's going on? And what did she mean when she told me you were trading?"

Bailey shrugged a large sack from off her shoulder. "Trading." She opened her sack. "We're not alone."

That hit him harder than anything Qi had instructed him in. He felt it like a kick to his gut. "What?"

"We're not alone. I haven't actually seen anyone yet, but we've been trading things back and forth. I've gotten blankets, food, and these tunic things . . ." She pulled a shirt-tunic out of her sack. "Maps."

"Let me see that!"

She pulled out a scroll. The paper looked like papyrus of some sort. He unrolled it carefully.

He'd unlocked the Gate to a world. Not just a corner, a small haven, a tiny place where they could be safe, but a world. His breath stuck in his throat for a moment. Why hadn't the dragon told him?

Or had that world existed only from the moment he unlocked the Gate? Numbly, he handed the scroll back to her.

"We can't stay here."

"Why not? I think it's cool other people are here. Otherwise this would be like, what, I dunno . . . *Gilligan's Island* or something."

Henry caught up to the two of them, dragging a much larger bundle. He dropped it. "This is supposed to be a tent or something if we can put it together. Bailey tell you?"

"Some of it. See anyone at all?"

"Nothing but squirrels and birds and a few skittery things in the bushes, but those tunics look like they'll fit most of us." He scratched his chest, and Jason realized Henry had no shirt. "Where is your shirt?"

Henry thumbed at the canopy hanging across several tree branches. "Same place the other guys' shirts are. And I, for one, will be glad to be wearing something." He took the tunic Bailey was waving about and shrugged into it.

She hid the look on her face a moment. Henry combed his fingers through his hair. "All right, I look like a refugee from a Renaissance Faire, but it's warm and clean." He glanced at Jason. "And you smell like you've been wrestling in a mud pit."

"That good, huh?"

"I think even Stef would be offended."

"Thanks. I think." He took a tunic Bailey pushed at him. Before the day got any cooler, he'd better go for a swim.

"I'll sit as lookout," offered Henry. "And then, I want to go home, Jason."

Jason peeled down to his jockeys. He threw himself into the pond, knowing it would be nearly ice cold, and it was. He came up gasping, and scrubbing at himself. The cleaner, the sooner, the better. "Home," he repeated then, as he sank back to his chin for a soak. "Are you sure?"

"Everyone got to say good-bye but me. They've gotta be awful worried."

"Time is different here."

"Not different enough."

"Are you coming back?"

Henry's mouth worked back and forth a bit. "I can bring some food and supplies back. I'm not sure if I should come back and stay, though."

Jason ducked under, and washed his head as thoroughly as he could with only water. He came back

up, spitting. Finally he climbed out and got his jeans
back on and the tunic that Bailey had given him,
roughly cut and sewn but of a soft, blue-green fabric.
He scrubbed his socks out and then trudged back to
the campsite with Henry. "You're one of us. You've
always been one of us."

"Oh, it's not that!" Henry shook his head vigorously, sending his glasses sliding down his nose. He
caught them before they did a ski jump off his face.
"It's just that—"

Whatever it was he was going to say got interrupted by the other boys sliding into camp. Actually,
it was Trent who slid, chin down, for he had been
riding Stef-cub rodeo style and lost his grip just as
they came around the corner. Rich staggered after
them laughing so hard he had to hold his ribs, as
Stef-cub let out a growling bawl, sat back, and
grunted in satisfaction. A ripple and Stefan sat there,
grinning ear to ear.

Bailey wrinkled her nose. Silently, she pointed at
the pond. All three turned around and trudged back.

Jason hung his socks over a tree branch. With any
luck, they'd be dry by midday tomorrow. In the
meantime, he'd have to suffer cold feet or wear his
shoes without, and for right now, with a fire going,
he could do without either. He sat down. "Mrs. Landau, whatever that is you're cooking, it smells great."

"It's stew. Hopefully, it'll be edible although how
we're going to eat it, I'm not sure. Bailey traded for
a pot, but we've no dishes or utensils."

"There's always fingers."

"I suppose. Feeling better?"

"I was." He grinned. Madame Qi looked to be napping under the canopy although with the others just roaring through, he doubted she actually slept. "I have a new Master and she is tough."

"Sometimes that's what you need."

"And sometimes you need all the help you can get." Jason lapsed into silence and heavy thoughts until everyone had returned. Then he looked up. "You all felt it. Even Ting felt it. Madame Qi here said she felt it, and insisted Ting bring her."

Rich nodded. Stef rubbed his nose which looked as if it had been bee stung and it probably had.

"Then why aren't any of the elders here? This is what we were all aiming for, and it's happened . . . and no one's here. Unless one of you has heard, and I don't know?" Jason looked from face to face. Each of them shook his or her head slightly.

"Not a nudge, nothing?" He felt stunned. How could Gavan and the others not know or care? After all he'd gone through. Up until that moment, he'd assumed they'd looked in while he recovered, and made plans to return.

Qi opened one eye. "Clever boys, but not clever enough." She swung the tip of her cane about, indicating the area. "It is blocked. Use your senses. Nothing in, nothing out."

"But Ting felt it . . ."

"Ting is one of us," Bailey protested. "We're like sisters, always connected."

"It's never been able to block before." Jason frowned. Trent traded a look with him before surveying the surrounding valley and mountains. Then he nodded in confirmation.

"You're the Gatekeeper here, Jason. That's your

magic, all about, except for a tiny sliver of an opening, more like a contact . . ." Trent hesitated, then
looked at Henry.

Henry lost all color and bolted to his feet. "I told
you I was bad luck! I shouldn't even be here!" He
cupped his gemstone with a citrine flare of heat
and power.

He was going. Or he was trying, but Jason could
feel him bouncing against the walls that *he'd* set up.
Only Henry couldn't stop himself. In a dead panic,
he flung himself against the blockade a second time,
and Jason knew he had to let Henry go through or
his friend would kill himself trying.

He let the Gate swing, and Squibb disappeared in
a brilliant golden flash.

32

RIGHT PLACE,
WRONG TIME

HE SHOULDN'T even be here, Gavan thought, as he turned away another attack, a trickle of sweat sliding down his temple and his arm trembling slightly. His beam flared and spit, spinning Isabella away with a sharp cry. She recovered and bared her teeth to face him. He retreated again, his back coming up against the cave wall. His left arm hung all but useless, flesh ripped from a Leucator attack, and worse, chilled to the bone. The cold made it useless. Even the blood that slowly dripped to the floor seemed barely thawed enough to ooze from the wound.

He could not Crystal unless he dropped the remnants of his Shield, but that Shield was all that kept the three Leucators from falling on him. They moaned at the smell of his blood and pain and hung

322

at the edges of their Maker's skirts, waiting for an opportunity to lunge. Isabella's eyes shone with a fierce triumph as she closed in on him.

The only thing he could do was Call, and so he sent it out, knowing that few if any could hear or would answer. FireAnn would not answer, being held to her promise to stay with Eleanora, and he did not even know how powerful a Call for help he could project.

He had one last resort. He could step into his crystal, imprisoning himself. Isabella would not be able to destroy him but neither would she probably ever allow his crystal to see the light of day again with any hope that another Magicker might be able to free him. Eventually, inside the gem, he would go crazy or die.

"One last offer," Isabella said. "Save yourself and the fair Eleanora, too."

"My opinion of you has not changed in the past few hours."

"I am wounded." Isabella allowed herself a bitter smile. "I offer you my wisdom, Gavan. I struggled for decades for it, while the two of you slept like babes, unworried, unknowing. I can't give her back the time she's lost, but I can show her how to seize another century or two. Living is sweet compared to the alternative."

"It doesn't appear to have sweetened you."

She gestured and tried his Shield again. It shuddered but held.

Gavan dug deep for more stamina and taunted her a bit more. "Backing Gregory against Brennard would have avoided all of this."

She made another noise of disdain. "Two men in a pissing contest. What else could be expected but that they would destroy everything for the rest of us. Stubborn and combative. And you, my dear boy, are showing the same traits." She lashed out, her power shoving his.

He stumbled. He fell on one knee, and a sharp pain went through it as he did. He glanced down to see a rock piercing his skin, nailed into his kneecap. That was going to hurt even worse later.

Gavan expanded his Shield to protect his suddenly open and vulnerable back. A Leucator hit him from the flanks, hard, and bounced off, but Gavan felt it, deep in every bone as the tackle rattled his teeth and knew, Shield or not, he was about done for.

He could retreat into his crystal or he could explode it. Exploding it might take out most of this cavern and the horrid things that resided within it. It wouldn't touch Isabella, for she had her own Shielding up although most of her energy was aimed at the offensive, at him. He hadn't much of a choice left.

A howling arose. It started thinly, at the edge of his nerves, and he struggled to stand. He made his mind up what he would do, and began to marshal the last of his energies to accomplish it. The keening grew. It came from without the caverns, and Gavan paused. He knew that sound.

Isabella dropped the hem of her gown, turning slightly. Then she let out a string of curses that would make a French stevedore blush. Perhaps even a cabbie. Gavan managed to get his back to the wall

again, even as a wind swirled inside the cave and
the lanterns in the sconces flickered wildly. Chaos
flooded in, with the beasts that always rode it.

Wolfjackals. Drawn by their duel and the Magick
unleashed, the beasts would tear them both apart.
Gavan did not know if he welcomed the distraction
or had simply attracted a new way to die. He dug
his heels in as the pack came in, snarling and slaver-
ing, and going after the Leucators with savage teeth.

Gavan braced himself for the new battle, then
looked up and saw in surprise that Tomaz Crowfeather was riding the lead beast. Tomaz raised one
palm, and a clear, blue light from the many turquoise
stones on his wrist cut the air. Isabella turned and
ran.

At the threshold of the great cavern, Isabella
halted. She let out a series of sharp, arcane words,
and the shackles on the Leucators shattered. They
shook themselves free of the chains with a low groan
of eagerness that grew louder and louder. In a great
swirl of colorful satin, the Magicker turned and fled,
her Leucators in her wake, crying her name as if she
promised them life. Only the one he knew as Eleanora hesitated, turning back for one last, longing look
at him, before fleeing the caves as the wolfjackals
went after them. Amid snarls of attack and hideous
screams of the unfortunate few caught behind,
Tomaz dismounted and caught Gavan up.

Rainwater nearly fainted as Tomaz took his arm
and tucked it inside his shirt, before lifting him onto
the back of a wolfjackal. The creature turned its head,
hot drool falling from its gleaming fangs, but allowed

Gavan to remain. Gavan knotted his hand in the thick-furred ruff, wondering how he was going to manage to stay on.

"Where in hell did you come from?" He looked at his friend.

Tomaz grinned. "I always wanted to be the cavalry come to the rescue." He swung up on the pack leader. "Let's get you out of here, and then we have much to explain to each other."

Henry landed in his kitchen. He immediately sank to the floor with a sob of relief and happiness at being home, his gemstone dropping from his hand. It rolled around and then lost its faint glow, and came to a stop against his leg. He picked it up and pocketed it, sighing. *Never drop your crystal.*

He looked about. The big family-style kitchen lay swathed in darkness. It must be the middle of the night. What night, he wasn't sure. A day or two or three after they'd left. Hopefully not longer. The trouble with Crystaling is that he was never quite sure when he was coming or going.

He never wanted to go back to Haven, but he knew he had to, if only long enough to drop off what supplies he could. The Squibb family believed in being prepared and the garage had boxes of powdered and freeze-dried foodstuffs against earthquakes or whatever other disasters might hit. His mom would go through once a year and donate the older stuff to the homeless shelter and restock, so he'd just be saving her that job. Not that freeze-dried beef stroganoff was the best stuff in the world, but it was better than stir-fried grass and onions. At least, he thought that's what Ting's grandmother had been cooking when he'd left.

He scrubbed away a tear with the heel of his hand. He couldn't be around any of them for long, he was too dangerous to them. He didn't know how or what was happening to him, but he feared that anything he could and did do might betray them. Henry vowed he'd never let that happen, even if he had to give up Magick again. Where he would go or what he would do, he didn't know. He had no idea what he wanted to tell his mom. So he'd get the supplies together, and while he did that, he'd think of something. Surely.

Gathering himself, he made his way out to the garage, fumbling here and there a bit, not wanting to snap on a light or even use his crystal. He found the mesh booty bags they used in camping and the cardboard boxes of supplies. The stainless steel storage unit held the newer cartons to the left, so all he had to do was go down to the right and pull a carton open. He gave up and cast a small Lantern spell on his crystal and set it on the top shelf where it glowed like a tiny harvest moon so that he could see what he was doing. He shoveled the packets into the bag as his eyes adjusted and nearly had the sack full when the side door creaked open farther.

He froze, spotlighted by the glow from his gemstone, as someone hesitated in the doorway.

"Henry?"

"Mom!" Caught, but he almost didn't care.

She rushed to him and gave him a great hug, her comfortable chenille robe surrounding him. She made one of those noises that mothers make when they're very very happy and trying not to cry and scare you because of it, and held him tightly.

"I'm sorry, Mom, I'm sorry, I didn't want you to worry."

She kissed the top of his head. "I wasn't too worried." She took a deep breath and made a little sniffling noise. "Joanna McIntire called me. I don't understand what's going on."

"Me neither," he said with heartfelt truthfulness. "And even if I did, I'm not sure how much I could tell you."

She held him away then, and searched his face. "But it's nothing bad?"

"I don't think it is. I mean, we don't mean it to be. It's not gangs or drugs or anything like that."

She glanced at the bulging mesh bag lying on the floor. "Are you leaving again?"

"I think so."

"Come into the kitchen and talk with me a moment or two." Her gaze rested then on the glowing crystal. She didn't say anything but led the way back into the house. He had to grab his crystal and drag the heavy bag back behind him.

"Is Dad awake?" he asked, as she fixed him an English muffin with peanut butter and jam.

"Your father could sleep through anything." She sat down on a breakfast chair and folded her hands on her lap. "I want you to know we love and trust you."

That made his eyes smart. He didn't deserve it, especially not with the battle he was having with himself. Henry shook his head. "I'm just trying my best, Mom."

She nodded. "But you can't tell me what's happening?"

"Can't. I want to, but . . ."

She put her hand out, smoothing his hair away from his forehead. "Does this have anything to do with summer camp, Henry?" She took his crystal from his hand gently, examining it. "And your powers?"

"Mom!"

She gave the crystal back. "Unlike your father, you are a restless sleeper. And you talk in your sleep." She touched his cheek lightly. "I couldn't help but listen, you were so sick with poison oak when you came home, but more than that, you were so unhappy. You'd lost your abilities, your talents, that you'd been so proud of."

"You never said anything to me!" He stared at her.

"And you never said anything to me."

"I couldn't! There's this Vow of Silence, you see, and it just locks you up, keeps everything bottled in, and then I had this drink to make me forget everything cause they had to send me away, but it didn't work right, and then I started remembering, and then the Magick came back and—" He plowed to an astonished halt. "And I shouldn't be able to tell you now."

"Maybe it's one of those protective things, that only works when there's danger." She laced her fingers together, watching him.

"Maybe." He rubbed his citrine. "Something happened and we had to run."

"Bailey? Jason? You? And the others?"

He nodded.

"Where can you go?"

"We're back at the camp, sorta. The trouble is . . ." He didn't quite know how to tell her. Henry stared down at the kitchen floor a moment.

"The world never understands people who are different."

He looked up. "Did I ever tell you I think you're the best mom in the whole world?"

She smiled slightly. "Yes, you did!" She held her arms out. He hugged her again. Her voice fell to a near whisper. "I'm very proud of you, Henry Squibb, and don't you ever forget that! Take whatever you need, and come and go as often as you can." She let go of him then. "Maybe someday you can tell everyone who and what you are."

"I don't know if that will ever happen."

"When it does, you be the first ambassador. Now, it looks like you have breakfast, lunch, and dinner to deliver!"

He rubbed his crystal. "Watch this," he said with pride as he took hold of the booty bag and disappeared from her sight.

Through the *between*, Henry searched for Jason. *Please, please, please, let me back.* He had to tell them what he could, and help however he could. It was the only way he'd ever be proud of himself, no matter what they thought, or his mom thought. He held to the hope that the tiny swing in the Gate Jason had given for him might yet be there. He searched so intently, he never felt the tiny nibble at the back of his mind.

Ah, there you are, my little Squibb. Where have you

been and what have you been doing, and where are you going?

He never felt a thing as Jonnard sifted through his mind and then sat back with a gloating laugh as, for the first time, he saw all and knew all that Henry did. Henry, in his eagerness to Crystal, had left his mind totally open. Even the delicious moments of stealing his Magick had never peeled the boy's thoughts open like a ripe fruit. And now, Jon knew all he could ever wish. He let Henry slip through, felt him bursting through the Dragon Gate into Haven, even as he stood with a triumphant yell for his father.

33

BATTLE STATIONS

TRENT eyed Jason. "You're taller than I am."

"I'm what? When did that happen?" Jason looked himself over.

"I have no idea. I think it happened overnight . . . about the same time that tunic last fit you." Trent jabbed a thumb at him.

Jason tugged on his tunic. It did, indeed, hang shorter and feel a lot tighter around the shoulders than he remembered which was sometime yesterday when he'd gotten it. His chin itched. He scratched it with one finger thoughtfully. He would have thought more of it if they had been anywhere but where they were. Rich and Trent were already tired of Haven, with little to do but try and set traps for Bailey's sight unseen trader friend: "Don't worry, it's capture and release," they told her when she found out and got upset. They'd tied Stef's sneakers to the top of the highest tree they could find, but the bear cub had merely scaled it and knocked them down. They'd hidden Madame Qi's cane at least three times but given it up when she had placidly opened her hand and called it back to her each time. Jason was of the opinion they would have tried something on Rebecca Landau, too, but as she seemed to be doing most of the cooking, they'd changed their minds. It had only been a few days and they were itching to explore.

Still, idle hands and minds . . . Jason came to the conclusion that it was obviously his turn. "I'm not falling for this," he said to Trent.

Trent widened his eyes innocently. "Falling for what?"

"Whatever."

"Okay, we'll call Miss Bundle of Enthusiasm herself over. Bailey! C'mere."

She looked up and wrinkled her nose before trotting over curiously. "What are you two up to?"

"Me, nothing. Trent here is trying to—" He never got a chance to finish.

"Jason!" Bailey let out a squeal. "You've got chin hairs." She stared at his face in fascination.

"Okay, now I'm P.O.'d. Taller than me with chin hairs." Trent squinted at him.

"Cut it out, you two!" Jason tried to yank his tunic into place about his body.

Trent put his hand on Jason's shoulder. "I'm not kidding, bud." He looked at Jason closely.

Bailey crossed her heart. Well, actually, it was Lacey she crossed who grumbled sleepily in her pocket as the gesture disturbed her. The little pack rat kicked about and bumped around a bit before resettling. Bailey tilted her face to look up at him. She wrinkled her nose again. "And taller."

"He is, isn't he? Am I right, or am I right?"

"You're right. The question is: why?"

"We're guys. We have these spurts of growth."

She shook her head. "Not in just a few days. And if we were all doing that, well, we'd all be taller or something. But we're not. Just you, Jason." She looked a bit worried.

"You're aging." Trent glanced at him.

"I don't feel older."

"I don't think Eleanora does either," said Trent quietly.

The impact of his words hit both Jason and Bailey. She paled. "From . . . the Magick?"

"Probably. His aging doesn't seem to be as drastic as Eleanora's, but still." Trent swallowed. "This can't be good."

He didn't feel different. His shoes were cramped and his tunic too small, and his chin scratchy, but he really didn't feel different. He walked over to the pond and looked down at its glassy surface. He didn't look more mature to his eyes, but the water didn't give him that clear a picture back. "It is what it is," he said, finally. He touched the image as if reassuring himself of what he saw.

Something rippled across the water as he touched it. Looking into it, he saw a pack of wolfjackals in the sky, circling, coming closer, riding a storm of black chaos as they always did. He looked back over his shoulder. Nothing behind him. The sky seemed a clear blue and undisturbed. Yet, as he stared back into the water, the vision became more and more distinct. To his surprise, the wolfjackals bore riders. At first, he saw Tomaz and Gavan. Then, as the water rippled, he saw Jonnard and Brennard and others. He rubbed his eyes. Who came? What was he seeing?

"What is it?"

"The water," he murmured, thinking.

Bailey leaned over. "Water mirrors are for prophecies."

"So?" Trent nudged her.

"So, Jason is a Gatekeeper."

They jostled each other, Jason barely aware of their bantering.

"You've got a peephole in your apartment door, right?"

Bailey eyed him suspiciously before nodding.

"All right then. This is Jason's peephole through the Gates." Trent jabbed his thumb at the deep blue water.

"You think so?"

Jason heard that last. He wondered himself. But a pounding inside his ears like the rolling thunder of a faraway storm told him he wouldn't have long to think about it.

"Get ready," he warned.

"What's wrong?"

He didn't have time to explain. He stood and yelled, his voice ringing over the small valley. "Get ready!" His crystal flared.

If they were going to attack, it would be on his terms. The vision of Tomaz and Gavan shimmered across the lake again. They looked caught, trapped within the maelstrom of chaos. The wolfjackals ran raggedly, their jaws dripping with foam from exhaustion. Did the creatures bear Tomaz and Gavan willingly? Possibly. If so, from what did they run? And why did the storm hold them against their will? If he blinked, he saw the Dark Hand commanding wolfjackals. They rode as warriors, bearing down on him, teeth bared. Who came after them? He wanted the true Seeing, and knew he would have to make a decision. He reached into the water and shook an image free. Power raged up his arm as he did.

They burst out of the lake. Water spewed up in great, foamy waves carrying the intruders on them. Wolfjackals heaved themselves onto the bank, their heated bodies steaming off the water, Tomaz clinging to the massive leader and Gavan trying in vain to hold to the second with one arm. He fell to the shore at the beast's second leap onto solid ground, three or four pack-mates on its heels.

"Thank the gods," Gavan said weakly, and closed his eyes.

Tomaz threw his leg over and landed lightly. Before anyone but Jason could react, he had Gavan up on his feet and one arm over his shoulder.

Wearily, Jason lowered his crystal to watch the wolfjackals circle. He waited for the familiar throb from his scar, but it stayed flat and cool. No menace came from them, this time.

"Good instincts, Jason," Tomaz said to him. "Let them go. They were as trapped in that burst of Chaos as we were."

In the wink of an eye, he opened a Gate and tossed them through, their howls of joy echoing back before the sound cut off abruptly, and it was as if the wolf-jackals had never come to Haven.

"You're bloodied," Jason said to Tomaz.

"Been in a fight, and a fire would be good." He nodded to Jason.

Later, Gavan would say, "I'd have been here sooner, lad, but I was a bit busy."

"Hold still," Rich muttered. He dabbed on some more peroxide and began wrapping gauze again. Gavan gave him a bemused look. "It'll scar," Rich told him, "but it's mostly just surface damage. You didn't bleed out much either, from the looks of it."

"Good news and bad news, aye?" He flexed his arm gingerly when Rich finished. "A handy kit you carry about."

"Won't do much if anyone gets really thrashed, but it's good for a cut or sprain." He clipped it back onto his belt.

"You've a talent there."

"Thanks. I mostly thought my Talent consisted of bear herding."

Stef snorted and dropped a load of deadwood onto the ground. He ignored everyone as he carefully fed another log into the fire. Gavan had finally warmed judging by the color in his cheeks, but he still leaned close to the flames.

Tomaz squatted across from them. He looked tired and worn, himself. His jeans sagged a bit about his body, and his bracelets seemed loose when he moved, as if he'd lost weight running with the wolfjackals. He'd said little about them, only that they were torn from Chaos and sought it to go back where they belonged. Jason had the feeling that there were volumes to be learned from the shaman but nothing he wished to tell at the moment. It was surprising enough to know that the wolfjackals could be entrapped by Chaos, and it was a near thing that he had freed them all.

Gavan straightened. He gave Jason a look of sheer pride. "You've opened the last Gate, lad. Good job. If Iron Mountain ever gets built, it'll be because of heroic acts like that."

"If? Not when?" Trent drummed his fingers on his knee.

Tomaz said quietly, "There are other matters at hand."

"We're going to be under attack." Everyone looked to Jason.

"Possibly," agreed Gavan slowly. "What makes you say that?"

"When I looked in the pool, I saw wolfjackals. Some bore the two of you . . . others bore the Dark Hand."

Bailey whistled. Rebecca reached out and grabbed her daughter's hand. Madame Qi tightened her grip on the cane across her knees. "It is a good thing," she said, "I have been able to teach Jason a few things."

"Very good," Gavan said to her. "As for what detained me . . ." He took a deep breath, wincing as if it pained him. In slow, halting words, he told them of the caves and the Leucators. "We've got to rally what's left of the Council, and Tomaz and I have to bring in Eleanora. I couldn't get through before."

"I've got it blocked."

"Can you open the Gates, Jason? Open and hold them, till we get Eleanora and FireAnn and what others we can in?"

"Jason won't be alone." Trent stood. A small piece of kindling snapped in his hands.

Gavan gave them a tired, lopsided smile. "From the first, none of you have ever been alone. You've always had each other. You are Magickers, more than we could ever have hoped for." He got to his feet carefully, his right arm tucked against himself like a broken wing. He held Jason's chin with his good hand, and looked into his eyes. "We will be back."

Jason shifted his weight. He said quietly, "I'm waiting for Ting and Henry, too. So I'll swing the Gates open every now and then, looking for you. We'll hold each as best we can."

"The Dark Hand will have tried the moment they felt the wave of the Dragon Gate being opened. Your blocking must have shut them out, as it nearly did me, and as it did Tomaz. I'm guessing they don't know where you're to be found."

"They will." Jason held an intense belief in the danger he'd seen in the lake.

"Then you'll have no choice but to guard the Gates carefully once they're open. When I get the Council in, we'll be able put up permanent wards, with pass runes." Gavan clasped Jason's hand. "Outstanding work, my lad. I can't wait to get Eleanora here."

*   *   *

After they left, it got very quiet. Bailey said, "It's not right without Ting and Henry."

"Ting will be here," Qi told her. "She is on the way now."

"I think Henry will be back, too."

"They'll be here," Jason said with certainty. "But this is what we have to do. There're three Gates in. Iron Gate, Water Gate, Dragon Gate. They'll have to be watched whenever I open them."

"Battle stations," agreed Trent. The Magickers all stood and walked to Jason and they slapped their hands in the air.

Ting tried not to fuss as her mother strapped together the last bundle and loaded it into her backpack. She didn't know how long she'd been gone from Haven, but it had been two days while lawyers drew up papers and made arrangements since Qi Zhang had said she would not be back. Jiao finally looked into Ting's face. "I know, I know," she said in soft answer to the rebellion on Ting's face. "You can go back and forth, but these are things she will need." She paused.

"And when everything is settled, I'll bring you to visit," Ting promised.

"You can do that?"

Ting nodded.

"Then I am content." Her mother held her a moment. "We'll stay here at the house until you can bring the papers back, and we know how she's really feeling. Sometimes, the health is a false promise."

"I know, Mom. We've been over this."

"Have patience with me, Ting. It's hard to lose a mother and a daughter in the same day."

"You won't lose either of us!" Ting promised fervently, and threw her arms around her mother's neck. "Now, I really have to go.

"I will wait," Jiao Chuu told her, and her mother's calm face was the last thing she saw as her crystal took her. She felt Jason's Gate waiting as if just for her, and slipped through quietly.

"It's time, my friend," the stranger said, and tapped lightly on Jerry Landau's car window. Jerry woke with a start. Sleeping again? He stretched, then groaned. He felt as dried out and crusty as an old mummy. How long had he been sitting there, watching the apartment building? He rubbed at his eyes.

"I never saw her," he muttered in disgust.

"It's all right. You should go home and wait. But before you go, I would like something small and insignificant from you to help in our quest."

Jerry looked at the man with a little bit of suspicion. He had little enough of anything to give away, and he thought uneasily that this man had never really been clear why he was at all interested in Bailey or Jerry's difficulties with her. As partnerships go, he hadn't really benefited one way or another. He brushed a paper off his dashboard and tried to straighten a bit in his seat, pins and needles in his legs from hours of not moving.

Antoine Brennard smiled thinly. "Don't worry," he

reassured. "You'll never miss it. Just a touch of your soul." He reached through the half-open car window and ripped it away.

Jerry Landau gasped. He shoved his legs out and went rigid against the driver's seat, his heart pounding, his body stiff as a board, his ears roaring. Heart attack! He had to be having a heart attack.

Brennard pulled his hand back filled with shadow. "Trust me. I can do much better things with this than you can. We'll have your daughter, one way or another." He stepped away from the car. "Now go home and forget." He made a gesture.

Landau's mouth moved open and shut like a fish caught ashore and trying to breathe dry air. Brennard stepped back and into the shadows before Landau could move at all and hurriedly started his car. He burned rubber getting away from the curb as the automobile screeched into motion. Brennard cupped the essence in his hands. A Leucator from this subject might come in very handy indeed.

Henry had forgotten how to breathe. The *between* held him gripped in its jaws and the plane of Crystaling stretched into a long black forever, and he knew he was doomed.

Suddenly, a tiny crick of light fractured across it. With a grateful sob, Henry dove toward it headfirst. The Gate! He'd finally found the Gate! He could feel Jason's presence, warm and welcoming, and clutched at it. Something broke inside of him, and he hurtled through with a grateful yell.

Henry landed on top of Stefan. Both boys let out shouts of surprise, Stef's breaking into the cub's voice as they rolled away from each other. With a bang and a clatter, they woke everyone else.

"Henry!" cried Ting in delight. "You came back!"

His head throbbed and Stef shoved him away with a good-natured grunt, and someone lit a Lantern spell, bathing the campsite in soft light. His booty bag had spilled open and Rich had already grabbed out a foil wrapped package of Rice Krispies treats and broken it open to share.

"Back, with treats," Rich noted.

"And that's not all," said Henry miserably. He dusted himself off. "Jason, Trent, I need to talk to you. If I can." He took a deep breath as they followed him off to a quiet place, and he said, "I've had Jonnard in my head." To his surprise, it came out, and he sobbed in gratitude.

Jason listened quietly as Henry spilled his guts. Trent did as well before putting in, "It isn't your fault. You didn't even know for sure what was going on, and I'm willing to bet he wasn't going to let you tell."

Henry puffed up his cheeks and then let his breath out slowly. "If only there was some way I could make it up." He looked at Jason.

Jason waved a hand. "Actually, I think you just gave us an unexpected advantage."

"I did? How?"

"Okay, Henry. This is what I need you to do. I need you to drain Jonnard."

"Me? But . . ." Squibb took his glasses off and cleaned them deliberately, thinking. "You're not going to just shut me off?"

Jason shook his head. Trent put his hand on Squibb's shoulder and shook him lightly. "Think about it, man. We may have a huge advantage here."

Henry looked at both of them, his round face slightly puzzled. "I've been a mole, and you guys are happy about it?"

"Not really, but . . . like Trent said, think about it. You've held the key all along. You kept muttering, tug-of-war, when Jon drained you. Henry, it *is* just like a tug-of-war. Only, this time, you pull back."

"I pull back."

"That's the plan."

Realization hit him. Henry put his glasses back on and pushed them into place. "How hard?"

"As hard as you can. Incapacitate him."

"I can do that?" Without waiting for an answer, he inclined his chin. "Of course I can. It goes both ways." Henry gave a delighted grin.

"It's not going to be quite that easy," Jason warned him. "We don't want Jon to know what you can do. You have to be light and quick about it."

Trent nodded vigorously. "No bull in a china shop," he added. "Got that?"

"I can do it." Henry's grin widened even more. "This is going to be fun."

"This is going to be dangerous."

"Oh, I know that. But it's still going to be fun. When do I do this?"

"Now," Jason told him. "Tomorrow may be too late."

"All right. It may be a long night."

"Not as long as it will be tomorrow."

Henry squinted up at him. "Did you get taller?"

"You think?"

Despite the pain in his arm, Gavan felt more alive and full of hope than he had in weeks, as Tomaz brought him to Ravenwyng. His feet touched the ground, and he could feel the spring air with the promise of summer on his face. He forced himself to think of unpleasant things, even though his heart sang with the hope he could bring to Eleanora at last.

"We'll have to deal with Isabella. Strip her of her powers forcibly, if need be, and then neutralize every one of the Leucators."

"That will take time but we shall get it done," agreed Tomaz. "Do you think there is any possibility at all Eleanora could be helped by that?"

"I think," Gavan said firmly, "she is being killed by it. As was Fizziwig and who knows who else? Isabella has to be stopped."

"Then that we will do." Tomaz paused. He stopped at the edge of the Gathering Hall building. "Did you not say you left the camp warded?"

"I did . . ." Gavan stepped around him. A haze of smoke and stench of burning hung like a fog. "Gods, no!" He broke into a shambling run for FireAnn's cottage, Tomaz on his heels. The front door lay in splinters. Inside, the smell of crushed herbs filled the air where they'd been trampled. The inside of the cottage looked thrashed as if a hurricane had hit it. It stood empty of all life. Gavan dropped into a squat by the empty bed where Eleanora had lain. He put a hand on the cold covers. He stared up at Tomaz helplessly.

"FireAnn didn't let her go easily."

"No." Gavan scrubbed the heel of his hand across his eyes. "What do they want of her?"

A shadow in the corner of the cottage shuddered and undulated and Brennard stepped out. His Shield of deep obsidian sparkled about him, carrying the shadow with him as he moved.

"Tell your boy to open the Gates and keep them open. If you want Eleanora alive. Otherwise, I shall leave her in Isabella's untender care."

"And FireAnn."

"And the redhead as well." Brennard waved his hand. "We will take Haven."

Gavan got to his feet. "And if I say no?"

Brennard crossed the cottage. With a word, he reduced the wall to rubble, and through its broken framework, they could see a convoy forming. Gavan managed a breath in spite of the emotion gripping his chest. He rubbed the head of his cane, and Tomaz's thoughts sprang into his own.

Let them pass. We will gather those we can and follow.

"Rainwater," said Brennard impatiently. "Get us passage."

"You shall have it," Gavan said, his voice dull, even though his mind churned with thoughts, and plans. "The boy is a Gatekeeper. I can ask him to open the Gates. I cannot keep him from defending them."

"I'll deal with him then."

"Leave Eleanora!"

"You'll have the two once we're safely across the

borders. Don't do anything, Gavan, that you will regret later."

Too late, he thought. He'd already brushed Jason's mind and told him to throw the Gates open and why, and what he and Tomaz planned to do.

He wondered if he'd put too much on Jason's shoulders, boy, not quite man.

He had no choice.

GUARDS AND WARRIORS

"REMEMBER," whispered Qi's voice inside his ear. "Wu Shu is an inner defense as well as an outer. Even more true for one such as yourself with the power. The enemy will press you on both fronts, but you will succeed." Ting's grandmother sounded confident and proud.

Jason drew himself together with those thoughts ringing through his mind. He knew he'd grown in just these few days, for the mysterious aging factor had only matured him, not weakened him. Not yet. Even more importantly, although he looked very much alone, he was not. Locked inside were the strengths of every Magicker he had ever touched, and every friend he'd ever shared with. The only thing he doubted was if his own strength would be enough, but it wouldn't be because he hadn't tried.

The corner of his mouth crooked up a little. He wondered what kind of brownie points against the Dark Hand he'd get for just trying.

He shifted his weight on the rock outcropping. From where he stood, he could see the four corners of this tiny pocket of Haven, which he'd once thought was the entire face of it. Now Jason knew better. A wind came through the valley, faint and clear, playing against his face and carrying the scent of spring on it, of green grass, a hint of faraway rain, and blossoms he had no names for because they were of Haven and no place he had ever been to before. After this was all over, he made a note, he'd ask FireAnn about some of those herbs and flowers. Or maybe he and Bailey could go on a walking tour.

He wondered about what the dragon had hinted at. As he fought here, when the battle came to him, would it be reflected elsewhere? Were all great battles in his world and Haven ripples of battles somewhere or somewhen else? And did the battles they started on their own create ripples that in turn carried grief and strife? Somehow he had always thought when war came to him, he'd be wearing a uniform and carrying a weapon of another sort, rather than a Chinese grandmother's cane.

Jason ran his hands over it. "Good, Chinese bamboo," Qi had said. "Nothing harder, not even a stubborn boy's skull." He wasn't sure what he'd do with it, other than what she'd shown him. His version of Wu Shu would have moves in it no master could have envisioned.

A trembling came on the wind. He felt it, more than heard it. Magic was even harder to define or see than the wind that carried it, but it pricked at his nerves. A storm rode the wind now. Jason swallowed. He was as ready as he could ever be, he hoped. He was to keep the Gates open, yet hold them here while Gavan and Tomaz gathered their allies and came from the rear. He was to let them in, but not to let them pass.

Or, as Bailey put it, "We're the cork in the bottle," which made sense in a Bailey sort of way. Jason hadn't thought to ask her whether the Dark Hand was breaking out of, or into, that bottle. He wasn't sure he really wanted to know. All that mattered was that he stood there, his face tilted to the wind, trying to catch the first glimpse of the attack.

He heard it first. Borne on the wind came an eerie howling that he knew all too well, the battle song of the wolfjackal. He shaded his eyes as the horizon darkened with clouds of storm gray and the wolflike beasts seemed to rip the very sky apart with their flashing teeth as they raced toward him. The back of his left hand twitched in pain from the long-ago scar, and he rubbed it slightly to distract himself. From Chaos itself, the wolfjackals seemed to obey no rule of time or space as they raced across the building clouds, descending to earth only when they drew near. That did not surprise him.

What immobilized him for a long moment was the sight of riders upon their shaggy backs. To see the Dark Hand mounted shot defiance into his heart. The dark powers would feed upon each other, making both more powerful than they would have been alone! Tomaz must have known this, even as Jason could sense it. Had he betrayed them to the Dark

Hand as well, as Henry had, as Isabella had, some in lesser ways, others in far greater? Had he shown them this fact unwillingly or willingly? Dare he trust Tomaz now, at Gavan's side, planning a rescue?

Jason narrowed his eyes after one fierce blink to chase away a bitter tear. He had no way of knowing and no time to guess. *I know what I know. Doubt brings weakness, and is the way of the enemy.* Tomaz had never failed him before. He would not believe the Magicker had failed him now!

He placed both hands on his bamboo cane once more and centered his thoughts. The crystal pendant at his throat answered with a flare of warmth. Strengthened by his exercises, he no longer had to cup it for Focusing. It answered him by sheer thought and will with a beacon of light that enveloped him in a luminous glow that muffled the ever sharper howling. The bamboo seemed to mold to his grip on it as he eyed the wolfjackal riders.

Jonnard moved to the fore, brandishing a black sword. Behind him rode Brennard and two of the Dark Hand he had seen before but whose names he'd never known or he'd forgotten, young men, pale, angry, wearing long duster coats straight out of the *Matrix* movies, and the fifth rider of the Hand was a Leucator of himself. Jason inhaled deeply, his breath hissing through his teeth. Isabella had always thought herself so clever.

The galloping wolfjackals covered leagues of ground in bare minutes, coming toward him at a dead run. He could hear their hot breath between howls and snarls and the sound of the men riding them urging them after him. Jason stood on high ground, but that wouldn't protect him, and he bent his knees slightly for the force of the first physical attack even as he readied for the mental unleashing of power they would send against him.

The glow of his Shield took on a rainbow-edged hue as Ting and Bailey and Rich and Stef bent their own powers through the clever gemstone pendant Ting had fashioned. They were out of his sight, in strategic corners of the green vale, protecting the other Gates, like him, trying to hold an invisible line. Like linking hands, Ting had said hopefully, and he could feel it now as if they did and prayed it would continue to hold the bond she'd forged for him. Only Henry did not filter through his crystal for obvious reasons. Trent, for less obvious.

The wolfjackals and riders leaped up below him. He moved, raining tiny pebbles and sand downward, and scarcely felt the first stings of power they sent against him. His Shield made tiny spits as it repelled each attempt to touch him. He felt as though he wore a great suit of armor and they could not touch him. If only it would last!

The Leucator dropped to the rear of the pack, watching him with eyes that would have looked like his own, but they were flat with the lack of expression. Dead eyes, Bailey would say. Something odd caught his attention as the Leucator raised his hand to guide his surly wolfjackal into submission but exactly what it was escaped him.

Jonnard stretched upward on his wolfjackal mount. "Give us passage."

"The Gates were open. That is all we promised." His voice sounded braver than he felt.

"We don't need promises to take what we can take." Jonnard threw his hands up, lightning shivering between them. Jason reeled back, as he threw his hands up in response, barely holding onto his cane.

He let his Magick talk for him. He swung around, aiming his gaze at one of the dark riders he barely knew, and the power swung with him and shot out with a sizzle. A wolfjackal dodged with a yelp and snarl, nearly unseating its rider. The smell of burned dirt filled his nostrils.

He brought his attention back to Jon and Brennard. Brennard cuffed his wolfjackal to a crouching standstill. "So," he noted. "The boy becomes a man."

"Not man enough." Jon spit out a curse and gestured. Jason's feet went out from under him as the earth moved, tossing him, and he landed, rolling, on the sharp rocks. He came up on his knees and catapulted into a back flip, courtesy of Qi's teaching, twisting his body into balance as he did, settling firmly onto his feet.

The look of satisfaction on Jonnard's face bled away.

A rumble like thunder cut through the stormy sky and Jason looked up toward it. None of the Dark Hand did, and that meant they expected it. He frowned. Out of the depths of dark clouds great forms rolled forward and then halted, waiting.

Huge wagons with black canvas tarps over them appeared, with hooded drivers, their dull brown draft horses stamping on the dirt restlessly, the fittings on their harnesses jingling like bells. He could not imagine what they carried but was afraid they would all find it before this fight was over. Behind them, he could see human figures, also waiting. An army. Brennard had brought an army with him. Jason shook his head as though he could clear his vision of that sight.

On the seat of the leading wagon, Isabella sat brazenly, and she held a limp Eleanora across her lap as if she were a rag doll or already dead.

Just hold them, Gavan and Tomaz had said. *Hold them until we arrive.*

Jason tightened his hands on his cane, feeling as though caught in some heroic movie and knowing the outcome couldn't possibly be the same. He might stand against the five drawing nearer and nearer to him as though they were a noose and he the neck they would tighten around, but an army?

Panic shot through him. He considered the options they'd planned beforehand, getting Ting, and Grandmother, and Bailey and Rebecca to safety if anything happened. His hand jerked in a reflex upward to grasp his crystal and signal a retreat.

How could he hold against an army?

A bamboo splinter came off in his palm, sharply, as he moved. Jason bit off a cry at the surprising hurt, then stifled a second exclamation. Qi's voice cut through his memory. They will fight you inside and out, Jason. Remember that!'

Yes. He had forgotten that . . . momentarily. He bit his lip against the sting of the splinter and gazed at one of the wolfjackals who paced and snarled, and then Jason took aim. A shard of white fire exploded at its feet and the beast bolted with a howl of dismay. It took to its heels. The Hand riding the wolfjackal thrashed and whipped it, unable to halt it, and no one moved to help him as the beast whirled about. They disappeared back into the storm that had brought them. Jonnard put a heel firmly to the side of the shaggy beast he rode, reminding it who was in charge, and it paced sideways to flank Jason. The Gatekeeper moved to watch Jonnard. That was a mistake.

In a flash, they were on him from two sides. He felt a claw rip at him and the heat wave of a power surge. Jason ducked his head and let his body soar as Qi had shown him, diving into a tumbling somersault and coming up, swinging his cane. He connected even as he kicked about, pivoting out of range as a wolfjackal snarled at his ear. No time to look, just react. Let his body avoid the danger. His spirit sensed the blows before they would hit and carried him away.

He waved a hand, crying out for Light and the Magick gave it to him, flaring in the eyes of the beast snapping at him. The wolfjackal veered away yelping and stumbled down the small hill, pawing at its blinded eyes. It dumped its rider who put a hand out, then pulled back his duster coat and stood his ground. Jason shrugged a shoulder and sent a lance of song at him that vibrated through him. He stared in astonishment at his hand, at the spear he held, as it shook harder and harder and then disintegrated into metal dust and rained out from between his fingers.

Jason turned away from the backlash on that spell but it hit him anyway, the noise of drums bursting in his skull until his own Shield rattled under the turmoil and he could hear Ting gasp softly in her own pain as she tried to protect him. He brought his Focus back on himself to dispel the sonics and then stood, panting, feeling something wet drip down the side of his jaw.

Jason touched fingers to his face and brought them away crimson. Someone had marked him, Shield or not, Magick or not. How badly was he cut? Was it a gaping wound that would drain him of all his blood? The thought of flesh opening to his skull, exposing nerves and muscles, made him shake and he stared at his fingers.

Jason, stop it. That's what they want you to think. It's a surface wound, minor, or I'd be out there bandaging you! Rich's voice echoed faintly in his head. Jason shook himself. He couldn't take his eyes off the blood dripping from his hand.

Two of them jumped him at once. He went down between them, rolling and kicking, feeling his flesh tear and his soul shiver. He kicked them apart and got back to his feet, battered, and wondered how much more he could take.

Trent watched from his position beside Henry, and saw Jason sway with pain. He muttered to Henry, "Now." Jason hadn't yet given the signal, but he wasn't sure Jason could even think clearly. He saw his friend struggle to remain standing.

"Now?" repeated Henry. His own face had gone deathly pale, as Jonnard leeched power from him. Tiny drops of sweat beaded his forehead.

Trent gripped his shoulder hard. "If you're going to do it, Henry, it's now or never! Finish him!"

"Tug-of-war," Henry muttered with determination. He squeezed his eyes shut. "He shut me down earlier, but he won't this time!"

Trent watched anxiously. Jason traded more blows, as the wolfjackals and riders circled up the small hill toward him. He wouldn't have much of a defense left on the high ground when they reached him in another jump or two.

Trent pulled his crystal 'from his pocket. Of all of them there, he was the least. He knew it, they knew it. It was of no help at all to be able to see the Magick raging around Jason now. There were no subtle traps. He would either stand or he wouldn't, and the rest of them had the other Gates to hold. The only thing he could do was help Henry a bit, and damnit, he was tired of being the cheerleader.

He thumbed his rock. Beautiful but obscured, a clouded white crystal it had been when he picked it and that was the way it stayed. Yet, it had been out with all the others gems for bonding with the new Magickers. Surely someone should have seen it was a dud and cast it out, just like him. He rolled it between his fingers even as Henry groaned.

"Hang in there, Henry! You're stronger!"

He didn't even know if Henry could still hear him. They crouched in the Y of a tree, Henry having made cheerful comments about being in the arms of an Ent, one of Tolkien's fantasy tree people. Trent had tied him to the main trunk just to make sure he wouldn't fall out. He guessed it was just the way he saw things. He didn't trust the fantasy the way Henry did.

A wolfjackal howled as Jason let go with a mighty

blow, the bamboo cane KER-AKing as it hit. Rider and mount fell heavily on the hill and slid down to a quiet heap at the bottom. Trent could see the effort trembling in Jason's torso as he stood, and steadied, and readied himself for yet another assault from Brennard and Jon. And the Leucator that was Jason's double waited to the rear, an eerie apparition. It was so like Jason that it had already fooled Trent once or twice at a glance.

Where were Gavan and Tomaz and whatever others they could reach?

Henry let out a sharp cry as he bit his lip and crimson ran down his chin. Trent gripped the other's shoulder again. Henry opened his eyes and said weakly, "I've got him!" He managed a grin.

Trent didn't think it would be enough. "Good man, Henry," he answered in spite of his apprehension. "Just don't let go!"

Stef fought himself. He could feel the bear cub trying to burst through the seams of his body, and he shook with the effort to stay human. The Magick rolling about him tore away his control and he could not help himself. He let out a deep, groaning sound from the very depths of his body, before turning a helpless look at Rich. "Rich . . . I'm sorry . . ."

"It's all right, man." Rich's face stayed pale against his freckles, his shock of brilliant red hair standing disheveled about his head, all his thoughts bent on the Water Gate. He could feel the caravans rolling into the valley, feel the sting of their corruption as it pierced the goodness that had been Haven's heart. The bear cub stood on its hind legs, weaving, and growled heavily. Then it dropped to all fours and lumbered to where Jason had chosen to take his stand.

"Stefan!" cried Rich after his friend, but the burly bear cub never looked back. His growling rose in intensity, sensing a fight.

Brennard looked down the vale and saw the half grown bear shambling toward them. He gave a chill smile. "We've broken the first," he said to Jonnard. "Now after the others." He circled his wolfjackal about, riding back to the black wagons and waving his hand in a signal. The tarp rolled up. A single Leucator got down, and looked about, nostrils flaring for a scent. Then with a low hissing, it loped away.

Qi collapsed with a tiny sound and fell to the grass. Ting immediately knelt at her side, pulling her grandmother to her, feeling her face. Qi took Ting's hands in hers, saying weakly, "This battle is not for the old. I am very, very weary."

"I'll take you home!"

"This is my home now. Only let me rest. Do what you must, Granddaughter, or . . . or I'll never forgive you!" Qi tried to squeeze her hands hard, but the effort proved too much for her, and her fingers just trembled about Ting's.

"You can't stay here."

"I can and will." Qi struggled to sit up, pulling her black, quilted jacket and pants straight.

"Back in the grove then," Ting insisted, getting her grandmother to her feet. "I'll be back!" she called to Bailey as she helped Qi hobble toward the safety and shade of the trees.

Bailey had felt the weakening of their Shields the moment Ting let go, but she said nothing. She bit her lip in concentration, knowing that somewhere beyond this curve of Haven, a battle to keep the Dark Hand at a standstill raged. She could feel it in her crystal and in the jewelry Ting had fashioned.

Lacey let out a series of worried chirps, ran out of her pocket, and climbed onto her shoulder, nestling against the curve of her throat. Her tiny furred body felt incredibly warm and comforting as the pack rat clung to her. Rebecca gently laid her hand over Bailey's, saying, "I don't know what I can do."

A strengthening surged into Bailey where her mother touched her. "Wow! Mom . . . you're a battery!"

"A battery?"

"You're like stored energy. I can feel it!" Bailey grinned at her mother, the moment of uncertainty when Ting left her gone. She felt its glow and goodness wrap about her, helping to fill in the gap Ting had left behind. She beamed her power to Jason, feeding him, feeling the tremendous need he had for whatever help she could give him. Her eyebrows lowered.

"What is it?"

"I don't think it's going well," said Bailey quietly.

"It will," Rebecca told her with a fierce pride in her voice. "You've got to believe the others are coming to help."

"If they can."

Rebecca leaned against her daughter, trying to will belief and hope into her, not truly understanding the battle they were waging except that much of it came from inside, and that could surely be encouraged by positive thoughts.

Neither of them heard the third person approach until his voice rose around them.

"Wife and daughter."

Rebecca swung about. "Jerry!"

"They told me you were hiding here. They told me they'd help me find you." He put a hand out, walking slowly toward them, but his chest heaved as if he'd been running. "It's time to be a family again."

Bailey turned wildly toward them, and then began backing up. "Mom! Mom, that's not Daddy. Don't let him touch you!"

Rebecca put herself between them. "Jerry?"

"Mom, don't!" Bailey's hand jerked. "It's not human."

"Is that any way to talk about your father? Who carried you around when you had colic? Who took you to your first pony ride? Baseball game?"

Bailey's mouth twisted. "You took me to the ball game because it was Nickel Beer Night."

"A man deserves a little reward now and then." The thing stopped, mouth working at a smile.

"Bailey, stay behind me."

"Look at its eyes, Mom. That's a . . . a Leucator. It's a made thing."

"All you've done is twist her against me, Becca. What a horrible, horrible thing for a mother to do. You should be punished!" He lunged at her.

He grabbed Rebecca. She screamed at the chill pain that jolted her at his touch, her arm going numb, as he pulled her away from their daughter. "Come to Daddy," he said to Bailey. He threw Rebecca away, on the ground, where she went limp with shock and lay there, dazed.

"Mom!"

He batted at her. Their hands connected even as Bailey tried to dart away, and her amethyst went flying. *Never drop your crystal.* She fell backward and scrambled to get away from the thing that looked like her father. Her Shield, her power, winked out, leaving her very much alone. Lacey squeaked in her ear and then bit her earlobe, *hard.* "Ow!" Bailey shot to her feet and the Leucator lunged past her, just missing. The chill of its body passing felt as if someone had opened a freezer door.

Bailey danced back. She removed Lacey from her neck and gently tossed her to the grass. "Go get it!" The fuzz ball squeaked off, tufted tail twitching in her quickness.

It wasn't quite alive. Therefore, it couldn't be quite as fast as she was. Bailey dodged and danced, staying just out of its reach, drawing it away from her mother who lay quite still below. She was wrong.

The Leucator was deadly quick, like a striking cobra. It came after her again, and she twisted out of its hold, icy hands leaving white brands on her wrists as she got clear. Both arms screamed with the pain and hot tears blurred her eyes. She dodged again, barely escaping it. She felt the soft ground give as it leaped at her again and Bailey fell.

It knocked the wind out of her. She lay gasping a second, then heard the panting and frantic chirping of her tiny familiar as Lacey hobbled toward her, laboriously dragging the amethyst. She caught both up and swung about, just as the Leucator came at her with a deadly embrace.

Purple fire split the air. It sizzled deep into the being, and her father's double opened its mouth, crying wordlessly. Then it began to melt into itself, and the sight made Bailey stumble away, choking. Her father's face looked at her, crying out, "Baby gurrrlllll," the voice melting with it. When it was done, and nothing left but a heap of smudge on the ground, she turned her head and vomited.

"Oh, Bailey!" Rebecca crawled to her and stood, wavering, one arm and shoulder limp as she pulled her child close with all the strength remaining in her uninjured arm. Lacey let out a squeak of protest then quieted as both mother and daughter cried. Then Bailey made a strangled noise and looked up. "Jason!"

She took off at a run, headlong into the fray of the battle on the other side of the hill.

Jason staggered back, spent. He took a moment to spin around, as if looking uselessly for his supporters scattered about Haven, and finding no reserve, turned back to Jonnard. Trent could see the despair in his face. Stef-cub barreled into the wolfjackals with a bawl, sending them wheeling about, dumping their riders to the ground. With a deepening bear yowl he ran around the lupine beasts, chasing them back into the inky pass of the Iron Gate.

Trent rubbed his stone again. He looked into its useless depths. The milky white cloudiness reminded him of the energy he'd seen surrounding George, Aunt Freyah's dancing service tray.

Jason let out a sharp cry. Trent's head snapped up to see Jason and Jon locked in deadly combat, hand-to-hand, toe-to-toe. They traded blows, somersaulted away, and drove back in, their hands and feet moving like blurs. It was more brutal than anything he'd ever seen before, and he knew it would kill one of them.

Brennard made a pass with his hands, and darkness ribboned the valley. He could feel its oppression, its workings. The Dark Hand had begun to block Haven off as the Gatekeeper failed.

Trent shoved at the dead stone in his hand with all his anger and frustration. Nothing! He was worth nothing, he could do nothing to help!

The gemstone warmed and then its interior swirled. A nova of a thousand stars spun in the palm of his hand, then cleared away. A transparent quartz rested within his fingers, marked only by a few mica and pyrite flecks along one facet.

Trent's jaw dropped.

He stood up in the tree. His gaze scanned the bowl of the valley. He could see the bright, shimmering band of energy that surrounded it. He always had seen it, since they'd tumbled in desperately looking for the dragon. He tapped into it.

The sky ribbon shimmered. Then it filled him. It shot through the darkness of the gathering storm, blazing it away, with a Light of its own, and a fierce kind of singing filled him.

Noise sounded in his ear. He could hear Bailey's whoop and Ting's excited squeal, in his thoughts, *in his freaking mind!*

Trent stood in amazement, his crystal clenched in

his fist. He pushed against the darkness being wrought by the Dark Hand, and he could feel it give!

Jonnard reeled back. Sweat slicked his black cloth to his body and he panted heavily. His hands moved in defensive mode, and welts striped his face.

Jason pressed forward. "Henry isn't there anymore," Jason said. "You're on your own."

"No!" Jon reached out, and a charcoal lash of power rayed out from his hand, striking the ground wildly. "Father!"

"Fight as you've been trained. You have him!" Brennard raised a fist in rage, crystal flaring, missing Jason as he swung on him.

Jonnard sank to his knees, sucking breath through clenched teeth, gone so pale his skin was gray. Jason drew near, prepared to take him out. Jon hissed and raised a hand toward his father. A snake of energy roped through the air, latching from one to the other. Antoine Brennard, who sat at the bottom of the crest, looked up in sudden surprise as his son took everything he had from him. He raised his hand to his chest, where the energy snake was sucking his life from him, and then looked at Jonnard in anguished surprise.

Jon roared in rage and leaped at Jason.

Jason met every blow with pain jolting through him. The bamboo cane took one last hit and then shattered in his palms. Splinters sprayed everywhere. He somersaulted backward and landed for a split second before kicking out and letting his crystal's power loose.

It knocked Jon down. The other rolled off the crest,

screams of hatred and anger spewing as he fell. He flailed in vain to get up and could not, quivering like a broken animal. Jason dropped to his knees and tried to breathe. His crystal flickered at his chest and went dim.

He kicked out. He caught Jonnard in the side of the head and the youth fell as if axed. He rolled over and over and over and came to a limp halt. He flailed once. He put his hand up, and cried, "Mother."

Someone shouted a command and the great wagons rolled forward. Isabella sprang down from the wagon to haul Jonnard into the shelter of the wagon bed. Then she snapped out a command, and rough hands gathered Brennard's body and heaved it up, so that he, too, disappeared into the depths of a wagon.

She snapped off a word. Jason blinked, and then rolled to his side, as his Leucator fell on him. He shrieked at the cold fire as it tried to devour him. He stared into his own face, as it put its hands to his neck, and began to choke him.

She threw a great cloaking over the caravan, as it rolled past him and disappeared into the depths of Haven. The other black, long wagons followed, and three troops of grim faced soldiers after. They stared at him as they marched past. He could not stop them.

He wrestled with the Leucator, feeling the strength in his body drain away, heartbeat by heartbeat. He could feel the hands on his throat grow stronger and stronger.

"Which one?"

"Take them both out."

"No!" Bailey cried. "One is Jason, one is not."

He struggled and tried to kick free. His hand

throbbed on the other's neck. The very touch of the Leucator sent burning chills deep into him. He could feel his neck bruising, collapsing, his breathing slowing.

Suddenly Bailey cried out, and the amethyst in her hand arched into a sword blade and she swung with all her might, and one of the Jasons stopped moving.

He sat up, gasping, after a very long moment.

"What . . . took you . . . so long?" He crouched, shivering uncontrollably.

"I had to know which was which." She reached down and tapped his hand. "His scar was on the right hand. And his was all white and flat."

His hand throbbed. The crescent scar flared red and angry, as it always did when evil came near. Jason tried to stand, and couldn't, and flopped down.

Trent climbed the hill, took Jason by the elbow, and helped him up.

"You won."

Jason looked at him a moment, trying to comprehend the two simple words. Then he shook his head.

"Brennard is dead."

"Jonnard lives. And they got through." Jason leaned heavily on his friend. Bailey came up and gently bolstered him from the other side. "They still have Eleanora and FireAnn."

Trent said quietly, "We lived. They didn't expect that. They used their hostages to get passage. And they've paid a heavy price."

"So did we!" He could barely stand. He could feel the pain and hurt in every fiber of his body.

"We'll get them back."

He had failed, ignoring what the dragon had tried

to tell him. He thought he'd understood it all, and now he realized he understood nothing. Yes, the others who stood with him were safe, and for that he could be thankful, but he'd failed himself and Gavan. He had become the warrior instead of the guard, and had let war into a world he scarcely even knew.

"Whatever it takes," he told Trent. "I will get them out of Haven."

Trent held him up. "Then that's what we'll do. Tomorrow."

Emily Drake

The Magickers

A long time ago, two great sorcerers fought a duel to determine the fate of the world. Magick was ripped from our world, its power kept secret by a handful of enchanters. The world of Magick, however, still exists—and whoever controls the Gates controls both worlds.

Book One:
THE MAGICKERS   0-7564-0035-X

Book Two:
THE CURSE OF ARKADY   0-7564-0103-8

Book Three:
THE DRAGON GUARD   0-7564-0141-0
(hardcover)

To Order Call: 1-800-788-6262

MERCEDES LACKEY

THE GATES OF SLEEP

The *Elemental Masters* Series

Evil portents have warned that Marina Roeswood will
be killed by the hand of her own aunt before her
eighteenth birthday. Hidden in rural Cornwall,
Marina has no knowledge of the dark curse that shadows her life. Will her half-trained magic prove powerful enough to overturn this terrible prophecy of
death?

0-7564-0101-1

"A wonderful example of a new look at
an old theme."—*Publishers Weekly*

And don't miss the first book of
The Elemental Masters:
The Serpent's Shadow
0-7564-0061-9

To Order Call: 1-800-788-6262

MERCEDES LACKEY

The Novels of Valdemar

Exile's Valor

Once a heroic captain in the army of Karse, Valdemar's traditional enemy, Alberich became one of Valdemar's Heralds. Despite prejudice against him, he becomes the personal protector of young Queen Selenay. But can he protect her from the dangers of her own heart?

"A must for Valdemar fans."
—Booklist

0-7564-0206-9

To Order Call: 1-800-788-6262

DAW 24

MERCEDES LACKEY

The Novels of Valdemar

To Order Call: 1-800-788-6262

Mercedes Lackey & Larry Dixon

The Novels of Valdemar

"Lackey and Dixon always offer a well-told tale"
—*Booklist*

DARIAN'S TALE

OWLFLIGHT
0-88677-804-2

OWLSIGHT
0-88677-803-4

OWLKNIGHT
0-88677-916-2

THE MAGE WARS

THE BLACK GRYPHON
0-88677-804-2

THE WHITE GRYPHON
0-88677-682-1

THE SILVER GRYPHON
0-88677-685-6

To Order Call: 1-800-788-6262

DAW 26

Kristen Britain

GREEN RIDER

As Karigan G'ladheon, on the run from school, makes her way through the deep forest, a galloping horse plunges out of the brush, its rider impaled by two black arrows. With his dying breath, he tells her he is a Green Rider, one of the king's special messengers. Giving her his green coat with its symbolic brooch of office, he makes Karigan swear to deliver the message he was carrying. Pursued by unknown assassins, following a path only the horse seems to know, Karigan finds herself thrust into in a world of danger and complex magic....   0-88677-858-1

FIRST RIDER'S CALL

With evil forces once again at large in the kingdom and with the messenger service depleted and weakened, can Karigan reach through the walls of time to get help from the First Rider, a woman dead for a millennium?   0-7564-0209-3

To Order Call: 1-800-788-6262